MW00647368

Blood Song

Warriors of the Five Realms

Book Three

Hollee Mands

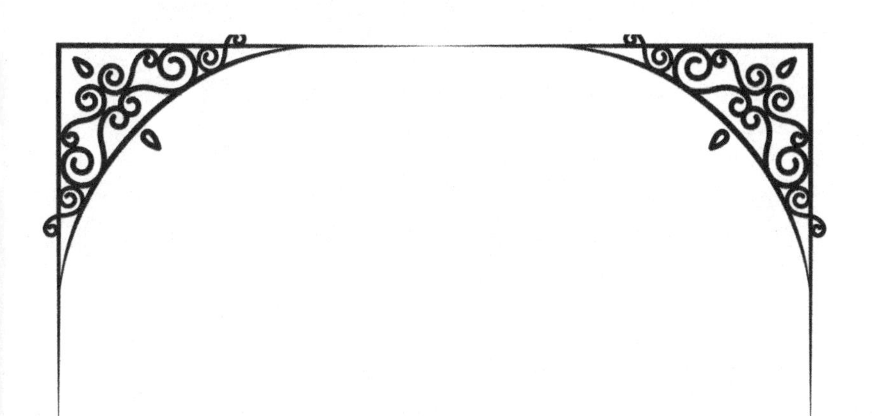

BLOOD SONG

WARRIORS OF THE FIVE REALMS

HOLLEE MANDS

Blood Song Copyright © 2023 by Hollee Mands.

All rights reserved. This book is a work of fiction. Names, characters, places, and incidents are the product of the author's imagination or are used fictitiously. Any resemblance to actual events, locales, or persons, living or dead, is coincidental. No part of this book may be reproduced in any form or by any electronic or mechanical means, including information storage and retrieval systems, without written permission from the author, except for the use of brief quotations in a book review.

Editing and proofreading by Kelley Luna

Proofread by Spell Bound

Cover design by Covers by Christian

To Kelley Luna
My darling sister from another mother,
Look at how far we've come together,
From self-publishing to shared secrets and laughter,
Thank you for being here for me beyond the happily ever after,
For never judging me for who I am,
And believing in me for all the things that I can,
My formidable editor and bookish soulmate,
Meeting you must be the grandest of fate,
I will always thank God and all my lucky stars,
Without you I would never have come this far.

CONTENTS

Author's Note ix
A Cautionary Tale from the Bard's Compendium xi

Prologue 1
Chapter 1 7
Chapter 2 16
Chapter 3 30
Chapter 4 43
Chapter 5 53
Chapter 6 66
Chapter 7 78
Chapter 8 92
Chapter 9 102
Chapter 10 111
Chapter 11 122
Chapter 12 132
Chapter 13 141
Chapter 14 157
Chapter 15 172
Chapter 16 185
Chapter 17 201
Chapter 18 214
Chapter 19 219
Chapter 20 225
Chapter 21 234
Chapter 22 253
Chapter 23 265
Chapter 24 271
Chapter 25 281

Chapter 26 293
Chapter 27 307
Chapter 28 321
Chapter 29 330
Chapter 30 336
The Prophecy 341
Chapter 31 343
Chapter 32 352
Chapter 33 360
Chapter 34 376
Chapter 35 386
Chapter 36 393
Epilogue 409

The End 413
Reader Bonus 415
Acknowledgments 417
Also by Hollee Mands 421
About the Author 425

Author's Note

Sign Language

Like all languages, signed language exists in variations. For example, American Sign Language differs from Australian or British Sign Language. For the purpose of this fictional novel, a universal signed language (much like Faerian, Animatish, Magerian) is used across the five realms as Handspeak.

It is also worth noting that the grammar of signed languages is not similar to most spoken and written languages. All signed language represented in this book is a creative interpretation of the hand signals the characters make. Contractions in dialogue were used to indicate fluency.

A little note on scene setting

For those who have read Book 1 (*Little Fire*), you may recall that the five realms are mirror images with varying creatures and geological differences.

In Book 2 (*Winter Sun*), you followed Evangeline and Declan to the peak of Arksana—the crown of a dormant volcano.

In *Blood Song*, I'd like to take you *under* said dormant

volcano (even if it is the mirror image of the same mountain in a different realm) and explore dormant lava tubes, blowholes, and a subterranean sea. (No, I did not pull that last one out of a hat —google it!).

While those are actual natural phenomena, I am conscious they probably do not work the way my overactive imagination has threaded them together. If you happen to be a seismologist or geologist, please suspend some disbelief as you follow Gabriel and Shyaree on their journey, quite literally, deep into the mountain's core.

Happy reading!

A Cautionary Tale from the Bard's Compendium

There once lived a king of the Winter Court,
Heart soured by grief and consumed by rot,
Soul devoured by hate until it became an empty shell,
Vengeance became the only place he could dwell,
Bathing in blood he believed was his due,
He broke spirits as well as bone and sinew,
Grisly experiments did he perform,
On little children he tried to transform,
Into living vessels to anchor his every breath,
Untouchable even by the god of death.

Prologue

Amereen Castle, Mage Realm

A mellow breeze sighed through the gardens, infused with the scents of fresh grass, springtime blooms, and a deadly stranger. Shyaree canted her head toward the footsteps approaching from the shadowed corridor. Male, she decided. And judging from the prickling of the little hairs on her skin, he was also fae.

Dark fae.

Only the Unseelie inspired such disquiet in her. Their unholy magic whispered of shadows and rot and secret things lying in the bowels of the earth that were better left unspoken. Theirs was a devious and dangerous race. Shyaree would know. She was, unfortunately, acquainted with one of the worst of their lot.

Ruthless.

Mercenary.

Assassin.

Gabriel Blacksage, a man as lethal as he was insufferable. And presently, the man was also obnoxiously late. Gabriel should have arrived half a candle past, or as the mages and their little ticking time tellers would say, over three hours ago. The tread of the stranger's boots on the cold stone told her he was not the man she awaited. This man's strides were subtle but soldierlike. Nothing akin to Gabriel's quiet footfalls and his tendency to slink about like the shadows he manipulated.

She wasn't the only one who noticed.

"That's not Gabriel," Evangeline commented with a frown.

After the first hour of wearing out her soles—and her scowl—Shyaree had earned both the mage queen's sympathy and company. Evangeline had taken to reading to her in one of the castle's many charming courtyards, joined by one unnerving other. An archmage, who radiated such extreme power that his presence was near suffocating, had occupied the stone bench beside his queen, listening to her read a child's fable with the look of a man utterly bewitched.

"It's Gabriel's second-in-command," the archmage replied. "Arkas Ironfall."

Evangeline set her book aside and leaned into her mate. "Strange. I expected Gabriel to take Shya home."

A comment that only compounded the niggle growing in Shyaree's chest.

Eight moons ago, Shyaree would not have understood enough of the mage tongue to grasp Evangeline and Declan's exchange. Eight moons ago, Shyaree would never have thought to be acquainted with an Unseelie assassin, much less wondering about his absence.

The fae—Arkas—must have felt the weight of the archmage's focus, because he wisely halted ten paces shy of Evangeline and sank to one knee. "Lord Archmage and Lady Thorne."

Shyaree found herself under the brief scrutiny of a lavender-hued gaze before the dark head lowered in a silent show of subservience.

Toying idly with his queen's fingers, the archmage kept his attention fixed upon the kneeling fae, who didn't speak. Or so it seemed.

Arkas was clearly conversing with the archmage through the mind. Once, Shyaree would have found the ensuing silence strange and unsettling. Now she appreciated—envied, even—telepathic conversations.

The archmage finally flicked a viridian gaze to Shyaree, but his expression gave nothing away as he spoke in fluent Animatish. "Gabriel is aware you're due to return home today, but he is indisposed." He nodded at the fae. "He's sent Arkas to take you home in his stead."

The niggle burrowed deeper beneath her breastbone, like a millipede crawling under a rock. Indisposed? Had Gabriel gotten into another fight? Was he . . . hurt?

But Shyaree crushed her questions in her fists along with the unwarranted worry.

Gabriel Blacksage was deadlier than a starving pack of wolverai. He could take care of himself. Even so, something must have shown on her face, because Evangeline reached over to squeeze her arm.

"I'm sure he's fine," the queen whispered with a reassuring smile.

Mortified by her transparency, Shyaree lifted a shoulder in an attempt at nonchalance.

Evangeline's lips took on a wry curve. "He's just caught up with . . . work. You know how he can be."

That was the problem. After eight long moons, Shyaree *did* know.

Gabriel could be as persistent as a hound on a hunt when

he got caught up in a task, but he wasn't one to go back on his word. He'd said, albeit teasingly, that he wouldn't miss the day of her departure. So she'd expected, however grudgingly, for him to be here.

Then again, whatever Arkas had conveyed to the lord archmage and Evangeline did not appear to concern them—so why should it concern her?

Shyaree nodded her understanding and forced a small smile for good measure.

Gabriel didn't need to be the one to create a portal. Any portal maker would suffice. But Gabriel had served as her unofficial interpreter for the duration of her stay in the mage realm. Despite their propensity to clash like flint and friction, she had grown a little attached— She bit into her cheek. Accustomed. She was accustomed, *not* attached to him.

She would have liked to bid him farewell, that was all.

But clearly, Gabriel did not think *she* warranted a goodbye.

Evangeline rose on her tiptoes, scattering Shyaree's thoughts to draw her into a tight squeeze. The mage queen was as slight as Shyaree was tall.

"I'm going to miss you," Evangeline murmured, her voice wavering with emotion. "Thank you for coming here, and for everything you've done for me all these months." The magnolia flowers in the large ceramic pots around the pavilion seemed to droop in tandem with the queen's downturned lips.

Despite her melancholy, Shyaree chuckled in her usual breathy, voiceless way. To think she'd once thought this waif of a woman frail and her affinity for magic feeble. Eyes misting, she pulled away from Evangeline's embrace in order to speak with her hands. *"Please don't cry, Evie, or you'll make me do the same."*

Evangeline bit down on her lips with an earnest sniffle, her nose turning the same shade of pink as the surrounding magnolias. "I'm sorry, but I just can't help it."

Shyaree scrubbed hastily at her own eyes while she smiled at the irony.

Once, she'd resented being sent here. And now she loathed to leave.

"We will meet again, won't we? Won't you come visit me?"

Evangeline would not be accompanying Shyaree on her return. The castle's lead healer, Mailin, was so overdue in her gestation that she was apt to go into labor at any moment, and Evangeline was understandably eager to remain close. Flowers weren't the only thing the mage queen could control.

"I would love to show you my home and for you to meet my people," Shyaree signed enthusiastically, trying to shake off her gloom. *"I think you will like the rainforest and—"* She slowed her hands as she noted Evangeline's increasingly mystified expression. Though the queen had taken the time to learn, she hadn't grasped beyond the basic motions of Shyaree's sign language.

Evangeline's brows puckered, and she blew out a breath. "I'm sorry, Shyaree. I think you've lost me." Clearly concerned about Shyaree's comprehension of Magerian, the archmage repeated Evangeline's response in Animatish.

Shyaree lowered her hands with a resigned shake of her head. The archmage might speak her people's tongue fluently, but he was not versed in Handspeak either.

Unlike Gabriel.

At the thought of her absent interpreter, Shyaree's mood further soured. She pasted on a cheery smile and forcibly tamped down all thoughts of an inconsiderate male who couldn't be bothered to bid her a final farewell.

And why did it matter?

Their paths would never cross again.

Chapter 1

Present day
The Red Den, City of Evenmere, Fae Realm

Gabriel sauntered from shifting shadows onto solid stone, his footfalls silent against the cacophony of delighted fools and despairing drunks.

The Red Den was as packed as always.

Carousers reveled while patrons occupied the card tables, reeking of alcohol, false hope, and desperation. The ones with deeper pockets milled in private alcoves where they could while away their coin under the eager attention of succubi. Those with a thirst for more grit crowded the fighting pits, cheering and jeering at witless trolls and bloodthirsty satyrs.

Avoiding all eye contact, Gabriel slid behind the bar to help himself to a bottle. The barman took one look at his face and wisely kept his mouth shut. Gabriel grabbed the most potent liquor he could find, took a hearty swig, and grimaced. Liquid fire coursed down his throat. Perfect.

He made it halfway across the Den before he caught the attention of one of the croupiers. The fae straightened at the sight of him and promptly signaled for another to take his place. Damn it. Gabriel had been hoping to slip away unnoticed. As the man elbowed through the crowd, Gabriel made a beeline for the stairs.

"Gabe!" Arkas yelled, nearly tripping a barmaid in his haste to catch up to him. "Where in the five flaming hells have you been?"

"Wouldn't you like to know?" Gabriel ascended the stairs two at a time, wishing the other man would take the hint. He was not in the mood, his patience frayed and flimsy like a gambler's self-control.

A portal flared on the steps to emit a stone-faced Arkas, who rooted himself squarely in Gabriel's path. Gabriel narrowed his eyes in warning, but Arkas merely folded his arms. "I've reviewed our manifests. You have no jobs scheduled, and we both know you haven't been to Amereen. Where have you gone?"

With his menacing scowl and an array of glinting knives decorating his brawny chest, Arkas Ironfall probably induced a healthy amount of fear in most. Gabriel sidestepped him with a shrug. The most fearsome thing about his second-in-command was his incessant ability to henpeck like a scorned wife.

"Have you nothing better to do than check up on me?"

"I worry about you."

Gabriel took another pull from the bottle and smirked. "And there's your problem. You worry too much. Maybe you need to take a break. I'm sure Malakai or Caspian can look after the guild operations while you're away."

Arkas's lips hardened. "Stop it."

"Stop what?" Gabriel cocked a brow. "Putting up with you and your nagging?"

Arkas moved to obstruct his path again, this time with a firm hand planted on the wall. "I'm serious, Gabe. Do you think I'm the only one who's noticed your absences? Two Silverbeaks were loitering near Windswept Alley yesterday, looking—"

"Please." Gabriel rolled his eyes at the mention of mercenaries from a rival guild. "You don't need me to deal with a couple of rookheads."

"No. But they seem to be taking your repeated disappearances as a pass to slide into Evenmere. Is that what you want?" Arkas cocked a challenging brow. "Silverbeaks strutting on our streets? Dealing dreamsmoke in our alleys, preying on our people?"

Arkas was tearing at his sense of responsibility. Gabriel knew that, yet he couldn't help the edge creeping into his retort. "Back off, Ironfall. What I do with my time is nobody's business but mine."

"Maybe if you hadn't made a habit of this, but it's been close to a *year*. A year of you disappearing at a whim to gods know where. Why can't you just tell me where you've been going?"

Gabriel eyed his second-in-command over the rim of his bottle. "Should I file a report every time I head out, then? Do I need permission next time I take a piss?"

Arkas exhaled heavily. "You know that's not what I'm asking. The rookheads aren't only lingering but also causing trouble. Vandalizing. Harassing shopkeepers. Small offenses, but enough to make our people restless."

Ever since Zenaidus Balvaris had ascended to the throne, his lapdogs—the Silverbeaks—had grown bolder and brasher by the day, backed by the unofficial patronage of a king. The rival guild's encroachment on Red Knight territory wasn't unique, however. There had been grumblings of the rookheads causing trouble at Duskhall and Nightgate, making a similar nuisance of themselves in other guilds' territory.

"Trust me. I have everything under control." Gabriel took another pull of his drink.

"Trust you?" Arkas snorted. "Look at you! You haven't touched liquor since . . . " Arkas ripped the bottle from his hand and sniffed. "Mujarin? You're downing Mujarin straight from the bottle now?" Disapproval oozed from the man's self-righteous pores. "Ozenn's blood, Gabe, what—"

"Enough." Gabriel snatched his bottle back, dribbling an exorbitant amount of liquor in the process. Whatever patience he had dissipated like alcohol in his bloodstream. "You're my second, not my mother."

The Red Knight flinched, and shame flooded Gabriel's gut. Arkas wasn't just the guild's second-in-command, but his comrade. His *cousin*. One who had been with him since the cradle, and one who had been ensuring the guild operated seamlessly in his absences of late.

Arkas didn't deserve his bullshit.

Gabriel sighed. "Just stop worrying. I have everything under control." Perhaps he'd gut a few in the morning. Spilling Silverbeak blood and painting his streets scarlet might be crude, but crude was fine as long as it was effective.

Arkas looked ready to belt him with more questions, but Gabriel pushed past him without another word. He needed to get to the attic, his personal haven where he could seek solace and sort out his thoughts, or he'd inadvertently end up *there* again. Arkas was certainly right on one count.

Evenmere needed him here.

"There's also someone waiting for you in the parlor."

Gabriel paused. "Deal with him yourself, or throw him out."

"Calls himself Hydra," Arkas added, and Gabriel nearly missed a step. "He's been coming here three days now. Refuses to deal with anyone but you. Are you sure you want me to see him out?"

Gabriel's mouth had gone dry, but it wasn't from magerian liquor.

"I'll see him."

Gabriel turned down the dim corridor to the private parlor with restlessness brewing in his chest. Hydra's appearance in the Den could only herald trouble—he just wasn't sure of what kind.

Creaaak. Gabriel grimaced and took more care with his footing. The floorboards should have been replaced years ago, and the carpets were worn thinner than a whore's slip. Blacksage Manor, now known as the Red Den, had served his family for countless millennia. But unlike the other Unseelie aristocrats, Gabriel could never seem to find the funds for the structural restoration the manor needed. It stung his pride, but at the very least, Blacksage Manor still belonged to a Blacksage.

He chose to believe his parents would be satisfied with that.

Pausing at the parlor door, he slipped a diken—a four-pointed throwing star—up his sleeve for easy access. He did not truly believe himself in danger from Hydra, but some habits had saved his ass more times than he could count.

He eased the door open.

The gas lamp flickered, casting dancing shadows over the man watching him with deceptive idleness from the armchair at the darkest end of the room. Hydra straightened and rose. His ice-white hair and clear violet eyes contrasted starkly with the black of his cloak. He appeared almost ordinary, with his coloring fairly common among Unseeliekind.

He wasn't.

Hydra wore many faces. This was merely the one he donned whenever he played the part of the spare but precocious heir of the Winter Court.

"Zion," Gabriel said without preamble. "What are you doing here? Has something happened . . . to *her*?"

Prince Zion of the Winter Court—or by his lesser-known alias, Hydra—lifted an innocent brow paired with a faintly mocking smile. "Her? Who?"

Gabriel tightened his jaw. "Don't play games with me, princeling."

"I'm not a telepathic mage, guildmaster. But given your recent *proclivities*, one could hazard a guess . . . " A sinister chuckle. "Shyaree?"

Every fiber in Gabriel's body froze.

That was *not* the name he'd expected from Zion's lips. Suddenly the prince's appearance in the Den spelled more torment than simple trouble. Gabriel stalked over to the sideboard and pulled out two glasses, using the time to gather his wits. He poured the prince a glass of fae mead and kept his tone curt and casual.

"You've been following me?"

The prince accepted his offering with a shrug. "I believe in doing my due diligence on the people I work with."

"I'm not interested in working with you."

"No? I would have thought Iolanthe makes us . . . friends of sorts."

Iolanthe. Gabriel had to fist his hand around his glass to keep it from shaking at the mention of her name. For years, he'd believed himself the single surviving Blacksage. For years, he'd worked ceaselessly to strengthen the Red Guild and, in his own way, right wrongs and pay his dues—until *that* day.

The day of Shyaree's departure from the mage realm.

Tasked by Declan to investigate Zion's claim of being the illegitimate son of Nathaniel Strom, the archmage of Flen and Declan's father, Gabriel had infiltrated the prince's stronghold. The secrets he'd uncovered had sent him sinking to the bottom of a bottle—a bottle he'd continued to spiral into every time the past got the better of him.

"Friends," Gabriel repeated with a scoff as he eyed the prince over the rim of his glass. "I wouldn't call us that. What do you want with Shyaree?"

"Ah, straight to business and not a single inquiry after Io's welfare . . . I'd thought your sister meant more to you than that." Zion's smile held a soft and placid veneer, but the underlying taunt grated at Gabriel's patience.

"Why are you really here, Zion?"

He only received another chuckle. The bastard was baiting him.

Too bad Gabriel was in no mood for games.

The diken sailed from his grip to slice the air between them. One silver prong embedded in the wall a hairsbreadth from Zion's throat. "I'd stop wasting my time if I were you." A fool might question his aim, but Zion was no fool.

Just demented.

The prince threw his head back in a laugh as though coming a whisker from a severed jugular were a particularly exhilarating experience. "Gods! Now I know why Io behaves the way she does. Are you Blacksages all so violent?"

"Did missing out on the crown give you brain rot? Or do

you believe you're somehow untouchable because you're Iolanthe's guardian?"

Zion didn't appear the least bit fazed. "We both know you can't kill me."

"You must be naive if you think death is the only torment to be had. Perhaps you'd like a tour of the Den?" Gabriel flashed his teeth. "I assure you the gambling tables aren't the only source of amusement around here."

Still chuckling, Zion removed a hefty pouch from his cloak. A jingling shake proved it was filled with coins. "I'm here because I have a job for you, guildmaster."

Gabriel set his glass down on the sideboard with a dull thud. "Then you've wasted your time and mine. I'm not taking marks."

It didn't matter that he could use the coin. He would never work with a man whose head he yearned to mount on a spike and watch the crows pick clean.

"I'm not asking for a kill. I'm asking for a woman."

Zion paused with another one of those aggravatingly placid smiles while sickness writhed in Gabriel's gut like a pit of snakes. The prince did not need to say her name for Gabriel to know whom he wanted.

"And who better to retrieve the pantherai female than the portal maker who knows exactly where her clan is?" the prince added with a small smirk.

Gabriel's fingers itched for the blades strapped at his back. How easy would it be to relieve Zion of his head? To feel the snap of tearing muscles and the satisfying crunch of bone . . . but what good would come of it?

They were at a stalemate as long as Iolanthe was in his *care*.

Gabriel clenched his fists and clung to a semblance of civility while he served the prince a sneer. "You're in the wrong guild, princeling. We don't do that kind of thing here."

Zion moistened his lips. The movement vaguely reminded Gabriel of a cobra scenting the air with its forked tongue just before striking its prey.

"Even if I told you she is the key to freeing your sister?"

CHAPTER 2

Pantherai Clan, Jijunga Rainforest, Animati Realm

Perspiration licked at her nape, and impatience strummed restless fingers along her breastbone. Rainy season lorded over the jungle in a sweltering haze, trapping both heat and humidity beneath curling ferns and the ancient boughs of the Great Kilinjiri tree.

The congregation of sweat-slicked bodies within the clan's ceremonial hollow caused children to fidget like fish on hot sand, but the adults managed a semblance of serenity, fanning themselves with palm fronds as they feigned interest in the clan elder's rote speech.

"We are gathered here today to witness the husungai of Shyaree, daughter of Baleen, to Hesok, son of Rogesh, through the tethering . . . "

Shyaree grimaced inwardly.

Husungai could be a day of dreams—or dread. A day when

a female was claimed, or more appropriately, *tethered*, to a male that would be her lifemate. For Shyaree, it was neither. Husungai was only another day of duty.

One she was determined to complete.

"To enhance the chances of a clan's continuity, Thurin blesses every warrior twice over . . . " As Dapa Jetossi droned on about the importance of husungai for the survival of their species, Shyaree plucked discreetly at the ropes digging into her collarbone.

The infernal ties were everywhere—crisscrossed all over her limbs and torso like parasitic vines clinging to a tree. Beneath the knots, she was allowed to wear only a bandeau over her breasts and scraps of cloth that hung from her hips like the petals of a wilted flower. It was a ceremonial outfit, meant to symbolize the submissiveness and sensuality of the bride, the ropes to be undone only by the groom at the end of husungai.

But gods above, how they *itched*.

She had no idea how other brides had made it to sundown suffering this abomination of a fishnet. And they were still expected to glow with happiness, while grooms wore their usual leathers with the addition of only a single rope at their wrist. One attached to the bride's *throat*—like a leash.

There was a reason husungai was deemed a tethering of the bride and not the binding of a couple. A female was tethered to her warrior, but not the other way around, because every warrior was assigned not one, but *two* brides.

One for each wrist.

"Husungai is a reward for our warriors. Each bride, a priceless gift from Thurin himself," Dapa Jetossi continued.

Shyaree snuck a glance at her soon-to-be lifemate kneeling on the moss-padded ground beside her. Shafts of sunlight spearing through the canopy cast a near-ethereal glow across Hesok's rugged features. He'd made an effort to trim his beard and even had his usually shaggy black mane braided into a neat queue. Broad-shouldered and brawny, he was pleasant on the eyes. Handsome, even. Many untethered females would be thrilled to be one of Hesok's arranged brides . . . Unfortunately, Shyaree did not share even a sliver of that feminine excitement.

Idly fiddling with the rope connecting them, Hesok's gaze searched the crowd until he found Emalia. His other arranged bride, still several seasons too young to be tethered. His gaze lingered on the bronze beauty, while Shyaree had not received a single genuine smile since their husungai ceremony began. Shyaree did not blame him.

If she were a warrior with a choice, she would not have chosen herself for a bride, either. Her *condition* meant no male wanted her, despite her place in the clan's hierarchy.

Fortunately for her, Hesok was decent enough to honor their late fathers' arrangement. Shyaree did require a lifemate.

Not for the companionship or the fact that husungai would allow her a hut and hearth of her own. She had always been content—happy, even—living in the longhouse amid the other untethered females. She needed Hesok for a very specific purpose—his help to gain an audience with a Tribe elder.

That, and she did not wish to go through another heat cycle without a male to ease her. And her next cycle was imminent.

Despite her own carefully laid out rationales, her heart grew heavier with each breath as she watched Hesok and Emalia exchange covert smiles through the crowd. Swallowing the lump in her throat, Shyaree turned from her groom to search for the reason she needed to see a Tribe elder in the first place.

Reiken.

Her twin sat at the very front, every inch the proud primus, except for the glazed look in his eyes and gauntness to his face. Flags of red colored his cheekbones, a clear sign of a rising fever. Of the *curse*. Worry wormed its way into her rib cage, causing a heaviness in her chest. She shrugged it aside and drew comfort in that husungai would bring her a step closer to the solution. A step closer to the items she required for the elixir to rid her brother of his curse.

Reiken caught her gaze and shot her a chiding glance. *"Stop fidgeting,"* he signed. *"And sit up straight."*

Dutifully Shyaree straightened her posture, ignoring the itch of her ties amid the humid heat. Thank the gods, Dapa Jetossi had finally reached the end of his speech.

"Hesok, son of Rogesh, now you may place your bride upon the altar and remove her bindings before Thurin."

A more enthusiastic groom would have scooped her up and carried her to the altar, but Hesok only gave her an apathetic nod.

"Come." He stood swiftly, and the uncoordinated pull of the rope between them caused Shyaree to stumble, inciting murmurs from the crowd and a warning growl from Reiken.

Her brother glowered openly at her groom, and only then did Hesok lift her off her feet. Shyaree plastered a gracious smile on her face, not for her groom or the crowd, but for her brother's benefit.

Hesok set her upon the altar, and the irony that she sat upon the very same spot where a goat had recently been slaughtered in the name of Thurin did not escape her.

As her groom worked on the ties at her ankles, Shyaree curled her hands into fists. Every cut of the ceremonial knife relieved her from the physical bindings but intensified the weight within her chest. Every slash was a severance of her independence, condemning her to a life as the unwanted bride. She struggled not to squirm as Hesok worked his way up her thighs, battled the desperate urge to leap from the altar and flee whenever his fingers brushed her bare skin. Perhaps that aversion would change when she was in heat . . .

An abrupt shout from the crowd jolted her. Blood welled from the knife's edge, but she was too dismayed by the commotion to care.

No, no, no . . . Gods above, not again.

Reiken thrashed on the ground, snarling and clawing at the air as though combating a phantom adversary. He released an agonized roar before his back bowed, seemingly from change, but not. A normal change would have taken him less than two breaths, but Reiken's pantherai did not show. Instead, random patches of fur repeatedly rippled and receded over his skin. He clutched his skull and screamed. His body spasmed and seized, his inner beast vying for dominance, but his two-legged form refused to yield.

Shyaree leapt off the altar, but the rope that tethered her to Hesok jerked her to a stumble. She tugged at her groom, who appeared too stunned to move. Reiken had never suffered such a bad episode before the entire clan. Shyaree pulled again, this time with enough force that Hesok staggered.

He hissed in a breath. "It's the curse! There's nothing you can do!"

"Let me go to him," she signed frantically. *"He's my brother!"*

"You shouldn't be touching him!"

Reiken's bone-chilling howl raised every hair on her skin.

"Please! That is your primus!"

Hesok remained motionless. Shyaree gave up seeking his permission. She simply lunged for her brother, half pulling, half dragging her lifemate-to-be along as if she were a mule saddled with an oversized cargo.

Her clansmen had formed a ring around Reiken, too fearful of the curse to actually lend a hand. Some invoked the protective sign of Thurin by running three fingers down their foreheads as though their primus's malmorphic seizure were an evil to be guarded against. Even Dapa Jetossi kept a wide berth, muttering useless prayers while he left Shyaree to deal with Reiken alone.

Shyaree attempted to seize Reiken's thrashing arms by the wrists. A near-impossible task. Not only was she constrained by the rope that kept her tethered to a very resistant Hesok, but her twin was more than twice her size. Ironic, considering their father used to say Shyaree had taken more than her share in the womb, leaving Reiken barely alive at birth.

With another roar, Reiken lashed out. Something sharp glinted within his grip. A dagger. It wasn't just any dagger—the draga sul. The wicked instrument would have carved into her cheek had she ducked a moment slower.

"Stop!" Dapa Jetossi cried. "Someone stop him before he spreads the curse!"

Shyaree attempted to wrench the weapon from her brother. She would have succeeded if Reiken hadn't rammed his elbow into her midsection with enough force to empty her lungs. She landed on her hip, pain shooting through her pelvis.

Hesok dove in with a growl when Reiken inadvertently slashed at him with one of his uncoordinated blows. The rope at her throat jerked, towing her like a boat in stormy waters as the two warriors tussled. Shyaree was yanked this way and that, catching the brunt of stray elbows and fists until a feathered dart whizzed through the air and sank into Reiken's shoulder.

Shyaree winced.

Huntersbane. The effect was almost instantaneous.

Reiken staggered, then slumped to the ground in a senseless heap, drugged by the paralytic the hunters used on large prey.

Hesok backed away, pulling Shyaree with him as he anxiously checked himself for injuries. The curse wasn't a transmissible disease, but everyone acted as if it were, fearing they might catch it if they were so much as nicked by the draga sul. Or as the mages called it in their tongue, the soul catcher.

"I told you to stay away!" Hesok exclaimed thunderously. "He could have cursed me!"

Shyaree gave him no response. The selfish coward deserved none. She crawled as far as her rope would allow to check on her twin. Reiken's skin scalded as though the mana in his marrow were afire, and even though he was unconscious, the dagger remained in his white-knuckled grip.

"Reiken should never have trusted the archmage!" Dapa Jetossi declared, finally reappearing from behind two clan warriors, both hands planted indignantly over his hips. "He should never have agreed to the deal. The draga sul is black magic, and the archmage meant to curse him."

Shyaree almost laughed. The archmage might be frigid and fearsome, but Declan Thorne hadn't struck the deal with Reiken to pass on a curse. No. Reiken had done that part on his own. He had misused the dagger, triggering a magical backlash that would slowly but surely drain the mana from his bones and render him malmorphic. When it came to that, the clan would have no choice but to shun him.

As the clan shaman, as Reiken's *sister*, she would not allow that to happen.

Still on her knees, Shyaree cast an imploring glance at the male who was to be her lifemate. *"Reiken's condition has worsened much faster than I'd expected. We must leave for the Tribe at dawn."*

"The Tribe?" Hesok repeated aloud, acting like he knew nothing of her plans. "Why in Thurin's wrath would we present ourselves before the Tribe?"

Hesok's pretense caused her teeth to grind, but Shyaree schooled her features and kept her motions calm as she explained herself before the clan. Before Dapa Jetossi. *"You know why. To create the curse-breaking elixir for Reiken, I will need three things from Thurin's Mountain."* And no one went up the god mountain without a Tribe elder's consent. No one crossed the Wall without permission.

This was the primary reason she'd agreed to husungai even though she felt nothing for Hesok, and knowing full well she was the last female in the clan he wanted.

The Tribe would never receive an untethered female. Even if she somehow managed to gain an audience with the Tribe elders without a warrior's backing, Shyaree doubted they'd allow her across the Wall on her own. She needed Hesok to get to Thurin's Mountain, even if it was only to sway the elders into giving them passage through the Wall.

"You would air our troubles before the Tribe? Disgrace our clan?" Her groom gaped at her with such incredulity that it would have convinced even her had she not discussed this with him just days prior. "We shouldn't have to pay for his folly and dark perversions."

The lying cur . . . She clenched her fists but didn't try exposing him. It would be his word against hers. She didn't need to be a soothsayer to know how that would play out. She glanced around, seeking support, but found none. Even Reiken's most trusted warriors kept their heads bowed, none daring to speak a word of reproach, because Hesok was not wrong.

Her brother *had* dabbled in the dark arts in spite of her pleading. Reiken had triggered a curse in his desperate, flawed attempt at raising the dead when he hadn't had the proper means to do so. But the fault was not his alone.

Shyaree was equally culpable.

"What are you suggesting, then?" She drew in a fortifying breath, but she was still unable to disguise the fury that fed a tremble into her movements. *"That we stand by and do nothing? Allow the curse to run its course? Reiken is not only my*

brother but your primus! You are his second, yet you show such indifference over the life of a man you have sworn to protect."

Most of the clan could understand Shyaree's sign language and read her open criticism, which further fueled the furious blaze in Hesok's eyes. He jutted his chin and raised his voice, unequivocally commanding every listening ear. "Precisely. I am his second, which is why I must act like one. Reiken hasn't acted like a primus ever since he gained possession of the draga sul. Who do you think has been leading the clan over the last sun cycle while your brother busied himself with false hopes of raising dead brides?"

Shyaree blanched while murmurings of agreement sounded among the clan. Clearly bolstered by the attention, Hesok swept his gaze over the crowd and beat his unbound fist to his chest. "I believe it's time we choose a new primus. A stalwart warrior who'd put the clan's needs before his own."

Shyaree curled her lips, not bothering to hide her disgust. *"You may be his second, but you are no primus. You could never beat my brother in a fair challenge"*—she punctuated her final words with a scoff and a mocking flourish of her hand—*"stalwart warrior."*

Hesok's palm cracked across her face so abruptly she didn't have a chance to blink. Shyaree brought a shaking hand to her stinging cheek, and whatever flitted across her expression caused Hesok to take a wary step back. The effect only lasted for a moment, because a self-righteous sneer curved his lips. "Do not forget your place, female. You are my bride. Disrespect me once more and I *will* forsake you, honor be damned."

It seemed she would always be the scapegrace of the clan.

Beneath the sea of judgmental stares needling her skin, Shyaree turned to her unconscious twin and peeled his fingers open to relieve him of the draga sul. For a relic of such staggering power, the dagger hardly weighed anything. She tested the sharp end with her fingertip, and the scarlet stones in the hilt seemed to wink at her.

Hesok retreated warily, but he could not get far. Not with the rope binding them together. "What are you—"

Shyaree held his gaze and very slowly, very deliberately, lifted the dagger to her throat. The snap of the rope was the sweetest relief.

Gasps chorused, followed by a wave of shocked and scandalized whispers. Hesok gawked with the disbelief of a male who had never expected to be spurned, especially not by one such as *her*.

"Daughter of Baleen, what do you think you're doing?" Dapa Jetossi demanded. "Forsaking your intended before you've even completed husungai is *not* done!"

Shyaree only lifted a defiant shoulder and leveled her eyes at Hesok. *"I just saved you your honor."*

And she'd saved herself the disgrace of being the first female in pantherai history to stab her lifemate in his sleep.

Shyaree wrapped the kaftan securely over her shoulder, one she'd snagged from Reiken's hut when she'd detoured to return the draga sul. She had placed the relic back in the fur-lined chest where Reiken kept his most prized possessions—her brother would be distraught if he regained consciousness to find the dagger missing—and traded it for a creased and crumpled parchment.

Reiken treasured the draga sul the way Shyaree treasured their mother's writings. And where his botched use of the necromancer's dagger had resulted in a curse, their mother's instructions would guide Shyaree in creating a cure.

She unfolded the parchment gingerly, running her eyes and

a finger over the nearly faded words that were long etched into her mind. The leaf litter crunched beneath her soles as she hurried down a familiar track. Moss-covered boughs, coiling ferns, and flowering orchids framed her path to a spot by the river she frequented whenever she needed a moment of solitude.

Or a good cry.

Shyaree was two steps from the gentle meandering waters when the river stones clacked beneath angry footsteps. She quickly folded and slipped the parchment into her bandeau, obeying an irrational urge to keep secret a precious piece of her mother that made her feel both strong and strangely vulnerable.

Hesok stood amid a cluster of rocks crowned by lichen, arms folded like a contemptuous king. "You will return to the clan with me this instant and make a public apology."

He looked ready to drag her back by her hair. Indeed, had she been any other female, she was certain Hesok would have already done so. But she wasn't.

Not with her *condition*. A silver lining in every situation, as her father used to say.

"Apology? I deserve one for the way you acted ignorant of my plans for Thurin's Mountain."

He didn't even look embarrassed. "I never agreed to take you to the Tribe. I only agreed to marry you as duty demands, ingrate."

"Well, I just freed you from your duty. You should be thanking me."

"*Thank* you?" Hesok's complexion turned an unseemly shade of puce. "You just humiliated me before the whole clan! You owe me an apology. And if you won't give it, I will claim it while you're on your hands and knees."

She snarled even as a horrified shudder racked her spine. *"Stop your lying! We both know you don't want me."*

"Want you?" Hesok scoffed. "I don't need to want you to do my duty. You are my arranged bride. A supposed gift from Thurin! I will have what is mine, Shyaree, even if you are more bane than blessing."

"I only agreed because I needed your help to cross the Wall, but now—"

"Your agreement was never necessary for me to take what is my birthright." He spoke over her signals with open impatience. Then his lips formed a knowing smirk. "Besides, we both know you need me for far more than that. Tell me, how many heat cycles have you endured alone, hmm?"

Shyaree had come into full maturity over thirty seasons ago. Every cycle had been torture, to say the least, but they did not last long. If Hesok thought three days of easing twice a year was enough to sway her to husungai, then he was sorely mistaken.

She ignored him with a haughty lift of her chin. *"Now I know you have no intention of assisting me with the Tribe, I no longer have* any *reason to tether myself to you."*

With or without his help, she'd find a way onto the god mountain.

"Do not be foolish! Thurin's Mountain is fraught with danger. Even if you did get the Tribe elders' consent, you'd be dead the moment you stepped beyond the Wall. Killing yourself won't bring back Reiken's brides."

His last words were shaped like barbs, and they found their mark. A mortifying heat rose to prick the backs of her eyes, but she forced the tears down with a tightening of her lips. She would not give him the satisfaction of seeing her cry.

"I won't give up without trying. The elixir is Reiken's last chance."

And perhaps, the price of her penance.

Reiken had never outwardly blamed her for his brides' demise, but Shyaree knew better than anyone that unspoken wrongs were not forgiven wrongs. Silence did not cleanse sin. If anything, Reiken's silence on the matter only magnified Shyaree's guilt. And perhaps that was what she deserved. Her shame was a weight she had to carry for the rest of her life.

Clouds must have drifted over the sun above the canopy, because a sudden gloom shrouded them as though dusk had arrived prematurely. The air felt heavier, too. Charged.

Her skin prickled.

Hesok must have felt the odd shift in the air, too. He rolled his shoulders with restless energy.

"Enough of this senseless talk. The elixir is nothing but a fool's errand, and you know it. Come now." He caught her by the forearm with a firm grip. "I am willing to forgive if you're willing to apologize. We will resume husungai and leave this unpleasantness behind us."

Shyaree ripped her hand from his hold. *"I will not!"*

Anger flashed over his face, quickly replaced by a heavy sigh and a weary tone. "Do you care nothing for your father's wishes? Baleen chose me to be your warrior. Do you not fear angering the gods? A bride does not spurn her intended warrior without being shunned, Shyaree."

As if she weren't already shunned. *"I'd rather face Thurin's wrath than spend the rest of my life tethered to you."*

She saw the exact moment he realized she would not be manipulated into completing husungai. He raised a hand to strike her again. She flinched . . . but the blow never came.

Hesok stared at a point behind her shoulder, his eyes wide with shock. Gooseflesh crawled all over her skin. The burbling stream showed a distorted shadow looming at her back.

Before she could turn, a large hand caught her lower jaw. Long fingers clamped around her throat while an arm banded at her midsection, keeping her immobilized. A gray fog rose from the ground like mist on a sunbaked morning. Shadows coiled, phantom chains around her body. Shock burst from her in sharp breaths. She knew enough about the fae to recognize a *portal.*

Gods above, this couldn't be happening! But the shadows thickened with every spike of terror stabbing panic into her chest. She threw her head back, trying to thrash from his hold. But her captor's arms could well be forged of iron.

Shyaree reached for Hesok, pleading for an intervention, but the warrior only took a stumbling step back as he ran three shaky fingers down his forehead in the sign of Thurin.

His dumbstruck expression was the last thing she saw before the spiraling shadows darkened to ink, eclipsing her sight and ripping her from the world.

CHAPTER 3

Heat and humidity morphed into a chill, causing a shudder to rattle her bones. The shadows blindfolding her unraveled to reveal . . . a fjord. Shyaree blinked.

A painting.

One so intricately detailed that for one heart-stopping moment she had believed herself atop a summit, teetering at the edge of the precipice, staring down into a narrow channel that bled between twin granite cliffs. The canvas hung across a wood-paneled wall, the reality of its illusion dispelled only by dancing dust motes and the mismatched scents of aged vellum, dried ink, and something darker and deadlier.

Something intrinsically *male*.

Her abductor remained at her back, one hand still clasped over her throat, another binding her to his chest. It was like being chained to a brick wall. Alarm choked her. She threw a frantic, sweeping glance at her surroundings. Writing desk. Curtained windows. Dresser. A stately four-poster bed. She was in a bedchamber of sorts, which only served to intensify her terror. She bucked wildly, but her efforts were about as effective as a breeze puffing into a mountain.

"Easy, Shyaree."

Another shiver ripped through her. He spoke the tongue of her people, albeit thickly accented. And gods above, he knew her name. She brought a foot down with all the might she could muster, and her bare sole connected with a thick leather boot. His unmoving stance told her she'd probably hurt herself more than him.

"Calm down. It's me."

Shyaree stilled. That *voice* . . . No, it couldn't be.

His hold at her throat softened, as though he wanted to release her but wasn't quite sure if he should. She took full advantage of his hesitation. She jerked her head down and bit into the fleshy part between his thumb and index finger. *Hard.* It was gloved, but the leather was thin enough that he grunted.

"Fuck!" He released her completely.

She whipped around and gaped. Magic oozed from his pores, wafting off him like smoke from a bonfire. His hair had grown longer, and the disheveled moonlit strands framed an angular jaw and cheekbones more like cut glass than ever. The shadows beneath his eyes seemed darker, and his customary smirk was conspicuously missing.

As if his height and breadth weren't imposing enough, an alarming collection of throwing knives, daggers, and wickedly shaped blades decorated his lithe form. The weapons glinted, daunting in their own right, but they did little to distract from the tightly muscled physique beneath the black leathers. A form so lethally honed that his presence reminded her of an unsheathed blade.

Gabriel Blacksage.

She was hallucinating. She had to be. After an entire year,

he couldn't possibly be *here,* staring down at her with such rapt intensity and such . . . quiet.

Shyaree poked a wary finger into his chest. Firm. He tilted his head but made no protest, which further convinced her she must have somehow fallen into the river, hit her head, and was now suffering from some form of concussion. The Gabriel she knew was not prone to silence. She jabbed again, stronger this time.

Very solid. Hard, even.

Her hallucination chuckled. A darkly roguish and faintly familiar sound. Her body responded to his voice as if to a rough hand stroking down her back.

"Oh, I assure you I'm real. And shouldn't you be pinching yourself instead of poking at me?"

Shyaree's gaze snapped up in disbelief. Her hands jerked with stupefaction. *"You?* You! *Why did you take me? Where are we?"*

Amusement sparkled in his eyes. Bright and crystalline, they were the shade of violet petals in the full glory of spring. Absurdly pretty and utterly out of place amid masculine features.

"Hello to you, too, wildcat."

She sniffed. She detested that moniker. *"Hello, Gabriel Insufferable,"* she shot back, taking care to sign the last word with a vehement roll of her eyes.

Her response only seemed to deepen his amusement. "I knew I was unforgettable."

"Absolutely. You're about as unforgettable as a run-in with a bear." She canted her head in mock consideration. *"Or maybe a nest of wasps."*

His grin was as swift as it was unsettling, so she tore her sight from his face and took another glance around the room. The sun had been pinned at the highest point in the sky while she was at the river . . . but the light filtering through the semi-drawn curtains appeared muted here. Weaker. As though the sun had just risen and was barely yawning at the horizon. She took a step toward the recessed window, wanting a better look at the outside world, but then decided against turning her back on her captor.

"Where are we? Why did you take me?"

The movement of her hands seemed to draw his attention away from her face, because his head lowered, and his gaze took a slow roam over her body before dropping to her bare feet. She curled her toes in self-consciousness. The kaftan had fallen off her shoulders during their tussle. And while her bridal attire was hardly brow raising in the clan, somehow it felt wholly inappropriate before *this* male.

Gabriel must have felt it, too, because he took a hasty step back, his lips thinning as though she wore manure instead of bridal garments. He kept his eyes firmly averted as he moved to the bed, snatched up a blanket, and tossed it her way. Clearly she appeared so distasteful it hurt him to glance in her direction.

"I'll explain after you cover yourself," he muttered.

All remnants of fear dissipated like ash in the wind. Foolish, of course. Gabriel was a cutthroat who killed for coin. A male who could savage and sunder with a blink of his eye, something she'd witnessed firsthand. A male who could saunter through the five realms at a whim, and one who had just torn her out of her world the way a child plucked the petals off a flower. She *should* be afraid.

But she wasn't.

The only emotion she could muster while looking at his chiseled profile was irritation as the memories of their time together in the mage realm surged to the forefront of her mind. Arrogant. Obnoxious. Inconsiderate.

Spine stiff, Shyaree wrapped the thick woolen blanket around her body, tucking the ends beneath her arms so she could continue to sign. *"Maybe next time you kidnap someone, you'll have the consideration to bring the rest of their clothes, too."*

Indignation actually flared in his eyes. "I didn't kidnap you."

Thurin give her strength. *"You snuck up on me! Snatched me from behind and stole me right out of my realm."* She shouldn't be this surprised. This was exactly the sort of thing his insidious kind was known for. *"What do you want from me?"*

She expected a cutting retort but received a tightening of his jaw. "I . . . " He snapped his mouth shut, seemingly at a loss for words for the first time she'd seen. Ha! Gabriel Blacksage struggling for words. If she weren't so incensed, she'd laugh. Then again, his somberness was so unlike him that something else struck her.

"Is it Evangeline?" Concern hastened her motions. *"Is she all right?"*

"Evie?" Gabriel frowned as though the mage queen were the last thing on his mind. He waved a hand. "Oh, I'm sure she's fine." He leaned one shoulder against the wall he'd retreated to, keeping clear distance between them as if she carried some foreign plague. He couldn't even seem to look her in the eye. His eyes followed her hands whenever she spoke, but his gaze darted to the wooden floorboards frequently, as if it disgusted him to look in her direction for any length of time.

"If it's not Evangeline, then to what do I owe this pleasure?" She lanced him with a sneer, lest he mistake her signals for anything less than sarcasm.

"I need your help."

He needed *her* help? He hadn't even thought to bid her goodbye, and after an entire sun cycle, he thought he could abduct her because he needed her *help*?

Shyaree shot him a universally lewd sign with a finger.

To her annoyance, it only caused his lips to twitch. "Look, wildcat. I know you're upset with the way I brought you here, but I had no choice. Prince Zion is looking for you. He knows who you are, and he'll find you sooner or later." His focus dipped from her face to her chest for a brief moment before dropping back to the ground. The floorboards must have been a dark polished oak once, but time had weathered the grains into a mellow walnut shade. "I took you for your own protection," he added almost in a grumble.

As though he'd performed an act of service at his own expense.

Shyaree stared in disbelief. *"The Unseelie prince?"*

But Gabriel didn't respond, seemingly fixated on his boots. She snapped her fingers impatiently to draw his attention back up to her hands.

"Why would the prince want me?"

"You have something he . . . needs."

"And what is that?"

"He—" Gabriel shut his eyes, pinching the bridge of his nose with a deep exhale. "Could you please keep the blanket on? It's falling off."

Scowling, she yanked the sagging blanket back beneath her arms. It wasn't her fault she needed to use her hands to converse and the blanket was too thick and stiff to stay in place.

"I need you to take me home right now."

Gabriel's lips flattened. "I just told you that you were in danger."

"I don't need your protection! I can protect myself."

"Right." A smirk slid over his lips, and suddenly he was the Gabriel Blacksage she remembered. "Like how you protected yourself when I *kidnapped* you?"

Shyaree bristled. *"You caught me by surprise, that's all."*

He arched a brow. "And your point?"

Oh, he hadn't changed one bit. Infuriating male with those irritatingly pretty eyes. *"Did it ever occur to you to ask me nicely?"*

A shrug. "I didn't think you'd come with me even if I did."

Hard to argue with that.

"What does this prince of yours want from me? Is it the draga sul?" She took the time to fingerspell D-R-A-G-A-S-U-L, unsure if Gabriel was familiar with the hand signal for a relic so specific to animati lore.

"Draga sul," he signed back, indicating his awareness before he switched to verbal speech with a sour curl of his lips. "Also, Zion is no prince of mine."

Shyaree huffed. She wasn't here to discuss fae politics. *"So he* does *want the draga sul? If that's what he wants, then he can try to get it from Reiken himself."*

Both her brother and the dagger were safe behind the clan's barriers erected by shieldmakers. No one—neither animati nor fae prince—could breach those walls.

"He'll want the draga sul eventually, but that's not what he's after right now. It's you he wants . . . or perhaps I should say, your blood."

Shyaree blinked. *"My blood?"*

A curt nod. "Before the last seer perished in the Winter War, he left behind a prophecy. One that states the blood of a voiceless twin is the key to the draga morli. The prophecy was also explicit in stating the twin was sister to the guardian of the draga sul."

Shyaree sniffed. The fact that she was nonverbal and Reiken's twin meant that her blood was the key to finding the draga sul's counterpart? Preposterous!

Though it was hardly a surprise the Unseelie prince wanted both those daggers. According to animati lore, the daggers were the sacred tools of the necromancer, Mekari the Unholy One.

Many believed that anyone who possessed both could not only defy death and spurn the laws of nature—they could raise an army so fearsome that the five gods would tremble.

Except the draga morli had been lost for an eon.

"If the draga morli still existed, it would have been found a long time ago," she signed impatiently. Her brother, for one, couldn't find the means to locate it even when he had the draga sul at hand.

Gabriel shook his head. "You're not listening, wildcat. Before Reiken had it, the draga sul was in the keeping of the Echelon of Archmages for centuries. The draga morli was never found because Declan is not a twin, nor was the archmage Alejandro before him. But your brother . . . "

Was a twin. Hers.

She took an unwitting step back at the intensity in his gaze and the conviction in his words. *"That can't be true. Reiken couldn't do it."*

Her brother had been obsessed with raising his dead brides. If there had been a way for him to find the other dagger, Reiken would have.

"He didn't have the prophecy from the necromancer's manuscripts." Gabriel's throat bobbed again, and his next words came unbearably soft. "He couldn't have known that his sister was the key to it all along."

Shyaree shuffled back even farther, her veins turning to ice.

If Gabriel spoke the truth, if this prophecy was true, then Reiken's dream of raising his brides from the netherworld could actually become a *reality*. Shyaree shuddered. The animati lore also held that the Risen did not always come back the same.

The lore was so steeped in the dark arts that just thinking of it curdled her blood.

"How much blood would it take?"

She was no stranger to bloodletting. Many animati rituals involved it. After all, their species bore mana in the marrow and the veins. Shyaree, by the nature of her changelessness, was mahalwei, which meant the mana in her blood was richer than most.

Gabriel paused long enough to make her uneasy.

"I'm not sure," he said finally.

"You're not sure? What does this prophecy of yours say?"

His throat worked as though he were trying to keep the words from escaping his lips before he said, "Mekari's runes will have to be carved into your skin, and your blood needs to run from it."

She shuddered, but that didn't sound *too* bad. *"Do it, then."* She stuck an arm out at him.

Gabriel blinked.

"Take what you need, and send me home."

"You're willing to . . . do it?"

"What choice do I have? You are clearly not willing to let me go unless I give you what you want . . . and I need to return home. So just do it. Quickly."

She had never heard of the necromancer's manuscripts. Nor had she heard of any such prophecy. It was probably a myth to begin with. If such a prophecy did exist, why had the archmages not capitalized on it sooner? Why only Zion, only now? It made no sense. And *if* the prophecy was true, if her blood was key to the draga morli . . . well, no one would be raising any army—not without the draga sul. And that dagger was safe behind her clan's shieldmakers' walls.

Shyaree didn't have time to spare on an unsubstantiated myth. No. She needed to return home and concoct another plan to gain an audience with the Tribe elders before Reiken's curse escalated any further.

Gabriel's lips formed a grim line. "I'm afraid it's not that simple. There are twelve runes that need to be carved along your spine . . . "

Shyaree flinched. Gods above, *twelve* runes?

"And according to the prophecy, your blood will need to be collected under the blood moon . . . and the next one falls in exactly twenty-seven days."

She frowned, but he wasn't done.

"And there's the matter of Zion. I don't trust him to leave you alone. At least, not until the draga morli is found." Gabriel nodded as if he had already made the decision on her behalf. "You'll stay here until the bloodletting . . . until it's safe for you to leave."

"I can't stay here for twenty-seven days!"

A muscle twitched in his jaw, but he said nothing.

The resulting silence was terrifying.

"No." She stepped back until the table's edge bit into her back. From the intensity of Reiken's last episode, she shuddered to think what would become of him in the next five days, much less twenty-seven. *"I refuse. Take me home this instant."*

"That is not an option, wildcat."

Panic seized her like claws. *"You can take me home and come to me on the night of the blood moon. But I need to return to my clan. Now."*

"I wouldn't have brought you here, today, if I believed there was another way. But Zion knows the location of your clan. He knows your identity, Shyaree. He wants the draga morli, and he believes your blood is the only way to find it."

She stared at him, sudden suspicion dawning. *"You want it, too, don't you?"* A mercenary like Gabriel Blacksage didn't do anything out of the goodness of his heart. *"You didn't bring me here just to protect me, did you? You took me because you want to use me. Just like him."*

Gabriel began pacing as though he could escape her questions. An oddly comical sight because the length of the wall took him fewer than five paces before forcing him to turn around. His restlessness drew her attention to the second canvas on the wall. A string of islands cradled in a perfect, pellucid blue, painted from a bird's-eye view. So masterfully done, it was doubtless from the same hand who had painted the stunning fjord.

When Gabriel ceased his pacing to meet her gaze again, it was with the eyes of a coldhearted assassin.

"If I don't take you, he will."

She bit into her bottom lip, and her hands trembled. Not from fear but rage. *"Am I supposed to be grateful? Am I supposed to believe you're somehow the better option?"*

He blanched. "I understand you don't have much of a choice, but—"

Shyaree snatched the slim vase from the desk and threw it at his head. He dodged with remarkable alacrity. The vase shattered into jagged pieces on the ground.

"Take me home! Now!"

He appeared aggrieved. "Was that truly necessary? That was an heirloom."

The nerve of this male! Shyaree reached for the next closest object. An ornamental box with contents that rattled.

"Stop," he warned sternly. "You put that—"

She sent it sailing across the room. This time, he caught it in an impressive show of reflexes. "That's enough, wildcat. You're acting like a faeling."

Her jaw hung. *"How dare you kidnap me, tell me your plans to keep me hostage while you bleed me . . . and call me a child?"*

She grabbed the only other thing left on the desk. An intricate lamp with a shade shaped like downturned petals. It was almost a work of art. She hurled it at his head. He caught it, but the shade toppled askew. She snarled. The bastard had barged into her life at a whim, made egregious demands involving her blood and body, and she couldn't even hit him across the head with a lamp. She prowled on her side of the wall until her foot snagged on the leg of a marble-topped stool.

A stool!

She picked it up, staggering from its substantial weight, while the blanket pooled at her feet.

Gabriel hissed and held up both hands. "No. Stop, Shyaree, please . . . I *need* the draga morli. There are lives at stake." The words came out pleading, slowing her anger. "Innocent lives."

She set the stool back down with an angry thump. *"Innocent people die every day! I'm not any more responsible for them than I am for you and your needs! But I am responsible for my own family."*

Reiken was all she had left.

She needed to go back, find a way to break the curse before he became incurably malmorphic. Before the clan cast him out. She couldn't desert her own brother just because Gabriel believed her blood to be the key to the draga morli. For all she knew, the prince had misinterpreted the prophecy! And Gabriel was just the mercenary carrying out his orders. A mercenary who hadn't even spared her a *goodbye*. He did not deserve a wink of her time.

"I won't do it. Now take me home!"

Her resolve must have shown, because his eyes hardened to amethysts. A muscle in his jaw ticced. "Everyone has a price, wildcat. Name yours."

"You can't buy me!"

Gabriel ran his fingers through his hair, ruffling the strands with such frustration that she almost felt sorry for him. Almost.

"Then I'm sorry." He turned and slipped out the wooden door, smooth as the snake he was. Shyaree lurched forward, but before she could reach him, the door slammed in her face. An incriminating click sounded. Shyaree rattled the knob. Locked. Thurin's wrath! She pounded against the door. If she had a voice, she would have screeched. As it was, she could only assault the wooden barrier to express her fury.

"Calm down, Shyaree." Gabriel's muffled voice drifted through the door.

Shyaree banged her fist twice to convey her *fuck you* sentiment.

"Think about what I said . . . " A sigh. "And keep the blanket on."

Silence. She didn't even hear his footsteps fading away.

She sank wearily to her knees. Tears threatened to spill. Damn the bastard to the five hells! She curled into herself, wishing for the ability to shift into her pantherai, break down this blasted door, hunt the insufferable bastard down, and rip him a new asshole. Shyaree sniffled, wiping the back of her hand under her nose, and stared at her surroundings balefully. The damned fae hadn't even told her where they were. Were they still in Thurin's Realm? She doubted it. Her kind didn't live in dwellings with brick walls and paneled wood. Her chin dropped back to her knees as she stared at the dappled light playing over the floorboards.

Dappled sunlight.

She looked up at the source.

The window.

Chapter 4

The door thumped with another angry kick. Gabriel shut his eyes and sagged against the wall outside the guest chamber. Blazing hellfires, he'd known it wouldn't be easy to convince Shyaree, but the wildcat was even more feral than he'd remembered.

He rubbed his palm with a wince. Thank the gods Shyaree was changeless, or he'd probably have lost a finger.

Kidnapped, she'd claimed. A self-deprecating scoff escaped his lips. She wasn't wrong. He had not planned on abduction, but when he'd seen the pantherai warrior raising a hand as if to strike her, Gabriel had simply acted. And now he was no different from the lowlife rookheads running the slave-trade cartel . . . only he had a furious female ready to spill his guts locked up in a guest room.

Ozenn's blood. Gabriel scrubbed a hand over his jaw. He couldn't have devised a worse blunder if he'd planned it. Damn it to all the five hells.

He *could* keep her locked up until the blood moon. He

could easily overpower her. He didn't *need* her cooperation . . . Sickness greased his innards.

He might be an assassin, but even he had lines.

How in Ozenn's blood would he get her to cooperate?

"Innocent people die every day!" she had signed, her hand motions sharp, her expression incredulous and indignant. *"I'm not any more responsible for them than I am for you and your needs! But I am responsible for my own family."*

"So am I," he whispered.

Gabriel didn't have much. Not anymore. Whatever he did have, he would fight for. Iolanthe was his sister. His flesh and blood. If her freedom meant he had to act the villain . . . so be it. He had done worse for far less reason.

Locked. The window was locked. Of course it was.

Shyaree shook the lever with a scowl, and the thick woolen blanket slipped off her to pool around her feet. Thurin's wrath! She wrapped the blanket back around herself with a bad-tempered huff.

There had to be a way out of here. She paced the room. The empty wardrobe implied she was locked in an otherwise unoccupied bedchamber. A spare room? There was a mirror, the bed, a desk, and the stool . . . Her eyes widened. The stool! As she attempted to lift it, the blanket fell from beneath her arms again. Blowing out a frustrated breath, she marched to the bed and stripped off its covering.

If she did manage to break the window, she didn't want to run off in a foreign realm clad in her bridal attire.

The white sheet was much thinner than the blanket and far less cumbersome. It was also wide enough that she had to wrap it twice around her body before she could easily tie the excess into a thick knot at the back of her neck. At the very least, she didn't need to worry about it falling off her shoulders.

She hefted the seat and smashed it into the window. The stool, in all its lacquered glory, crashed through the window frame like a rock. The resulting noise was deafening. She cringed and counted three fevered breaths, but no one barged through the door. A peek through the broken window showed the stool swallowed by the bushes below, which appeared quite a ways down.

Green lawn stretched for a good distance before it met a row of thin-limbed trees and a tall iron fence. She poked her head farther out for a better view and noticed a street at what must be the front of the building. More ochre-brick buildings with dark, pointed roofs loomed like a row of dour-faced sentinels guarding the street. Uneasiness stamped fidgety feet over her chest. The last time she'd been in a large settlement, it had been the Amereen capital. Quaint shops and merry street vendors filled her memory. She would have been lost that day if it hadn't been for Gabriel.

How could she hope to escape this place?

Shyaree sucked in a steadying breath. She would figure it out one step at a time.

If she could change, she could have made the jump easily, but in her two-legged form? She'd probably break a limb. Which meant she had only two options.

One, stay and play captive for the next twenty-seven days until Gabriel bled her like a sacrificial goat.

Two, climb out the window and figure out a way to get home.

There was no contest.

After hastily shoving the thick blanket over the window sill to cover the broken glass, she reached for the ledge. Pain sliced into her palm—she'd overlooked the shards sticking out from the side of the frame and now the window frame was stained with bloody palm prints. Grimacing, she retreated into the room.

Gods above, this wasn't as easy as she'd thought.

She had also wrapped the bedsheet too tightly around herself, and she could barely bend her knees to climb out. She loosened the tie at the back of her neck and adjusted the sheet to allow her legs more movement, then clambered precariously over the sill, taking care to avoid the glass at the sides as she stepped onto the thin outer ledge. There were no other footholds in the smooth brick wall, but the ledge extended far enough that she might just be able to reach the window beside hers—one that appeared blessedly *open*—if she leapt.

And if she failed, well, hopefully the bushes below were less prickly than they seemed. A slight breeze tugged at her hair, whipping it around her face and shoulders as though to warn her of her perilous position. She pressed her body against brick, her fingers into mortar, and shuffled bit by small bit until she neared the end of the ledge. She had to jump. A quick look below caused her toes to curl and her heart to palpitate almost hard enough to knock her off balance.

"Hoy!" The voice startled her so much she nearly lost her grip. Another glance showed a boy standing by the stool in the bushes. A shock of black hair. Pointed ears. Fae. A stream of Faerian flowed from his mouth, nothing intelligible to her ears. But from his bewildered expression and taut stance, he must think her an intruder. He was also yelling, which meant he'd attract more attention.

Or worse, Gabriel.

Thurin help her. It was now or never.

Shyaree lunged.

By some small miracle, she found herself clinging to the ledge of the window she was aiming for. When she managed to pull herself up, she wasted no time squeezing through the window's opening, only to curse when she got stuck at the hips. The boy below was shouting up a storm. Thurin's wrath!

Shyaree wriggled, shoving hard at the window to pry it wider.

It finally gave way.

She tumbled face-first into a carpeted corridor. To her left, many doors, and a curving staircase to her right. Should she hide in another room? Run up the stairs? Run down? The boy would likely alert Gabriel soon, and if the damned Unseelie found her, her chances of escape would dwindle from low to none.

Out. She needed to get out *now*.

Instinct sent her barreling down the stairs. At least she wouldn't have to worry about climbing out any more windows. Holding onto that thought, she reached the bottom step, which opened into a vast hall.

Arched windows spanned one side of the room. Sunbeams bounced off the varnished floors onto the alarming collection of weaponry mounted to the walls. Crossbows, swords, maces, blades of different shapes and sizes—all polished to a sinister shine. Recessed alcoves with plush seats took up the other side of the room, while an odd assortment of tables dominated the center.

Her gaze latched onto the exit at the opposite end of the hall.

Two stately hardwood doors with an intricately carved crest of snarling wolves and soaring hawks surrounding two crossed swords. There was almost an eerie anticipation to the room. As though the space were meant for a crowd and it awaited motion, conversation, and laughter. She scampered past two large rectangular tables and a semicircular countertop containing a series of glass cabinets. Bottles of varying sizes, cups—

She tripped over a boot sticking out from under one table and crashed into the adjacent table.

A drowsy grunt, followed by an exclamation in a melodious language that could only be Faerian.

Gods above, the boot was attached to a *leg.*

An ashy-haired male rose from under the table, squinting at her with a look of utter bafflement. Shyaree darted for the door.

Only two more males sauntered through an open doorway, blocking her path to the exit. She froze like a frightened possum.

All three males reminded her of Gabriel in some form or fashion. They all had uncanny eyes of varying shades of purple, sharp-tipped ears, and similar leathers that clung to strapping frames. Wicked-looking blades and swords were secured to each broad back. If they were anything like her captor, she was in a lot of trouble.

One of the newcomers barked out stern, incomprehensible words.

Shyaree shrank back.

He reminded her of a bristling bear sizing her up, and he definitely didn't sound friendly. The one beside him appeared equally daunting but less austere. The brows above his hawklike eyes furrowed as he spouted words dripping with confusion.

Shyaree shook her head and hands, trying to indicate that she couldn't understand them, all while edging toward the double doors.

The one from under the table scratched at his nape,

studying the sheet covering her body in a way that made her uncomfortable. If the first two were a bear and a hawk, this one definitely reminded her of a snake—one that looked at her as though she were a juicy field mouse.

Bear, Hawk, and Snake all closed in on her simultaneously.

She bolted for the doors, praying they weren't locked.

Just as she reached the handle, the door flung open, cuffing her in the chin. She fell on her rear, wincing at the pain radiating through to her jaw.

The boy who'd caught her window escapade burst in. When he spied her on the ground, he jabbed a triumphant finger at her. "Fir! La fain!"

Only the boy wasn't really a boy. He was lanky and clean-shaven, which had given her the impression of youth, but up close, he was something else altogether. His skin held a faint iridescent shimmer, and there were *ridges* on the sides of his neck that reminded her of gills on a fish.

As if things weren't dire enough already, Fish Boy had brought another male with him. She glanced up and gasped. A fae with a dagger tattooed across his cheek, the sharp end pointing to the corner of his mouth. The air gushed from her lungs. This was the male who had brought her home a year ago. She racked her head for a name. Arkas Ironfall.

A *portal maker*.

She scrambled to her feet, signing frantically. *"Help me!"*

Arkas's eyes widened with a spark of recognition. "Shyaree?"

Shyaree nodded enthusiastically, elated to see a man who could be her key home.

Arkas blinked and scratched his beard, obviously dumbfounded. "What are you doing here?" he asked in heavily accented Animatish.

"I don't want to be here!" Gods above, she didn't even know where *here* was. *"Please help me. Take me home!"*

Arkas stared at her motions, his expression increasingly perplexed. "I . . . I'm sorry, but I don't understand you."

Frustration cawed in her chest.

The other males had all crowded around her, and they were speaking over each other, some even belting out words in Animatish. Arkas responding in her tongue had obviously clued them in, and apparently, they all spoke her language. Some more fluently than others.

"How you here?" Bear asked.

"Not speak why?" Hawk.

Arkas interrupted in their tongue, and if he clarified her nonspeaking nature, it didn't stop the questions.

"Where did you come from?" Snake demanded.

Fish Boy piped up in rapid Faerian. Judging from his animated motions and inflection, he was undoubtedly recounting her window escapade. Someone grabbed her elbow, spun her around.

Snake.

He tugged the sheet at her shoulder. "What are you wearing? How did you break into the Red Den?"

Shyaree jerked her hand from his grip and bared her teeth in a snarl. *"Don't touch me!"*

Snake might be the most fluent in Animatish, but he clearly did not know Handspeak. He seized her forearm and gave her a hard shake. "Answer us!"

Idiot. Obviously, he did not understand her hand signals, so what manner of answer did he expect from her? She mimed writing, hoping these males could interpret the gesture . . . but even if they did allow her a writing instrument, could they read Animatish?

"Can you not speak, or can you not hear?" Snake cocked

his head with a sneer. His teeth gleamed like the myriad knives strapped to his person. "Answer. Us."

Shyaree stepped up to him, and being a typical male, Snake didn't step back, even though surprise flared in his expression. It was all too easy to lift one of his slim blades from its holster. She flipped it deftly in her hand and slapped the flat of it against his cheek before pulling back into a defensive stance.

Snake hissed.

"Caspian!" Arkas snapped in a warning tone before continuing in a string of Faerian.

Shyaree had no idea if Arkas was warning Snake—Caspian—or if he was rebuking *her*. Whichever it was, she couldn't back down. The first rule of survival as a changeless female in an animati clan—never show weakness. Shyaree brandished the knife, making it clear she knew her way around a blade and wouldn't hesitate to use it.

Snake's eyes narrowed. "I'd give that back if I were you."

She very deliberately took a step back and pointed at the door. If they allowed her to leave, she would gladly return the weapon.

"You think you can sneak into the Den and leave, just like that?"

Sneak in? Ha! Shyaree held up a derogatory finger.

Hawk made a noise that sounded like a smothered laugh. Caspian didn't seem to find it amusing, because his canines sharpened at an alarming rate.

Shyaree widened her stance and braced herself, but the attack never came.

Someone pushed past Hawk and Bear, grabbed Caspian by the collar, and shoved him sideways as though he were made of cotton and not muscle. And this someone suffered no retaliation for it. In fact, the ring of males eased away, leaving Shyaree to face the brunt of a blazing violet gaze.

"What in the five blazing hells do you think you're doing, wildcat?"

Low words spoken in her language, underscored with such deadly intent that her grip on the knife slackened. She swallowed.

Gabriel looked ready to maim.

Chapter 5

Gabriel ground his teeth, tasting blood. His canines had distended of their own accord, and his heart still pounded a feverish beat.

He'd only been gone long enough to fix Shyaree a plate of food from the kitchen, but he'd returned to broken glass and scarlet stains on the window frame. He'd trailed the bloody fingerprints with his heart lodged somewhere in his throat, only to find her in the heart of the Den, snarling at his men as though she truly were a wildcat . . . while wearing a ridiculous white sheet that was one knot away from unraveling.

Shyaree took one look at him, and her face paled.

She bolted.

Gabriel caught a handful of the damned sheet flapping around her like an oversized sail on a mast. With that single yank, the knot came free, causing her to stumble to her knees. Cursing, he gripped her elbow to help her up, but she flipped around and lithely jabbed her other elbow at his abdomen. Gabriel jumped back, but pain scored his forearm. "Damn it!"

Where in the five hells had she gotten a knife?

"Get that out of her hands!" Arkas yelled.

Before the others could intervene, Gabriel pulled her to her feet. For all her feistiness and fire, it was easy enough to disarm her. He threw the knife out of her reach and wrapped the sheet firmly around her to immobilize her arms. The wildcat made an enraged huffing noise in her throat and snapped her teeth.

"Bite me again, wildcat, and I swear I will bite back."

Eyes flashing with disdain, she stilled. For someone who lacked the ability to vocalize, the woman certainly conveyed contempt with ease.

"Now where exactly did you think you could get to?" he asked, belatedly realizing her hands were trapped. He loosened the sheet enough for her arms to slide out to sign.

She formed a ring with one hand, fingered the circumference and jabbed at him with such vehemence that her denigration was obvious even to those who couldn't understand Handspeak. *"You're an asshole!"* Scorn oozed from her every motion.

When it became clear she was about to belt him with more derogatory Handspeak, he shoved her arms down and tightened the sheet again, flashing a grim smile. "I never claimed to be a gentleman."

Shyaree's lips thinned, and her chin jutted with stubborn defiance, showcasing the discoloration spreading across her jaw like rot. What the fuck?

"Who *did* this?" Gabriel grated the words in Faerian because the bruise didn't look like something she'd acquired from a fall. It streaked diagonally across her jaw, as though she'd collided with someone's knuckles.

"No idea." Hector shrugged. "The wench appeared out of nowhere."

"She broke out of a second-floor bedchamber window!" Isidor supplied unhelpfully.

"Bedchamber?" Mordecai scratched the stubble on his cheek. "How did she get into one of the bedchambers? Well, that explains the sheet . . . "

"Maybe one of the patrons snuck her in last night," Caspian said with a sneer as he picked up the knife from the ground and slipped it back into its sheath. "Had their fun and left her here."

"I'm not asking who brought her here." Gabriel damned well knew *that*. "I'm asking who hit her."

Unblinking silence.

Gabriel cupped Shyaree's jaw, careful to keep his fingers away from her vicious teeth, and ghosted his thumb across the bruise darkening her skin. "Explain!" he barked.

Isidor startled as though he'd been doused headfirst in a tub of ice. "I didn't mean to! I opened the—"

"*You?*" Of all his men, Gabriel wouldn't have expected the gentle mer healer to raise a fist against a woman.

"I-I . . . it was an accident!"

Gabriel seethed. "How could a bruise this shape and size be an accident?"

Arkas cleared his throat and stepped forward to shield the mer from Gabriel's wrath. He had been quiet throughout, no doubt observing and drawing silent observations as usual. "It was an accident. She ran into the door just as Isidor and I were entering. It was the *door*, Gabe. Ask her yourself." Without giving him a chance to react, Arkas harrumphed. "Why are you growling at us anyway? Shouldn't the question be *why* she climbed out a window on the second floor?"

Gabriel scowled. "Isn't it obvious? She's trying to escape."

"And why is that?" Arkas tilted his head with an assessing gaze. "What's an animati female doing in the Den in the first place?"

Every fae gaze swung in Gabriel's direction, speculation

gleaming in purple-hued irises. There weren't many portal makers in the guild, and Arkas had not touched a female since the death of his mate.

Hector gaped as if Gabriel had sprouted horns. "*That's* why she's wearing nothing but a sheet?"

"Fuck me, is this why you've been disappearing for days on end?" Mordecai guffawed.

"She's obviously more trouble than she's worth," Caspian said with a roll of his eyes.

Gabriel exhaled. "Gods, it's not like that!"

"Tell us, then. What is it like?" Mordecai grinned.

For a crew of cutthroats, the men behaved alarmingly like a gaggle of fishwives.

"You really should've kept her out of the Den," Hector muttered with a shake of his head. "The succubi won't be happy when they find out they've been replaced. By an animati female, no less."

"Right. What manner of animati is she?" Mordecai asked, his gaze roaming over Shyaree with unconcealed interest.

Disgusted, Gabriel swept an arm beneath Shyaree's knees and scooped her up against his chest. It didn't help his current reputation, but damn the gods, dawn had already arrived, and the gambling tables never opened too early for some. Shyaree was in the presence of his most trusted circle, and that had already sharpened his fangs. For reasons Gabriel couldn't explain, he didn't want anyone else seeing the wildcat in little more than a bedsheet. Without another word, he hauled his fuming cargo up the stairs with the loons hooting in his wake.

Shyaree contemplated sinking her teeth into the taut tendons of Gabriel's neck.

The only thing stopping her was his earlier warning. Since his fangs were considerably sharper than her canines, Shyaree seethed in silence while Gabriel carted her back up the stairs as though she weighed no more than a babe.

Gabriel was guildmaster. A fact she was reminded of by the way he interacted with the others. Even the other portal maker, Arkas, seemed to defer to him. What were her chances of returning to her home realm without Gabriel's consent? Probably none. She had to convince him to see reason.

Biting, no matter how satisfying, was out of the question —for now.

The lout surprised her by surpassing the second floor and going up another two flights of stairs before opening a door in yet another dimly lit corridor. She didn't need to ask to know this room was *his*. It smelled distinctly of polished steel, crisp shadows, and something annoyingly sensual and male. But instead of alarm, Shyaree felt a grudging spark of interest.

Gabriel's chamber was filled with *things.*

Many, many things that piqued her damnably curious heart. A dresser, a wardrobe, and a sizable desk took up almost half the room. Memorabilia her fingers itched to touch littered every available surface. Glass jars full of feathered instruments, stacks of books, random knives, strewn coins, and loose buttons. A somewhat deformed skull partially covered by a pile of parchment. The unmade bed occupied the remaining space in the room, with clothing draped haphazardly at all edges.

Shyaree side-eyed her captor with a snort. The man was a *mess.* Not that it came as much of a surprise. Gabriel had always exuded a chaotic sort of energy.

He dumped her unceremoniously onto the mattress.

The moment she was free of his arms, she wriggled free from the sheet. *"How dare you!"*

"How dare I?" Violet eyes narrowed. "*You* put a hole through my window!"

"What did you expect? You locked me in!"

"I told you I brought you here for your own safety!"

For her safety? Ha! Dung did not need to sing to make its presence known. *"You took me because you need my blood to get the draga morli!"*

A muscle twitched persistently in his cheek, drawing her attention to the scruff contouring his strong jawline. "I asked for the price of your cooperation, didn't I?"

Did he think that absolved him of abduction? *"And I told you I don't want anything but to go home! My brother needs me."*

Gabriel planted fingers against his temple and drew in a deep breath as though dealing with her caused him a headache of epic proportions. He turned to the dresser and retrieved a small bottle and a washcloth, then beckoned her.

"Come here."

Even though she itched to approach the dresser to better examine the scattered objects, Shyaree folded her arms and remained exactly where she was.

Gabriel exhaled audibly. "I just want to clean up your cuts."

Shyaree glanced down at her forearms. Her wounds didn't need tending. They'd already stopped bleeding. That was one of the perks of being changeless. She healed faster than the average animati, and her kind was arguably the hardiest race in the five realms to begin with.

She told him so, but Gabriel didn't seem to care.

When she remained unmoving, he prowled over to settle one knee on the edge of the bed, igniting a frisson of panic. Shyaree thrust out her forearms to prevent him from coming any closer.

His lips quirked. "Good girl."

She curled her fingers to curb the urge to scratch the self-satisfied smirk from his face. Gabriel was clearly no stranger to wounds, because he cleaned her cuts with surprising care and efficiency. Head bent, he muttered something beneath his breath that ended with "wildcat." Then he leaned forward in the most unexpected manner to brush his lips against the longest cut on her forearm.

Almost like a kiss.

Only it wasn't.

His breath warmed her skin even as a chill seeped like an icy hook digging into her marrow. Shyaree jerked her arm away. *"What are you—"*

Her breath stuttered.

Darkened veins stood stark in Gabriel's throat as though his blood had somehow turned to ink. The inky lines spread like roots beneath his skin, crawling down his neck and all over his face. His irises were no longer the clear violet that reminded her of amethysts but a soul-stopping black that spilled into the whites of his eyes. So black he could have been the god of death in the flesh.

Shyaree blinked, and just as quickly, it was all gone. No ghostly veins, no eerie black eyes. Just Gabriel, staring back at her with questioning brows.

Shyaree would have thought she'd hallucinated if not for the weighted chill that seemed to have sunk into her flesh. She glanced at her forearm, and her mouth dried. Beneath the pink cuts, a web of black veins spread from where his lips had touched. As though he'd imparted rot straight into her flesh.

She ran a trembling finger against the writhing shadow veins, barely daring to breathe. *"What did you do to me?"*

The slow smirk on his lips was no longer annoying, but wholly hair-raising. "I don't like you jumping out windows, wildcat, nor do I want you threatening my men with their own knives."

Shyaree sunk her nails into her skin so abruptly that blood seeped from the cut.

Gabriel hissed. "Stop that. It's only a shadowmark."

She could only stare.

"It's a piece of my shadow. It will"—a dark chuckle—"help me keep track of your movements."

He spoke as if it were the most natural thing in the world to embed *pieces of his own shadow* into another's body. Shyaree sucked in rapid breaths. Her arms grew rigid. If she moved, she feared she'd do something stupid, like slap him.

"I can't have you acting so recklessly again, so the shadowmark will remain until you see reason."

"You put a piece of your shadow in *me? And you think* I'm *the one who needs to see reason?"*

He sat down on the edge of the bed with a sigh, and Shyaree fought the urge to shrink from him. She might have known him from before, but it had become obvious she knew next to nothing *about* him. And what she did know only painted him in an increasingly alarming light.

She'd always known Gabriel to be obnoxious and arrogant, but she'd never known him to be high-handed or unreasonable. She'd known he was capable of shadowmagic, but she hadn't known he could actually brand others with a shadowmark.

He peered at her from beneath silvery lashes. "Are you thinking about how we can be of use to each other?"

She jerked up her chin and narrowed her eyes. *"I'm thinking of all the things I know about you and how none of them are flattering."*

His lips flattened. "I know this is hard for you to accept, but it doesn't change the fact that you're the blood—" He cleared his throat. "It doesn't change the fact that your blood is necessary to locate the draga morli. And like it or not, Zion would have come for you if I hadn't . . . and he wouldn't be asking the price of your cooperation."

Shyaree would have replied with a choice finger, but he *shushed* her by seizing her hands. His grip, large and warm and unapologetically firm, enveloping her own was so unexpected that a shudder rippled down her spine. And it wasn't borne of fear.

The contact clearly had a different effect on him, because Gabriel released her as though he'd caught the scalding end of a heated iron. He sprang to his feet, jammed both hands into his pockets, and began to pace.

"What about the Tribe elders?" he asked abruptly. "Is there someone you wished to see? Your . . . friend didn't seem too agreeable, but I can help you."

Shyaree was fighting the urge to rub her skin where he'd touched, so she almost missed the implication. Then it sank in, and her lips parted.

"You spied on me? You watched me the whole time with Hesok?" Long enough to eavesdrop, it seemed.

"What is . . . " Gabriel repeated her hand signal for Hesok with a questioning frown.

She fingerspelled H-E-S-O-K for clarity, and Gabriel's ears flattened.

"Hesok. Is that the coward by the river?"

She did not disagree. Gabriel sniffed and paced to the window, seemingly uncomfortable now that he'd admitted to spying. "I would have shown myself, but since you had company . . . I waited."

Shyaree's cheeks warmed with each breath as she recalled her conversation with Hesok. She snapped her fingers, drawing his sight back to her. *"You heard everything?"*

"Well, I didn't hear *everything*," he said defensively before curious lines formed between his brows. "What's husungai?"

Shyaree blew out a mortified breath. Gods above! *"How did you even know where to look for me? How long have you been lurking near the clan?"*

"I'm a portal maker." An imperious shrug. "I go anywhere I want, anytime I want. And I can get you wherever you need to go a lot faster than any of your warriors ever could, wildcat."

The sudden possibility crushed the air from her lungs. It was so obvious that she felt stupid. With a portal maker, she didn't need Hesok. Gods above . . . she didn't even need a Tribe elder. She could traverse leagues in the time it took to draw a single breath. When he'd abducted her, all she'd thought of was escape.

She'd never stopped to consider what he was proposing.

Thurin's wrath, she could never seem to *think* when Gabriel was involved. His presence was a disruptive force that rattled her thoughts, raised her hackles, and evidently . . . rendered her senseless.

"If I agreed to the bloodletting . . . would you help me get to Thurin's Mountain?"

A slow grin broke across his face. "Is that your price, wildcat?"

Shyaree's lips pinched. *"I haven't agreed to anything yet."*

"Well why don't you think on it and tell me your terms?"

When she hesitated, he turned to the door. She climbed onto her knees and slapped her hand against the bed frame to capture his attention. *"Where are you going? Don't you dare lock me in again!"*

"Ah, that's a mistake I won't be repeating. In fact . . . " Gabriel strode to the windows and flung them wide open.

She glared at him warily. *"What are you playing at?"*

"I'm only going to get your food, but there'll be no more

locked doors from now on. Or windows." He shot her a wink and thumped a fist over his heart. "Fae's promise."

And the fae couldn't break their promises.

It had to be a joke of some sort. *"You're really leaving?"*

"I told you I'm getting you some food." His sight slid over the sagging sheet around her body, and she felt it like a literal touch. Hers wasn't a modest race. Her people bathed together in the river all the time, and nudity didn't bother her as much as the cold, but something about Gabriel's scrutiny made her feel as though he saw beyond the shell of her body to the secrets she kept locked inside. Somehow, his gaze made her feel exposed. Vulnerable.

She didn't like it. Not in the least.

Shyaree yanked the sheets higher and scowled.

"No more throwing things out the windows, wildcat." He paused with his hand over the doorknob. "Or there *will* be consequences."

Then he shut the door, leaving her blinking after him. Had the bastard truly left the door unlocked? Shyaree crawled from the bed and tested the knob. She sucked in a breath when the door swung open. She peeked out cautiously, half expecting Gabriel to pounce from the shadows and herd her back in.

No one appeared.

He was truly gone.

A thrill shot through her spine, but a cold wash of trepidation followed. Surely this was because he'd *shadowmarked* her? To *help him keep track of her movements . . .*

What did that even mean?

Would he be able to find her wherever she went?

She rubbed at the spot his lips had brushed, and her skin tingled from the memory. But the shadows had long since receded, and the icy sensation was gone. An inkling of hope had her biting down on her lower lip. She was changeless, after all, and her blood brimmed with unused mana. Could she possibly be immune to his unholy fae magic? She stared at the corridor that led to the winding staircase, which continued upward.

Running was futile without a portal to take her back to her own realm. But at the very least, she could learn the layout of this place, if only to aid in her eventual escape. Decided, she took her first step into the corridor. And froze.

Something moved in her periphery.

A quick glance told her the corridor was perfectly empty, only a dim hallway mottled with stray sunbeams from the circular window at the end. Yet something rippled in the shadows. It took her another shuddering breath to realize the *shadows* were writhing. Or more accurately, darkness was. Shadows were see-through. Whatever moved was opaque, like a piece of the sky on a starless night. It glided along the walls like an owl winging through the sky before it swooped in and swallowed her whole.

Terror was a scream chained within her throat. She could almost feel it, whatever *it* was. Amorphous and cold, it was as intangible as air but somehow *more*, and for one terrifying moment, she was lost in nothingness. Her sight dimmed, and the ground dropped from beneath her feet. Then Shyaree was falling . . . onto messy blankets.

Gods help her.

She was back in Gabriel's room, sprawled in the middle of his bed.

She stared, mouth agape. What had just happened? Tendrils of inky apparition wafted around her. She swatted her arms, and the apparition vanished. This couldn't be happening. Shyaree bounded off the bed.

If she ran fast enough, perhaps *it* couldn't catch her.

Wrong.

The moment she dashed out the door, it crashed over her

like an inky wave. Only to spit her back onto the bed. In exactly the same spot.

Son of a beast!

Shyaree sprang from the bed again, fixing her sights on the window this time. The sun was shining bright outside. There were no shadows. No places for dark and aberrant things to lurk. Shyaree stuck an experimental arm out the window.

Nothing came for her but the sun's rays warming her skin.

She pulled herself onto the ledge, and suddenly she understood why Gabriel had left the windows wide open. There was nowhere for her to go but down. Unlike the room on the second floor, this one had no other windows nearby. Shyaree wouldn't be going anywhere. Scowling, she moved to retreat, but the sheet snagged on something. She fumbled for balance, but too late. She toppled through the window.

Or she would have.

Under the sun's rays, *it* appeared no more substantial than a specter. Nebulous. Translucent. Feathery darkness wrapped around her in a whisper of crows' wings, just as the world tilted and blurred . . . and she fell.

Face first into the bed.

Chapter 6

Gabriel returned to the guest room to retrieve the plate he'd left in his haste when he'd first found Shyaree missing. He paused at the doorway, but it was too late to back away.

"It's going to cost us to replace it," Arkas murmured without looking away from the broken window. The glass itself had been a work of art, handcrafted by a family of firesprites in Glendowen. A proper replacement would cost Gabriel thirty heads at the very least.

"Board it up," Gabriel said as he picked up the abandoned plate. It was filled with bread, sliced meats, and an assortment of fruit he knew Shyaree preferred. As if presenting her with her favored foods would somehow alleviate the guilt gnawing in his chest.

Arkas finally lifted his head. "We could always use regular glass."

"It's Glendowen fireglass or nothing."

Blacksage Manor was already a far cry from its former glory. The very least Gabriel could do was retain its original fixtures. *And with Shyaree, you would not only free Iolanthe but also demand a sum enough for a hundred fireglass windows from Zion,* a sly voice whispered in the back of his mind.

Gabriel ignored it while Arkas shook his head. "What's really going on, Gabe? Do you want to explain what the shaman is doing in the Den?"

The shaman. Arkas clearly remembered Shyaree from before.

"She has something I need," Gabriel muttered.

Arkas snorted. "Try telling me something that isn't obvious."

Shadowmagic tugged like tiny fishhooks against Gabriel's skin, suggesting the wildcat must be attempting escape. Again. Gabriel's lips twitched. What wouldn't he give to see the expression on her face when she met his phantasma?

Arkas caught his amusement, and his glower darkened. "Abducting and keeping a half-naked female captive is Silverbeak bullshit. Not ours. Not yours."

Indignation and insult flared in his chest. Arkas had known him since the cradle. Did the other fae truly believe so little of him?

"I've been trying to convince her to work *with* me. I've done little else."

"Work with you?" Arkas's brows furrowed. "On what?"

Gabriel was ready to retreat from the room, evade the question, but he paused. He owed Arkas the truth. He'd kept Iolanthe's survival from him for far too long. His cousin had never forgiven himself for Iolanthe's *death*, even though Gabriel only had himself to blame. And he feared Arkas would be so driven for atonement that the truth would send him into a reckless frenzy and only jeopardize his life.

Dragging his second-in-command into this mess with

Prince Zion was the last thing he wanted. Zion could cross him at any time.

"It's complicated," Gabriel said finally.

Arkas's gaze dropped to the plate in Gabriel's hand, and his jaw tightened. "Is this Rebekah all over again?"

Gabriel snorted. "Of course not—"

Crash.

The muted sounds of breaking furniture and angry shouts drifted from downstairs.

Gabriel and Arkas abandoned their conversation for the gambling floor.

They arrived in time to see Caspian thrashing a dark-haired fae against the bar.

Arkas broke up the ruckus, hauling Caspian back with a firm hand. Gabriel jerked the other man away with a hank of stringy hair in need of a wash. One look at the silver rings decorating the man's fingers and Gabriel's jaw clenched.

"What's a Silverbeak doing in the Red Den?"

"Just strolled right in like he had every right . . . " Caspian straightened his jacket with a snarl. "Demanding an audience with you."

The rookhead arched his back, twisting around. When he caught sight of Gabriel's face, he beamed like a fool who'd won his first hand. *"Your Grace!"*

Gabriel flinched. Dreamsmoke wafted from the man's breath, pungent and sickly sweet, but that wasn't the reason his lips curled.

"Your Grace, I come bearing wonderful news!"

"Address me as guildmaster or lose your tongue."

The wastrel only giggled, too strung out on dreamsmoke to care how perilously close he was to tasting the edge of a steel blade. "But the king insisted the message is meant solely for the duke of—"

Arkas's boot connected with the rookhead's gut without warning. The guild's second-in-command didn't stop with a single kick. Gabriel stepped back. Arkas never did tolerate reminders of the past. When his rage finally dulled, Arkas shook out his fists. "Deliver the message, or I'll relieve you of more than your tongue."

"H-His Majesty, the new king Zenaidus . . . " The wastrel wheezed out a breath, crimson-tinged saliva dripping from split lips as he regurgitated a message. "Is prepared to forgive the past. Wipe the slate clean, so to speak, should His Grace"—the rookhead glanced to Arkas, and his throat bobbed—"g-guildmaster. Should the guildmaster pledge and prove his loyalty."

Gabriel laughed. "Zenaidus's hold on the crown must be far more precarious than I'd thought if he's seeking the Red Guild's loyalty."

Zenaidus had recently been crowned the king of the Winter Court given his father's continued absence—though Gabriel knew *exactly* where the mad king Zephyr was. Imprisoned in a Soul Tree tucked away in the mage realm, Zephyr had finally met his retribution in the wrath of a Summer Court princess. And while Zion, the second-born prince, had vied for the throne, he had never managed to sway the nobles in his favor.

Dreamsmoke might have bolstered his courage and blunted his fear, but the Silverbeak seemed to measure his next words. "Deny this opportunity, guildmaster, and you will not be offered another. Unlike the late king Zephyr, His Majesty will not show leniency to those who remain against the Crown."

The implication was so outrageous it was almost laughable. "Leniency?" Gabriel circled the wretch with a sneer. "Is that what they told you? That the Red Guild prevailed throughout Zephyr's reign because of his *leniency*?"

"I can only say what His Majesty intends." A slight bob of his throat. "And His Majesty intends to restore your ducal rights, Your Gr . . . guildmaster. The king is ready to acknowledge you before the High Lords as the duke of Evenmere . . . "

The air seemed to grow heavy. Grim eyes settled on Gabriel while he regarded the Silverbeak emissary. What a joke. The duke of Evenmere. A title that should have *never* been his in the first place. A title that had long since lost its meaning.

"I've heard enough of this drivel." Gabriel swallowed the bitterness in his throat and turned toward the stairs. "Get him out of my sight."

"Guildmaster!" The rookhead launched to his feet only to be kicked back to his knees. "Do not squander this opportunity!" he cried amid the blows raining down on his back. "You have no idea of King Zenaidus's powers! Evenmere can be yours again if you only share the loca—"

Arkas's next blow had the rookhead spitting out a tooth. "Evenmere *is* ours."

"We should return him with his tongue shoved up his ass," Caspian added with a dark laugh. "That'll get the king's attention."

Gabriel didn't plan to watch. He started up the stairs. His shadowmagic hadn't tugged for a while now. What was the wildcat up to?

Despite having curled into himself, the rookhead continued to spew garbled words, as though his life depended on reciting the entirety of the king's message. It probably did. " . . . location of the pantherai . . . "

Gabriel halted on the steps, his blood running cold in a single instant.

" . . . clan's location . . . " A rattling cough.

"Pantherai?" Arkas asked sharply. "Why is the king searching for an animati clan?"

But the emissary never got a chance to reply.

His head rolled to the ground, a grotesque ball in a sticky puddle of gore.

A silence descended over the Den while Gabriel calmly wiped the blood from his blade on the Silverbeak's tunic. If anyone was shocked, it wasn't because Gabriel had relieved the messenger of his head. It was because he rarely sullied the Den.

But a little blood was worth the silence. He would not disclose the contents of the prophecy and involve his men—at least not until he had a solution.

"Dispose of his body, but put his head in a nice box." Gabriel shot his men a grim smile. "I think it's about time we sent the new king a coronation gift."

Arkas's gaze was sharper than a lance through the gut. "It's Shyaree, isn't it? It's her the king wants."

"Shyaree?" Caspian frowned. "The firebrand in a bedsheet?"

Gabriel shrugged.

If the king was also searching for Shyaree, it could only mean he had learned of the contents of the necromancer's manuscripts. Zion was either dead or a master manipulator.

Gabriel was willing to wager his manor on the latter.

"It doesn't matter what the king wants . . . She is mine." He sidestepped the growing scarlet pool, careful not to soil his boots. "Get someone to clean this up. Don't let the blood dry, or it'll stain the floorboards."

When he'd collected himself, Gabriel returned to his bedchamber. Cautiously. He eased the door open without peering in, lest the wildcat attempt to use him as target practice. When nothing launched at the doorway, he ducked his head in, half expecting to see his room in shambles.

It wasn't.

Quite the opposite.

Not only was everything in place, but the bed appeared even tidier. Clothes he'd left scattered were folded into a neat pile at the foot of the bed. Shyaree snuggled in the middle of it, legs beneath the sheets, pillows at her back, while she studied something in her hands. A blanket tucked beneath her arms left her shoulders criminally bare, reminding him that she was dressed only in scraps of cloth while lying in bed. In *his* bed.

The notion sent a jolt straight to the dumbest part of his anatomy.

Gabriel scowled.

He needed to get a hold of himself. He marched in, brusquely set the plate on a clear spot on the table and tossed the random dress he'd pilfered from the guest chamber onto the bed. "Get changed and come have something to eat," he ordered, a little disgruntled that she'd barely looked up since he'd walked in.

Without lifting her head, she eyed him and arched a single perfect brow. Her gaze flitted past his offering with an obvious lack of interest and settled back on the book she held. She flipped a page, and Gabriel startled.

"Did your mother not teach you it was bad manners to go through people's private things?"

Calmly, she set the sketchbook down on her lap. *"Did your mother not teach you it was bad manners to abduct a woman?"*

He suppressed a smile. "She didn't, actually." He didn't think Shyaree would appreciate knowing his mother *encouraged* him in portal making, which had led to their current situation, so he offered no further detail on the matter. "But she did teach me not to pry."

With two sons and three daughters, Sylvia Blacksage had worked hard to instill clear boundaries between her children to keep peace in the household. But unfortunately for all, Gabriel had been born with the ability to create portals. Sticking his nose into his sibling's secrets had been a little too easy when one was a nosy faeling with the ability to portal into closets and hide without a trace.

"Give it here, and go get changed."

Shyaree's eyes narrowed. She clasped the sketchbook to her chest, causing the blanket to sag and drawing his attention to that scanty strip of cloth used in place of a proper chemise.

Gabriel dropped his hand and curled his fingers. "Now, Shyaree."

She tucked the sketchbook under one arm before signing, *"Go fuck yourself."*

A laugh escaped him. He'd been on the receiving end of that line a hundred times over, but never in Handspeak. Her hand signals were sharp and vehement, leaving no question as to her ire. But somehow, they appeared too graceful to be offensive, which made her lewd sentiment more amusing than it should be. But if gazes could sunder, Gabriel would have been slain.

Rancor radiated from her pores when she thrust her forearm at him. *"Get it out of me."*

He took the opportunity to snatch his sketchbook and set it in a drawer. She scowled, and he grinned. "The shadowmark will remain until I'm certain you won't be climbing out any more windows."

She looked ready to combust. *"You are an insidious and unholy creature."*

She wasn't far from the truth. The atrocities Gabriel had committed in his life were countless, but his shadowmark was not one of them.

"I am a being of Ozenn's creation. Shadowmagic is as natural to me as the change is to your kind."

"I hate you," she said, but there was little heat left in her movements. She slumped back onto the pillows with the stoic grimness of a warrior resigned to defeat.

Gabriel moved the plate to the bed. She eyed the food with disdain, but surprise flashed in her features when she noticed the kovi berries. She popped one into her mouth and released a little sigh that softened the firm set of her lips. Gabriel stood up and moved to lean against his desk.

"I thought kovi berries only grew in the mage realm."

They did. "Portal maker, remember?"

Eyes narrowed, Shyaree picked another berry and chewed so vigorously that Gabriel nearly winced on the fruit's behalf.

"So, what else can you do with shadows?" she signed before her hand hovered over a custard bun. She brought it up to her nose for a sniff before squeezing it between her thumb and forefinger as though fascinated by its spongy texture.

"Try it," Gabriel urged. "It's soft and sweet . . . like those cinnamon rolls they serve in Amereen Castle." And he'd once watched her devour four in one sitting. Then she'd licked the icing from her lips like a satisfied cat after a bowl of cream . . . He was making a mental note to get her some cinnamon rolls when a pink tongue darted from between her lips for a little lick of the custard filling.

Gabriel swallowed. Nope. No cinnamon rolls. No more custard buns.

He was going to avoid feeding her anything that inspired her to lick like that.

She took her first bite. The pleasure suffusing her face caused him to fidget. He should probably leave the room, leave her to her meal.

But she pinned him in place with a pucker between her brows. *"You didn't answer my question."*

It took Gabriel a slow blink before he remembered what she'd asked. "Shadowmagic?"

At her expectant nod, he slapped a restless hand over his thigh. "Right. Well . . . blackfire is the most basic form of shadowmagic, but not easy to master. It is very handy in combat as it requires minimal focus . . . "

She swallowed the last bite of the bun and proceeded to lick at her sticky fingers.

Gabriel scrubbed a hand over his jaw.

She looked up with a questioning frown, one glistening finger poised between lush lips. Gabriel cleared his throat and banished his gaze to the bedspread. "Uh . . . as I was saying, blackfire. Basic. And uh . . . there's vaporization. As you can imagine, turning our bodies into shadows isn't as simple as generating blackfire. It requires a lot of magic."

The bedspread was dense enough that it outlined her hips and legs, revealing that she was sitting in his bed almost nude. He dragged his eyes back up, only to see her biting into a slice of nectarine. Juice dribbled down her chin, and her tongue darted out again. No more nectarines.

"The longer one remains in shadow form, the more magic one requires. It's not exactly the smartest strategy in combat. And—"

Gabriel sucked in an agitated breath. Ozenn's blood. Was he rambling? But he couldn't seem to stop. "And if one can vaporize, one can usually possess animals, too."

"Birds?" she signed, clearly remembering the time she'd seen him possess a hawk.

Gabriel nodded. "Birds, bats . . . small animals. And then there's shadowbending, which can manifest as portals. Illusions. Or as you've just experienced firsthand"—Gabriel couldn't help a soft chuckle—"phantasma."

Shyaree's swallow was almost audible. *"And you can do all that?"*

"I'm Unseelie, aren't I?"

When her eyes rounded, Gabriel faked a cough into his fist to mask a smirk. He couldn't conjure blackfire. Not anymore. He could barely vaporize outside his home realm without a host. And his shadowbending skills? They were limited to portal making and shadowmarking. Nothing else. But he wasn't about to disclose the limitations of his shadowmagic, not when she was looking at him with equal parts disgust and *awe*.

She blinked at him uneasily and picked up another custard bun. This time half of it disappeared in a single voracious bite. Gabriel's smirk deepened involuntarily. She was far from ladylike. Wholly unrefined, really. But she was also unpretentious . . . and so utterly adorable.

His eye twitched. *Adorable?* Dreamsmoke from the damned rookhead must have somehow seeped through his skin, addled his brain. Or perhaps the Mujarin in his system was finally taking effect . . .

"Stop looking at me like that."

Gabriel jerked back with a blink. "Like what?"

"Like I have scat on my face." She chewed crossly. *"If you don't like what you're looking at, you can always send me home."*

Gabriel laughed. "Trust me, you wouldn't *be* here if—" He snapped his mouth shut before he could blurt the rest of the sentence.

You wouldn't be here if I could help it.

You wouldn't be here if you weren't the blood sacrifice.

You wouldn't be here if you weren't the key to Iolanthe's freedom.

Gabriel clenched his jaw and clung to thoughts of his sister. And his next words came out hard. Harsh. "Have you thought of your terms yet?"

He hoped she would ask for something that would exact a pound of his flesh. He would make her sacrifice worthwhile. Whatever she wanted, she would get. He would make sure of it.

She ignored him. It wasn't until she polished her plate clean that she finally signed, *"You're going to keep me here until I agree to the bloodletting, aren't you?"*

Bloodletting . . . and more.

Bile soured his throat, but he saw no point in prevaricating. "Yes."

Anger flashed across her face, heightening the color of her cheeks, but her shoulders slumped. Her hands fisted in the silken fabric of the dress, and when she looked up at him, her eyes were colored by an emotion he'd never seen her wear.

Bleakness.

It punched him like a knife in the gut.

"I'm sorry. Wildcat—"

The dress hit him squarely in the chest. *"I refuse to wear this. Find me something suitable for traveling, or let me go home and pack."*

Gabriel paused. "Traveling?"

Shoulders stiff, Shyaree eyed him as if he were a worm wriggling beneath her soles. *"You have a deal, you high-handed bastard. Help me get what I need from Thurin's Mountain . . . and I'll allow you my blood."*

Chapter 7

Thurin's Mountain, Animati Realm

Women should never be allowed to wear pants.

Or more specifically, *Shyaree* should never be allowed to wear pants. Gabriel gritted his teeth and tore his gaze from the hypnotic sway of her hips as she climbed over a moss-covered log. *Stop it, Blacksage.* He turned his focus to his surroundings.

Sunlight speared through the canopy to pattern the ground in alternating slivers of light and shadow. Thick, coiling vines suffocated gnarled trunks, while dense undergrowth smothered the forest floor in some form of fern or fungi. Gabriel slapped a hand at his nape. Damned mosquitoes everywhere. Ozenn's blood, he felt like a bug navigating a spider's nest, yet the wildcat refused to let him hack through any vegetation to ease their journey. *"How would you like it if I were to cut off your arm just to walk past you?"* she had signed indignantly. *"Something doesn't need to scream to feel pain."*

Since this was technically part of the *price* of her cooperation, Gabriel had acceded to her whims. While Shyaree had agreed to stay with him until the blood moon, she had given him hard terms.

One, he was to get her onto Thurin's Mountain.

Two, he was to aid in her quest to harvest three ingredients for an elixir.

Three, should she succeed in creating said elixir before the next twenty-seven—now twenty-*six*—days, Gabriel was to deliver it to her clan without delay.

Gabriel had agreed readily, even though he knew nothing of Thurin's Mountain or this mysterious elixir. It had sounded simple and straightforward enough, but he hadn't expected to be scaling hills, climbing logs, dodging vines, and skirting random holes—all while Shyaree prowled ahead in a pair of snug leather pants. Ozenn help him.

Was he to endure this for the rest of their deal?

When Shyaree had first mentioned going home to pack, Gabriel had politely declined. He would not allow her the chance to slip behind her shieldmakers' walls and disappear that easily. But since there was no way he was going to traipse through a rainforest with her in a bedsheet, Gabriel had wisely —or so he'd thought—entrusted her to Isidor. A male with no sexual appetite or appreciation for the female form.

What could possibly go wrong?

Shyaree had appeared hours later, wearing the broadest grin Gabriel had ever seen and an outfit that made him question his life decisions.

"I'll have the tailor make some clothes to her measurements, but it'll take a couple of days. For now, she'll have to wear some of mine. They are a little tight in some areas, but at least they fit," the mer had explained with a snide smirk, which made

Gabriel wonder if the healer had harbored some hidden resentment for him all along.

A *little* tight? A little *tight*!

To be fair, the tunic was loose and innocuous enough. But the mer imbecile had given her a holster belt—one with tiny hooks that fastened just beneath her bust, accentuating curves that needed *no* more attention.

"Obviously one can never carry too many blades," Isidor had explained cheerfully when Gabriel had queried the need for the holster belt. The mer had seemed entirely oblivious while he showed off the array of throwing knives strapped across Shyaree's shoulders. The wildcat had spun around, parading a machete sheathed at her hip with the same glee most women took in showing off extravagant ball gowns. Her obvious delight had chased a strange thrill through his bones.

Gabriel had not cared for it.

Not one bit.

"Carrying them is only effective if one knows how to use them," he'd said in Animatish while wearing a deliberate sneer. His only warning was a narrowed gaze before a throwing knife sailed past him and thudded into the wall, exactly two thumb lengths from his temple.

"You're right," she'd signed coolly. *"I'll need to work on my aim."*

Something in his chest had somersaulted, but Gabriel had managed a scowl. "Damage my property again, and you'll pay for the repairs."

And if the holster and weapons weren't damning enough, Isidor had also given her *pants.* Leather ones she'd probably have to peel off at night.

"Fuck," Gabriel muttered under his breath, and shoved the mental image firmly from his head. He risked a glance only to catch sight of Shyaree scrambling over yet another fallen trunk, this one desecrated with a profusion of oyster-shaped mushrooms. It was as though the gods had purposely set them upon an obstacle-laden path so he had the perfect view of her climbing up and down, up and down while the leather stretched and strained against a perfectly rounded—

She turned back.

Gabriel pretended to be captivated by the same towering trees they'd passed in scores since dawn. She clapped her hands, signaling for his attention.

By some miracle his voice came out flat and deceptively casual. "What?"

"Is the bag too heavy?"

"No." He shifted the rucksack over his shoulders. Their traveling pack wasn't heavy so much as it was cumbersome.

"Then why are you walking so slowly?"

Warmth crawled up his neck. "It's the heat." Not really. It might be humid, but a cooling breeze sighed periodically through the trees, rustling the understory of flowering arums and broadleaf ferns. "It's sweltering."

An outright lie, but it was preferable to admitting his pants had grown a little too snug for comfort.

"Just hurry up." She cast a wary gaze around. A macaw perched nearby, staring at them with unflinching curiosity. *"This doesn't feel like a good place to linger."*

"You brought us here," he reminded her as he pushed past shoulder-high thickets.

"I brought us to the closest point I've ever been to the Tribe's Wall," she corrected him with a frown. *"You brought us here."*

"Well, you wanted to get onto Thurin's Mountain. So I got you onto Thurin's Mountain."

While Gabriel could create portals to any location that wasn't magically or psychically warded, he could not open portals to places he'd never *seen*. So he'd taken them to the closest possible location with the help of a winged host. Securing a suitable host in the animati realm had proved a struggle, but eventually he'd managed to find a brown-throated hawk. Gabriel had scouted leagues until his host tired, but the flight had shaved days off their trek. Then, he'd portaled them within hiking distance of a massive rock wall—creatively dubbed the Wall by the locals—that rivaled the rainforest canopy in height. According to Shyaree, the Wall marked the entire perimeter of Thurin's Mountain and no one passed it without a Tribe elder's consent, but Gabriel was not an ordinary no one.

He'd searched until he found another suitable host—a hornbill. He'd seized control and simply flown over the rocky barrier. It had been easy enough to cast another portal once he'd gotten a clear image of the ground.

"Didn't we just pass this plant?" The cluster of little pink cups dangling from a spray of spiky leaves looked familiar. "Are we any closer to what you're looking for?"

Shyaree gnawed on her lower lip and rubbed her earlobe—a nervous tell that had him narrowing his eyes in suspicion.

"You *do* know what you're looking for . . . don't you?"

Her spine stiffened at his query, but her hesitant nod confirmed his fears. *"Sort of."*

"Sort of?"

"I am waiting for nightfall. I believe I can only find what I need under moonlight, but while waiting, I was hoping to begin by searching for an underground cave or a . . . " At Gabriel's blank look, Shyaree added defensively, *"It is what my mother's song says to do."*

"Your mother's song?" Gabriel cocked his head. "You said you were looking for three things, ingredients, for an elixir. You didn't mention anything about a godsdamned song."

Despite the stubborn tilt of her chin, her lips pursed into a sheepish line. *"The song gives instruction to find the items I require."*

Gabriel huffed out an incredulous laugh. "Are you telling me your grand plan for finding these three things is based on some random *song*?"

"It is not random!" Shyaree signed hotly. *"The song has been handed down for generations, shaman to shaman. My mother was a shaman before me, and she created this elixir before. So I know it is doable . . . "* The heat fizzled from her hand signals as uncertainty clouded her eyes. *"I'm just not sure if I know how to decipher the song."*

Gabriel swatted distractedly at yet another mosquito buzzing near his ear. The whole affair was sounding more and more questionable. "Wildcat, what exactly *are* you looking for in this dirt-infested mountain?"

The gnawing of her lower lip again only made him nervous. "If I'm going to fulfill the terms of our bargain, you'd best tell me what this song is about."

Shyaree surprised him by pulling a folded piece of parchment from her pocket. She unfolded it with near-reverent care, gingerly smoothing out the page. When he reached for it, she seemed to hesitate before relinquishing it into his hand. The parchment was slightly torn at the edge of one crease, and the ink had faded in spots, but the words were still legible:

Go, for all Thurin's creatures when malady prevails,
To the land kissed by the moon's silver tails,
Seek and harvest the seeds that glow,
Deep, deep in the canyon below,
Listen hard for the field that breathes,
And harvest the waters from between its teeth,
The moon's silver must turn to blood,

Only then will the tomb begin to flood,
Draw from the vein of the one twice blessed,
Only then will the cursed find rest.

Gabriel blinked. Then he reread the text. "Is this meant to be a joke or a cradlesong? Flooding tombs, Shyaree? Glowing seeds? What . . . breathing fields?"

When she had mentioned ingredients for an elixir, he had foolishly assumed she was after native plants—herbs, roots, or maybe even wildlife, not answers to some cryptic cipher he could barely understand. Five hells, it was obvious *she* barely understood it.

Gabriel rubbed his temple. He'd wanted her to ask him for something difficult, not impossible.

She curled her fingers before she exhaled. *"I told you, my mother followed these instructions and succeeded. It cannot be that difficult."*

"No? Then tell me, what exactly are the moon's silver tails?"

"Maybe it refers to a forked stream? Or perhaps it's a metaphor for moonlight shining through the trees?"

Gabriel's gaze shot to the dense canopy overhead. "We can barely see the sky! How do you expect to see the moon? Ozenn's blood! Did your mother give you any more information? How do you even know what you're looking for?"

She sucked in an audible breath, her lips tightening. *"I don't know. I learned the song from my father. My mother died . . . birthing me."*

Gabriel's incredulity deflated on an exhale. "Shyaree . . . "

She shook her head. *"I know it sounds ridiculous, but this elixir is Reiken's last chance. I can only try."* She sniffed. *"If you want to renege on our bargain, you are welcome to leave. I'll figure it out on my own."*

Her determination showed in the defiant jut of her chin . . . yet the slight curl of her shoulders did not escape him. Nor did he miss the way she wrung her hands together the moment she was done signing. Whatever Reiken needed this elixir for, Shyaree was clearly desperate to give it to him. She had to be, to name this as the price for her blood . . .

But no matter her bravado, she feared.

And her fear struck a chord deep in his chest . . . because he felt exactly the same. "Sometimes that's all you *can* do," Gabriel said quietly. "The world may think you've lost your wits, and even you may second-guess yourself . . . but none of that matters because the moment we stop trying is the moment we stop fighting." He brushed a stray strand of hair from her face. "And don't ever stop fighting."

She blinked up at him. The hard press of her lips softened to an uncertain curve that made him want to slide his thumb along the seam and coax a full smile.

He shoved his hand into his pocket. "So . . . let's start with the glowing seeds. You think they're somewhere in an underground cave?"

"A canyon deep below? What could it be if not an underground cave? There should be plenty of subterranean caves around these parts, and they are usually linked. We could start looking for one to begin our search."

They would probably have more luck spearing a quail for dinner by throwing knives into the sky, but Gabriel decided to keep his sarcasm in check. Glowing seeds, breathing fields, and flooding tombs. A sliver of anxiety crept up at the latter, but Gabriel batted it aside. He would do whatever it took to get her what she wanted.

It was not just the terms of the bargain.

It was the least he could do.

They had trekked for *hours*, and still the sun stayed stubbornly in the sky, bleeding brightness through the rainforest canopy. They had found no underground caves, no forked streams, or anything that could possibly be relevant to the song. But Gabriel had found yet another food item to revoke from the list of things he'd be offering Shyaree. No more oatcakes.

Or anything with crumbly bits that might cling to the sides of her mouth.

Shyaree climbed over a log, stepping cautiously onto the leaf litter as though she were liable to encounter hidden snares. Her head swiveled at every little sound, and she scanned the surrounding trees with enough wariness to lift Gabriel's brow. The deeper they ventured, the more guarded she seemed to grow.

"I know the Tribe governs this place, but are there any clans living here? Hunters?"

"No one hunts in these parts."

"Dangerous animals?"

"Likely. But if we don't bother them, they should not bother us."

"Then what are you so scared of?"

She looked at him as though he were daft. *"We're in the thick of Thurin's Mountain. I already told you what to expect!"*

She had mentioned it the night before, but it hadn't concerned him.

"Cragaliths?" Gabriel had heard tales about them, but he'd never actually encountered one. Legendary creatures part flesh and part stone, fashioned from Thurin's bone. "But aren't they guardians of sorts? A part of Thurin's army made to protect this realm?"

Shyaree's lips slanted with wryness. *"Perhaps they are, but they also used to terrorize the locals. The cragaliths are the reason the Tribe erected the Wall. They are the reason no clan settles around here . . . but they aren't the only creatures to fear in these parts. Rogues have no choice but to live here, too. The Tribe captures and keeps them here, behind the Wall."*

Gabriel snorted. "You're with *me* and you're afraid of outcasts?"

Her eyes narrowed to slits. *"Rogues are more feral than you think. They have lived outside the safety of their clan for so long that they exist permanently in their bestial form. A stray rogue wandered near my clan a few years ago."* She shuddered. *"It mauled three of our warriors before it was taken down."*

"Well, you have no cause to worry." Gabriel fingered the edge of a diken and flashed a smile sure to stiffen her spine. "You're safe with me, wildcat." The words rolled so naturally from his tongue that it took him another moment to realize what a hypocrite he was. The smile faded from his lips, but she didn't seem to notice.

"Are there no bounds to your arrogance?"

Gabriel smirked. "Arrogance is bullish confidence *without* the necessary skills or substance to back the claim . . . and luckily for you, I have both."

"Arrogance and *bullish confidence?"* She arched her brows. *"I already knew that."*

His lips twitched. "Wiseass. I've brought down ogres taller than some of these trees with a simple dagger."

At her blank gaze, he realized belatedly that ogres did not exist in her realm. He was on the verge of citing more *relatable* examples of his past vanquishments until he realized he was behaving like a schoolboy eager to impress. Five blazing hells.

He was Gabriel Blacksage, guildmaster of the Red Knights. He didn't need to impress anyone.

Especially not *her*.

He shouldn't be doing anything with her apart from carrying out the terms of their bargain. In the next twenty-six days, he would do whatever he could to aid in her pursuit of the items for the elixir, then he would bleed her on the night of the blood moon. But what happened *after* their bargain?

She still had no idea . . .

A snap of her fingers brought him out of his dark reverie. She pointed at a strange rocklike structure that punched out from the ground.

"Is that . . . an anthill?"

"It looks more like a termite nest, but I have never seen one so large."

Neither had he, but it didn't surprise him. Critters seemed to grow larger in this dirt-laden realm. Mosquitoes were practically the size of wasps. He showed her the many coin-sized bumps on his skin he'd collected so far with no small amount of disgruntlement.

She laughed.

Her throat made no sound save hearty chuffs of breath, but he could almost *feel* her mirth radiating into his marrow. Gabriel had seen her smirk and chuckle countless times over, but he'd never seen her throw her head back in a genuine laugh. Her eyes crinkled into adorable crescent moons while her shoulders shook with glee.

He tripped, staggering abruptly to the ground.

He pulled himself up with a scowl.

"Are you all right?" Merriment continued to sparkle in her eyes, coaxing his lips into a curve he would not permit. He grunted in response. He couldn't remember the last time he'd tripped over his own feet.

She reached for his hands and turned his palms as though to check for grazes.

"I'm fine," he said sourly.

Hilarity faded from her face. *"I am sorry. It is just that I have never seen anyone stung so badly . . . and you just looked so . . . "* She clamped her lips together as she dissolved once more into laughter.

Amusement tugged at his lips until his attention snagged on an unruly bead of sweat sliding down the graceful column of her throat. It trickled along her clavicle, slowly, teasingly, only to slip into her cleavage. He swallowed involuntarily.

Oh, for fuck's sake!

He ripped his gaze away with clenched teeth. What in the five flaming hells was wrong with him? He was planning her *sacrifice*, yet he was ogling her at every turn like a lecherous satyr. The next time he was in the Den, he would plow the nearest succubus into oblivion and spend himself dry. He was clearly due for a release.

But now he needed to remove her from his sight. He marched forward, leaving her to trail after him. It wasn't long until she snapped her fingers.

"Look, there is another." She peered up at a large mound spearing from the ground like a giant stone spire. *"It is so strange, and termites do not usually nest on soft land."* Every graceful sweep of her hands continued to snare his attention. Trapping his focus, stoking his lust.

"Though it looks like the soil—"

"Enough!" The word shot from him with more bite than he'd intended. She startled, and Gabriel leveled his tone. "That's enough. Why don't you focus on looking for that underground cave instead? I don't need a lesson on termites or land formation."

He needed to *stop* behaving like a randy hound in need of a rut.

Her lips parted with a frown. *"I was only trying to show you—"*

"I don't care. Stop playing the guide. I'm not a tourist. This isn't a leisure stroll. I have no interest in spending any more time in this wretched, mosquito-infested realm than necessary, so if you don't mind, let's just keep moving."

Hurt leached into her face while shame flooded down the back of his neck.

"I—"

She was already storming away. But instead of forging ahead, where the path looked relatively muddy but clear of foliage, she chose to climb up a cluster of fallen trees, prickly branches, and overgrown ferns.

He sighed. "Wildcat."

She didn't turn around. If anything, she moved faster as though to escape him. She climbed a series of branches to jump atop a log, prowling with the ease of an acrobat on a trapeze rope. She didn't spare him a backward glance before disappearing from his sight.

He rubbed the space between his brows and drew in a steadying breath. Good. He would take this path instead. He could certainly use the space. He stepped around a bunch of riotous ferns, and the deceptively smooth ground cracked to reveal slick mud. Frowning, he took another cautious step forward, only for the crack to widen. *Squelch.*

He sank boot-deep.

Damn it. The ground was a lot softer than he'd thought. He yanked himself free, but the motion only muddied the ground even more. Growling an imprecation, he hopped over to a patch of dirt that appeared less slick.

Bad, bad idea.

His foot sank ankle-deep. He jerked his legs up, but the mud emitted a sluicing sound before sucking him even *deeper*.

"This has to be a joke."

Only then did he realize this was what Shyaree must have meant by *soft land*. She'd meant it literally. Quicksand. No wonder she'd climbed atop those logs.

And now he was knee-deep. And still sinking.

Chapter 8

Shyaree fought the urge to look back. She refused to. The insufferable beast. He'd just reminded her exactly why they'd never gotten along.

Gabriel had always had the uncanny ability to draw down her defenses only to make her feel like an utter fool. Maybe it was those pretty eyes and spun-silver hair that never failed to charm her. Or maybe it was his prowling gait, or his intoxicating scent that had always made her want to lean closer for a better whiff. Maybe it was just his broad-cut frame and the way he dominated every space with such ease it made him impossible to ignore. Whatever it was, she hated it.

Hated *him*.

Her cheeks heated at the recollection of Gabriel's disdain. *This isn't a leisure stroll. I have no interest in spending any more time in this wretched, mosquito-infested realm than necessary . . .*

Of course he didn't. Why would he? He was only here for their bargain. For her blood. Nothing else. She would be foolish to think—

Gabriel's distant growl stilled her steps.

She shut her eyes with a weary sigh. The brute couldn't be daft enough to step into a sink pit, could he? She backtracked and found that the brute *could*, in fact, be daft enough.

Gabriel was lodged to the hip in soft land. The very land she had just tried to warn him about. The arrogant boar had clearly chosen to disregard her caution and had trampled right into quicksand.

He glanced up at her with a scowl. "This has to be the most inhospitable realm in all the gods' creation!"

A snicker escaped her lips in a puff of air.

She made her way down to the edge of the pit. How had he managed to get himself submerged to the hip in such a short span of time?

He stretched a hand toward her, as though she were beholden to help him even though his own bullheadedness had led him to this predicament.

If Shyaree were a cruel woman, she would have served him a rude gesture to show exactly what she thought of his obnoxiousness before leaving him to his sticky fate. But she wasn't the malicious sort. Well, rarely. She raised her brows at his outstretched arm and very leisurely folded her own.

He hissed. "Shyaree."

The corners of her lips lifted. She might not be cruel or malicious, but she could be petty. She cupped her ear with one hand and signed, *"What's that? I can't hear you."*

Violet eyes narrowed.

She smirked. Served him right. If he'd heeded her, none of this would have happened. Perhaps she should leave him here. After all, he was a deadly assassin. Surely he could find his way out of a sink pit.

He lunged up, his arms reaching skyward as though to reach the looping vines hanging from a branch overhead. How curious. Did the fool not realize his struggling only served to quicken his submersion?

Idly, Shyaree settled on the ground and crossed her legs as she observed his futile attempts. She'd always found the fae a strange, alien race, but she'd never thought them dense. Perhaps she'd given them too much credit. Only fools exerted strength where strength only worsened their predicament. Soon enough, he'd worked himself waist-deep.

Shaking her head, Shyaree snapped her fingers. When he looked her way, she signed, *"Portal."*

Violet eyes narrowed. "A portal requires me to walk through it. If I opened one here, it would only transport the unsubmerged part of me."

She flapped her arms in a flying motion. He couldn't literally fly, of course. But she was referring to his disturbing ability to render himself amorphous, to nothing more than a slinking shadow. Surely that would free him.

"I can only vaporize if I have access to a vast quantity of magic, or if there is a suitable host in the vicinity—and I sense none!"

Ah, for all his otherworldly command of magic, the man was thwarted by a simple sink pit. Mud speckled his face, and clumps clung to his usually pristine moonlit hair. His chest heaved with agitation. When she made no move to help him, he glowered and continued his pointless efforts to free himself. Did he not realize he was in no real, imminent danger?

Sink pits were rarely deep enough to swallow a man whole —and Gabriel was a very tall man. In fact, sink pits were rarely lethal. Unfortunate victims who failed to free themselves died the slow death of dehydration, not suffocation.

She cocked her head, shamelessly watching his struggle with no small amount of amusement. She even enjoyed the sounds he made—the grunts of exertion punctuated by melodious words she understood to be profanities.

After another drawn-out moment, Gabriel finally ceased his mudslinging. Visibly panting, he scrubbed a hand over his forehead to shove the silver strands back—inadvertently painting a streak of mud across his face.

He had the nerve to glare at her before he finally coughed out a single word that must have gouged his pride. "Please."

Gratified, Shyaree chuckled and rose to her feet. She motioned for him to relieve himself of the weapons at his back. They were only weighing him down.

He frowned but didn't contest her order. He unsheathed his swords and flung them one after another, displaying impressive throwing skills. The blades landed just at the cusp of solid ground. Shyaree darted over to gather them and deposited them on safer ground.

Next, she motioned for the rucksack he wore. With a low grunt and a heft, the pack crashed paces shy of her boots. Shyaree retrieved it quickly and dragged it away before it began to sink.

His holster belt was not so easy. The lower part of it was already submerged with his torso, and he couldn't undo it without reaching into the mud.

Gabriel motioned her aside and emptied his holster belt of throwing knives and dikens in a quick series of thunks into a nearby tree. Shyaree winced.

Satisfied that they could no longer make him weigh any less, she scoured the circumference of the pit until she found what she was searching for—a broken branch of sufficient sturdiness and length.

"Slowly. No abrupt movements," she instructed before extending the branch.

Gabriel grabbed onto it, pulled, and nearly dragged her in.

Thurin's wrath, perhaps she shouldn't have waited until he was waist-deep before intervening. Shyaree thrust all her weight back, but she hadn't anticipated how hard it could be to haul a full-grown fae male from a sink pit.

With every inch he gained, they had to wait a moment to allow the mud to fill the space his body had occupied. It was a painstakingly slow process, but soon Gabriel came close enough to touch. She tossed the branch aside in favor of grasping his arm. Shyaree gritted her teeth as her muscles strained with exertion. Every breath passed with excruciating slowness. It was like trying to extract a deeply rooted weed from the earth. Just a little more . . . Just a little . . .

He lurched from the pit—and right into her.

Shyaree landed on her back with a gasp. The male weighed like a boulder. She tried rolling out from under him, but the mud-slicked bastard kept her pinned.

"Found that funny, did you?"

Clumps of mud splattered onto her.

Shyaree shoved at his chest, but he didn't budge.

"Hold on now. Where's the hurry? You were pretty content sitting by the edge before. Besides . . . what ill-mannered brute would I be if I didn't say thank you, hmm?" A slow, teasing smile lifted his lips while mud dripped, dripped, dripped all over her. "I'm so grateful that I might just give you a hug."

Son of a beast! Shyaree swatted and squirmed with a half-hearted snarl while wayward laughter tickled up her throat. She wriggled her hips until his grin faded and a low growl rumbled from his chest. The sound vibrated her very bones.

She stilled.

Suddenly she was exceedingly aware of every muscled part of him pinning her to the ground. The teasing light in his gaze had melted away, replaced by an abrupt darkening that made her heart flounder in its cage.

She parted her lips to draw in a deeper breath, but it seemed to draw him closer, too. His pupils dilated, his irises riveted to her mouth. He was saturated with sweat, mud, and grime . . . yet he smelled strangely delicious, and his solid weight pressing into her . . . divine. Something in her groin coiled, and the muscles between her thighs clenched, reminding her that her heat was imminent. Her heat. Shyaree swallowed nervously. She would come into heat in a matter of days . . . and when that happened, she shouldn't be anywhere near *Gabriel*.

She should shove him away. This was not real attraction. It was simply her body reacting to the nearest male. But her hands seemed to have grown a will of their own, because they landed over his ruggedly chiseled arms . . . and stayed there.

His head lowered until their lips were a hairsbreadth apart and their breaths kissed. Tingling sensation bloomed everywhere, dandelion heads brushing over her skin. Just as she thought her heart was about to lurch from her chest, Gabriel reared up.

He turned sharply to the trees, his body tensed like a boa before it lunged.

Only then did she notice a strange new scent. Perspiration mingled with leather, musk, and male. No. *Males.*

Danger.

The hairs on her skin stood up just as a gleam of silver shot out from the undergrowth.

Gabriel's ears twitched at the subtle whoosh of a blade cutting through the air. He threw himself over Shyaree, shielding her. A second slower and a diken would have penetrated his temple. As it was, it sank into bark. More followed.

Gabriel rolled off her and dragged her behind a fallen log.

A three-pronged diken embedded in the trunk of a tree just above them was inscribed with Faerian: *Victory over glory.* A Silverbeak weapon. And it was flecked with blood.

Shyaree huddled beside him, cupping her forearm. Blood dribbled from between her fingers and dripped off her elbow.

They'd hurt her.

"A flesh wound," she signed, appearing more stunned than fearful.

Gabriel shifted closer, his heart drumming a violent beat in his chest as he glanced at the rest of her for more cuts. They'd *hurt* her. One head would roll for every drop spilled.

"Beheading the emissary was a mistake, Blacksage," called a male voice in Faerian. "You've angered the king."

"Don't bother running," said another from the opposite side. "We have you surrounded."

"Who are they?" Shyaree signed.

"Pests." Gabriel signed back with a strained smile. *"I'll handle them."*

She didn't look reassured, because she reached for a throwing knife in her holster belt.

He stayed her hand. *"Stay here."* Gabriel peered from their hiding spot. His weapons lay out in the open, along with Shyaree's abandoned machete. They had the three throwing knives strapped to Shyaree for two Silverbeaks—and counting.

"You can't outrun us," drawled a third voice. "You know what the king wants. Hand us the female, and we'll let you go."

"Maybe," quipped a fourth.

Bawdy laughter erupted from all around. There were more than four.

Shyaree clenched his arm. Panic showed in her eyes. They were fenced in by Silverbeaks. Two against five, maybe more. Gabriel had faced worse odds. Shyaree was handy with knives, but could she fight? If the rookheads' objective was to capture her, they would swarm him and take her.

Gabriel's jaw clenched. No. As much as he wanted all the heads to roll, he'd settle for the ones he could take in one minute. One minute for his portal to take hold and her to slip away. But one minute was a lifetime in close-range battle. Unless . . .

"Come on, Blacksage," called an uncomfortably close voice. "Is this what you've become? A coward hiding behind a log?"

Leaves rustled. Boots crunched as the Silverbeaks closed in on them. Blood continued to drip from the gash on Shyaree's arm, down her elbow, staining a crimson patch in the dirt.

Fuck it.

Gabriel's fangs tingled as he turned to Shyaree and signed, *"Do you trust me?"*

She nodded warily.

He didn't give her a chance to object. He drew her hand away from the weeping laceration on her forearm, lowered his head, and wrapped his lips over her wound. The moment her blood touched his tongue, Gabriel fought the urge to groan. He hadn't drunk from another since Rebekah, and Shyaree tasted *nothing* like a fae female. A potent magic—*mana*—something Gabriel had never tasted before. Two heady swallows and pure undiluted magic pulsed through his veins like an eagle soaring through the skies.

He pulled back, aware that Shyaree was one breath from bolting.

"Trust me," he repeated in a harsh whisper, wiping her blood from his lips just before his body dissolved into shadow.

He flowed over the ground, seeping into shaded crevices, wending over dry leaves, dead twigs, and small rocks. He glided past little saplings and large ferns, tunneled through upraised roots, a shadow guided by instinct alone.

He found the first Silverbeak easily. The Unseelie crouched beneath the underbrush, utterly oblivious to his presence. Gabriel solidified at his back and slit the man's throat with his own weapon. The rookhead crumpled without a sound.

Gabriel vaporized again, moving on to the next. Mana burned through his veins, flaming like fire fed with ale. He managed to fell another before the Silverbeaks wised up. His time was up, anyway. Even with Shyaree's blood in his system, Gabriel couldn't maintain shadowform beyond a few precious minutes in a realm not his own.

He slunk to his discarded swords and solidified. He had barely managed to arm himself before a series of dikens whistled toward him. Gabriel spun his blades and deflected them with a well-timed pivot. No more dikens followed.

One by one, the Silverbeaks revealed themselves from their hiding places.

Seven.

Gabriel pulled his lips back in a snarl. Tearing the threads of magic he could find from every shade and shadow in his vicinity, he formed a portal close to the log where Shyaree hid. At the sight of his nascent portal, a Silverbeak lunged in her direction. Gabriel herded him back, blades slashing just as Shyaree darted out from her hiding spot.

One of her knives struck a Silverbeak in the chest.

"Get the whore before she escapes!" growled the apparent leader.

"Now, Shyaree! Go!" Gabriel yelled.

She released another knife, but Gabriel didn't see if she hit her mark.

The rookheads charged him in a flurry of sharpened fangs and flashing steel. Gabriel blocked the first blow with his swords, allowing the momentum to drive him back two paces before he kicked upward. His boot connected with his opponent's jaw in a satisfying crunch even as he dodged left and deflected another blow. A full spin of his swords bought him some distance from his opponents. His curved blades were best for close-range combat—exactly what he preferred. But trying to keep five rookheads from Shyaree made it trickier.

Gabriel had always enjoyed challenges.

He jammed his elbow into a gut and sank his blade into flesh. "What are you waiting for!" he roared at the wildcat. "Go now!"

His portal was complete. He couldn't keep them all away from her for long.

He watched her run in his periphery. But not into his portal. She dashed *past* it, disappearing through the trees like a deer skirting a hunter.

Two Silverbeaks exchanged a smirk before rushing after her.

Chapter 9

Shyaree ducked low-hanging vines and dashed past a cluster of bromeliads without a care for the thorny leaves tearing at her tunic.

Two. She'd managed to draw two from the throng—hopefully Gabriel could handle the rest on his own. For now, she'd have to find a way to hide.

Running full tilt in the rainforest was near impossible. Fallen leaves and other forest detritus hid stumps, holes, and dead branches. She couldn't even run in a straight line. She skirted trees, hopped past ridges, and scampered over logs. But the forest discriminated against no one. It must make the chase equally fraught for the fae on her heels. If anything, she had the upper hand. She'd grown up in this terrain, and she unconsciously charted a path most advantageous for her speed and size.

The males after her might be nimble, but they were also considerably larger.

A wall of shoulder-high thickets beckoned in her periphery.

Shyaree veered toward it and squeezed through the first opening she found, scurrying in like a rabbit into a burrow.

The sloped ground limited visibility beyond the copse. If her pursuers couldn't tell if they could intercept her from the front or lose her in the midst, they had no choice but to follow to keep her within their sights. She only prayed the thicket did not grow so dense as to trap her within.

One of her trackers hissed what sounded like an imprecation before breaking branches echoed through the forest. They were cutting a path for themselves.

Spiny branches snagged her hair and clawed at her like bony fingers. She brushed them aside, only to stumble over a hidden stump. She landed hard on her hands, scoring her knees and cutting her palms. Stomping footsteps propelled her to her feet.

Shyaree pushed past a spray of wild ferns, leaving a smattering of red on the broad leaves. Thurin's wrath! Blood dripped from the lacerations on her palm. She pushed forward, keenly aware she was leaving a scarlet trail for her hunters. She had no choice. The foliage was too thick to traverse without touching.

Instinctively she pushed in the direction where the branches grew more tangled but were finer. Softer. Younger. Covering her head with her arms, she shoved through the curtain of saplings, ignoring the little scratches to her skin. Her pursuers' pounding footfalls grew louder. With their hacking swords, they would find her soon enough.

Outrunning them was not the answer.

She had to find a way to disappear.

She stumbled from the copse, and her ragged breaths almost drowned out the distant gush of running water. Almost.

A short distance down a dangerously open path and she saw it. A wide riverbend. She sped alongside it and found its source. Boulders piled high in a sharp incline, rising like a rocky castle amid the thick hardwood trees. A wide strip of frothy white cascaded through the middle—a waterfall. A godsend.

Spying a depression behind the heavy fall, she slid swiftly behind the thick covering of water and flattened herself against the rock face.

Water misted everywhere, drawing a damp chill down her spine. She listened hard for her pursuers but heard nothing. Were they stuck in the maze of thickets? She had no way to tell. Thurin must be smiling down on her, because the depression offered a narrow pathway that led deeper into the heart of the fall. The water was a sheet of white that would obscure her from sight.

She came to a halt when knobby protrusions dug into her palm. She squinted, her eyes adjusting to the dim light, as she ran her fingers over the uneven surface. She startled.

Not bumps.

It was the *spine* of some large creature embedded in the rock. And she had inadvertently smeared her blood over it. Her heart ratcheted anew. It couldn't be . . .

A disembodied voice came in rapid Faerian before switching to smooth Animatish. "Come out, come out, kitten . . . we know you're here."

Shyaree held her breath. She wiped her bloodied and clammy palms on her pants before reaching for the last throwing knife she had. Which was more horrifying, her pursuers roaming out front or that she was here, clinging to a fossilized—

"We'll make it worth your while . . . " The voice muffled as he moved too far for her to catch the rest of his words.

She allowed herself a shaky breath. Where had they gone? Had they left? Or were they just waiting for her to come out of hiding? She was so focused on the sounds of her pursuers that she almost missed the subtle crack-crack-crack of shifting stones. But it was hard to ignore the debris and tiny pieces of rock raining down over her head as though a giant hand sprinkled spices into a pot. And impossible to miss the bony ridges *undulating* at her back like an anaconda shedding its skin.

Shyaree's breath caught.

Crack. Crack. Crack . . . More fractures riddled the rock face. Thurin's wrath, this couldn't be happening. The *thing* wasn't fossilized. There was only one creature fabled to live hidden in the gaps and crevices of the earth.

Cragalith.

Shyaree tore out from behind the falls and into the open, not taking her eyes off the bony tail partially free from the rock.

A shout from her pursuers. "There she is—"

Crack-crack-CRACK!

Chunks of rock crumbled and crashed into the river.

The fae were merely ten paces away, but even they stared, open-mouthed, as rocks dislodged, altering the flow of the massive fall in a sudden spray of water. A tremble of the ground jolted Shyaree from her stupor. She turned and fled. Only one of the fae caught up to her and seized her by the arm.

"What the fuck is that?"

CRAAAACCCCK!

It was the deafening noise of a boulder being crushed from the inside out. The ground shook with enough abrupt intensity that they all lost their footing. Shyaree took the opportunity to shake off her captor and bolt.

She didn't get far.

A hand grabbed her elbow.

She was ready for him. She whirled back, aiming her throwing knife at his throat, but he blocked her with his elbow, so she carved up a chunk of his arm instead.

"Rutta!" He growled, raising a hand to strike.

"A-Adrian!" shouted his companion.

The sheer disbelief in his voice had them all freezing. Even though Shyaree *knew* what she was looking at, her jaw still hung.

Long legs, segmented and spindly, pushed out from an explosion of rocks. An abominably large spider . . . Except this creature had six legs instead of eight. Each leg was thicker than a tree trunk, and it stood close to the height of four grown men stacked together. Bulbous red eyes swiveled, then came a low, screeching whine. The creature didn't move except to snap its forearm-sized mandibles.

Shyaree jerked out of the fae's hold and fled.

Adrian followed her cue. So did his companion. But the moment they started running, the cragalith released an earsplitting wail. And the ground trembled as though a stampede of wild horses charged after them.

A strangled scream had Shyaree turning back.

Adrian's visage was the shade of whey as he stared down at the black spindle jutting where his stomach should be. A spindle with a bulbous tip covered in bristly hairs and blood. A *lot* of blood. The shaft protruded further from Adrian's torso with a gruesome squelch before the tip flared open like the petals of a carnivorous plant. The serrated ends dug into the surrounding flesh, and the whole thing retracted, dragging Adrian with it.

The fae did not even manage a scream while the cragalith's mandibles snapped him in half. Shyaree couldn't seem to move. Fear shrieked through her, but her blood had turned to ice and immobilized her limbs. It wasn't until she heard the sickening slurp—the cragalith sucking its meal from the inside out—that she regained control of her faculties.

Run, run, run!

Only to stumble in her haste.

The other fae beside her, who had been equally transfixed

by fear, yelled something unintelligible. He hurled a knife at the cragalith. Steel clanged off its stonelike carapace. Shyaree didn't stay to watch this time. She ran and didn't turn back. Not even when she heard bloodcurdling screams and more nauseating slurping.

A high-pitched wail.

The ground quaked, then came the sound of uprooting trees and tearing boughs.

Her boots skidded on mud. She steadied herself, not daring to look back. Where could she go? Where could she hide from a creature that could pulverize rock? She couldn't think. Not when panic clogged her chest and fear choked at her throat. She pushed past a low branch only to realize she had an open wound on her palm. Her hands were stained with blood. Gods above, was it following her because it could smell her blood?

The river.

She needed to hide in water or at least wash off the blood.

Shyaree swerved to her right, catching a glimpse of the gargantuan monster skidding as it tried to follow her. It collided with a copse of trees. The cragalith screeched in apparent fury, its tail swiveling erratically while it swung itself around.

Shyaree ran as fast as she could, trusting her instinct to take her back to the river.

Ice prickled along her forearm. She had barely noticed her shadowmark pulsing beneath her skin when a shadow bounded into view. Too close, too soon. She slammed into the figure, and they both hurtled to the ground, rolling in a tangle of arms and legs. Shyaree was still gasping for breath when the man disentangled himself and loomed over her.

"Are you all right?" Rough hands cupped her face in a startlingly protective manner. "Are you hurt?"

Shyaree could only shake her head. Blood stained his

clothes and skin, and she had never been gladder to see him. Relief struck her so hard she released an involuntary sob.

Gods above, Gabriel was alive.

"Did you think you could escape me?"

He was alive. And furious.

"Did you think I wouldn't find—"

Shyaree launched herself into his chest, wrapping her arms around him. That seemed to startle him into silence. She pushed back to sign, *"Make a portal! Take us away!"*

At her urgency, his head swiveled, looking for danger. "Where are they?"

"Dead!"

"You killed them?"

As though in response, the cragalith shrieked in the distance and the ground quaked. Gabriel's gaze widened. "What was that?"

"It killed them! Take us away. Take us away now!"

When he did not immediately obey, Shyaree pounded her fists against his blood-soaked shirt. *"Make a portal! We need to leave!"*

Gabriel hissed. "I . . . I can't."

Nearby trees toppled. The cragalith must have picked up their scent.

"You can't make a portal?!"

"Used too much magic, too quickly," he said. "I need time."

Thurin's wrath! Shyaree half ran, half dragged him along. Gabriel must have caught a glimpse of the cragalith, because soon he took her hand in his and picked up speed. Only he led them in the wrong direction—away from the river.

Shyaree redirected him, dragging him by the arm as she pointed toward the river.

He didn't argue.

When they reached the water's edge, he halted.

Shyaree motioned at him. *"Get in!"* He was covered in as much blood as she, maybe more. The cragalith would find them both.

Gabriel shook his head and repeated the same two words that nearly had her tearing at her hair. "I can't."

"It is tracking us by the scent of blood. Water will wash away the scent."

His jaw hardened. "I'm not going into the water."

Thump! Thump! Thump! The river's placid surface rippled.

"You can't swim?" she signed incredulously.

"I can, but . . . " He shook his head and gave her a soft shove toward the river. "You go."

Breaking branches resonated, then came a high-pitched chirrup.

"What about you?"

"Get in the water and hide behind those rocks. I'll distract it."

Thump! Thump! Thump! Ripples overlapped as though even the river babbled with fear.

"Are you out of your mind? You can't fight it!"

"I'll find a way."

"You are covered in blood! You can't outrun it! You can't— "

Gabriel caught her by the shoulders with firm hands. "Hey, hey. Shyaree. Look at me." He tipped up her chin. She met his gaze and found amusement in his eyes.

Amusement.

Shyaree had a sudden urge to box his sharp-tipped ears.

"I can take care of myself, wildcat." The sheer confidence in his tone was reassuring. It was also utterly terrifying. He nodded at the water. "Now get in and keep yourself hidden. If you get a chance, run and don't look back. I'll find you."

She shook her head, ready to drag him in with her, but he

wouldn't budge. Nor would he release her shoulders or give her the space to sign her worries. To list all the reasons he would soon die a horrible death.

He shot her a knavish smile that seared itself into her mind's eye and a reassuring squeeze that only made her want to wrap her arms around him and never let go.

"I can take care of myself. *Trust* me."

Chapter 10

Gabriel waited until Shyaree was safely in the water before he jogged off. Closer to where the earth trembled. Shyaree had said blood drew the creature.

That made things easy.

He was already covered in the blood of his kills, but he needed more. He drew a knife and sliced his palm—his only exposed skin. A calculated risk that allowed him to drip fresh blood away from the pool. Away from Shyaree. It would work. It *had* to. He'd used a similar tactic with a basilisk once. The serpent had nested a little too close to the slums of Evenmere, and Gabriel and his men had lured it out with cow's blood, then they'd trapped and slain it.

The only difference here was that he didn't have the other Red Knights with him. Or a cow.

A deafening chirrup, then its thundering steps.

Thump! Thump! Thump!

Sounded like the cragalith had taken his bait.

Gabriel chanced a glance over his shoulder and caught a glimpse of the colossal creature between high branches. His eyes widened, and his stomach sank. Five blazing hells. No wonder the ground shook. His plan had felt a lot more solid before he'd realized a cragalith was double the size of a basilisk. He swallowed his rising trepidation and cracked his neck. He'd faced worse and survived. This was nothing but an oversized spider.

An overgrown arachnid with a taste for blood.

And his vest and shirt were drenched with it.

Thump! Thump! Thump!

Gabriel ripped off his baldric and his swords. Tossed them to the ground. Next, he unbuckled his holster belt. He glanced up at an ancient tree so tall he couldn't even see its top. Perfect. Freed from his restraints, he peeled off his blood-soaked clothes, running the blood from his still-weeping palm along them to thicken the scent. He launched them as far as he could away from the tree.

Thump! Thump! Thump!

He made a split-second decision to leave his weapons on the ground. They would only slow him down. The knife in his boot would have to do.

He began to climb.

Up and up he went, until a breeze flitted across his skin and the ground quaked. The cragalith charged into view. Its front legs might be reminiscent of a spider's, but it also had the segmented back of a beetle and a long tail with a disturbing slew of wriggling legs that brought to mind a horse-sized centipede.

It snarled before lunging at the bloody pile Gabriel had left as bait. The giant arthropod wasted no time spearing and tearing at his clothes.

Now or never.

He was bleeding from a laceration somewhere on his back. Once the nightmarish pest was done ingesting his clothes, it would doubtless sniff him out. Gabriel didn't fancy being a snack on a stick.

He leapt from his perch and landed squarely on the cragalith's back.

It hissed and flung its head back and forth. A jarring crash. It slammed into a tree, dislodging a hail of leaves and twigs. Branches whipped into Gabriel's face and struck his back.

He clung doggedly to a fistful of bristly hairs.

His other hand was useless at this point. Blood made his grip slick, and even if he managed a hold, the cragalith's hairs were so fine and tensile that they cut into his wounded palm. His clinging seemed to enrage the creature even more, because its leg-riddled tail struck upward in a scorpion-like move. Gabriel swerved, narrowly avoiding the mean end shaped like a lance. Another strike. This time he dodged a second too slow. A sharp edge scored his thigh, ripping through his pants and tearing flesh.

"Fuck!"

Gabriel reached for the knife in his boot. He plunged the blade into the beast's thorax, and the jarring impact nearly lost him the blade. Its hide was hard as rock. And it bucked like an enraged stallion. Gabriel tightened his grip, the stiff hairs cutting into his skin. Soon he'd slip and get trampled. Or worse.

The tail swooped in again, missing Gabriel's head by a handspan.

Time to end it.

Wedging his boot between the segments of the creature's exoskeleton, Gabriel hoisted himself higher. The cragalith shook its head like a dog with ticks in its ears. Gabriel laughed. He was the tick from hell. When the protruding red eye came into view, he didn't hesitate.

He drove the dagger in—scalding gunk splashed into his face.

The cragalith shrieked with enough gusto that Gabriel's ears rang. It staggered, tripping over saplings and slamming into a tree. The impact sent Gabriel hurtling through the air. He smashed into something hard. His lungs emptied. Pain seared through his leg. Then he was falling, his descent slowed by reedy branches.

He collided with the ground.

White spots speckled his sight; an incessant ringing filled his ears.

Was the ringing canceling out all other sounds? Or was the overgrown bug conspicuously quiet? Gabriel pulled himself up groggily. His head spun as though the world were shaking. Perhaps it was. Nausea rose in his throat in the form of iron-tasting bile. He spat, then scrubbed sluggishly at the sticky mess obscuring his vision. Ozenn's blood. He couldn't see *anything*. Where was the damned creature? Was it dead?

A presence brushed up against him. Gabriel jerked, scrambling to get away while still on his back. Footsteps. Hands on his face and his shoulders.

Not monstrous feelers or spiky bristles but gentle hands. Feminine hands.

"Shyaree?" he croaked.

He received a firm squeeze on the shoulder.

Gabriel rubbed his eyes. "Where is it? Is it dead?"

Another reassuring squeeze.

Gabriel sucked in a shuddering breath and allowed himself to fall back to the ground. The infernal ringing in his ears turned to a steady hum, and his skin stung as though he'd suffered a bad burn. She wiped at his eyes, helping him remove the rest of the gooey fluid from his face until he could finally blink. When his lids opened, Gabriel had never seen a sight more staggering.

Shyaree signed something, but all he could focus on were her eyes. He'd always thought her irises a plain gray. Only now did he notice the flecks of lustrous blue. They reminded him of the sea before a storm. Tempestuous. Wild.

Glorious.

He scowled. "Damn it, wildcat. Didn't I tell you to stay hidden?"

She responded with a frown of her own. She tried to pull him into an upright position, but the searing pain had Gabriel cursing aloud. Shyaree promptly eased him down to his back. Gabriel groaned. Was he on the ground? It felt like he lay on a pile of stones. Everything hurt.

Snap! Snap!

Shyaree's face came into view again.

Snap! Snap!

She was snapping her fingers in his face.

"Look at me," she signed. *"Focus."*

"Focus . . . ," Gabriel mumbled. "Focus on what?"

His head felt heavy. He lifted it to study the source of the pain radiating from his leg. He should be shocked at the sight, but he only blinked. Blood oozed from a gaping patch of his thigh.

"Is it dead?" he asked again, though this time he wasn't sure if he was asking about the creature or his own leg.

Shyaree nodded to the side.

Gabriel followed her gaze and found his answer sprawled on the ground, six spidery legs akimbo and its rear end curled up like cooked shrimp. Releasing a shaky breath, Gabriel shut his eyes and allowed himself to relax, but she patted his cheek once more, demanding his attention.

He lifted his lids with a frown.

"Don't shut your eyes," Shyaree signed with another pat to his cheek. *"Look at me."*

Gabriel didn't want to obey her, but looking at her was no hardship, either. With her gaze locked on his, she ripped a length of fabric from her tunic. She tied it above the wound on his leg like a tourniquet, but the wound continued to seep. Not good. A pervasive ache made itself known at the back of his head, and his hands started to shake.

"Need rest," he managed. "Just a nap."

He needed Sleep, the restorative slumber all fae fell into when they were egregiously wounded.

She reached out to curve her palm over his cheek. The unexpected tenderness in her gesture brought a crease between his brows. Then she scurried off into the bushes.

Gabriel shut his eyes. Just as he wondered if she'd deserted him, Shyaree returned with their rucksack, a handful of mushrooms, and . . . a small piece of wood?

"What's all that for?" he asked, and his tongue felt thick in his mouth.

She mimed biting into the nondescript brown mushroom, indicating that it should be consumed, before holding it to his lips.

When Gabriel eyed her offering warily, she set the items down and signed, *"To numb the pain."*

He accepted a mushroom and grimaced as he chewed. Vile. He detested mushrooms. Still, Shyaree pushed more into his mouth, persisting until he consumed every last one. Then she broke the branch in half and held one part to his mouth.

Gabriel shook his head. "No way—"

Shyaree flicked him beneath his chin. Gentle but firm, it was akin to a schoolteacher's rap to his knuckles. The last rap he'd received had been . . . he couldn't even remember. It had been centuries since he'd been a boy.

Gabriel hissed, baring his fangs.

Shyaree paid him no heed. She captured his lower jaw and worked his mouth open with firm insistence. It was half shock and half disbelief at her handling that Gabriel parted his lips.

She stuffed the wood between his teeth.

"Ngggh!"

Gabriel was about to spit out the damned thing and take a bite of *her* when she *jabbed* a needle through the skin around his wound.

"Agh!" Gabriel clamped his teeth over her makeshift bite guard. Where in the five hells had she gotten a fucking needle?

He gnashed his teeth at her first tug of the thread.

The wood wasn't such a bad idea after all.

With every prick and pull of the needle, Shyaree kept her hand steady and her face composed. Gabriel's complexion grew chalky and his skin clammy, but he kept his chin up, defiant violet eyes fixed on her every move as though daring her to go faster.

She could not distract him with banter or soothe him with words. She could do nothing more for him than finish up as swiftly as possible.

So she made quick work of the task, stitching up the worst of his wound.

When Gabriel had lured the cragalith away, she'd washed the blood from her body at the river the best she could. Then she'd detoured to where they'd been ambushed, seeking weapons to arm herself. She'd found the remains of the fae that had been left to face Gabriel. Not only had he *handled them*—he had not been merciful.

She'd also found their abandoned rucksack.

The same one Isidor had packed in front of her. Food, water, and essentials, which included needles and thread. *Better go prepared than be sorry,* the healer had said with a smile. He'd had no idea how right he was.

Unfortunately, he had failed to pack alcohol. Shyaree had only a canister of water she'd use to rinse the injury to the best of her ability.

It took fifteen stitches to close the wound in Gabriel's thigh. A thorough examination revealed a particularly deep laceration near his forearm. Two more stitches. There was also a gash on his back and another slit along his palm, but those were shallow enough that she tore strips from the hem of her shirt for bandages. Good thing Isidor's shirt was oversized on her, or she would be running short on fabric.

When she was done, Gabriel spat out the wood.

He'd been painfully conscious the whole time, even though his eyes had taken on a drugged glaze—the mosswort taking effect. Prone on the ground with his chest rising and falling in shallow breaths, he appeared more vulnerable than she'd ever seen.

The notion was disconcerting until he muttered, "Ozenn's balls, you are *terrible* at stitches." His eyes slid shut, but not before he added, "I'll probably scar."

Shyaree's lips thinned. Perhaps she should have stabbed him harder with the needle.

She snapped her fingers at his face, but he didn't stir. Alarmed, she slapped lightly at his cheek until his eyelids lifted.

"We need to go somewhere safe," she signed.

The longer they stayed out in the open, the more risk they ran. Cragaliths aside, many other dangers lurked in Thurin's Mountain. Rogues, or even regular predators, would be drawn to the scent of blood.

Gabriel nodded sluggishly. He pushed himself up, and she slipped an arm under his shoulder. Together, they hauled him to his feet. Shyaree blew out a breath. His arm hung like a log over her shoulders.

He shuffled and blinked as though struggling to keep his

eyes open. Worry gnawed at her. Perhaps she shouldn't have fed him so much mosswort.

Step by slow step, she helped him forward.

"Where . . . ?" he mumbled.

She was looking for a Kilinjiri tree, like the Great Kilinjiri in her clan used for ceremonial purposes. But Shyaree had one arm wrapped around Gabriel's back and her other securing his arm over her shoulder. She could only mouth *shelter* and hope he understood.

He seemed to, for he didn't pose further questions. They moved with agonizing slowness. Gabriel's labored breaths whistled in her ear. Shyaree huffed and puffed until she finally spied a towering tree with stiff, raised roots.

They made their way toward the Kilinjiri, and Shyaree lowered Gabriel to the ground. She motioned for him to wait, then circled the tree, looking, *praying* for the telltale opening of a rotted hollow.

A Kilinjiri was not actually a tree at all, but a network of parasitic lianas that had grown around some poor tree and strangled it. Over time, the lianas drained the host, creating a hollow chamber beneath. The network of overgrown lianas masquerading as a giant, soaring tree often served as a hideout for animati children.

When she found the lip of a long-wilted liana, Shyaree gave a little clap of excitement. Using a knife, she pried it open. Hopefully this one wouldn't be already occupied by some unfriendly critter. She peeled the liana back so she could pry it apart with her hands.

"What is it?" Gabriel slurred.

Shyaree grimaced. His skin was ashen, and his lips were too pale. He looked like a corpse. Maybe she had overdosed him. Her innards tightened. Gods above, could mosswort be poisonous to the fae?

She tugged at his hand, motioning for him to climb into the hollow.

"In there? In this . . . tree?" The note of unmistakable shock in his voice had her glancing up. He swallowed, his breaths shallowing. "We bury our dead in Soul Trees, but I'm not dead yet, wildcat."

Shyaree blinked. That had never occurred to her. But this wasn't a fae's grave. It was a Great Kilinjiri, revered by the animati. To her, it was a symbol of sanctuary and safety.

"It's shelter," she signed.

Gabriel peered inside warily, his lips parting. "It's . . . hollow."

Precisely. It was the perfect hiding space.

"Like a tomb."

"It's a place for you to rest."

Gabriel mumbled something inarticulate, but he shuffled in, wincing every time he put weight on his leg. He lay down with a groan, stretching out his long legs the best he could, but Gabriel was a tall man. The Kilinjiri hollow was not wide enough to accommodate his full height, so he was forced to lay on his side, curling his spine. Shyaree crawled in and shoved the stiff lianas back in place, shutting them in darkness. Her eyes adjusted almost instantly, but from the way Gabriel blinked, he couldn't make out a thing. His hand reached out as if seeking her presence.

Shyaree caught it and gave it a reassuring squeeze.

His breaths came in short, irregular pants. She shuffled closer until her body cradled his much larger frame. Somehow, his discomposure was more frightening than the wound in his leg. At least that would eventually heal if tended properly. But this . . . Shyaree placed a palm over his cheek. She stroked the smooth plane of skin that tapered to the shadow of a beard near his jaw.

She lifted her hand to stroke again, but he cupped the back of it and pressed it in place, as though he didn't want to lose even a moment of contact with her skin. Gradually his breathing slowed and tension seeped from his muscles.

Lulled by his nearness and the secure cocoon of the Kilinjiri, Shyaree was almost asleep when he mumbled, "I'm sorry. I'm so sorry."

She tilted her head at him, but his eyes were closed.

Chapter 11

Dawn seeped through the cracks like a gentle melody. Shyaree licked her lips, painfully aware of her parched throat. Every part of her body throbbed. She shifted, and the prickle of phantom pins assailed muscles too long in the same position.

Gabriel remained curled on his side. Shyaree grimaced. His leg appeared even worse in the morning light, and her makeshift stitches macabre. It was as if a long and skinny centipede had decided to make its residence on his thigh. Blood had dried in rust-colored streaks over his face and around his wounds and crusted the tattered edges of his pants. But he seemed peaceful.

His breathing was long and regular, and the slight part of his lips made him appear almost boyish . . . if one could discount the bristles darkening his jawline. She brushed her fingertips against his forehead but jerked back in shock.

Gods above, his skin was overheated.

She patted his cheek, determined to rouse him. He stirred with a low groan and muttered something inarticulate, but his eyes remained obstinately shut.

Shyaree patted his cheek again until a single eyelid opened in a slit.

She sighed with relief and rummaged through their rucksack for a canister. Then she raised his head over her thigh so he could drink. Once he was done, she took a large pull from the bottle herself.

"How do you feel?"

He blinked blearily. "What . . . ?"

Shyaree shifted back and re-signed her query.

"Like something that came out of the rear end of a troll . . . Where are we?"

"Inside a tree," she reminded him.

He attempted a stretch, then winced. "Ozenn's blood. How long have I been out?" His eyes had strayed, scrutinizing their surroundings in the stray patches of sunlight filtering through the roots.

Shyaree waited patiently until his gaze returned to her before signing, *"It's morning. You slept through the night."*

"The whole night?" He frowned, as though surprised. "And you . . . stayed?"

"Where else could I have gone? I am too far from the clan to find my way back alone."

His visage darkened. "Maybe you should have considered that before running off yesterday."

It took several heartbeats before she understood what he meant. Then her eyes narrowed. *"I didn't* run off. *I was trying to divert some of those men."*

"That's why you refused my portal?" The crease between his brows deepened. "You wanted to . . . what? Even the odds for me?"

"Did you think I would leave you to face those males on your own?"

He stared. He stared for so long she began to wonder if

there was something unsightly on her face. There probably was. Probably blood and gunk and gods knew what else.

Discomfited by his unerring scrutiny, she held up her forearm. The one he'd shadowmarked.

"Besides, what's the point of running?" She added a sneer for good measure. *"You'll find me eventually, right?"*

He reached out unexpectedly to wrap long fingers around her forearm. His thumb caressed the shadowmarked spot in a strangely gentle manner. He couldn't have spooked her more if he'd sprouted horns. "I could have taken them, you know. I've faced worse odds in battle. You should have left."

Her back stiffened, and her motions turned taut and choppy. *"Next time I will, even when it looks likely you'll get slaughtered."*

"Good. Self-preservation is always sensible." His lips tilted into a wry curve, but something in his tone wavered.

Shyaree swallowed, suddenly contrite. She *had* inadvertently awoken a cragalith. And he'd taken it down. With a single dagger, no less.

"Who were they?" she ventured with less heat in her movements. *"And why were they after us?"*

"Silverbeaks. A mercenary guild that works for the new king." He moistened his lips, and Shyaree fed him some more water. "I think they were here for you."

She blanched. *"Does everyone want me for . . . my blood?"*

His answering smile was almost apologetic. "For a prophecy, it was pretty straightforward."

"They only want me to get the draga morli, right? If we find it, they'll leave me alone, won't they?"

The smile faded from his face. "One would assume so." He sat up. Or attempted to. He was clearly still discombobulated, because his forehead crashed into the top of the tiny enclosure. *"Sipa non!"* He sagged back with a groan.

Shyaree reached for him reflexively. He lowered his head into the crook of her shoulder, his nose trailing the curve of her neck. His breath warmed her skin and roused a sudden shiver. She had a distinct impression he was breathing her in, that her scent brought him comfort. The tip of his nose grazed the length of her nape and up to her ear. She shivered again, her skin tight with awareness. She was about to pull away, but he leaned closer. He pressed his cheek against her temple with a weary sigh, and the sound was so miserable that she had a sudden urge to stroke his back. To rub her own cheek against his.

Thurin's wrath, what was wrong with her?

This was *Gabriel Blacksage*, not some child in need of coddling.

She pulled away.

An emotion that looked a lot like dejection flashed over his face, but it cleared so quickly she wondered if she'd imagined it.

"Sorry," he muttered, rubbing at the injured spot on his forehead as he leaned back to the ground.

She reached for him again, then curled her fingers and forced her unruly hands back to her sides. *"You are overheated,"* she signed instead.

Gabriel's throat worked. Then he nodded, as if heated skin were of minor consequence. He shut his eyes and resumed his fetal position, rearranging his legs as though seeking a more comfortable angle.

Shyaree shook his arm.

"I just need a little more Sleep."

His eyes remained adamantly shut, so she snapped her fingers at his ear.

He squinted up at her with a beleaguered sigh. "I want to go home as much as you do, but I can't do any magic right now. Give me a few more hours, and I'll have a portal ready."

She shook her head. *"You need more water. To cool down."*

"I don't think I can move right now."

"Your skin is too hot."

"Don't worry. Another nap and I'll be good as new."

She couldn't decide if he was serious, so she cupped his cheek and put on her sternest expression. *"Many die from overheating."*

Even in his current state, he chuckled. "It's called a fever. And I think my wound is infected. But I don't think Ozenn's taking me back yet."

She peered at him skeptically. A fever? When an animati had a fever, death often followed if it was not treated properly with herbal brews. Shyaree was unable to give him those. But his eyelids drooped as if the simple act of speaking wearied him.

Shyaree nudged him until his eyes reopened. *"What can I do to make you feel better?"*

His lips curved in the faintest of smiles. "Let me sleep."

"How long?"

But his eyes had already drifted shut.

Shyaree blew out an exasperated breath. Sleep. He'd already slept the entire night, and he needed more? How would sleep cure heated skin? Then again, he was fae. She recalled Gabriel sleeping for *days* in the infirmary after a bad altercation with the archmage. Something inside her settled.

Perhaps this was normal for him.

With that in mind, she crawled from the hollow and into the open, stretching her back and limbs. Hiding in a Kilinjiri hollow was a lot more comfortable when you were a small child.

She backtracked to the site of the fallen cragalith.

To her shock, a crumbly layer of stone had grown all over the carcass in gray clumps. Its tail had curled back into itself, and granite formed a protective shell around the creature—no different from the layered rocks by the waterfall. And stranger still were the *snails*. There had to be over a hundred of them, tiny little ochre-shells gliding in apparent peace over the cragalith's rocky form.

A shiver licked down her spine. Was it even dead?

Gods above, if it wasn't, she certainly didn't want to wake it again.

Giving the rock-crusted creature a wide berth, she made her way back to the waterfall and halted in her tracks. The grisly remains of the two fae—the Silverbeaks, as Gabriel had called them—were strewn about, staining the ground with dark patches.

She signed a prayer to Thurin. The fae might not worship the god of war, but they had certainly met a gruesome end in his realm. Shyaree drank from the pool and washed herself as swiftly as possible. Scrubbing the filth from her skin, her thoughts wandered to Gabriel's refusal to get into the water. The male had shunned the river in favor of battling a cragalith with his bare hands.

Come to think of it, it wasn't the first time he'd avoided water.

Once, Gabriel had taken Shyaree to the beach in the mage realm. He'd been tasked with watching over her at the capital bazaar while Evangeline tended to some mysterious business, and he'd protested and grumbled like a reluctant child with a hated chore. Eventually, he'd ushered Shyaree from the bazaar to the seashore because he had no patience for her gawking. She'd never been in the capital, never seen so many eclectic wares on display. She could have whiled the whole day away just studying the little curios the mages sold in that thriving marketplace. But Gabriel had rolled his eyes and taken her to the beach instead.

She hadn't complained. In fact, she had been secretly overjoyed. Because it was also the first time she'd seen the sea. Overcome with excitement, she'd beckoned for him to join her in wading the briny waters, but Gabriel had refused.

"I prefer to keep my feet dry, thank you," he'd said.

She hadn't thought much of it then, but perhaps Gabriel had an aversion to water.

When she deemed herself suitably clean, Shyaree proceeded to search for her missing weapons. She'd lost the machete and throwing knives the kindly Isidor had given her. She didn't want to return to the Den missing half her borrowed weapons. But she couldn't find them. Instead, she found *Gabriel's* weapons.

The discarded holster belt holding a myriad of throwing stars. His baldric and his twin blades. She collected them all, hefting them over her shoulder. The weight of the steel was staggering. How did that male manage to swagger about, surefooted and spry, while carrying such a load?

Crack!

Shyaree jumped at the sudden crunch beneath her soles. Gods above, she'd unwittingly crushed a snail beneath her boot! Why were they everywhere? She wiped her feet fastidiously on a patch of grass, trying to remove the slimy goo from her sole while issuing a mental apology to the unfortunate critter.

When she stooped to scan for more weapons, her eyes widened. The snail must have been a sacrifice sent by the gods, because she would never have noticed the thatch of prickleberries otherwise. Dark berries clustered near the ground. *Edible* berries.

Shyaree ate her fill. She wasn't one to turn down a favor from the gods. Then she collected more in the hem of her untucked tunic. Who knew how long Gabriel would continue to sleep? Satisfied, she juggled the berries and the weapons and made her way back to the hollow.

By the time the Kilinjiri came into view, dusk was a gray pall across the horizon. Storm clouds shadowed the sky, billowing close to scrub the moon from its spot.

Her steps faltered, and her heart thudded.

A figure crouched beside the Kilinjiri roots, a dark outline against the shadowy forest. For one brief, blinding moment, she'd thought Gabriel had woken and crawled from the hollow. Except Gabriel didn't have wings jutting from his back, nor would he scrape at the roots like a badger clawing for grubs. Her breath thinned. She took a shaky step backward, but the subtle jangle of weapons on her person snared the creature's attention. It lifted its head as though to sniff the air, and the first drop of rain hit her cheek like a celestial warning.

Run.

Skeletal hands dragged him beneath the thick layer of ice and into the watery depths of oblivion. Gabriel thrashed violently, but they clawed at his arms, raked at his ankles. Sharp teeth gnawed his calves and tore at his neck, but the agony was nothing compared to the frigid water burning in his lungs. Bubbles escaped his mouth, carrying with them the echoes of his dying screams. Glowing eyes surrounded him. They were eerily beautiful, almost like fireflies illuminating a starless night . . . until they swam close. Close enough for him to make out each leathery crease on their malicious faces and count the serrated teeth that would soon rip him apart . . .

Gabriel woke up with a start, cold sweat coating his skin, screams echoing in his ears, and water sloshing around him. He jerked up, and the pain searing his leg tore him from the nightmare and grounded him in the present. He wasn't in the lake, but the hollow of a damned tree.

Why the fuck was there water everywhere?

It took him another shuddering inhale to recognize the rumble and roll of thunder. *Rain.* It was raining outside. Gods, it was only rain. He sucked in gasps of air, willing himself to breathe past the memories and leave them in the past where they belonged. When his breaths came easier, he groped about in the damp darkness.

"Shyaree?" His voice came out a hoarse whisper. He had drifted in and out of consciousness to the feel of her pressed against his side. She had been a constant and comforting warmth cuddling his back, the sound of her breathing a soothing lullaby in his ear.

But where was she now?

Gabriel shifted his wounded leg experimentally and grimaced. He needed to get out of this damned hole. Forcing himself up, he groped at the roots until he felt the opening and crawled out into the deluge of a wailing sky.

"Shyaree!" Another crack of thunder muffled his shout. Ozenn's blood, where could she possibly be? He shuffled about blindly, ignoring the sting of rain hitting his skin and the jarring pain streaking up his leg with each step. "Shyaree, where are you?"

A flash of lightning forked the sky, illuminating a glimmer on the ground not ten paces away. The rivulets running down his skin chilled to ice with each step.

His weapons lay scattered amid clumps of something black and pulpy.

His heart seized so violently he couldn't breathe. He staggered to his knees, ran his hand through the horrifying gore.

Then he laughed, dazed with relief.

The substance on the ground was not blood or bile but berries.

Mushed berries.

As though someone had dropped and trampled them in haste.

Chapter 12

Lightning impaled the sky while the heavens roared in protest. The wind howled in her ears as though to spur her forward, but like a capricious child, it rustled twigs and rattled low-hanging branches at her every turn. Shyaree stumbled, nearly twisting her foot in a shallow pit obscured by thready roots.

A screech sounded hair-raisingly close at her back. She threw herself to the ground, narrowly avoiding the score of unforgiving talons. Wings swooped close enough to ruffle her hair. So close, the creature's snarl echoed in the surge of air against her skin.

Shyaree tore her foot from the tangle and dashed beneath a row of close-knitted trees. The rogue couldn't follow her through cramped spaces, not with those large feathery appendages. It must have been a griffi—its distorted wings bore the recognizable gold-and-black plumage. A majestic animati meant for frigid, snowy mountains, not a sweltering rainforest. But the Tribe worked to secure all rogues in Thurin's Mountain. This was meant to be a sanctuary for the outcast, and she was trespassing.

Rain pelted her skin. The dirt turned to slippery mud, and grounded leaves acted like grease beneath her frantic soles. Water trickled down her face to further obscure her vision. She slowed and slid behind the curved bough of a low-limbed tree. Her heart thundered in time to the storming sky as she clutched one of Gabriel's swords to her chest. The wicked blade's solid weight gave her a small measure of assurance, but she hoped she wouldn't have to use it.

A rogue was still animati. She didn't want to have to kill one of her kind afflicted by malmorphism—a condition due to excessive buildup of mana in their marrow—if she could avoid it. She understood better than anyone how debilitating it was to be stuck in between forms, to be neither man nor beast. Ironically, she was a shaman who healed mana buildup in the marrow . . . when it was still curable. This rogue must have suffered from malmorphism for years, because it no longer appeared civil but wholly aggressive and animalistic.

Agonizingly slow moments crept by in the form of whistling wind and whipping branches. Perhaps the rogue had tired of its chase and had left in search of other prey. Dread writhed like a nest of snakes beneath her breastbone. What if it circled back to the Kilinjiri? It must have scented Gabriel in the first place or it wouldn't have been clawing at the roots.

Gods above, what if it was digging Gabriel up right now?

Fear sluiced down her spine, propelling her to move just as another bout of lightning speared the skies. A single flash showed a hunched silhouette perched on a branch overhead.

The rogue.

And it was staring down at her with eerie stillness.

Fear kept her frozen like a fawn in the face of a hunter.

The rogue's gold-tipped wings were folded almost regally at its back, the only discernible proof of its origin before malmorphism had taken and twisted it into a monster. Most of its torso appeared human . . . a painfully emaciated one. Its ribs and hip bones protruded beneath taut sinew and leathery skin, while its hindquarters appeared twisted and furred, and its feet like lion paws. Judging by the phallus hanging from its crotch, it was male. Brown feathers covered its crown, and a beak jutted where its nose and mouth should be. No humanity remained in its eyes. Only feral, bestial hunger.

Shyaree darted just as the rogue leapt from its perch.

Panic spun blind spots in her eyes.

An enraged screech caused adrenaline to spike in her bloodstream. She tightened her grip on the hilt of Gabriel's sword. Flee or fight. Flee or fight . . . There was no outrunning it—

An imposing kapok tree came into view, its umbrellalike crown so heavily draped with creeping vines that they hung like crisscrossing ropes. A furious beating of wings at her back spurred a fresh sense of clarity.

She didn't need to flee or fight.

She could snare it.

She ran beneath the vines and threw herself between the kapok's buttress-like roots, praying the rogue would follow.

It did.

It crashed into the vines, flailing like an enraged wasp trapped in a spider's snare, screeching as though to compete with the booming thunder. It snapped its beak, baring rows upon rows of razorlike teeth. Even its tongue was thin and avian sharp.

Only the creature was much stronger than she had anticipated.

Its gaunt frame lunged, again and again, until the vines

snapped from sheer force. She scrambled back until her spine hit the kapok's curved bark. The vines had proven an ineffective snare. The rogue trilled with seeming excitement.

Its prey was trapped.

Another horrifying snap, another vine giving way. Taloned fingers snatched at her calves. Shyaree lashed out with Gabriel's blade, but the claws grazed her arms, gouging flesh. Pain escaped her in a hiss. She recoiled, gritting her teeth and clenched the sword's hilt.

She could not get past the rogue's swiping talons.

It could easily break free from its entanglements if it thought to shred the vines, but it seemed to be ruled by base instinct. Its pupils were hugely dilated, so black they almost consumed the whites of its eyes. There was no higher awareness in its eyes, no echo of the warrior it must have once been before its current state.

She had no choice. Perhaps killing it was a mercy.

Shyaree tucked her knees and bided her time.

She only had one chance. She had to drive the blade through its throat or heart, and the only way to do that was when it came right upon her.

Snap! The final vine across its torso broke.

Wings flared just before it sprang forward. Sword poised, she braced herself—only the creature never reached her. It belted out a high-pitched scream instead, stumbling as though jerked by an unseen force before it was flung aside.

Thunder rumbled high above, seeming to herald the towering figure with silver-spun hair who blotted out her view of the sky.

Her breath came out in a quivering gasp. Gabriel's gaze swept over her in one shuddering instant and darkened to a malignant hue. He turned back to the rogue, sword twirling deftly in his grip. If it were not for the limp in his gait, she would have never guessed he had been injured.

The rogue circled in an airborne swoop.

A glint of the sword and something fleshy landed with a frightening thud—a bony hand tipped with talons. Before the rogue could shriek, Gabriel slashed again. And again. It spread its wings in a desperate attempt to flee. It did not make it off the ground. Gabriel hacked at it like a woodcutter at a block of wood. Relentless. Merciless.

Shyaree had never known the sound of breaking bone could be louder than a scream.

Gabriel butchered the creature until its wings unfurled like a blanket of dirty feathers soaked in a puddle of gore. Still, he continued to hack.

Shyaree shivered, suddenly free from the stillness of shock. She rushed over to seize his arm and stay his hand. His chin jerked up to reveal his expression wilder than the billowing storm. Then his eyes seemed to finally focus, his pupils dilating on her.

"Shyaree." The sword clattered from his grip.

He pulled her into his arms, and thunder pounded in her ear. Not from the storm in the sky, but the furious beat from within his chest. Faerian poured from his lips, hoarsely whispered words that made no sense to her save the relief cradled in each syllable. He held her in much the same way, clasped to his chest as though she were something unbearably precious he'd almost lost. And just like before, he lowered his head and pressed his cheek against her temple.

This time, she didn't pull away.

Gabriel held her until the sky's deluge slowed to a hazy drizzle. His pulse regulated, and with it, his sanity returned in a storm of sensation. Aching muscles. Lethargy. Confusion.

They were huddled in the middle of a land that had proven to brim with monsters. He should conjure a portal, take Shyaree back to the Den where it was dry and warm and safe—but he was not ready to release her.

Nor did she seem to mind.

In fact, she was nuzzling her face against the side of his jaw in a slow, rhythmic manner, as though she were both offering and seeking comfort. Her arms had curled around him, holding him as he held her, and she fit so seamlessly against him that they could have been two halves of a woven tapestry. She was tall enough that if she shifted her face, their lips would meet. Gabriel had to halt himself from bridging the distance.

"Shyaree . . . stop," he whispered.

She stilled instantly. Her arms unwound from his waist, and utter embarrassment filled her face as if she had been caught doing something scandalous. Despite his intentions, his arms tightened before she could fully withdraw, his body contradicting his logic.

She had released him, and her arms hung limply by her sides, but she made no move to shed his embrace, either. Instead, a tremor ran through her willowy frame. It echoed through him like a quake to his bones. The world seemed to tremble beneath his feet. She clutched him abruptly, and her lips parted, not with desire but shock. Only then did he realize the ground was *truly* shaking.

An earthquake? But the tremor stopped just as quickly as it had begun, and he wondered if his fevered brain was playing tricks.

"What in the five flaming hells was that?"

Shyaree pushed from his arms with a small hitch in her breath, eyes narrowed at the ground. Gabriel followed her gaze with a frown, but all he saw was dirt and forest detritus and the tiny rivers of red trickling from the mangled body behind them. Nothing spectacular.

"What is it?"

Very gingerly she pointed at a snail making a slow journey over a cluster of fist-sized rocks.

Gabriel's frown deepened. Had she never seen a snail before? "What—"

She shook her head absently and traced the lustrous slime trail the little creature had left behind, rubbing it between her fingers, as if the goo were a fascinating discovery. Then she pointed at the bushes where the snail was ostensibly headed . . . toward a cluster of *more* snails. She sank to her hands and knees, and the moon chose that moment to peek from behind the ebbing storm clouds, beaming bright as though its sole purpose were to illuminate the sleek lines of her rear.

Ozenn's blood. "What are you doing?"

Had the woman seriously gotten on her knees for a trail of snails? She paid him no heed as she crawled beside the critters. Gabriel shuffled after her, and admittedly, there *were* an inordinate number of them. A tiny congregation of shells gliding slowly but steadily in a single direction until they disappeared over . . . a cliff?

Gabriel's lips parted.

A shallow cliff, barely two feet deep, but it marked the margin of an entirely different terrain. The wind whistled, shafted from between tightly knitted trees into an abrupt empty stretch of horizontal granite. Devoid of dirt and foliage, the rocky platform held boulders arranged like a series of jagged teeth.

Uneven crevasses formed black veins in the ground.

But most startling were the shimmering streaks of silver lining the granite floor. Under the full glare of the moon, unobscured by rainforest canopy or storm clouds, the snail tracks looked like a thousand glistening ribbons draped over rock. As though the gods had taken a fine-tipped brush and scribbled moonlit lines over the ground with no rhyme or reason.

"Have you seen anything like this?" Gabriel asked, but before Shyaree could respond, a deep-set tremble shook the earth beneath their soles.

A loud, droning whoosh!

Water gushed from a distant fissure like a fountain, shooting an impressive height of over a hundred feet before falling in wet splashes over rock.

Gabriel blew out a breath. A geyser?

Rumble and whoosh. Water arced unexpectedly from a crevasse close enough to mist the air and shower them in droplets. Gabriel released a startled laugh, sharing a grin with Shyaree, who was mopping water from her face. The water was not hot, as he'd expected, but strangely cool as if it came from a fresh spring trapped underground. Not geysers, then . . . but blowholes.

They stood in momentary silence, watching water erupt from random crevasses with a near-playful cadence. Every so often, the ground shuddered and sent water exploding with a deep rush of air, as though it *breathed.*

His mouth parted on a sudden realization. "Shyaree . . . "

From the sheer giddiness in her expression, she had already worked it out for herself.

To the land kissed by the moon's silver tails . . .

Listen hard for the field that breathes,

And harvest the waters from between its teeth . . .

They had found the first of the three items from her mother's song.

Chapter 13

"I must admit she did a remarkable job," Isidor said as he inspected the stitches on Gabriel's thigh. "But you could have saved yourself the infection if you'd returned a day earlier," he added with a disapproving tsk. He daubed the area with something astringent that stung both Gabriel's nose and wound.

Exhausted and irritable, Gabriel curled his lips. "Do you think I chose to camp inside a tree with a hacked-up leg for fun?"

Shyaree's stitches might have kept the gash in his thigh closed, but the surrounding skin had grown inflamed, and Isidor's resulting nagging was something he could do without.

"There," the mer said, tying off the bandage. "A few more days of Sleep, some karro salve, and you'll be good as new."

"Where's Shyaree?" Gabriel asked when he was able to hop off the bed, but the healer had already bustled from the room.

"Here." Isidor reappeared, not with Shyaree, but a spare pair of pants. The mer held it out to him then pulled it back, seeming to think better of it. "Do you need help putting these on?"

Gabriel scowled. "Just give them to me." He would be damned if he needed help pulling up a pair of pants.

Isidor shrugged and tossed the garment at him. "Just keep the weight off your leg." He swept up the wads of bloodied bandages littering the ground.

"So where is she?" Gabriel asked again, easing the pants on with a grimace.

The mer looked up from his cleaning and blinked owlishly. "Who? Miss Shyaree?"

"No. The Seelie queen," Gabriel deadpanned.

At Isidor's confused frown, Gabriel exhaled. "Yes, Shyaree. Where is she?"

When Gabriel had retreated to his bath chamber for a wash, Shyaree had been whisked away without his knowledge. Isidor had calmly reminded him that Shyaree needed a bath, too, so Gabriel had relented. But surely she was done by now.

Isidor shrugged. "I'm not sure. I believe she's with Kai."

Gabriel's hand stilled at the tie of his pants. "*Malakai?*"

Isidor bobbed his head, but amusement dashed across the healer's obsidian gaze. "Kai volunteered to tend to her when it was obvious I was needed here."

That deplorable skirt-chaser. Gabriel gritted his teeth. This whole time, he had assumed Shyaree was with Arkas, the only male apart from Isidor he'd trust around her. Arkas was dependable. Steadfast. And most importantly, Arkas had never expressed interest in a female since his mate's passing.

"Miss Shyaree wasn't really hurt. Just some scratches here and there. I handed Kai a jar of karro salve that'll—"

"Where's Arkas?"

Isidor sighed. "There were a couple Silverbeaks loitering near our perimeter. He went out to clear them off when you and Miss Shyaree failed to return to the Den after the second day." The mer shrugged. "You know how he is."

Gabriel suppressed the urge to groan. Without another word, he fastened his pants and summoned a portal. He strode through it with the healer yelling after him, "Where're you going? You should be resting in bed!"

Using magic at his current state would only slow his body's regenerative ability, but limping down two flights of stairs would have taken far too long. Besides, Isidor did say to keep weight off his leg.

He could have used his shadowmark and portaled to Shyaree's exact location, but he couldn't risk walking in on her while she was still in a bath . . . or worse. Gabriel strode into the second-floor hallway, growling at the thought of Shyaree within the same walls as the Den's most notorious philanderer. Malakai's room was the first on the left.

Gabriel rapped an impatient fist on the blackguard's door.

Silence.

He pounded with more urgency. "Kai!"

The adjacent door opened to reveal a surly-eyed Caspian. "He's downstairs. In the kitchen."

The tightness in Gabriel's chest eased. The knave hadn't smuggled her into his private quarters, then. "He's with Shyaree?"

Caspian leaned against the doorjamb with an answering roll of his eyes. "Of course he is. How else will he compete with me if he doesn't try to hump everything that walks?" A wry snort. "Now if you don't mind, will you cease the banging? I've had a long night, and I'd like some sleep." The door slammed.

Fuming, Gabriel portaled to the ground-floor kitchen. He pushed past the door into a chamber lit by a warm crackling fire. Hector—the Den's unofficial, self-appointed chef—shot Gabriel a distracted nod before he resumed whistling and stirring a bubbling pot. Gabriel's stomach stirred at the aroma of simmering stew accompanied by freshly baked bread, reminding him that he hadn't eaten anything more substantial than oatcakes for the last two days.

"There he is! Gabe!" Malakai grinned at him from behind a kitchen bench. "All patched up now?"

Seated across the table from the degenerate womanizer, Shyaree turned to beckon him, appearing more at ease than Gabriel had ever seen. He limped over and halted.

"How are you feeling?" she signed, and scooted to the side as though to make space for him on the bench. But Gabriel remained rooted to the ground, his fingers fisted. Her cheeks were flushed and rosy, and her hair was unbound, hanging past her shoulders like damp ribbons as she nursed a steaming mug in her hands. The contentment on her face should have coaxed the same from him, but it didn't.

She was wearing a *bathrobe*.

An overlarge one that looked suspiciously like something out of Malakai's closet.

A muscle twitched in Gabriel's jaw.

"Where have you been?" he demanded with enough gravel in his tone to scrub the idiotic grin from Malakai's face and furrow Shyaree's brows.

"Uh, you hungry, Gabe?" Malakai asked with an awkward laugh. "I don't think the stew is ready yet, but there's some bread—"

"You took her into your bedchamber?" Gabriel couldn't quite keep the snarl from his voice, and his words came out more as an accusation than a question.

"Ah . . . yes." Malakai's throat bobbed. "Shy wanted a bath, you see. So I gave her one."

Shy? Gabriel gritted his teeth. "You *gave* her a bath?"

"I allowed her to use my bath chamber," Malakai amended hastily. "She bathed herself, really."

A gentle touch at his wrist. Shyaree placed a palm over his forearm, waiting for his attention. Irrationally triggered by the confusion on her face while she wore Malakai's bathrobe, Gabriel snapped. "What?"

Her lips pursed, and irritation glinted in her eyes. *"Why are you so agitated? Is your leg hurting?"*

"I'm . . . " Why *was* he so agitated? Fuck. "Tired," he muttered finally. That was not a lie. He *was* enervated. His body ached, and if he were to shut his eyes, he would fall into Sleep. He should be in bed, not here, creating a scene and drawing the curious glance of a now-silent Hector.

Gabriel exhaled. Why did he care if Shyaree had been in Malakai's room at all? She was here. Safe. Alive. Cooperative.

That was all he needed from her. For now.

Shyaree's skeptical gaze roamed over him, but the annoyance in her expression softened. She gave his forearm a little tug. *"Come, then. Sit. How is your leg?"*

"Fine." Gabriel settled grudgingly beside her, feeling a little too much like a bear in need of hibernation. "I just need to Sleep it off."

"Some food will help, too." Malakai snagged the breadbasket from the kitchen counter and shoved it unceremoniously under Gabriel's nose before shooting Shyaree a conspiratorial grin. "The guildmaster gets cantankerous on an empty stomach."

That was when Gabriel noticed the jar of karro salve between the two and the washcloth in the man's hand. Malakai tipped the jar and soaked it with a generous amount, but instead of handing Shyaree the washcloth, he leaned over the narrow table to daub the grazes on her knuckles as though she were incapable of dressing her own cuts.

Shyaree pulled away with a wince.

"There now," Malakai said with a chuckle. "You're not afraid of a little sting are you, Shy?" He pulled her arm back in place, thumb rubbing lightly over her wrist. Shyaree's lips parted, and a slight flush rose to kiss her cheeks, but she didn't pull away.

"Shyaree." Gabriel clenched his hand before he gave into the irrational urge to shove the other man off his seat. "Her name is Shyaree."

Malakai paused to give Gabriel an odd look. "Yes. Yes, I know that."

"She's animati," Gabriel added, seemingly incapable of keeping his mouth shut. "She heals fast enough. She has no need for karro salve."

Malakai frowned. "No?" He turned back to Shyaree, avid curiosity in his gaze. "What does your kind usually do to dress wounds, hmm? I can do whatever you're used to."

Shyaree ducked her head with a small shrug, but Malakai only grinned. "We may be mercenaries, but we know how to treat a lady. Tell us what you need. There's no need to be shy, Shy." He laughed, as though he'd made a particularly fine joke.

Shyaree peered up at Malakai from beneath her lashes, a small, soft smile lighting her face.

Gabriel scowled. "Oh, for fuck's sake. Just because she can't speak, it doesn't make her shy."

The smile on her lips faded, and the flush on her cheeks intensified.

Malakai's eyes narrowed before he turned abruptly toward the stove. "Hector, is that stew done? Bring Gabe a bowl, will you?"

Gabriel's lips thinned. "I'm not hungry."

"Of course you are," Malakai insisted. "You need to eat before you make a bigger ass of yourself."

Cursing under his breath, Gabriel hobbled from the bench toward an amused Hector, because Malakai was probably right. But Gabriel did not need to be served. He could damn well serve himself. Besides, he didn't need to sit and watch Malakai mollycoddle the wildcat. Gabriel was not usually annoyed by the other man's charm, but to see Shyaree reciprocating with a smile had riled him like nothing else. He had spent half a season with her in the mage realm, playing her interpreter. When was the last time he'd been on the receiving end of such a tender smile? He ground his teeth.

Never.

Shyaree *never* smiled at him that way. Malakai rubbed on her wound, and she smiled like he'd hung the moon? Gabriel ladled up a bowl of stew and spooned the broth with gusto—and spluttered. It scalded his tongue. Feeling the fool, he snagged a nearby flask and took a swig of water. When his mouth cooled, he shot a furtive glance back at the table. To his annoyance, Hector had taken *his* spot on the bench.

But . . . Shyaree couldn't speak.

Gabriel returned his attention to his bowl with a small, perverse smile of his own. The wildcat could not communicate properly with his men. She would need *him* to interpret sooner or later.

A burst of laughter sounded.

Gabriel glanced over to see Malakai and Hector speaking in broken and stilted Animatish, pressing her with questions about what had happened on Thurin's Mountain. The nosy lot. Instead of receding into her usual shell of austerity, Shyaree wore a congenial curve on her lips and responded with nods or general hand gestures. She did not appear to require his assistance. Gabriel spooned up another mouthful with ill-natured grace.

Specks of silver freckled the air, as though the sky suddenly rained smelted metal. Gabriel continued with his meal, unperturbed. He did not always recognize his men's portals, but Arkas's were unique.

Soon the little globules melded, an amorphous mass of liquid silver that opened into a portal. A black boot stepped through, followed by the rest of the man. Arkas appeared like a hound on a hunt. "Ozenn's blood, Gabe. I was looking everywhere for you."

Gabriel only grunted. "Relax."

His second-in-command cast a cursory glance around the kitchen. Hector and Malakai beckoned him over, while Shyaree shot him a small smile of acknowledgment, but Arkas ignored them. Instead, he loomed over Gabriel and lowered his voice.

"Do you know what she is?" Arkas jerked a thumb at the table.

Gabriel followed his gaze, where Malakai and Hector seemed to be entertaining each other with stories in botched Animatish. Shyaree must find them entertaining, because she was *still* smiling.

"A wildcat," he muttered.

"I'm serious, Gabe. Do you know what you've brought into the Den?"

Gabriel regarded Arkas with narrowed eyes. Had the other assassin somehow learned the contents of the necromancer's texts? Did Arkas realize Shyaree was the blood sacrifice?

Worse, had Arkas found out about Iolanthe?

"She's a damned *hybrid*!" The last word exploded from Arkas with enough vehemence to draw the attention of those at the table. He hissed and lowered his voice to a low, angry octave. "A hybrid with enough venom in her bite to poison an entire village! She needs to be returned to her mate. Immediately."

His cousin could well have spoken gibberish for the sense he was making. Gabriel set his bowl on the counter with a calm that belied the ire simmering in his blood as he latched onto the point that abraded most.

"Shyaree doesn't have a mate."

"I went to her village, Gabe." Arkas crossed his arms with an upward glance. "I spoke to her people. Her *mate*."

"Hey, everything all right over here?" Hector had partially risen from his seat with frown lines between his brows.

Arkas gave Hector a curt nod before lowering his voice, pitching his next words for Gabriel's ears only. "Whatever you think she is, whatever you want from her, it's not worth it. She is not who or *what* you think she is."

Gabriel clenched his jaw as his ire boiled to anger. "You were supposed to be monitoring the Silverbeaks. Watching the slave traders. Instead, you went to her clan? I worked with Shyaree for eight months in the mage realm. I know exactly what she is."

Arkas's snarl showed a hint of fang. But before his second could say more, Malakai made his way over.

"What's going on with the two of you?"

Shyaree had turned around on the bench, peering at Gabriel as she signed her concern. He reassured her with a stiff nod, but Arkas released another hiss as though he couldn't stand the sight of her. He stormed over and jabbed a commanding finger at Hector. "Get away from her, Hector. Now."

"Why? What's wrong?" Hector asked, even though he vacated his seat, clearly unused to the open aggression from the second-in-command.

Malakai laughed awkwardly. "Easy there, Arkas. She's just a girl."

"She's not *just a* anything." Arkas swung his gaze to Shyaree and promptly switched to Animatish. "You're coming with me."

Shyaree merely stiffened her spine and curled her lips. Her silent derision aggravated the second-in-command enough that he seized her boldly by the wrist.

Everything in Gabriel tensed. He darted over and squeezed Arkas's shoulder in warning. "Release her."

Arkas shrugged him off, reverting to Faerian in the next breath. "She's dangerous, Gabe. An abomination. One with deadly venom in her system. A single bite could end you!"

Shyaree ripped her hand from Arkas's grip with an angry huff that had him grating words in her native tongue. "Your mate wants you back, mongrel!"

Slap! Shyaree's palm connected with Arkas's cheek. He growled and made a move to grab her again.

Gabriel jerked the other man back by the collar. "Do *not* touch her again, Ironfall. Do you hear me?"

Arkas hissed, and his ears flattened. "Hear you? Are *you* listening to *me*?"

Shyaree gave them both a look of disgust. There was no way she understood their exchange. Arkas spoke Faerian unless addressing her directly. But Shyaree had clearly read enough from his tone and body language.

She pulled up her knees and slipped off the bench before storming for the door.

But Arkas seemed insistent on testing Gabriel's patience, because he swiftly dodged between the tables to bar her exit. He seized her again, this time with a vicious yank of her forearm.

Gabriel's fangs sharpened. *"Arkas!"*

Shyaree whipped around to knee her captor in the groin. He recoiled without releasing his hold, twisting her arm. A horrifying pop sounded just before Shyaree's expression crumpled with pain.

Darkness exploded into the room.

Gabriel's phantasma enveloped Shyaree in a protective

shroud of shadows that drew her from Arkas's reach and back to his side on the kitchen floor.

Gabriel didn't realize he'd started until his fist plowed into Arkas's jaw.

His second staggered, toppling a bench. His hand went to the reddening spot at his chin. "Mordida sipa!" He spat a wad of crimson-laced spittle to the stone floor. "Did you just hit me? For this murderous little bitch?"

Arkas was both his cousin and companion since the cradle. A man who had fought countless battles with him since the Winter War and one he trusted to manage his guild in his absence. A man who had just assaulted Shyaree in his presence.

Gabriel's knuckles collided with his second's face forcefully enough that something cracked beneath his fist. Blood spewed from Arkas's nose, but Gabriel wasn't done. He dragged the man up and hauled him to where Shyaree huddled on the ground, not liking the way she panted like a winded rabbit who'd narrowly escaped the jaws of a wolf. Shoving Arkas to his knees, Gabriel whipped a knife from its holster and held the pointed end to the man's jugular.

"Apologize."

Arkas hissed, and blood trickled from the hand cupping his broken nose as he dared contest Gabriel with a disbelieving glower. Hector and Malakai stared, making no attempt to intervene. No Red Knight in their right mind would challenge him. It was just as well, since he considered these men to be vinaro —brothers of different blood.

But Arkas was no ordinary Red Knight. He was his second-in-command. His cousin. Clearly, the man thought himself above reproach.

Gabriel lowered to a crouch so he met the challenge in Arkas's gaze with a warning of his own. He ran the blade along the man's throat, not to sever but with just enough force for blood to well in a threatening line.

"I won't repeat myself."

Arkas swiftly lowered his gaze and mumbled in Animatish, "I'm sorry."

A disingenuous apology, drawn by a hard hand of dominance. It was the best Gabriel could wrench from the man without breaking him. For now.

"Make no mistake, Ironfall. Touch her again, and there will be no opportunity for apologies." He released the man and allowed him to rise.

Arkas wiped the blood from his nose with the back of his hand. He held Gabriel's gaze for a tense moment before spinning on his heel and slinking through a portal. Gabriel shut his eyes on an exhale before turning his attention to the wildcat.

He had expected an icy glower or a heated scowl, but he received neither.

Her gaze was downcast as she cradled her assaulted arm, her breaths ragged, and her body trembling.

Malakai, who had snuck to her side, did the glaring on her behalf. "Will someone tell me what in the five hells that was about? Arkas, the bastard. He dislocated her shoulder."

Shyaree could not stop her body from shaking. Dimly, she was aware of Gabriel barking out orders in a stream of Faerian, but she could not seem to bring herself to her feet, so she remained crouched on the stone floor. Her arm was numb, but her shoulder was afire. The muscles surrounding her assaulted joint spasmed, and she felt every little twitch like a knife cut.

She shut her eyes and forced herself to breathe.

She was no stranger to this pain. *Breathe, Shyaree.* She could almost hear her father's voice in her ears. *Breathe, and it will be better, I promise.*

She sucked in shallow gasps until she managed deeper inhales. She breathed and replayed the ghostly echo of her father's soothing baritone in her mind until a deeper voice jarred her focus.

"Malakai is going to fetch Isidor. He'll be able to twist your shoulder back into place." When she gave no visible reaction, he continued, "I should keep you locked up." His words were harsher than broken glass and just as cutting. "You're a hazard to yourself."

In spite of the pain, or perhaps because of it, she whipped her chin up with a snarl. His own man had attacked her, dislocated her shoulder, and it was somehow *her* fault? Warmth pricked the back of her eyes. She quickly averted her gaze, but he must have caught it, because his expression softened, and that was even worse.

Her eyes began to leak.

The muscles of his throat worked. "Don't," he said, as though the tears were within her control. If they were, no one would ever see them fall. But she tried to obey anyway, squeezing her eyes shut in an attempt to stymie further humiliation. Except now she'd started, she couldn't seem to stop. Worse, she couldn't even bring herself to wipe her face, because somehow it hurt to move her uninjured arm. Such agony rippled at the slightest movement that she could only scrunch her eyes and wait for her tears to dry.

His callused thumb traced the damp tracks on her cheeks in a disturbingly tender manner. It only instigated more tears. Thurin's wrath, she just wanted him *gone.* But she couldn't move, she couldn't sign, she couldn't speak. She could only sit there and suffer his ministrations and listen to words that unraveled her further.

"I'm sorry I let him touch you," he whispered gruffly. "I'm sorry you felt the need to fight him. You shouldn't have to. I would have protected you . . . You know that, don't you?"

She glared up at him, tearfully, balefully.

Of course he would. He needed her for her blood.

But there was something in his voice, a sincerity that made her think he would have protected her regardless. As though she were worth protecting. As though she were safe . . . with him. And that notion, with *Gabriel*, was so unprecedented that her tears surged into a mortifying flood.

Footsteps echoed across the stone floor, then came Malakai and Isidor's voices.

Shyaree turned her face before they could witness her discomposure, and the motion caused fresh pain to writhe up her shoulder. Gabriel rose heavily to his feet, intercepting them with words. She didn't know what he said, only that they spoke long enough for her to steady herself. She was still sniffling when Isidor crouched beside her to inspect her arm, but at least she was no longer bawling.

The healer tsked sympathetically and motioned toward her shoulder, indicating that he wanted to force her arm back into place.

Shyaree cringed and shook her head.

"I know you have superior healing, but I doubt even the animati can heal a dislocated shoulder naturally, Shyaree," Gabriel said, as though she lacked common sense. Rationally she knew it had to be done, but she'd damn well do it when she was ready.

"Isidor said the longer you wait, the more you risk further injuries and muscle strain," he added. Shyaree shook her head again with more decisiveness and bared her teeth for good measure. Tremors still racked her frame. The harder she tensed, the more she shook. She needed time to lick her own wounds before she subjected herself to more agony.

Gabriel crouched on her other side with a sigh. "What are you so scared of, wildcat?"

With her ability to communicate now restricted to her facial expressions, Shyaree could only scowl.

"You were ready to take on two Silverbeaks before, but you're afraid of this?"

"Gabe," Malakai chided. "The girl is already in a lot of pain."

Gabriel only scoffed, all traces of his earlier tenderness gone. "I never took you for a coward, wildcat. Maybe I was wrong. You're nothing but a trembling kitten."

Shyaree slammed her head forward. Right into his face.

Gabriel's muffled curse was worth the pain radiating through her skull. She might not have access to her voice, but she always found a way to express herself—even if she had to resort to headbutting someone.

But she'd inadvertently allowed Gabriel close. So close, his body now trapped hers against the wall, and his arms kept her in place. Before she could wriggle away, he seized and straightened her assaulted arm. Rotated it. A loud snap. The ache at her forehead dulled, overshadowed by the searing jolt to her shoulder.

A grim smile filled Gabriel's face before her vision dimmed.

Shyaree sagged like a rag doll, and Gabriel secured her to his chest before she could fall face-first to the ground.

Isidor studied her limp form with a tight jaw. "Was that truly necessary? I would have coaxed her into bed first."

"Did the job, didn't it?" Gabriel scooped her off her feet, making sure not to jostle her arm and shoulder while his own leg protested beneath the added weight.

"Give her here," Malakai said, parting his arms.

Gabriel's eyes slitted. "What did you say?"

Malakai had the audacity to glower before he enunciated his next words as though Gabriel were hard of hearing. "I said give her to me. You're injured, aren't you? I'll take her to the guest room. The window is boarded up now."

Gabriel's arms tightened around her reflexively, daring the other Red Knight to challenge him with a show of fangs. "I'm fine."

"Ozenn's blood!" Isidor exclaimed irritably between them. "Miss Shyaree's not a bone, and you're not dogs." He pinned Gabriel with a hard stare. "Take her if you must, but get her some ice for the swelling." The healer marched to the door with a disgruntled huff. "And get off that leg if you want to recover any time soon."

Malakai and Gabriel exchanged a glance, all tension dissolving into sheepishness at Isidor's outburst. It took a lot to ruffle the mild-tempered mer.

"So . . . what in the five hells was Arkas going on about?" Malakai asked.

Gabriel's throat constricted. "The fuck if I know." Shadows pooled into a doorway, and Gabriel tossed Malakai a side glance. "You heard Isi. Get her some ice and send it up. My room."

Malakai raised his brows. "Yours?"

"Yes." Gabriel cradled her closer to his chest. *"Mine."*

Chapter 14

Shyaree blinked, fighting the grogginess. She lay on a bed, cocooned in a soft blanket and shifting shadows. She tried rising and immediately sucked in a breath. A silhouette of a male loomed over her. When she realized who it was, her fear abated . . . but her pulse did not slow.

"You were out for a good three hours." Gabriel peered down at her. "How are you feeling?"

She felt . . . Gabriel was holding something deliciously cool at her shoulder. She rounded her shoulders experimentally, relieved the burning sensation was gone, replaced by nothing more than a persistent ache. She had never enjoyed being mahalwei more than now, when the amount of mana flowing in her bloodstream accelerated her healing. Changelessness was both a blessing and a curse.

"I hate you," she signed, remembering his taunts and how he'd forcibly relocated her shoulder.

Instead of offense, she received a soft smile. She scowled. Gods above, she remembered more than his taunts. She remembered the whispered words that were both gruff and gentle, his callused touch, and the tender brushing of her tears. The memory inspired a coiling warmth in her abdomen.

Refusing to acknowledge her body's traitorous reaction, Shyaree turned to her uninjured side, ready to be left alone.

Surprisingly, Gabriel obliged, leaving the room without protest. Only to reappear just as she was about to doze off.

"Sit up."

A sidelong glance showed him with a steaming bowl on a tray. She sighed and shook her head.

"You haven't eaten," he said.

She frowned and made a shooing gesture with her good arm.

His lips twitched, but his voice brooked no argument. He placed the tray on the table, drew a chair to her bedside and picked up the bowl. "You can sit up and eat, or I'll pour it down your throat. Your choice."

The son of a beast. She knew that tone. He would not concede until he got his way, and this time she was too tired to fight him. She pushed up from the bed to take the bowl, but to her surprise, he kept it in one hand and ladled a spoonful of stew to her lips. She reached for the spoon, but he pulled it away.

"I can feed myself."

"Best if you don't move your arm. Healer's orders."

"I feel fine now."

His lips firmed. "If you're fine to use your hands, then you can explain Arkas's accusations."

She tensed. *"I don't see how it matters. You want my blood for our bargain, and you'll get it."*

He twirled the spoon in the bowl, stirring up a fresh waft of steam and an aroma that actually made her mouth water. "It matters because he seems to think you're a danger to me."

Shyaree snorted. *"Do you* feel *like you're in danger, guildmaster?"*

He raised his brows and brought the stew to her mouth again. Reluctantly, she wrapped her lips around it. Despite the rolls she'd eaten earlier, she was still hungry. When the rich flavor of braised beef and vegetables met her tongue, she sighed. Delicious. Scooting closer, she looked up at him expectantly, but his attention seemed riveted.

To her mouth.

Shyaree gulped involuntarily, and his gaze followed the movement of her throat. She licked her lips, and he drifted ever so slightly forward, as though her tongue were a lure. Her heart rabbited in its cage, each beat thumping in her veins as he leaned closer and closer.

Shyaree leaned back a smidge, and he recoiled like a man snapping out of a thrall.

Frowning, he dipped the spoon back into the stew and twirled it jerkily before scooping another mouthful. He narrowed his eyes, and his jaw tensed. One moment he stared as though she were the most beguiling thing he'd ever beheld and the next as if she were something dredged from the bottom of a stagnant pond.

"That's the thing about danger. It's deceptive. A letter opener can kill just as well as a knife if wielded the right way."

It took Shyaree a slow moment to process his response. She'd practically forgotten her own query. *"While that may be true, a letter opener will require far more force than a sharpened blade to kill a man."*

His lips twitched. "Not necessarily. All it takes is a little skill and the right opportunity."

Shyaree bristled. It was one thing to be compared to a letter opener and another for him to insinuate possible murder. *"Might I remind you that you were the one who kidnapped me?"*

He chuckled. "Fair enough. Still, I cannot ignore Arkas's claims about your bite being venomous."

The stew in her stomach curdled. Venomous. The second-in-command had also called her a mongrel. He *knew*. Arkas had clearly paid a visit to her clan and asked pointed questions to glean so much about her.

"What else did he say about me?"

While Arkas had snarled at *her* in Animatish, every heated word he'd spoken in the kitchen had been in Faerian. Shyaree didn't know the extent of his knowledge of her *condition.*

Gabriel brought another spoonful to her lips, refusing to respond until she swallowed. "He said you were not what you seemed." His shoulders tensed, and the spoon dropped into the bowl with a dull clink. "Apparently he'd spoken to your *mate*, who called you an abomination with enough venom in your blood to poison an entire village."

Shyaree squirmed.

Arkas had spoken to Hesok, then. Had her supposed lifemate told him everything?

Gabriel scraped the spoon along the bottom of the bowl while a muscle jumped in his jaw. "You have a mate, Shyaree? Why haven't you told me this? How long have you been mated?"

Shyaree blinked. The man had been warned of her venom, yet he seemed more aggrieved that she had a mate?

"Hesok is not my mate! He was my arranged lifemate, but we never completed husungai."

"Hesok?" Gabriel repeated in a dangerously low voice.

Shyaree nodded slowly, a little alarmed by his sudden outrage. His knuckles whitened around the bowl until the contents sloshed precariously close to the rim. She reached for it to prevent him from spilling stew all over himself. He must have mistaken her gesture for impatience, because he clamped his mouth shut, visibly restraining whatever he wanted to say.

He raised another spoonful to her mouth.

Shyaree shook her head. She had lost her appetite at the thought of Arkas speaking to Hesok . . . digging up her shame and secrets. No wonder he had looked at her like he'd discovered a rat in the pantry.

Gabriel eyed her irritably. "We both know you're hungry. Eat."

Shyaree leaned back into the pillows with a huff. *"I am not an invalid who needs to be fed!"*

But he did not relent. It was only when she swallowed the last bite that he set the empty bowl aside and spoke in a voice that seemed to have turned to gravel. "He didn't even try to help you."

"Hesok has never seen a fae portal before," she signed. *"You must have spooked him."*

"Spooked him?" Gabriel sneered. "Is that the excuse you're giving him for not coming to your aid? The woman who was to be his lifemate?"

Shyaree looked down to her hands. *"I may be his arranged bride, but he never wanted me. I was just a responsibility he never asked for."*

Gabriel rose from his seat to plant a hand on either side of her legs, looming over her with such malevolence gleaming in his violet-hued irises that something inside her shriveled.

"Why is that?" he asked quietly. "Why would the bastard not want you?"

She was all too aware of his large body poised over hers and his hands bunching the sheets beside her hips. All too aware of the outrage simmering in his eyes—on her behalf.

Shyaree managed a shaky laugh as she repeated Hesok's

words with her hands. *"Because I'm an abomination with enough venom in my bite to poison an entire village."*

Gabriel's eyes narrowed, but he didn't back away, as though daring her to divulge the worst.

Why not? Arkas had already begun digging . . . Sooner or later, Gabriel would learn the truth.

"Do you know what happens when animati from different clans crossbreed?"

He shook his head with a frown, clearly not expecting the sudden change in the conversation's trajectory, but he didn't interrupt her. Instead, he eased back to settle on the edge of the bed, his thigh a touch too close to her hip, but she didn't feel the urge to widen the distance between them.

"My mother came from the serpenti clan from the Aesagi Sea. The pantherai and serpenti were at war at the time, and my mother was a war prize. My father eventually took her as his bride because both his arranged lifemates had died from the war."

Gabriel blinked. "Your mother was a . . . serpent?"

"A sea snake," Shyaree signed wistfully. In her serpenti form, Mother'd had the most beautiful yellow stripes and diamond-shaped scales along her back—or at least that was what Father had said. Shyaree wouldn't know.

She had never met her mother.

"Crossbred children take after their father's inner beast." She sneered. *"Or at least that is what Thurin intended. Sometimes, nature does not obey the gods."*

Shyaree licked her lips and shut her eyes with a brief exhale. Her shoulders had grown so tense she had to consciously relax them to avoid aggravating the ache in her joint. When she opened her eyes, Gabriel had moved from the bed to pick up a flask buried in the clutter on the table. He returned with a glass of water and held it to her with questioning eyes. Shyaree accepted it gratefully. The brute could be strangely considerate at times.

"Is it hurting you to handspeak?" he asked, and somehow she knew he was not only referring to her arm.

She shook her head. Now she had started, she wanted to finish. She would rather he hear the truth from her than receive a regurgitated version from Hesok through Arkas. If Gabriel were to look at her with the same disgust as his second by the end of it, at least she'd have had her chance to say her piece.

"I was polymorphic."

Gabriel repeated her hand signal with a questioning frown. *"Polymorphic?"*

Shyaree fingerspelled the term for clarity before explaining, *"Some animati suffer from malmorphism . . . it happens when mana builds up in the marrow inconsistently to fuel their change and they become stuck in a malformed state. Half human, half animati. Just like that rogue that attacked me."*

"Just like Byrne," Gabriel murmured, referring to a pantherai outcast he'd recruited into the Red Guild.

Shyaree nodded. *"And some crossbred children may be stuck between three forms. Polymorphism."*

At Gabriel's blank gaze, Shyaree's fingers curled, hands sinking to her lap before she pushed herself to continue. *"My mother suffered trying to birth me. She* died *trying to birth me. Reiken would have died, too, if they had not cut her open because I was stuck in the birth canal."*

She had been a bane even at birth, born with a panther's tail and serpent scales.

"I thought you were born changeless."

Shyaree gave a shaky laugh. *"No animati is born changeless. As a child, I* could *change, but I could never do it right. Sometimes it was a missing tail. Mismatched ears. Fur on my cheeks when I didn't mean to change, or claws that refused to show when*

I tried. Sometimes I had scales instead of fur. That made me odd. The other children laughed at me. Called me names."

Mongrel.

Abomination.

Monster.

Shyaree fisted her hands at the memory.

"You were bullied because you couldn't change right?"

Bullied. Such a prosaic word for so much *pain*.

Shyaree nodded, and Gabriel's indignance showed in the tightening of his jaw, as though he couldn't understand how or why that could have happened. She leaned back into the headboard and regarded him with a wry smile. Of course he couldn't. She could only imagine what a beautiful boy he must have been, with his silver-white hair and his bright violet eyes. Gabriel wouldn't have merely fit into his world as a child; he had probably been the standard of perfection. Why would he understand the pain of growing up feeling odd and ugly and out of place?

"Children can be cruel. But one day I just got sick of the taunts . . . and I snapped." They had mocked her relentlessly. Pushed her around. Scratched her. Bit her. So she'd bitten back. Except by some quirk of nature, Shyaree had inherited her mother's ability to excrete venom. But *unlike* her mother, Shyaree's bites had proved fatal.

"I killed two girls that day." And proved herself to be a hybrid neither pantherai nor serpenti. An abomination not only to be ridiculed but feared.

It would have been enough to cease her recount there. She'd already given Gabriel the truth of her monstrosity, but something inside her wanted to share some of the weight on her shoulders. *"Those girls were Reiken's arranged brides."*

Gabriel stared, incredulity etched in every line of his face.

Shyaree donned a sardonic smile in an attempt to disguise

the shame pinching at her cheeks and the guilt gnawing in her chest. *"Don't worry. I am only venomous when I change."*

Any moment now his shock would sink in. He would flinch with disgust. He would back away and—

He hissed with open outrage. "This is why you're risking your life for Reiken? You think you owe him his brides?"

"I do owe him."

It was because of her Reiken was obsessed with the draga sul and necromancy in the first place. Every animati warrior was only arranged with two brides within the clan. Irreplaceable ones. Usually if a male lost one or both brides, they were forced to take war prizes or negotiate brides from other clans. But Reiken had seen firsthand what could come from taking nonpantherai brides. After what had happened to their mother, how could Shyaree blame him for not wanting to father possible atrocities like her? How could she judge him for wanting what should have been his?

Gabriel ran a hand through his hair, ruffling the quicksilver strands. He muttered something in Faerian before he met her gaze again. "Is that why you are changeless now? Because you fear your own venom?"

She laughed, and if her laughter had a sound, it would have been hollow. Gabriel had phrased it in such a magnanimous way. As though she had sacrificed her pantherai as penance.

"I only stopped changing because the urge was beaten out of me."

It was near impossible for animati to *not* change, especially during adolescence. But after the death of those girls, every time Shyaree had succumbed to the urge, Father would hurt her until she'd learned to suppress it. But it had taken many torturous years, a lot of pain and tears, before she'd finally learned to stop.

"It was *beaten* out of you?"

"It was the only way I was allowed to live. Had I been any older, I would have been hunted down for killing those girls. But my father was primus at the time, and he did everything he could to keep me alive. Even if my punishment hurt him more than it hurt me."

Because despite her monstrous nature, her father had *loved* her.

Every time Baleen had taken a hand to her, his anguish hurt them both like a double-edged sword. But he had done it anyway. And Shyaree begrudged him none of it. It wasn't his fault she'd been born this way—Reiken had never had trouble changing into a perfect pantherai.

She was flawed.

She had been flawed in the womb.

She tried her best to explain, but judging from Gabriel's thunderous expression, he didn't understand.

"But you are changeless now," he said finally. "Why does Arkas think you're still a threat to me?"

A flush rose to her cheeks. *"Does it matter? If I wanted to kill you, I would have while you were sleeping in the Kilinjiri."*

Perhaps Gabriel was right. She *was* a trembling kitten. A coward. Because she desperately wanted to disappear beneath the blankets.

"Tell me, Shyaree, or I can't protect you from Arkas."

She pinned him with a disbelieving gaze. *"I do not need your protection. All I need is for you to keep your end of our bargain."*

"And I need you alive if you're to hold up *your* end of the bargain," he said wryly. "Like it or not, I will protect you, so you might as well tell me, or I'll get the truth from Arkas." His expression soured. "Or Hesok."

After a tense moment, Shyaree conceded, shame slapping scarlet on her cheeks. *"I'm about to go into my next heat cycle."*

He blinked. "What?"

Shyaree squirmed deeper into the blankets, but she could not turn away from him while signing her words, so she signed with her eyes downcast. *"I've been going into heat for a few years now . . . and every time I do, the compulsion to change intensifies."*

She had clearly taken him by surprise, because his mouth mimicked a fish's when out of water. "So you'll . . . change?"

Shyaree shook her head sharply. *"I will not. I have controlled myself before, and I can control it again."* Even if it was nothing short of torture. She glanced up at him, willing him to understand. *"Hesok thinks husungai will keep me from changing, and that is likely the impression he has given Arkas. But I can control myself, Gabriel. Believe me."*

She snuck a glance at his face, half expecting to see disgust or fear—not anger.

His jaw squared. "What is . . . " He mimicked her hand signal for *husungai,* brows furrowed.

Shyaree clarified by fingerspelling the word.

"Husungai," he enunciated, and hearing the word in his deep, accented voice sent a shiver down her spine. "What is it, and what does it have to do with anything?"

She couldn't look him in the eye as she signed. *"Husungai is . . . mating. Most believe sex would sate the urges to shift . . . "*

A faint flush climbed up his neck. "That was why you were barely dressed that day?" He growled as though the recollection offended him. "That was your mating ceremony?"

She bent her knees beneath the bedspread, curling them into her chest. *"It was . . . but I ran away halfway through."*

He leaned closer. "Why did you run, Shyaree?"

She sighed. She didn't want to talk about Hesok. *"Because he wasn't who I thought he was . . . I do not want to be tethered to him."*

The answer must have satisfied him, because Gabriel leaned

back with a small smile to his lips. "He clearly wanted you. He chased you down to the river, asked you to return with him."

She scowled. *"Only because I hurt his pride."*

"So I did you a favor, didn't I?" He smirked. "Appearing when I did."

The smug bastard. *"You did Hesok a favor,"* she corrected. Had Gabriel not intervened when he did, Shyaree would have probably stabbed the warrior.

Whatever she expected, it wasn't for Gabriel to laugh. But he laughed until his eyes watered, as though everything she had just confided were a joke and not her life's shame and scars.

Stung, she pulled the blankets closer to her chest before signing, *"I am glad you found that amusing. Please get out because I would like to get some sleep now."*

He rose to his feet, and when she thought he would leave the room, he opened his closet. Rummaged through it. Then he threw a bathrobe at her, one that did not look too different from the one she had on.

"Take that off and change into this one."

Shyaree frowned. *"What's the difference?"* Malakai had given her a spare robe because none of his clothes fit her. Shyaree had meant to look for the kindly healer for more clothes, but she'd never gotten the chance.

"Just do it." Another crisp command that left no room for argument. He turned, keeping his back firmly averted, making it clear he would not leave until she obliged.

Sighing, she shrugged out of one borrowed robe and into another. It wasn't until she secured the sash around her waist that she realized *this* robe smelled distinctly of Gabriel. A perverse quiver racked her frame, and it wasn't caused by revulsion.

How she despised herself.

How she hated him for making her do this.

She crawled back into bed and snapped her fingers impatiently to indicate she was finished. *"Done. Happy? Now get out."*

Gabriel hobbled over to swipe the other bathrobe to the ground as though it harbored contagion. "Scoot over, wildcat."

Without warning, he yanked his shirt over his head.

Shyaree gawped, twin spots searing her cheeks, but she couldn't seem to peel her eyes away. *"What are you doing?!"* Her first night in the Den, she had slept in his room while Gabriel had slept gods knew where.

"I told you I won't let Arkas near you again, so I'll be sleeping here tonight."

"I am not sharing a bed with you!"

He snorted. "I don't exactly like sharing, either, but a promise is a promise."

She knew fae could not break their promises, but this was ridiculous. *"You think he will come for me in my sleep?"*

Gabriel only shrugged. "Arkas can be pretty determined if he sets his mind to something. And I need Sleep if I'm to recover—don't you want to find the next item for your elixir?"

Heart pounding irrationally fast, she pulled the blankets tighter around herself. Gabriel must have mistaken that for consent, because he climbed onto the bed.

Shyaree would have squeaked if her vocal cords allowed it. *"Why take off your shirt?"*

"Because I'm used to sleeping without a stitch on. But don't worry, I'll keep my pants on tonight," he said in a grumbling tone of a man making some grave sacrifice.

Without another word, he leaned over to the side table, doused the oil lamp, and drenched them in darkness. "Good night, wildcat."

The bastard sounded almost self-satisfied.

Shyaree shrank beneath the blankets and curled into herself, squeezing her eyes shut as the mattress undulated while he settled.

Sleep.

How was she supposed to *sleep* wrapped in his scent while he stretched out beside her not one handspan away? She was used to sleeping in the longhouse amid the other unmated females. She held herself still, but her heart could not seem to, because it jounced and jangled like a mad, uncontrollable thing. Only when Gabriel's breathing evened did she allow her eyes to open.

Gods above, she had never considered her ability to see in the dark a curse.

He lay atop the bedspread, seemingly content to sleep without a blanket, inadvertently showcasing his body. A tingle stole down her spine as she stared. He was honed to a husky vigor that dried her mouth. She had the strangest inclination to scoot closer, and . . .

Another shiver shook her down to her bones.

Gods above, she was going mad.

She had seen scores of naked male torsos. Her entire clan bathed in the river during the warmer months—sometimes together if the water level ran low. She had seen enough to know her own preferences. She found brawn particularly pleasing, but she'd never seen a physique that made her fingers itch *this* much or her eyes fixate in *this* way.

The dusky line trailing down the middle of his torso to disappear into his pants seemed to beckon her. She couldn't seem to look away from the two perfectly symmetrical rows of abs on his stomach . . . Thurin's wrath, were they as hard as they looked?

"It's rude to ogle, wildcat."

Mortified heat stung her cheeks. He had one arm tucked

under his head, and his eyes were ostensibly shut. He couldn't *possibly* see her in the darkness anyway . . .

His lips curved. "You know one of the reasons my kind is called the dark fae is because our magic is strongest in the dark." His eyes cracked open with a sly, sidelong glance. "But we see pretty well in it, too."

The humiliation was enough to swallow her whole, but it was his rumbly chuckle that had her reaching over and pinching his bicep. Only the muscle was so hard she couldn't pinch him properly.

"Oh, ow," he said with an infuriating smirk. "Was that supposed to hurt?"

She reared up from the bed.

"I wasn't ogling, you obnoxious beast!" she insisted in a desperate attempt to save face. *"I was only thinking of how much I hate being here. Of how much I hate you!"*

Her outburst knocked the smirk straight off his face, replacing it with a stifling soberness. She turned to give him her back, belatedly realizing she was lying on her sore arm. With a huff, she rolled onto her back and squeezed her eyes shut, trying to calm her rapidly beating heart . . . all while feeling like the biggest liar in all the five realms.

Chapter 15

Shyaree's eyelids lifted with a languorousness that could only come from a night of solid sleep. She sighed and nuzzled into the soft bedding, savoring the cozy warmth and the soothing scent of a heady, masculine musk—

Her eyes popped wide.

He was gone. But gods above, she was burrowing into his pillow. Sometime in the night she must have rolled from her side of the bed over to his. Thank Thurin the bastard wasn't here to witness her nuzzling . . . but where had he gone?

A faint scratching sound alerted her that she might be alone in the bed, but she was not alone in the room.

She lifted her head to find the bastard in question—still bare chested—seated on the ledge of a recessed window, crowned by a halo of sunlight. The curtains seemed strategically drawn to emit a swath of light over the sketchbook propped on one bent knee, as though he were trying to keep the rest of the room shaded while he . . . drew.

The scratching was a charcoal nib running against parchment.

He appeared so engrossed he did not seem to realize she had awoken. Shyaree laid her head quietly back onto the pillow, wearing a grudging smile. She had never seen him like this except in sleep, with his hair ruffled and his face devoid of calculation or cynicism. Instead, he wore an adorable smudge of charcoal on his cheek and solemn concentration between his brows. Her gaze dipped to the distracting breadth of his shoulders and the mesmerizing flex of his well-thewed arms as he worked. There was something annoyingly appealing about the tendons and veins cording his forearm and his knuckles. Something indescribably sexy . . .

She squirmed, and suddenly the bathrobe no longer felt cozy but stifling.

Gods above, was she already in heat? Why else would she feel aroused by the simple sight of his arm? Her stirring must have drawn his focus, because he glanced over.

"Good morning," she signed while faking a yawn. He smiled, and the slow curve of his lips sank into her like a hook in the chest.

"You slept well."

Not a question but a statement.

Warmth spread across her cheeks. Thurin's wrath, she was still lying on his side of the bed. She managed a nonchalant shrug. *"What are you doing?"*

He paused before rising from the ledge. Then he made his way over, slightly limping, and handed her the sketchbook.

Shyaree's lips parted. It was a sketch . . . of the Tribe's Wall. From a bird's-eye view, the Wall looked like a spine. Branches reached from either side of it like lovers trying to touch.

"Why would you draw the Wall?"

He settled on the edge of the bed to recline against the headboard while Shyaree shifted back to keep distance between them.

"Sketching is my way of preserving the memory so I can find my way back to these places, if I ever need to." Because portal makers could only cast portals to places they'd been—and it must hinge on their memory of the place.

Shyaree quirked a brow. *"Does every portal maker do this?"*

Gabriel shrugged. "I'm sure every portal maker has their own way of keeping track of important places. Arkas, for example, makes it a point to return daily, until the location becomes a memory etched into his mind."

She ran a finger over the top of the page. *"Why would the Wall be important to you?"*

"It's not, but it is to you."

The words came out of his mouth so swiftly they seemed to catch him by surprise. The implication sank through her skin, stirring a strange warmth in her blood. She offered him an appreciative smile, and something peculiar happened.

The sharp tips of his ears turned the faintest shade of pink.

He rose abruptly from the bed. "Hungry?" Without waiting for her response, he turned for the door. "I'll get us some breakfast."

She clapped her hands, stalling his exit.

When he turned back with a questioning glance, she pointed at her cheek.

He frowned in confusion.

Perhaps it was the warmth still simmering in her chest, but she pushed out of the bed and padded over to him. *"You're wearing charcoal,"* she signed before reaching up to wipe the smudge from his cheek . . . much like he'd rubbed the tears from hers the day before.

Gabriel's throat worked, and for one heady moment she almost believed he relished her ministrations . . . until he jerked back like a man burned by a hot brand. He ran a thumb over where she'd scrubbed as though to wipe off the residue of her touch.

"Thanks," he mumbled, and disappeared through the door, leaving her feeling foolish and flustered.

Why had she done that? She curled her fingers. Just because he'd made a sketch of the Wall? Annoyed with herself, she ventured to his bath chamber for her morning ablutions. When she was done, he had not returned.

She picked up the sketchbook again and flipped idly through it from the front. Now she knew the significance of these sketches, there was a near-voyeuristic thrill in looking at them, knowing she was seeing the places through his eyes. That these locations were of significance to him. A cityscape with spiraling towers. Twin mountains shrouded in fog. A tranquil field dotted with wildflowers. A domed building with the most intricate carvings . . . and Gabriel had recreated them all with stunning clarity. The first time she'd seen these sketches, she'd wondered if Gabriel was the artist. Now she knew. Her lips twisted in a wry curve. How strange that the hands capable of such lethality could also create such beauty with something as simple as a stick of charcoal.

She flipped the page and stilled.

Every sketch in the book featured landscapes or architecture but no faces.

Until this one.

A lone woman peered out a window as though longing for something only she could see. There was something intimate about the scene, with the woman's hair unbound and her attire looking like a nightgown. Was this her bedchamber? Gabriel must have been there, standing exactly at this angle, basking in her wistful beauty, to render each detail of her so perfectly . . .

Something in Shyaree's chest tightened.

Limping footsteps heralded Gabriel's return. She flipped

the page over just as he entered, her heart thudding like a child's when caught prying where she shouldn't.

He placed a heaping platter of food before her, the awkwardness from before seemingly forgotten. Two cinnamon rolls, two custard buns, kovi berries, sliced mango, and nectarines. Either all food in the Den was made to her liking or Gabriel had an uncanny way of picking her favorites . . . except the sight only soured her appetite.

It was on the tip of her fingers to ask him about the woman in the portrait when he leaned over her to study the page she had open. "That's the entrance to the library in Amereen Castle. Do you recognize it?"

Nodding, she mustered a smile and shut the sketchbook.

Whoever the woman was, she was undoubtedly important to Gabriel . . . and it was absolutely none of her business.

Whoosh! Water erupted from a blowhole with a force that mimicked the flare of Gabriel's disbelief. "You want us to go down there?"

They had returned to the blowholes, or as described by Shyaree's mother's song, the field that breathed. Sharp-edged boulders jutted randomly across the odd stretch of granite and gushing water, some taller than others, giving them a saw-toothed appearance. It seemed like the most logical place to begin their search for the next item. But it was a few hours to dusk.

The snail tracks had proved much harder to discern without moonlight, or maybe they disintegrated under the sun or in humidity, but Shyaree had industriously studied the damp granite with an adorable pleat between her brows. The remnants of the sticky slime trail had led them winding past jagged boulders and exploding blowholes up to one of the larger craters. A closer look showed a funnel-like opening, and judging from the dryness of the surrounding rock, it wasn't a blowhole, but a hole, nonetheless. One large enough for them to crawl into.

And apparently, the evidence of snail slime and the fact that the hole wasn't spewing water were reasons enough to crawl in.

"The snails have gone in, so it must lead somewhere," she signed, her hand signals stiff with impatience.

Gabriel did not blame her.

He had promised to help her retrieve everything she needed before the blood moon, but he had slept more than half of it away. His leg wound was now nothing but a scar, but they were also left with a little over ten days to find the remaining two items she needed for her elixir.

Ten days to help her before she saw him as a liar.

Ten days before her sacrifice.

Every time his thoughts wandered to the prophecy, sickness twisted his insides and coated his mouth with ash.

Shyaree had been oblivious to it all, sleeping in his bed, allowing him to rest and recuperate, undoubtedly thinking she would be home at the end of their bargain.

But Gabriel would not be taking her home.

He would permit her to make her elixir, allow her to accomplish what she'd set out to do, but he would deliver the elixir to her clan himself. If the prophecy was true—and as much as it nauseated him, it was—she would not be going home at all.

Shyaree was the blood sacrifice . . . in the most literal sense.

The ground shuddered in another whoosh-inducing tremble, as though the very earth shuddered from his insidious thoughts. Gabriel jerked at his shirt collar as his long-forgotten conscience consumed his innards like maggots on carrion.

Shyaree was nothing but another head. He had slaughtered hundreds, and for less reason.

She was the key to the draga morli—to Iolanthe's freedom.

Except . . . she was Shyaree.

Shyaree, who had faced two Silverbeaks for him when she could have fled. She had stitched up his wounds, taken him to shelter, and cared for him when another would have deserted him. Like Rebekah.

Instead, Shyaree had trusted him with the scars of her past . . .

She snapped her fingers, drawing him from his twisted thoughts. *"I know it looks dangerous, but it makes sense, don't you think? If the snail tracks are the moon's silver tails, then . . . "* She unfolded the creased parchment and tapped at the first verse of her mother's song.

Go, for all Thurin's creatures when malady prevails,

To the land kissed by the moon's silver tails,

Seek and harvest the seeds that glow,

Deep, deep in the canyon below.

She gestured to the tunnellike hole again, and Gabriel grudgingly agreed that it did look like it could possibly lead them *somewhere* underground.

"The snails went in . . . " She implored him with her eyes, and Gabriel folded his arms on an exhale.

"And what if we come face-to-face with another cragalith . . . or some other creature while we're down there?"

She frowned as though the response were obvious. *"You could portal us to safety?"*

Gabriel snorted. Perhaps if he were a mage with the ability to teleport in the blink of an eye. "Fae portals open slower when we are outside our own realm, Shyaree. Mine will take at least a minute to form here in Thurin's Realm. A lot can happen in that time."

She fed him a cajoling smile that seemed manufactured to stroke his ego, but it only piqued his amusement. *"You have slain a cragalith. Did you also not slay trolls and fell ogres? Gut basilisks? I am sure you'll think of something."*

She had clearly spent too much time with Malakai and Hector, who had been feeding her tales of Gabriel's past escapades, all in embarrassingly broken Animatish. And if he was honest, he had done little to dissuade them. Now he was secretly pleased she felt so sure of his abilities that she didn't consider a cragalith to be a relevant danger.

Gabriel exhaled. "If we're doing this, I'm going in first."

He didn't see her response because familiar feathers flashed in his periphery. They disappeared so quickly it could have been a trick of his imagination. But paranoia had saved him more than once.

Gabriel shoved Shyaree against the flat expanse of the nearest boulder and caged her body with his. If it was who he thought, he wasn't in danger—she was.

Shyaree's eyes rounded in astonishment. She shoved at his chest, trying to make space to sign her protests. And being the opportunist he was, Gabriel lowered his head and very swiftly, very lightly, grazed his lips against hers.

A geyser erupted nearby, and it might as well have exploded beneath his feet.

Awareness scorched down his spine, burning beneath his skin as though the barest brush of their lips seared him like the handle of an overheated iron.

Shyaree wasn't unaffected, either. If it weren't for the warmth of her breath and the softness of her skin, she could have been stone. He was well and truly a bastard because it only made him want to deepen the kiss. To slip his tongue between her lips, sweep through the cracks of her stiff-necked rigidity and crumble her walls.

"Relax," Gabriel whispered against her tightly sealed lips, and the ground seemed to rumble in agreement. "We are being watched."

Water sprayed into the air nearby, shrouding them in mist. Shyaree sucked in a small breath, and somehow that little inhale was far more erotic than it had any right to be. Gabriel pried himself from her mouth only to trail his depraved lips along the smooth and stubborn curve of her jaw. She shivered.

"Don't stare, but I want you to look at the rocks behind me. Can you see a crow?"

Gabriel moved his head down the column of her throat in the guise of kissing her neck so she could look behind him. Of course he had to make it look convincing, so he trailed the tip of his nose along her skin. Something thundered between them, so loud Gabriel wasn't sure if it was her heart or his own. She reached for his arm and squeezed it with a trembling hand, nodding imperceptibly.

"Look at its wings. Are there silver tips?"

Another squeeze. *Yes.*

Gabriel pressed his forehead against her temple. "Any other crows you can see?"

Shyaree leaned into him, shaking her head, pretending to playfully burrow into his chest. *No.*

Gabriel snuck a hand between them, as though to grope at her breast while he retrieved a diken from his baldric. He caught a frisson of trepidation in her gaze. "There's nothing to fear. But when I turn around, I want you to stay behind me. Do you understand?"

Her jaw tensed.

He leaned into her ear, perversely aroused by the hitch in her breath and the rapid rise and fall of her chest. "Listen to me for once, won't you?"

She narrowed her gaze but nodded.

"Good girl." He allowed himself another featherlight brush of his lips against hers—for no reason other than that he was a wretch without self-control. Only this time her lips parted ever so slightly, like an inadvertent invitation. Gabriel had never claimed to be a gentleman. He would burn in the five hells soon enough anyway.

He molded his lips against hers and ran his tongue along her parted lips for a single shuddering moment. He expected her to taste tangy or tart. Piquant. Instead, she tasted like the damned honey cakes he'd procured for her breakfast and something unmistakably feminine and sensual and so, so decadent. A groan nearly escaped him. Five flaming hells of torment, he'd never tasted anything sweeter. He wanted to push his tongue deeper, steal more than a taste but . . .

He wrenched himself away and sent his diken sailing into the boulder behind them. Fae steel pinged off the rock as the silver-winged crow coasted from its perch with an angry screech. It spiraled twice before swooping to the ground not ten paces from where they stood. Shadows slunk from the bird's form to solidify into the figure of a man.

Gabriel folded his arms.

If he'd wanted to kill, his target would be dead by now, and the voyeur knew it, too.

"Spying, Arkas? Is this what you've become?"

Arkas's gaze tracked to Shyaree and narrowed as though he viewed a thriving wasp nest at Gabriel's back. "Can you blame me? She could kill you with a single bite, and here you are sticking your tongue down her throat! If you had—"

A nearby blowhole drowned out Arkas's tirade.

The second-in-command cast a leery glance around. "What are you even doing here, Gabe?"

Gabriel scrubbed a hand over his face with a heavy exhale. Since their altercation in the kitchen, Arkas had stayed away.

Gabriel hadn't had a chance to confront him, explain how Shyaree was not as dangerous as the bastard Hesok had made her out to be. Gabriel hadn't tried to seek out his cousin, either. He hadn't been particularly driven to reveal his reasons for bringing Shyaree into the Den. But now that Arkas was tracking them into the animati realm? It was going too far.

He only hoped the truth wouldn't send Arkas into a reckless spiral.

"Shyaree is helping me secure something I need," Gabriel began carefully while another geyser gushed, this one close enough to spit cool droplets at them.

Arkas wiped at his face irritably. "From what I've gathered from Isidor, it seems like you are here helping her secure things *she* needs."

Gabriel sighed. "Shyaree is the key . . . to Iolanthe. She's alive, Arkas. Io—"

"You cannot be serious!" Arkas exploded. "Are you listening to yourself, Gabe? You sound utterly delusional."

Denial. A natural stress response.

Gabriel took a step closer and offered his second a conciliatory smile. "You wanted to know what's been occupying my mind the past year . . . and now you do."

Arkas's fingers clenched until a tremor shook his hands. "This isn't amusing. Not in the least."

"I wasn't jesting."

Arkas's gaze snapped up. "Iolanthe is . . . dead. She's been dead for centuries! You know this. You saw her die yourself. You were there. Whatever Zion told you, it's a lie."

Anger. Another expected reaction. Gabriel had gone through the same emotional flux over the past year. "I saw her, Arkas. I snuck into Duskhall Castle . . . and I *saw* her. I saw Iolanthe." His sweet little sister had grown to look so much like their mother that Gabriel couldn't deny her even if he wanted to.

Arkas shook his head, disbelief bleeding into his eyes. He jammed both his hands against his temples as though to compress his skull. "Io can't possibly be . . . She's dead! That's the only reason I left her behind!"

The latter came out with such vehemence it rivaled the force of a blowhole.

Gabriel grimaced. "*We* left her behind."

Arkas shook his head. "Iolanthe was my ward."

"And she is my sister, Arkas," Gabriel said softly. "It was *me* she sought that day, not you. The fault is mine to bear."

Arkas sliced his palm through the air as if he could cleave Gabriel's words from his ears. "It's her." He pointed at Shyaree with the desperation of a man seeking a scapegoat to ease his anguish. "She's made up this elaborate ruse somehow. She is just using you to get what she wants. Can't you fucking see that?"

Gabriel stepped into Arkas's line of sight to block Shyaree from his view. "If she is, she's using me as much as I am using her. She's the key to Iolanthe's freedom. Her blood is the key . . . do you understand?"

"You're delusional, Blacksage! She is manipulating you." As though reacting to Arkas's anger, the ground trembled with gusto, and a distant blowhole shot water high into the sky. Arkas barely noticed. "Her mate said she'll be going into heat soon, which will make her uncontrollable. Dangerous. She needs to be returned to him!"

Arkas made to rush past him, but Gabriel snagged him by the collar before he could take another step in Shyaree's direction.

"I wouldn't go near her if I were you."

There was no need for harsh words on his part. His second

knew him well enough to know the next time Gabriel struck, he wouldn't miss.

Arkas released a cynical laugh. "This is what we've come to? After all these years . . . after all I've done for you and the guild . . . You choose a wench over me."

Gabriel's eyes narrowed, and he shoved his cousin in the chest. "If I'd chosen her, you would already be dead, you idiot."

Arkas laughed again, and hysteria muddied the lavender in his gaze. He pounded a fist into his own chest, as though to mimic the stab of a dagger.

Silver globules bled in the air, dripping into the form of a portal. The moment it coalesced, his cousin stormed through it without a backward glance. Gabriel didn't stop him, nor did he blame him—Arkas needed time to come to terms with the truth, hopefully *without* doing anything foolish in the meanwhile.

Gabriel turned around and found a flushed-faced Shyaree. He inclined his head and switched to Animatish. "Don't worry, wildcat. He's gone."

She didn't look reassured. Who could blame her? She understood none of their exchange, and the last time she'd seen Arkas, the bastard had dislocated her shoulder. Gabriel mustered a faint smile for her benefit and nodded at the hole.

"I think we've wasted enough time now."

Chapter 16

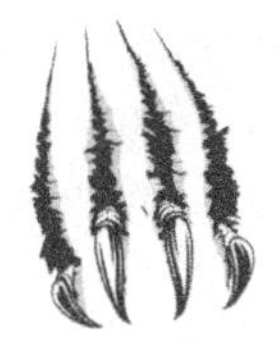

The rock was hard on her knees and hands, but all Shyaree could think about as she crawled down the tunnel was the feel of Gabriel's lips pressed against her own. The heat of his skin and the shape of his lips were all but imprinted onto her flesh, seared into her mind.

Her *first* kiss, stolen in a *farce*.

A particularly sharp rock dug into her palm, causing her to halt with a hiss.

"What's wrong?" His voice was hushed and frantic. He placed a hand over her shoulder, urging her to turn. Shyaree shrugged him off and shook her head to indicate she was fine, but she didn't turn back. She could barely look at him without warmth stinging her cheeks.

When he was retrieving the diken he'd launched at Arkas, Shyaree had obstinately fit herself into the tunnel's entrance so she could go in front. He had protested and even attempted to drag her out; she'd almost kicked him in the face. She refused to crawl in after him while her lips still tingled from the taste of him. She didn't want to look at him at all, or think of the way his body felt against hers, all heat and hard muscle, rousing sensations she didn't want. Not from him. Especially when he didn't seem the least bit affected by what had transpired between them. As though the kiss had meant nothing to him.

Of course it hadn't.

He had likely kissed hundreds of females. The notion brought another flush up her cheeks.

"Did you hurt yourself?" The concern in his tone skimmed over her skin like a caress. An involuntary shiver kissed her spine.

Sniffing, Shyaree shook her head again, brushed her hand over her lap and resumed crawling without a backward glance. She didn't need to look back to feel his frown. But it was hard for her to communicate when they were crawling on their hands and knees. The tunnel was tight enough that it was even hard for her to turn sideways.

"What's ahead?" he asked after a short pause, for what seemed like the umpteenth time. Shyaree might be in front, but the tunnel wended like a river, and she could barely see ahead, much less beyond the next bend, so she shook her head a third time.

But the snail tracks kept her motivated.

While they were wholly underground, the random patches of moonshine moss growing along the tunnel emanated a subtle bluish glow. The faint shimmer kept their surroundings dim, but it was enough to illuminate the silvery tracks of her shelled guides. Shyaree soon found them along the way—little clusters gliding down the circular tunnel like tiny comets shooting in slow motion over stone.

If Gabriel noticed them, he did not seem impressed. In fact, he had been grousing under his breath the whole time, grumbling about recklessness and danger. He spoke in Animatish, so clearly he meant it as a rebuke for her ears.

Shyaree tried her best to ignore the grouch at her back.

The tunnel was far too narrow to fit danger in the form of a cragalith. Besides, if there were approaching danger, the tunnel's hollowness meant she would hear it well before they met it. And while Gabriel's portals were not instantaneous, she felt confident she could buy him enough time with the weapons strapped to her holster belt. She could take care of herself for as long as he needed to create a portal.

Another stretch deeper and the air seemed to cool. The rock beneath her palms chilled, or maybe it was just the fear crawling over her bones. Pressure formed in her ears, sending more wariness to worm beneath her breastbone.

How far down were they? Where did the tunnel lead, and why would snails venture so far into the earth? Her ruminations came to a standstill because the tunnel opened abruptly into a much wider space. A cave of sorts.

A deep whoosh greeted her when she stepped into the area. She startled but quickly recognized it as the echo of the erupting blowholes. They sounded even louder down here, almost as though this chamber were the mountain's heart.

Gabriel stepped in after her, and try as she might to ignore him, his proximity served as a steady, calming reassurance.

The cave was eerily dark, lit only by thick clumps of moonshine moss that allowed her to see the space ahead. She moved forward and looked up.

The hairs on her skin stood on end.

Leglike appendages dangled from above.

At her sharp gasp, Gabriel wrenched her into his chest. He secured one hand over her front while his sword glinted in another. He looked ready to slay whatever hung above them. Except . . . roots.

A breath of relief gushed from her lungs. Gods above, thick roots, threaded with finer, hairlike structures had somehow speared through the rocky ceiling. And for one bloodcurdling moment, she'd mistaken them for a mass of dangling cragalith legs.

Gabriel followed her gaze, but she could practically feel him bristling at her back.

"You could have been attacked," he growled close to her ear over the echoing rumbles of the blowholes. "I should be at the front. Defy me again, and I'll chain you to—"

Shyaree whipped around to shove him in the chest.

"Chain me? I am not your lifemate! You don't get to chain me . . . or kiss me! You shouldn't even be touching me!"

Her vehemence seemed to surprise him, because he rocked back on his heels. "I . . . I didn't mean it like that."

Shyaree made a rude gesture and stalked down the space, suddenly more angry than spooked. He caught up to her easily. "Where are you—"

Another rumble echoed through the cavern, canceling the sound of his voice.

Gabriel switched to signing. *"How do you even know where to go?"*

"Does it look like there are many directions to choose from?" she signed back. The cavern was elongated, and there was only one direction they could take.

His jaw tightened, but he matched her pace.

The snail tracks had disappeared altogether, or if they were around, they were obscured by the roots. Shyaree suspected the little critters were drawn to the moonshine moss growing liberally down here, but could the "glowing seeds" in her mother's song also be a reference to the moss's glow? Either way, the signs motivated Shyaree to move forward while Gabriel kept close to her heels.

In the dim blue light, he appeared almost otherworldly. Ethereal, with his chiseled profile outlined in a blue halo and his silver hair glinting like a star on a moonless night. He looked like an angel, she decided. A fallen one.

Shyaree stumbled against an uneven rise of the ground, but Gabriel caught her deftly by the elbow, steadying her. She was about to pull her arm away, but he pointed to the ground. Randomly dispersed mounds littered the rock floor.

"Watch your step," he signed. She hadn't taken more than five steps before he stopped her again with another tug at her arm. *"I'm sorry about before. I did not mean to kiss you."*

Shyaree stiffened, something in her rib cage unreasonably stung. She straightened her spine and batted the air with feigned nonchalance. *"Just don't do it again."*

He averted his gaze, and his hands lowered to his sides. With relief, no doubt.

An awkward tension filled the air amid the mountain's resounding breaths.

"Why was Arkas spying on us?" she asked, trying to redirect her thoughts as she navigated the bumpy ground. *"How did he even know where to find you?"*

Tension seemed to seep from the air into Gabriel's shoulders. *"Arkas is my cousin. Our shared blood makes it easier for him to find me. He has means to scry for my location across the five realms if he truly wants."* A scowl. *"And he has done so in the past."*

The thought of anyone checking up on the likes of Gabriel as though he were a child in need of a nursemaid was faintly amusing. *"Have you not told him I am incapable of excreting venom in my two-legged form?"*

"Since that day in the kitchen, he's made himself scarce. I have not seen him until now. And he seems convinced you might . . . " He scrubbed the back of his neck before leaning over to her ear to speak aloud. "He thinks you might change when you go into heat."

She squirmed in place. *"It's not that time yet."*

Not for another week, at least.

Gabriel appeared equally uncomfortable with the subject. *"He doesn't know that."*

They reached the end of the cavern and a bend that seemed to bring them even lower in elevation, because the subtle pressure returned to her ears. But strangely, the blowholes no longer sounded as loud.

She glanced around, unsure if they should keep moving forward. Apart from the roots penetrating the rocky ceiling above and patches of moonshine moss, it didn't look like any vegetation grew down here . . . How could there be seeds, much less glowing ones?

"Shyaree . . . ," Gabriel began.

Half afraid he would insist they turn back, she tried to revive their conversation. *"Even if I did change, I wouldn't attack you without cause."*

"Arkas can be a little hardheaded, especially when it comes to my safety."

"That's ridiculous. You are not a child in need of protection."

"No, but I suppose old habits die hard. It has been ingrained in him since birth that his purpose is to protect a Blacksage."

Shyaree arched her brow. *"I thought you were cousins."*

"We are . . . but Ironfalls have served the Blacksage family for too many generations. Our blood mingled when my aunt, a Blacksage, decided to marry her bodyguard—an Ironfall."

"Your aunt decided?" Shyaree frowned. *"She got to choose for herself?"*

"In my culture, the women choose their own mates, wildcat."

Shyaree blinked. *"Your women get to choose their own mates . . . for themselves?"*

The idea was so preposterous, so radical, it sounded almost sinful. Scandalous. Glorious. Suddenly, Shyaree wished she were born fae. How lucky fae females were to have *no* arranged lifemates. No haughty boy lording it over her that she would one day be tethered to him. No husungai. No need to pander to a female she wouldn't naturally be friends with because one day they would share the same male.

"Your aunt married for love?" What other reason could there be for a female choosing to marry a man who'd served her as a protector?

The skin around Gabriel's eyes crinkled, as though he were recollecting a fond memory from long ago. "She did. As most fae women do."

"And what if you are chosen by one you do not want? Would you be forced to mate with her anyway?" she asked, utterly fascinated by the concept of choosing one's own mate. Even the idea of being born without an assigned lifemate sent a forbidden thrill through her.

Gabriel laughed. "Ozenn forbid. No. While fae males do a *lot* of courting in hopes the one we desire chooses us, we aren't bound to accept any female's choice."

So fae females *and* their males had the right to choose for themselves. What a novel idea. Shyaree side eyed him with envy and a sudden blazing curiosity. *"How many females have you denied?"*

Gabriel blinked. Perhaps her tactless query had caught him off guard. Even the blowholes seemed to think she'd overstepped, because a larger eruption rumbled overhead. It was admittedly an intrusive question, but Gabriel had no mate she knew of. Surely a male like him would've rejected many . . .

"None, because none has ever chosen me."

Her lips parted.

Her surprise wrought a small chuckle. "Mercenaries hardly

make desirable mates. We may be good for scratching an itch or fulfilling a fantasy, but we're not the sort of men most would choose to settle down with."

Her cheeks flamed yet again. *"But you said you were a lord in your village,"* she signed hastily. *"I assumed . . . "*

The smile on his lips faded. "That a title somehow makes me more desirable?" He shook his head. "Besides, I was never meant to be the duke of Evenmere. My brother, Grayson, was the true heir."

Shyaree glanced up. *"You had a brother?"*

"I did." A weighty pause. "And three sisters."

"What happened to— "

They'd arrived at a steep cliff. Shyaree braved the edge, and vertigo seized her. A lagoon. She swayed back on her heels. It was so dark she could barely make it out by the faint shimmer of lapping water.

A series of stone platforms jutted from the watery depths like precarious stepping stones leading toward another plateau in the distance.

A plateau that held the pale promise of iridescence.

Her palms dampened. How would they make it across? The distance between each platform seemed small enough to jump, but far enough to inspire wariness. She turned to Gabriel, who was studying the lagoon with an oddly clenched jaw.

She touched his forearm, securing his attention before she signed, *"Shall we jump?"*

Gabriel snorted. "Why jump . . . " He snapped his fingers, and shadows slunk from the ground, swirling like skeins of black ribbon weaving together until a portal formed. A tiny black speck echoed on the plateau in the distance. "When you can walk across?"

At Shyaree's parted lips, a faint smirk touched his. "Come."

To her surprise, he held out a hand. She placed hers in it

and allowed him to lead her through the portal. A single step and she emerged on the other plateau. She gave a little happy jump at the ease with which they had crossed the watery chasm and beamed at her fae companion. As she glanced around, this plateau appeared no different from the last. The same heavy roots penetrated the rock overhead, except . . .

Shyaree snagged Gabriel's elbow, pointing animatedly at the ceiling. Fine and feathery roots carpeted the ceiling like a thick layer of cobweb, but that wasn't the reason for her excitement. *Nodules* were nestled within the web of tightly knitted roots.

She'd only noticed them because they shone the same bluish hue as the moss.

Gabriel whistled. "If that isn't 'the seeds that glow deep, deep in a canyon below,' I don't know what is."

Shyaree was inclined to agree. Still looking up with near-giddy excitement, she approached the closest hanging root. It was thicker than both her wrists combined, and long enough it was two handspans from touching the stone ground. The tree growing above must be ancient. She gave the root an experimental tug. It seemed solid enough to hold her weight.

Gabriel clasped a hand over hers. "I'll do it."

Shyaree released the root with a frown. *"You don't think I can climb?"*

"I'm sure you can, but I know I can do it faster," he said with a cocky undertone that had her both rolling her eyes and turning away to hide her smile. She had not seen this side of Gabriel in a while, and strangely, she missed it.

He gave her no chance to argue, scaling the root without so much as a grunt. Shyaree grudgingly agreed. The man made the feat appear easy. It did not take him long to reach the top where the nodules clustered in a mesh of plumy roots. He tossed one down at her, clinging to the vine like a reincarnated monkey.

She studied the glowing nodule that reminded her of a mango, covered in fuzz.

The rumbling blowholes muted his voice as he asked, "How many?"

Just like with the water from the blowholes, Shyaree had no idea how much to collect. Her mother hadn't been particularly prescriptive.

"As many as you can get," she signed. Better to harvest more than less.

Gabriel gave her a mock salute and proceeded to collect the seeds. It was not until he hoisted himself higher to reach another cluster that a subtle movement in her periphery caught her attention.

Shyaree's brows pinched. The younger roots grew so thick at the top that it was almost a canopy, and she could have sworn something had *moved* behind it. Had a breeze ruffled the roots? She tensed.

They were deep underground. There was no breeze.

She stepped sideways until she nearly fell over another one of those stone bumps. Hopping atop the mound, she squinted overhead. Gasped.

A root *squirmed.*

The movement was so subtle that she would not have noticed if she hadn't been looking for it. Another miniscule undulation caught her eye. Then another. Her heart thudded with enough force to nearly topple her from her perch.

The entire ceiling *writhed.*

Gods above, those feathery bits weren't just a tangle of young and tender roots. Some of them were attached to larger shapes—oblong creatures—camouflaged and clinging to the ceiling.

And Gabriel was climbing closer and closer to the top.

One of those creatures wriggled past the mesh of roots,

little tentacles twitching on its rounded crown. Her breaths came out short. A worm? A giant one that outsized Gabriel in both width and length. It bore distinctive slate-gray markings, allusive to a cragalith's. Trepidation shredded her next breath.

Was this . . . cragalith larva?

Thurin's wrath! The entire ceiling was crawling with them. The one closest to Gabriel stuck its head past the cover of roots as though to stare at the intruder.

An intruder who remained unaware as he filled his rucksack.

How to warn him?

Shyaree clapped her hands frantically, but he did not seem to hear her. The constant echo of the blowholes must be even louder near the top. Shyaree hefted the nodule he'd launched at her back up at him. It hit him squarely between the shoulder blades.

Gabriel glanced down at her. "What?"

"Get down! Get down now!"

Panic must have shown on her face, because he looked up with a frown. The terrifying creature had slid its bulbous head far enough from the lattice of tender roots that its wormlike face was impossible to miss. Gabriel must possess the gall of ten men—he did not startle.

Despite being mere handspans away from the face of an unexpected creature, his only visible reaction was the flexing of his arms before he calmly tightened the rucksack's tie and dropped the sack of nodules to the stone floor.

Shyaree didn't go for it. Her heart was lodged in her throat, her feet rooted to stone as she watched Gabriel steadily distance himself from the creature. The larva did not appear happy with the intruder's retreat. It only trundled closer and bared its maw. Even from her vantage point, she made out the rows of startling little teeth reminiscent of a giant lamprey's.

It was large enough to swallow the guildmaster whole . . . and it appeared agitated enough to follow through. Gabriel must have come to the same realization. He unsheathed his sword in one fluid move and slashed upward.

Shyaree cringed.

His sword scraped against the larva's paunchy underside. Instead of dealing damage, it only seemed to anger the creature. Worse, the motion attracted *more* larvae. They glided toward Gabriel, a mass of gray tentacles drifting through the canopy like shark fins cutting through water.

Shyaree dragged her hands through her hair, helplessness eating her from the inside out. She couldn't shout warnings or do anything to help him. All she could do was watch while the nightmare unfolded, with a scream locked in her throat.

The agitated larva reared from the roots, an unearthed worm in a wild dance, shaking the webbed construct until debris rained.

Gabriel lost his grip. He slipped a short, heart-stopping distance, sword clattering to the ground. By some miracle, he regained his hold. He clung to the swaying root with both hands, dangling like a precarious pendulum. But before he could climb the rest of the way down, a second larva clamped massive jaws over the head of the root.

A single snap and it severed as though cleaved by a machete.

Gabriel plummeted like a stone. He landed somewhere amid the bumpy ground with a horrifyingly hollow thud to haunt her nightmares. Shyaree darted forward without a care for the unforgiving spray of sharp stones and dirt clumps raining down. An ominous crack sounded. She glanced up just in time to leap out of the way.

A large fragment of the ceiling descended, a blanket of knitted roots tied to slabs of rock. Dirt plumed in the air. Shyaree coughed into her hand, eyes watering as her head swiveled, frantically searching for signs of Gabriel. Where was he?

Thurin's wrath, was he completely buried?

Was he . . . crushed?

Her boots caught, and she stumbled, only to realize the ceiling wasn't the only thing that had collapsed. A larva had fallen with the crash.

The creature's centipede-like legs squirmed for purchase as it writhed on its fleshy back with a mournful sound that could only be described as a moan. Its many legs wriggled in waves until it finally rotated to its feet and raised its head.

Shyaree brandished her machete, but the creature didn't seem inclined to confront her. It bared rows of tiny sharp teeth before retreating to the wall to climb back up the ceiling.

As soon as she was certain the creature meant her no harm, Shyaree sheathed her machete and returned to her knees, pulling and peeling apart roots tied to slabs of rock thicker than her wrist and larger than her person. They were near impossible for her to shift, much less sort through. Panic squeezed like a boa constrictor around her chest while a sob wound up her throat. Gods above, where was he? Where—

Pain sliced through her palm. Blood welled to grease her hand.

A muffled cough.

Shyaree jerked up, looking around until she spied a hand reaching from beneath rock and a tangle of roots. She hurried over, nearly tripping over a stone mound in her haste.

She didn't dare climb atop the rubble in fear of adding more weight to Gabriel, so she paused at the side, grasping for his hand.

She threaded their fingers together and squeezed.

He clutched her hand as though she were a lifeline. "Shyaree . . . ?" His voice sounded rough and muted, but otherwise all right. "Shyaree . . . are you"—another muffled cough—"are you all right?"

She squeezed again in response, whimpering her relief while she tried to peer into the gap his hand stuck through.

She could barely see, but hints of light outlined his quicksilver hair. He appeared trapped but not crushed. The mounded ground with its natural undulation must have saved him from being completely buried.

She patted his hand to reassure him before pulling from his grip.

He protested with a grunt. "Where's that thing? Are you safe? Shyaree?" The frantic note in his tone had her reaching for him.

She gave him another reassuring squeeze.

He must have understood, because he quieted when she pulled away the second time. She started tearing at the roots closest to the gap, removing smaller fragments of rock she could manage lifting. Once she cleared everything she could, she peered down, pleased to see his head and part of his shoulders now in her direct line of sight. Dirt streaked his face while grazes scored his cheek and forehead, but his expression was of stark relief as he squinted up at her.

She leaned over the gap and signed, *"Are you hurt?"*

He appeared trapped on his back, prone beneath a large slab of rock. She wasn't sure if he could read her hand signals from his angle, but he responded soon enough.

"I don't think anything is broken."

Another wave of relief struck her hard. Thank the gods.

"Can you try to get out?" she signed even though she knew it wasn't likely. She had cleared the surrounding rubble, but she could not remove the slab over his midsection. It was wider than the length of her and thicker than her thigh. It would be

impossible for him to move from beneath, much less for her to lift from above.

"Where's the worm?" he asked again, concern thick in his voice.

The creature was already halfway up the wall, its short legs striking stone with click, click, click sounds that raised every hair on her body.

"Don't worry . . . It does not seem aggressive," she signed.

Skepticism lined his face. "What in the five hells was it?"

Shyaree put her whole weight against the slab in an attempt to slide it off him instead of explaining her suspicions—the larvae probably pupated into cragaliths. Gabriel helped her from the bottom, grunting his exertion.

The slab shifted infinitesimally.

Gods, how would they free him? She gave the slab another shove before blowing out an exhausted breath. She checked on the larva. The creature had made its way back up to the ceiling. She stared up at the new crater above with a shudder. Now that a chunk of the ceiling had fallen, some of the larvae had wormed close to the rootless expanse as if to explore the new terrain. She wondered when they pupated . . .

She tensed. Where were the pupae?

Thurin must be laughing at her, because a crack sounded distinctly just as the unsettling thought crossed her mind. She had heard this sound before—by the waterfall, just before the cragalith had emerged from rock.

Shyaree whirled around.

One of the larger stone mounds on the ground, patterned with moss and . . . painted with her bloody handprint shuddered—cracking. As though something clawed from the inside, trying to get out . . .

Hatching.

She stared dazedly at the mounds all around. Eggs? Gods

above, this whole time, they'd been walking on *eggs*? Her pulse accelerated, then she checked her panic with deep breaths. The larvae did not seem aggressive—or at least the one that had fallen did not appear so. Did it matter if they hatched?

Something black and spindly shoved from the cracks, and her blood chilled to ice in her veins. Eggs hatched into larvae. But these were not eggs . . . they were *pupae*.

And the creature crawling out was not larva but a full-grown cragalith.

Chapter 17

Gabriel shook his head, trying to clear the incessant pounding.

While his whole body throbbed, the fact that he felt every part of his aching anatomy told him he was not seriously injured. It had to be divine intervention that he wasn't crushed—the thick slab over his chest could have easily squashed him.

Instead, it rested over him like a granite tabletop. He had fallen between two stone mounds that created a valley for his body. Tucked in the rocky cleavage, he had space enough to move his head and arms but not to cast a portal to free himself. A portal, just like a physical door, required space to open.

But he could still cast a portal *for* Shyaree and send her to the Den for help.

He was about to voice his intent when she froze, staring at something well beyond his line of sight, like a rabbit face-to-face with a fox.

"What is it?" he asked in a low voice. "What's wrong?"

She gave a near-imperceptible shake of her head, not taking

her eyes off whatever she was staring at. Slowly, her arm edged toward her hip. Toward her machete. He craned his head, shoving and straining within his stone prison, but he couldn't move enough to push himself up. He couldn't see what was scaring her. He couldn't protect her, but he heard it—the ominous sound of breaking stone.

The cracking intensified, then came a dissonant screech.

Oh, *fuck.*

He'd heard that sound before.

"Shyaree!" Gabriel shoved at the slab caging him with renewed fervor. But the stone barely moved, and he was already panting.

He would send her back to the Den, and no matter what followed, his men would slay it without question.

"I'll pool my magic just to your left. And when I tell you to go," Gabriel whispered harshly, "you *go.*"

That caught her attention. She shot him an incredulous look.

"For once, just listen to me!"

Gabriel pulled the threads of magic from the surrounding shadows to form the gateway as close to Shyaree as possible. He didn't know where the cragalith was, or if there was more than one, but he knew one thing for sure—he needed to get her *out.* Now.

The chirping grew louder. Chorused.

More than one.

"Now," Gabriel shouted as his portal solidified. "Go now!"

She ran. Once again, she bolted in the opposite direction. Her sudden movement must have inspired the cragalith to charge, because the ground trembled.

"Wildcat!" Gabriel roared. "What are you doing?"

His shouts alerted the creature to his presence. Gangly legs flashed across his vision, followed by an insectoid maw hissing through two pincerlike fangs. Gabriel jerked his head as far as space allowed just before the cragalith stabbed a leg downward. It missed his head by a hairsbreadth. It reared back and struck again.

It climbed directly over the slab, the stone straining heavily over his torso, compressing his chest. Gabriel wheezed as he swiveled left and right, narrowly avoiding the cragalith's lancing foreleg. He spat a slew of profanities.

The slab cracked right over his chest.

The jagged ends slid into his rib cage and dug into his flesh. Gabriel slammed both his palms up in a weak attempt to stop the two sides of the slab that were slowly but surely slipping down. Directly into his midsection.

If the cragalith so much as stomped, he would most certainly be—

Clank! Clank! Clank! Steel against stone.

The cragalith drew back abruptly, snarling at the source. It could only be Shyaree causing a distraction. She succeeded, because the crushing weight on his chest lessened, the cragalith charging from his line of sight.

"No! Shyaree!" Panic was a crushing weight worse than rock. Gabriel punched up, using sheer strength to push his way from beneath the slabs.

"Shyaree!" He bellowed, with muscles trembling.

Clank! Clank! The wildcat was nothing if not stubborn.

Cla—

A deafening snarl.

Gabriel's heart seemed to tear from his chest. "Fuck! Shyaree! Shyaree!"

No more clanking.

On a guttural roar, Gabriel shoved his entire body upward. One slab slid down, scraping the side of his torso, tearing skin. Pain seared up his arm, but he didn't have time to think. The other slab rammed into his midsection. The ragged edge was thicker than both his palms put together, but he maneuvered to the side, shifting out of its way. He pushed up. His head pounded with renewed dizziness, but the surrounding rubble still caged him in. He stuck his head through the widened gap, but his shoulders remained too broad to fit through.

Two cragaliths growled at each other as though fighting for dominance. And just beyond the scramble of spindly legs was his wildcat. She clutched her machete—clearly what she'd used to cause the clanking noise—and teetered at the edge of the plateau just before the cliff. Trapped.

The larger cragalith flipped the slightly smaller one sideways and shoved it over the edge with a triumphant screech.

"Hey! Hey! Over here!" Gabriel yelled, shoving hard enough to widen the opening. He squeezed his shoulders through. The cragalith paid him no heed, its attention fixed upon Shyaree, its segmented tail coiling like a wound spring.

The opening parted just a little more. He would never reach her in time. He wrenched at every thread of magic accessible to him and flung his shadows in her direction, even though he could barely see to know where to cast.

He was still a moment too slow.

The cragalith lunged, but Shyaree didn't even try to avoid it.

She jumped—over the edge.

Shyaree dangled by her fingertips at the precipice with her heart lodged in her throat and her name a thundering echo through the cavern. Gabriel's cry rang with such vehemence it stained the air with frenzy. Debris sprinkled over the edge, raining into her eyes, causing her to sputter.

"Shyaree!" he howled, again and again, until it became a keening sound in the shape of her name but underscored by so much fear she could hardly believe it came from Gabriel.

Her fingers strained, her hands trembling. She gritted her teeth, clinging for all she was worth until her boots found purchase. A small blessing in the guise of a divot that allowed her to anchor her weight and strengthen her grip. Little stones whistled down from the ledge to sprinkle into the darkened depths below. There was an indeterminate splash, echoed by a cragalith's furious chirrup. The creature had lunged at her and fallen into the lagoon.

Could it—*they*—still be alive? Could they swim? The one in the rainforest had hidden behind a waterfall. Gods above, could it crawl vertically? How long would it take for them to ascend? She grappled with fear while she struggled not to lose her hold. She scanned either side of the cliff face, searching for an overhang or anything she could use to help her climb up.

The barest glint caught her attention.

Something that wasn't rock or root but an entryway cut into the cliff. It was far down, just shy of the lagoon. A doorway cut into rock?

A hand seized her wrist and hauled her up. Then she slammed into the broad expanse of a hard, heaving chest.

"*You*." He spat the word like poison on his tongue. One hand secured her to him with the force of steel while the other cupped one side of her face with unnerving gentleness.

"You stayed *again* when you should have gone! You jumped off a cliff! A godsdamned cliff, Shyaree!" He yelled some more, but she was too distracted by the painfully tender way he cradled her head to his thundering heart. He pressed his forehead against her temple, his body still vibrating with rage even as his tirade quieted. That was when she realized his skin was scraped and bruised, parts of his shirt torn and tattered. She pushed away from him with alarm, inspecting the fresh cuts on his face and arms.

"Why didn't you use my portal?"

"I couldn't leave you behind."

He wasn't the only one startled by her response.

"You little *fool.*" His mouth crashed into hers, hard and forbidding, as though her risking her life for him was a concept so foreign he could neither fathom nor tolerate it. Almost as if it were something he *feared.* This time, it wasn't a soft brush of his lips or a sly tease with the tip of his tongue. No, Gabriel molded his lips against hers with an angry growl, startling her enough that she gasped—not in shock or alarm, but a foolish, irrational, irrepressible *want.* He wasted no time invading her parted lips, teeth grazing and tongue plundering with a ferocity that should have frightened her.

It didn't.

She met every punishing lash of his tongue with her own until he groaned. Until she was no longer sure who was punishing whom. Every savage stroke of Gabriel's tongue against hers turned her blood thick and her muscles lax. He was a flame, and she, a candle melting into wax.

It wasn't until he slowed to a pause and the cold brush of air replaced the heat of their kiss that she realized she'd forgotten to breathe. He had consumed her so thoroughly that she would have asphyxiated without realizing. Or complaining.

"What were you thinking? You could have died!" He hissed into her ear, his own breaths fevered pants against her skin. "Not for me. Never for me. Do you understand? I'm not worth your life."

She did not agree and she didn't care to dissect the reasons behind her opinion. He *was* a blackguard. A mercenary with questionable intentions . . . and he was right on one account.

She *was* a fool, because all she wanted was to kiss him. She pressed her lips against his in an attempt to coax another taste.

He snarled against her mouth.

"You," he rasped. "Gods, you drive me—" His tongue delved between her lips as though he couldn't deny her. A rumble rose from his chest, vibrating into her marrow while he ravaged her mouth with an urgency that rendered her mindless. "Insane."

Shyaree wanted to tell him that he drove her equally mad, but she was pressed too close, and her hands were wrapped around him. So she responded the only way she could. She bit into his lower lip, and her body arched on instinct to mold itself against his.

Gabriel emitted a tortured sound, half growl, half groan. "How are you so sweet?"

Sweet? He was one to speak. The man was slick with sweat and grime, yet her body responded by pooling a perverse heat between her legs.

Another groan. "Stop, or you'll regret it."

A part of her rational mind agreed. There was a reason she shouldn't be doing this. But she couldn't seem to think.

Her hands found their way into the thick, silky strands of his hair. She pulled him down and pleaded with her gaze. *More.*

Desire bled black into his irises. She stippled his jaw with soft kisses and felt the remnants of his self-control shatter when she playfully nipped at his neck. He groaned, and his hand clamped over her throat. She found his hold more thrilling than threatening.

"You asked for this, wildcat."

Words both a warning and a promise.

Another thrill washed through her, along with a measure of wariness, her frayed rationality protesting. There was a reason she shouldn't want this. She shouldn't want—

A large hand snaked between her thighs; his palm pressed into the cleft between her legs, obliterating all rationality. She rubbed shamelessly into his palm. *More.* She wanted more. Needed more. She wanted—

Gabriel pulled his hand away.

She bared her teeth in frustration, digging her nails into his back.

He hissed. "Patience, wildcat."

Shadows slunk around them like a silken fog until their surroundings blurred and her thundering heart drowned out the distant roar of erupting geysers. Darkness obscured her sight, but she was already blind to everything but the man feverishly kissing, biting, and sucking his way down the hypersensitive skin of her neck while his hand ripped at the ties of her pants.

"Gods, I've been wanting to peel these off you from the moment I saw them." His hands roamed greedily over the curve of her rear. He groaned again before his mouth returned to hers and he feasted like a ravening beast intent on devouring her soul.

Devouring *her.*

Shyaree didn't care.

He was a scorching star in the dark of night, and everywhere he touched, her blood ignited like oil to flame. She had never been so eager to burn.

Rough hands ripped her shirt, scattering tiny buttons across the wooden floorboards. She gasped, raking her own hand down his back. He hissed again, this time not in passion but *pain*.

Shyaree pulled away to see blood on her nails. Nails that seemed to have somehow lengthened with sharp tips. Thurin's wrath. It took her another dazed moment to realize they were back in Gabriel's room. But they hadn't even made it to the bed. She was splayed on the floor, pinned beneath him, and her nails had sharpened to literal *claws*.

Startled, she curled her fingers and shoved her fists into his chest.

Gabriel didn't budge. Violet eyes heated with lust. "It's all right." His voice was a husky lull. He seized both her wrists and pinned them over her head with a devastatingly slow smirk. "I don't mind a little scratching."

Shyaree shook her head. *No.*

He attempted to kiss her, but she turned away. He haltingly released her arms, confusion marring his brow, but his body continued to cage hers.

"Let go."

His eyes narrowed. "I warned you, Shyaree. I want you." Blatant and unapologetic words that exhilarated and alarmed her in equal measures. "And now I know you want me, too."

"I do not."

"Don't you?" His gaze darkened with an intensity that made her pulse dance.

He clamped a hand over her throat in a dominant and proprietary hold that caused a flutter in her abdomen. He caressed her throat, strong and sure, then slowly roamed over her breasts and further south. She tried to scoot away, but he held her firmly in place as he slid a finger into the cove between her legs. A wicked curve cut across his lips when he found her wet and wanting.

"Are you sure?" He leaned close, his breath warming her skin. "Because it's obvious to me what you want."

She managed a weak scowl and was rewarded with a dark chuckle. She uncurled her fingers to show him her claws, but they were nothing but blunt nails. Had she imagined them? Perhaps. But she had still scratched him hard enough to draw blood. She was too close to her heat cycle, and Gabriel was *not* her lifemate.

"What if I change?"

"Ozenn's blood, I hope you do." He didn't give her time to process that reply, because he swooped down to claim her lips again. His hand returned to that secret spot between her legs, his fingers unerringly deft. He slid one finger back into her, rubbing with gentle insistence until her legs fell apart in surrender. She swatted at him half-heartedly, and her attempts to wriggle away soon turned to mindless writhing. She found herself gripping his strong shoulders, her head arching back with need. More. She wanted more . . .

"I know what you want, wildcat." Another maddening stroke before he slid a second finger into her wet heat. "I know what you need." His stifled moan could well be her undoing. "Gods . . . You're so tight . . . Let me . . . "

He had barely begun moving when her muscles tightened with a near-unbearable tension. Her head fell back, and her eyes squeezed shut as ragged breaths escaped her lips.

"Keep your eyes open," he commanded with another thrust of his fingers. "I want to look into your eyes while I touch you."

She obeyed.

It was impossible to deny him while he strummed a carnal rhythm in the most sensitive part of her, playing her body like an erotic instrument he was bent on mastering. His fingers pumped in and out, speeding and slowing in a maddening tempo that made her writhe and whine. She clung to him with a desperation that would have been mortifying were he not watching her with enough worship in his eyes to make her feel like a wanton goddess.

She couldn't escape his relentless assault or its overwhelming effect on her. Sensation built upon delicious sensation until it was all too much for her body to contain, until she spasmed and her breaths came in rasping gasps.

Only when she grew limp did he finally cease, leaving her breathless and bereft, only to lift his glistening fingers to his lips. Still holding her gaze, he licked them as though they had been dipped in the sweetest honey.

Gods above, she had never seen anything more sinfully erotic.

Her muscles tensed with fresh need, and heat coiled between her legs even though he had just gifted her release.

"Fuck . . . " He growled. "You taste divine."

She felt those rough words like his fingers back between her legs. The rumble of his voice sent shudders along her spine. He leaned down to kiss her, and his wicked tongue delved deep into her mouth as though to share her taste while he kneaded her breast languorously. She shivered, overwhelmed by the sensations he stirred with every stroke of his tongue. He was like a hurricane, and she was a fallen leaf caught in the storm.

He pulled away from her lips only to kiss down her throat, settling himself between her legs. With a devious gleam in his gaze, he parted her thighs and hefted her knees over his shoulders. Gods above, surely he wasn't going to . . .

He lowered his head, and sudden panic flared in her chest.

He'd already unraveled her with his fingers; she couldn't begin to imagine what he could do with his *tongue.* She barred him with a frantic shove at his forehead even as her body clenched with want. Desire sparked deep in her stomach, sending prickles of something akin to pain across her skin. As though her inner beast lay just beneath her skin, waiting to escape.

She pushed up to her elbows.

He caught her by the shoulder and eased her onto her back, a warning in his eyes. "I'm nowhere near done, darling."

Darling. Gods, that word hummed beneath her breastbone, further heating her blood. Her legs clamped uselessly around his neck, and her protest came out weak.

"I can't take more."

"Oh yes, you can . . . " The knave chuckled, and more wetness slid between her legs at the dark sound. "And you'll enjoy it."

She snarled with frustration. *"What if I change? What if I bite you?"*

He smirked, cocky as ever, while he ran hungry, possessive hands over her thigh to knead the curve of her behind. "You can't kill me with a little venom—"

"A little venom?" Shyaree stared at him in shock. *"The last time I bit someone in my polymorphic form, I killed! Arkas is right. You have no idea what you're dealing with!"*

"I don't care what you are, but I do know *who* you are . . . And it doesn't change the fact that I want you, Shyaree." His insistence unsettled her. Thrilled her. Alarmed her. How could he know her when he'd never seen what she was capable of with a single bite? Gods above, why would he even *want* her? It only proved he didn't know her at all.

She pulled her legs from his shoulders.

He scowled. "Look at me."

She shook her head. He caught her by the chin and tipped her face up so she was forced to meet his eyes. "Look at me and tell me you don't want me."

Gabriel kept a firm grip on her jaw, making it impossible for her to look away. Compelling her to acknowledge a need that would only bring her heartache.

"I hate you," she signed.

His jaw tensed. "I didn't ask for what you feel for me; I asked if you *want* me."

"Your arrogance is stifling. I told you I am close to heat, yet

you think my response is for you." She tore her chin from his hold and plastered a sneer over her face. *"My body would react the same to* any *male."*

He recoiled as though she'd slapped him, but it worked. He eased off enough to allow her to roll out from under him.

She wrapped her arms around herself and tucked her knees to her chest, desperately wishing she could run and roam beneath the canopy of her rainforest. To be anywhere but here, where she felt the near-painful urge to crawl back into his arms.

Gabriel stalked to the door, but she did not look up. She could not bring herself to meet his gaze lest he see the heat needling at the back of her eyes, or worse, the want.

"Lie to me all you want, darling . . . but don't go lying to yourself."

She glanced up just as the door slammed shut.

Chapter 18

Gabriel stormed from his bedchamber and straight to the bar on the first floor. For once, the riotous energy of the gambling hall did nothing to calm him. He snagged a bottle of Mujarin.

He must have carried death in his eyes, because everyone who saw him stayed wisely out of his way. He took a swill of Mujarin—the only liquor he'd found strong enough to allow him stupor—and hoped he'd succumb to its effects. Experience told him he'd have to down the entire bottle in less than ten minutes to achieve it.

He took another gulp and grimaced. Gods, how he hated the taste of alcohol.

The conversation with Shyaree replayed in his mind, as unwelcome as gnats on his skin.

Your arrogance is stifling . . . My body would react the same to any *male.*

Gabriel took another swig, but the sear of magekind's most potent liquor could barely compare to the burn of her words. She'd eyed him as though he were nothing more than a replaceable stud. Indeed, wasn't that what he'd been over the ages? Women always saw him for who he was, and they had always wanted him in their bed—but they would never keep him. None had ever chosen him, for good reason.

Shyaree had been right to stop him.

She was right to *hate* him.

Who was he to demand her submission? He was a selfish hypocrite, carried away by his own wants. He did not deserve a single kiss, much less her desire . . .

"Guildmaster," purred a soft, feminine voice at his back. A hand slid over his thigh. "You look like you could use some company."

Gabriel turned to see one of the succubi smiling suggestively at him. He studied the redhead over the rim of his bottle. Like all succubi, Arulla—or was this Jeniska?—was made to please the eye. And because beauty was in the eye of the beholder, succubus magic masked their true features and presented the most pleasing vision to every eye—creating an unmatchable walking fantasy.

And in Gabriel's eyes, Jeniska—or so he assumed—was stunning. Pale, creamy skin. Thick, wavy tresses that fell past a generous bosom, and curves made for pounding. Perhaps he should lose himself in her arms. It would be intensely pleasurable. It always was with the succubi. But . . .

"I'm not in the mood," he heard himself say.

Jeniska pouted. "Are you sure? The unspent energy you're radiating would keep me sated for days."

Gabriel shook his head with a chuckle and took another gulp of Mujarin. Blinked.

Jeniska's red curls were darkening as he watched, straightening to a sleek, glossy waterfall of black. Green irises turned a glorious stormy gray. Creamy, pale skin to a rich, brown tan. Her facial structures morphed, too. Her narrow jawline took on a stubborn tilt that made his fingers itch, and her lips widened to a luscious pout that caused his loins to throb.

Perfection had a face, and she wore it. Right down to the constellation of three tiny moles on her temple. Shyaree simpered and kneaded his thigh with one hand.

Gabriel reached for her dreamily. "Kiss me," he commanded.

She roped her arms over his shoulders and chuckled, her voice sweet and jarring, shattering the illusion. A fantasy. That was all it was. His wildcat didn't have a voice, and even if she did, she wouldn't sound syrupy. More, Jeniska smelled too floral. What had been pleasing was now pungent . . . totally at odds with Shyaree's earthy femininity.

Gabriel extricated himself from her arms and patted her head with an apologetic shake of his own, absently noting that she was far too short as well. "I'm sorry, sweetheart, but I've changed my mind."

Disappointment clouded her eyes, but Jeniska shrugged. The Red Den was never short on patrons to sate her sexual appetite, and she knew it.

"Well, whoever she is, she's got you bad," she said with a wistful sigh, still wearing his wildcat's face and features. Ozenn's blood.

Somewhere along the way, Shyaree had shattered his idea of the perfect woman.

She'd replaced it.

Gabriel downed the rest of his bottle, and just like always, it produced nothing but a faint hum in his blood. He wanted—needed—utter oblivion. Gabriel returned to the bar and scowled. That had been the last bottle.

Five flaming hells of fuck.

If he weren't worried about the possibility of Arkas showing up to kidnap Shyaree, Gabriel would have headed into the fighting pits for a few rounds with a troll. Getting beaten to within a gasp of his life was a sure way of inciting Sleep. And those were the only times he'd ever gotten reprieve from the chaos of the thoughts that assaulted him even now . . .

He gritted his teeth.

How ironic that *he* was protecting Shyaree from Arkas, whose intent was to return her to her clan, when it was *Gabriel* from whom she needed protection.

Nine days before the blood moon.

Nine days before he delivered Shyaree as the blood sacrifice.

He clenched the empty bottle until his knuckles showed white. Sickness manifested in his gut in a miasma of wretchedness and rage. How could he go through with it?

How could he not?

Iolanthe's freedom and so much *more* hinged upon the draga morli . . .

Bile rose in his throat, and guilt gnawed his innards while his mind tormented him with a recollection of Shyaree's pleasure-flushed cheeks, of her lips swollen from his kisses.

What if I change? What if I bite you? she had signed, fiercely and naively fearing for his safety. Worried over a wretch who deserved nothing but to rot in the five hells . . .

Gabriel sneered into the distance.

Perhaps her venom would be the poison to finally kill him, but even that would be a mercy. It would be more than he was due. He couldn't think of a better way to go than rutting between her thighs, with her lips on his skin and her venom in his veins . . .

My body would react the same to any *male.*

The memory of her graceful hands forming those words punched him with the force of a studded mace wielded by a rampaging troll. A pain he deserved. A pain he *relished*. It was poetic justice that she cared nothing for him, hated him, even.

Yet the thought of another man touching her . . .

Gabriel slammed an angry fist to the countertop, rattling the glasses and garnering leery looks from the patrons at nearby tables.

In his periphery, Caspian was making his way over wearing a furrow between his brows. Ozenn's blood, it must be bad if he'd garnered the concern of one such as Caspian. But Gabriel wasn't in the mood to discuss his unruly display of temper.

Or the cause of it.

He shook his head at the Red Knight, and the man slowed in his tracks.

Gabriel stormed up the stairs to the one place he could seek peace in the Den.

The attic.

Chapter 19

"It hurts, Dapa!" Shyaree howled, clawing at the moss-covered dirt so desperately that bits flew into her mouth. "It hurts!"

Her spine arched as her muscles spasmed to refuse her inner beast. It felt as if her pantherai were clawing beneath her skin, demanding to be set free.

"Please, Shyaree, no!" Baleen caught her head with one hand and her waist with his other, trying in vain to stop her muscles from contracting and shifting into her pantherai. "Please, please, control it! I know you can! Please, gods . . . Do not succumb to it!"

Shyaree shook her head. Tears scalded her cheeks as Baleen muffled her cries with a hand over her mouth. It had been over three moons since her last change.

Gods above, it hurt so bad.

But if she changed, the clan would kill her that very moment. She tried her best to heed her father's caution. Patchy fur receded, and her claws retracted. Shyaree released a soft whine, freed from the painful urge to change, but it only rose again like a current after a withdrawing tide. Her spine curved, and bones snapped as her tailbone lengthened.

Crack! Her ligaments tore apart, her bones disarticulating and reshaping while her muscles twisted to *stop*. Pain was the blood on her tongue, the white in her vision, and the torture that blazed across every fiber of her being. Pain was the feral screams in her ears—her own or her father's, she did not know.

Agony burned through her body, and in that moment, she no longer cared if she lived or died.

"No, Shyaree! Please!"

She dimly heard her father's pleas and the dull, half-hearted crack of his fist against her ribs. Baleen had never had the heart to use his true strength on her—and that had been his downfall. He should have killed her.

Thurin's wrath, he should have let them kill her.

Instead, he chose to keep her. She twisted around and sank her teeth into his forearm, ending the one person who had ever seen her as more than an abomination.

Tears dribbled down her chin and into the tub. As steam rose from the water, Shyaree pretended it was her shame wafting away.

Gabriel's words rolled in her mind like a never-ending echo. *Look at me and tell me you don't want me.*

Gods above, she wanted him so much it *scared* her. But everything inside her shriveled at the thought of killing him with her venom. It was a nightmare. A sin. A shame she'd lived over and over. She didn't want to live it again. Yet the memory of her father's last moments persisted with vicious clarity. The calmness on his handsome face as her venom spread through his blood, repeating, "It's not your fault," until the light faded from his eyes.

Ironically, that was the day she'd stopped changing—and speaking.

Her vocal cords had never aligned to produce words again. It had taken her father's life to stifle her inner beast, and now she was allowing simple lust for a single male to threaten her self-control. Shyaree fisted her hands. *No.*

Everything about Gabriel was wrong for her.

He was nothing but a conniving and cold-blooded mercenary. An arrogant, high-handed, and unscrupulous assassin who killed for coin.

One who had protected her again and again.

Shyaree pounded a fist to her forehead. *Fool!* It was sheer idiocy the way she tried to romanticize him and his actions. Thurin's wrath, Gabriel wasn't protecting her. He was protecting her blood because he believed he needed it for the draga morli.

She was nothing but a means to an end for him.

Her mind wandered over the things he'd said to her and selected one that had deeply unnerved her. *I don't care what you are, but I do know who you are . . . It doesn't change the fact that I want you, Shyaree.*

A shiver wound up her spine. Those were the closest to words of acceptance she'd ever heard from a male not her father. Gabriel had struck a chord with her deepest fantasy by that declaration.

She sneered. He didn't mean it.

If he *truly* knew her, he would never have said that.

She slid down into the tub so the hum of water filled her ears like a gentle lullaby. He'd only wanted her body just as she'd wanted his. Lust. That was all there was between them.

She stayed submerged until bubbles escaped her lips.

When her skin was well and truly wrinkled, she stepped out of the tub to face yet another conundrum. Gabriel had wrecked her shirt. Somehow the brute had managed to dislodge *every* button. She gritted her teeth and rummaged through his closet to pull on one of his shirts, trying in vain to ignore the delicious masculine scent that had the muscles between her thighs tingling.

She scowled. It was bad enough she had to sleep in his bed, but to be wrapped in his scent for the rest of the night? It would be impossible to sleep.

She pursed her lips until an idea came that made her smile.

Ever since they'd returned from the blowholes, Gabriel had allowed her to roam the Den at her leisure. His phantasma never reared up unless she tried to step outside the manor's walls. It would be easy enough to search for Isidor and beg the amicable healer for a new shirt.

Isidor's clothes were less baggy on her, and he also smelled a lot less virile and intoxicating. With that thought, she wandered to the second floor, where most of the other Red Knights roomed. She didn't know which room was Isidor's, so she knocked on the door she knew belonged to Malakai—the kindly Red Knight who had run her a warm bath.

"What in the five hells do you think you're doing?" asked a curt male voice too close to her back.

Shyaree startled, whirling around to the disapproving glare of Snake, whose name she'd learned was Caspian. She hadn't run into him since her first day in the Den, but she recalled his hostility.

His lips curled as his eyes ran down her form. He held a tray of food. "Have you no shame?"

What in Thurin's wrath was his problem? Shyaree glared and pointedly turned her back in hopes he would leave her alone. He only sauntered up to lean against Malakai's door and study her with open distaste.

"Cast your wiles all you want, but Kai has more loyalty than you think. He may be a libertine, but even he knows better than to betray one of our own."

What did that mean? Apart from Isidor, Malakai was the only one who had treated her with genuine warmth and decency.

"Do you know where I can find Isidor?" she signed before belatedly remembering Caspian did not understand Handspeak.

Caspian cocked his head as though trying to decipher her hand signals before he shook his head. "I don't understand you, woman. Anyway . . . " He shoved the tray unceremoniously into her hands. "Gabe sent me up with your dinner." He spoke with enough annoyance to tell her he did not enjoy the errand.

Dumbfounded, Shyaree stared down at the brimming tray. She inclined her head in thanks, but Caspian only snorted.

"You'd be wise to stay away from Malakai, or any other man for that matter. Gabe's been hurt by women like you before, and none of us would stand to see that happen again."

Shyaree frowned, too confused to take offense. Hurt? By women like her?

The sketch of the wistful female staring out the window flashed across her mind's eye. She tilted her head in clear question, hoping the Red Knight would explain.

But Caspian only narrowed his gaze, studying her for another drawn-out moment as if to gauge her sincerity. She must not pass muster, because he scowled.

"Just keep your damned wiles to yourself." Without another word, he retreated to the head of the stairs. Then he paused to shoot her a glance over his shoulder. "I don't know what you are doing together, but Gabe said to tell you he'll see you in the morning to resume the search."

Shyaree blinked. Was Gabriel not returning to his bedchamber tonight?

But Caspian had already disappeared down the stairs, leaving her alone in the dimly lit hallway with nothing but her churning thoughts and the laden tray. A steaming bowl of broth, slices of cut meats, hard cheese, bread rolls, preserved fruit, and fresh kovi berries—all her favorites, yet sickness greased her insides.

Somehow it felt worse knowing the female in his sketch had hurt him. Whoever she was, he must have loved her . . . Something bitter rose up her throat.

Did he love her still?

Chapter 20

Gabriel stepped cautiously from his portal onto smooth rock, silent darkness, and the overwhelming odor of excrement. He sucked in an instinctive breath between his teeth and grimaced. He could almost taste the ammonia staining the air—what was causing that foul smell?

He held still and listened for danger. Despite his natural ability to see in the night, his eyes struggled in complete darkness. There was no bioluminescence here, not even the faintest glimmer of light in this acrid hole his wildcat had insisted on exploring. They were in the opening to a tunnel or cavern of some sort cut into the rock face just above the lagoon. Gabriel could not find it in him to deny her wishes, so he had returned to the larvae-infested plateau, descended from the precipice with a grappling hook, gotten a visual of the entrance, and portaled them here.

Soft footsteps sounded at his back, then his portal ebbed.

Sensing Shyaree's presence, Gabriel reached unconsciously for her and threaded their fingers.

She might not need the reassurance of touch, but he did.

It wasn't because this entrance led into a pitch-dark cavern that smelled of piss and feces, but the fact that the inky lagoon was a short drop below them. Being a few backsteps away from what appeared to be a bottomless pit of *water* made his skin crawl and his chest constrict. The gentle murmur of the seemingly placid surface did nothing to ease him.

Ichor Lake had appeared placid, too . . .

An involuntary shudder trailed down his back, and Gabriel allowed it to pass through him. Fear was nothing but another emotion—one he refused to bow to. Unfortunately for him, drawing deep, centering breaths as was his usual practice was admittedly not as practicable given the surrounding stink.

Shyaree must have sensed his unease, because she squeezed his hand, almost in question. Gabriel squeezed back. He would have eased her with a verbal reply, but because he had no sense of what was ahead, or the cause of the stench, he would not draw unnecessary attention to their presence with any added sound. He palmed the walls on either side. Unlike the plateau above, the hand of nature had not carved this space. The walls were too smooth and the ground too flat. Not a cavern, then. His fingers brushed against indents in the stone just before light flared in a sudden blinding brightness.

Shyaree's breath hitched.

A flurry of furious flapping. High-pitched squeaks that hurt his ears.

She jerked from his grip.

"Shya—"

A torrent of leathery wings swarmed into him, a chaos of screeching and scratching, knocking him back with the force of a punch. He stumbled back, covering his face with his hands, but then his calves collided with a hard edge. He stretched out his arms for balance but caught only more flapping wings.

Then he was falling.

The water swallowed him whole. It was bone-numbingly cold. So cold, it felt like a thousand pins stabbing into his skin while his lungs seared from the unexpected intake of liquid. A few pumps of his legs and he broke the surface with a heaving gasp.

Fuck, he was *in* the lagoon.

His chest tightened until his lungs couldn't expand. *Breathe.* He needed to breathe. He needed to find the ledge. Where was the fucking ledge? Everything was so dark he couldn't see. The water tasted stale and salty with a faint metallic tang, and it lapped at him like a monstrous tongue tasting a morsel it would soon devour.

Fear dragged at his ankles, clawed at his flesh . . . He couldn't see below the surface. Was something lurking beneath him now, poised to strike? To drag him under?

Breathe, Blacksage!

He sucked in a ragged inhale, and a glimmer of rationality sparked—portal. He could portal back to the ledge. He opened his senses, pulling for threads of magic in the dark, only to be swarmed by horror.

He could *not* conjure a portal.

Something was blocking his ability to use magic . . . just like at Ichor Lake. Gabriel panted for air, but he couldn't seem to fill his lungs. Were the sirens circling him, waiting to tear at his flesh, gnaw at his bones? He sucked in a shredded breath. No, no, no . . . This was not Ichor Lake. He was *not* in Ichor Lake.

Then why couldn't he use shadowmagic?

He flailed and faltered, his legs tiring from the thrashing. Where was the ledge?

Everything was so cold, so dark. He couldn't see. He couldn't see below . . . just like Ichor Lake. Breathe! Breathe . . . Breathe . . .

Gods, he couldn't draw in enough air. Tension coiled so tightly in his chest that he could barely stay afloat and—

Something touched him.

Something with *hands*.

Gabriel jolted. He kicked wildly, splashing to swim away, but the creature latched doggedly onto his arm. Gabriel lashed out. His fist landed in the softness of a feminine chest. A hiss of pain halted his panic.

The creature touched him again. Hands on his face. Warm hands. Gentle hands. Firm, reassuring touches. He allowed the entity closer and reached for it haltingly. Instead of the slick, leathery skin of a siren, he found smooth, taut skin.

"Shyaree," he croaked.

His response was a sweet, breathy sigh and another squeeze at his forearm. She swept even closer, until they were chest to chest, to cradle his face in her hands as though willing him to calm. She stroked his cheek, and her presence was a shining lodestar guiding him from a nightmare. Somehow the air no longer felt so thin and the waters no longer seemed so insidious.

Gabriel pressed his forehead against hers, and finally the vise around his chest eased.

Finally, he breathed.

Flickering firelight from brass braziers cast dancing shadows over timeworn walls.

The previously pitch-dark entryway did not lead into a tunnel as Gabriel had assumed, but a chamber of unexpected design—a heptagon-shaped burrow hewn into the massive rock bulwark. Seven decorative lintels, each flanked by cracked and crumbling pillars, cut across the walls in perfectly symmetrical lines, and a passageway in each wall led away from the main chamber.

Intricate but faded frescoes of animati lore adorned each wall beneath cracked entablature and friezes depicting the seven original animati clans—panthers, wolves, snakes, stags, bears, condors, and griffons—all discolored by water and defiled by bat droppings. But even with guano fouling the space, an inviolable air of sanctity remained, as though the bats were merely squatters on holy ground.

Sopping wet, Gabriel studied his brightly lit surrounds with no small amount of bemusement. Whatever had magically lit the braziers had also blocked his ability to use magic. He hadn't been able to conjure a portal in the lagoon, nor could he cast one here.

They were stranded.

Shyaree, equally drenched, did not seem to share his consternation. She was understandably transfixed by the lore-etched walls, but Gabriel was too preoccupied to match her wonder. It had been easy enough to climb the short distance from the lagoon to the ledge, but how would they get back to the plateau without his portals?

The larvae-infested ground was leagues above them. It would be nigh impossible to climb the steep rock face with bare hands. He grimaced. He had left his climbing gear and grappling hook at the plateau, not anticipating the sudden loss of his magical ability.

Damn it! What was causing the blockage? He shut his eyes and spread his senses, feeling for the tingle of magic, a tremble in the shadows . . . He couldn't feel a godsdamned thing.

A gentle touch at his forearm drew his sight.

Shyaree wore firelight the way some women wore pearls, the warmth accentuating the radiance of her burnished skin and her sleek midnight mane. Despite the crinkle in her brows, the steady regard of her stormy gray eyes settled his agitation like a soothing caress. Gabriel reached out to brush away the little damp strands clinging to her face—and checked himself. He forced his hand back to his side.

If she noticed, she chose not to comment. Instead, she lifted a hand to show him a thin laceration on her finger. *"I think my blood caused the braziers to light."*

Gabriel frowned.

"I cut myself while groping in the dark. And the next thing I knew, light flared."

Her cut was no longer bleeding, but he inspected her finger as an excuse to touch her. "If so, you must have triggered a magical ward, because I can no longer cast a portal."

She jerked her hand back. Apprehension clouded her face. *"Maybe you just need some sleep like you did in the Kilinjiri before you can use magic again? You were quite distressed by the water."*

"I am not distressed," Gabriel said irritably. "And that was different. I needed Sleep for my body to recover, but this blockage has nothing to do with a physical wound . . . or the damned water."

She cocked a disbelieving brow. *"Water terrifies you."*

"It does not." The words shot from his lips too quickly, too defensively to be anything short of pride. And they both knew it.

"You chose to fight a cragalith barehanded rather than hide in the river. And just now you panicked even though you could clearly swim. Why?"

He broke eye contact, reaching down to yank off a squelching boot and drain it while he kept his words dry in an attempt to deflect the conversation. "Has it ever occurred to you that killing a cragalith barehanded was just another notch on my monster-slaying belt?"

"That is not just reckless but stupid!"

He scoffed. "I'm not the one who jumped off a cliff without so much as a plan. Nor did I dive into a lagoon not knowing if danger lurked within." A backhanded comment, given she'd done both on his account. But that was precisely what needled him. Her putting herself in harm's way . . . for someone like him.

"At least I'm not the one constantly pretending to be invincible."

Gabriel tensed. She had no idea. "And I'm not the one risking my neck for a brother who bartered me for a dagger, but here we are."

She flinched. *"You're such an asshole."*

He worked off his other boot. "Never claimed to be a gentleman, wildcat."

She snapped her fingers furiously when he was too slow to glance up. *"You could never be one even if you* tried, *but that doesn't mean you should behave like a bear with its nose stuck in a beehive."*

His eyes slitted. "What in the five hells is that supposed to mean?"

"It means your ass is showing and it stinks.*"*

It was no more than her usual serving of snark, but the emphasis on the last word with the tiny wrinkle of her nose stoked a dark urge. He couldn't decide if he wanted to kiss or spank her. Very possibly both.

He squelched the urge. "And here I thought it was my spectacular good looks that drew a woman's attention."

Her lips thinned. *"The most spectacular thing about you is the size of your ego. I am constantly surprised you do not trip over the weight of your own head."*

He caught her wrist in response. She pulled back, but he refused to release her. Instead, he ran a thumb over the vein on the inside of her wrist, watching with perverse satisfaction as heat kissed her cheeks. He chuckled. He couldn't help himself. She made it so easy.

He rubbed a slow, suggestive circle over her skin. "I can assure you that my ego isn't the only thing of spectacular proportions, wildcat."

Her spine stiffened, but her breaths shortened. *"Stop it."* She ripped her hand from his and staggered away as though he were diseased. *"Whatever this is between us, it's not real."*

She had jumped off a cliff . . . jumped into the damned lagoon to retrieve him—and still she preferred to pretend she cared nothing for him. "And I suppose you think what you have with . . . " A slow turn of his mind supplied a name. "Hesok," he spat. "Is that what you think is real?"

She grimaced. *"At least he knows what to expect from me. I could succumb to change, and a simple graze of my teeth could kill. Does that not faze you?"*

He tossed her a wry smile. "Careful, wildcat . . . you almost sound worried. For me."

Her throat worked, the delicate muscles constricting, but her eyes narrowed. *"Only because I need you alive to complete our bargain."*

A bargain. And that was exactly the reminder he needed. He pulled back, clenching his fingers. He hated how she was right, and he hated how her silent words had the ability to slap him like a physical hand.

"Once we both get what we want, our paths will never cross again," she signed with deleterious fervor. Dejection must have bled into his expression, because she paused. *"Careful, guild-master . . . you look like you may actually want more."*

She truly had no idea.

"Don't flatter yourself, wildcat." A cynical smile cut across his face, as though her words hadn't just cut through his chest. "Not every man looking for a fuck is asking for forever."

She flushed, eyes blazing. *"Well in case I haven't already made myself clear, I'm not interested in a fuck or forever. So let's just find the tomb so we can both be on our way."*

Chapter 21

The moon's silver must turn to blood,
Only then will the tomb begin to flood,
Draw from the vein of the one twice blessed,
Only then will the cursed find rest.

Shyaree turned the last verses of her mother's song over and over in her head as she studied the stone that blocked the middle passageway. It was carved with a circle and the words: *The moon only shines once into the same grove.*

What did that even mean? And why was this the only one mysteriously sealed?

She had explored the other six passageways. They all led into isolated spherical chambers, each one filled with hundreds of little alcoves cut into the walls like honeycombs in a beehive. Each alcove held a small urn, and each urn, ashes.

They were in a mausoleum.

And judging from the talmi-gold urns, carefully decorated altars, and lavish provisions, it was a mausoleum for the revered. For the Tribe elders, perhaps.

Oddly enough, not a single bat dropping besmirched the six chambers. It was as though the winged mammals knew to respect the dead by limiting their defecation to the main chamber. Even the prayer provisions remained intact apart from the touch of time. Half-used candles dripping tallow held their turgid formation upon the altars, and if it weren't for the thick coat of dust and cobwebs, they could have been freshly lit. Stone jars held age-hardened honey. Sticks of incense were still stuck to hanging censers. Porcelain pitchers and painted porringers occupied the prayer tables, while dried herbs wrapped in scrim and coated in wax were scattered about.

The mausoleum was hidden so far down in the depths of Thurin's Mountain that Shyaree would never have found it without Gabriel's portal. How did people even get here?

And what was behind the sealed seventh door?

The passageway walls were all etched with prayers and platitudes for the deceased, but the stone barrier had only a simple circle with faded patches of gray paint . . .

Shyaree leaned wearily against the wall.

She was wet, exhausted and, according to Gabriel, also stranded.

With a heavy sigh, she returned to the main heptagonal chamber to find the guildmaster mulling over one of the seven walls featuring a mix of pictorial carvings and etched text.

"What is this word?" he murmured at her approach.

Ikruisa. A word from Old Animatish.

"Gifted," she signed.

Gabriel grunted. "Gifted . . . "

He resumed reading under his breath, pausing to query her whenever he encountered a word he wasn't familiar with. It took her a moment to realize the wall depicted animati lore of the necromancer's twin daggers—the draga sul and the draga morli—which was probably what had drawn his interest in the first place.

The daggers were painted in silver and gold, clasped in the hands of a somber woman with heavily kohled eyes and a savage scar across her forehead. And directly behind her, the circle of a full moon. The inscription beneath the carving read: *Mekari the Unholy One*.

Shyaree shuddered involuntarily.

Like all animati, she was no stranger to the necromancer and the hell Mekari had once unleashed into the five realms through those infamous daggers, but Shyaree had never heard the story of how the necromancer came to *be*.

The tale, etched in stone, began simply enough.

There was once a maiden, Shasti, who'd spurned the affections of Thurin, the god of war, for the love of another. In turn, the animati god had ended Shasti's mortal life with a curse. She was to roam his realm as a shade for all eternity, kept apart from her lover. It would have been a tragic but typical tale. One of the many unfortunate accounts of mortal souls falling prey to the wrath of vengeful gods . . . except Shasti's lover had been no ordinary being.

Mekari had been a shaman with an affinity for the dark arts.

Driven by grief, Mekari turned to Draedyn, the god of death, and offered her soul in exchange for the knowledge of necromancy. Draedyn accepted her as his eternal servant, and by doing so, he created the first true immortal—Mekari the Deathless.

Using her god-gifted knowledge, Mekari went on to perfect the art of necromancy over the span of the next thousand years. Worshipped as a deity and revered for her immortality, she was called many names over the ages.

Witch.

Sorceress.

The Unholy One.

But Mekari remained best known across the five realms as the necromancer.

Through twin daggers forged from her own blood, Mekari raised Shasti from the dead. But her lover did not come back the same.

Still cursed from Thurin's wrath, Shasti returned to the living world with a ravenous hunger that could only be sated by blood and flesh. Unable to control or accept her own hellish urges, Shasti killed herself.

Mekari, distraught by her lover's desertion, sought retribution from the five gods. When none agreed to help her, Mekari resorted to raising an army so fearsome that her Risen surpassed even the god of death's control.

The Risen answered to no one but the Unholy One herself.

The hairs on Shyaree's skin prickled as she and Gabriel reached the next inscription paired with a pictorial carving of the five gods.

Draedyn, the god of death, watched the carnage of the Risen tearing into warriors with seemingly detached amusement shining from his one eye.

Thurin, the god of war, retaliated by gifting his people the strength of beasts and creating stone sentinels—cragaliths—to supplement his army and safeguard his realm.

Ozenn, the god of chaos, allowed the threads of magic to seep through all the realms for his people's use, enabling the fae to traverse and defend themselves wherever they might be.

Railea, the goddess of light, raised archmages to protect her world and cleansed the realms of the Risen through a Reckoning of stars falling from the skies.

Yet nothing kept the Risen suppressed for long. For every

victory gained, lives were lost, and every death only contributed to Mekari's undying army.

Until Chonsea, the goddess of life, approached Mekari for a truce.

The goddess promised Mekari an elixir that would break the curse over Shasti's fate. Mekari would be allowed to live a single mortal lifespan with her lover . . . but in exchange, the Unholy One must give up her daggers, her army, and be subjected to eternal slumber upon Shasti's next natural death.

Mekari agreed.

Gabriel shook his head. "I have never heard anything more . . . "

"Romantic?" Shyaree signed.

"Idiotic," Gabriel finished at the same time.

They stared at each other.

"How is it romantic to cause such devastation through the five realms, only to sacrifice everything for the sake of a woman who never asked to be saved in the first place?" Gabriel demanded with a snort.

Shyaree dipped her head, slightly sheepish. Gabriel was probably right. Mekari had rained literal hell across the five realms. It was vengeful and macabre, not romantic. Yet a part of her heart ached for the necromancer. Even from the stale depiction of a cold, stone script, it was obvious that all Mekari ever wanted was a lifetime with the woman she loved.

How would it feel to be loved so deeply by someone that they would go as far as to defy the five gods for you? It was a deep, dark sort of love that raised gooseflesh and inspired legends—the kind of love Shyaree would never know.

Gabriel returned to the wall, brushing his hand over the etched words. "Do you think all this is true? That Draedyn himself gifted Mekari the knowledge of necromancy?"

His fingers drifted over the word ikruisa. Gifted.

Mekari had not only been gifted knowledge from Draedyn but the curse-breaking elixir from Chonsea.

" . . . recognize it as the twelve runes of the necromancer?"

Shyaree shot him a distracted glance. Gabriel was frowning at the script on the next wall. "Do you see this? The rune of *life* to raise the dead, but the risen will not come back the same. Not without a seer's blood . . . "

She barely registered Gabriel's musings because she was still pondering ikruisa. The modern word ikru—blessed—was an abbreviation of ikruisa.

"It's true, then," Gabriel muttered, seemingly to himself while he continued to study the inscription. "The necromancer's daggers may be able to summon the dead, but in order to bring them back to life, a seer's blood is . . . "

Shyaree darted to the sealed passageway where the phrase *The moon only shines once into the same grove* was inscribed above the circle on the barrier, with paint faded from time. Paint that could have once been silver. Her heartbeat quickened as everything clicked into place like a perfect puzzle piece in her mind.

"Shyaree . . . ?" Gabriel appeared at her back.

"This leads to the tomb in my mother's song," she signed, barely able to keep from bouncing on her soles with sudden excitement. *"Draw from the vein of the one twice blessed? That line references Mekari, and this leads to her tomb."*

Gabriel cocked his head, and his eyes narrowed with perceptiveness. "Your mother's song used the term twice blessed, not twice gifted."

"Mekari was twice gifted by the gods, but the word ikruisa can be shortened to ikru in the modern tongue. And ikru means blessed. Blessed." Shyaree grinned. *"She was twice blessed."*

Gabriel frowned, but Shyaree didn't give him time to pose another question. She gestured impatiently at the words etched in the barrier. *"See this? The moon shines only once into the same grove."* She tapped at the carved circle beneath. *"This must be the moon. A silver moon. The necromancer's symbol."*

Going with her gut, Shyaree snatched a knife from his holster belt and cut her finger.

Gabriel hissed. "What are—"

She painted her bleeding finger over the circle, smearing her blood onto dry stone. It absorbed every drop thirstily, as though it were dehydrated sand.

"The moon's silver must first turn to blood," she signed when the blood on her finger began to ebb, the cut already healing. *"Do you understand?"*

After a long-drawn moment, Gabriel sliced his own finger. "Do you think fae blood is acceptable?"

Shyaree beamed up at him.

When they coated the circle in a dark, bloody red, she stepped back with eagerness and apprehension, waiting and waiting . . .

Nothing happened.

"Maybe this isn't the moon referenced in the song," Gabriel said contemplatively. "Or maybe this isn't the right tomb to begin with. Maybe there's another tomb we haven't discovered."

Shyaree palmed the stone barrier in frustration. Had they not used enough blood? Could there be a hidden mechanism? A latch concealed somewhere?

Gabriel clasped her shoulder. "Wildcat—"

A grinding noise hushed him—stone scraping against stone. The guildmaster jerked her away from the barrier as though by instinct. Dust plumed at the edges like a sudden cloud of smoke. Gabriel's sharp intake of breath echoed her awe.

With a low, creaking groan, the stone barrier began to lift.

The lifted barrier revealed steps cut into the sides of a steep rock wall that descended deeper into the mountain's core. Light leaked from somewhere high above, casting a faint, ethereal glow on the space. The wall was lush with foliage, brimming with broadleaf ferns and cockleshell orchids that drenched the air with tropical sweetness. A glance up showed the same greenery forming a domed top, not a sliver of the sky visible to the eye. But the fresh air and the sound of trickling water meant this wasn't an enclosed space.

Shyaree stared at the precipitous descent, overwhelmed by vertigo. It was as if they had stepped from the mausoleum into a vast, eggshell-shaped grotto.

And there was nowhere to go but down.

No balustrades or guardrails accompanied the weathered stone steps. No railings to prevent them from falling. An unwitting stumble and they would drop a long, long way down into a seemingly endless gorge.

A reassuring squeeze of her hand. "Afraid of heights, wildcat?"

She would be a fool not to be, yet the nerves in her stomach settled at the sight of Gabriel's wry smile. She shook her head but kept her hand in his, allowing him to lead her down onto the first of what must be a thousand staggered steps.

She traced her other hand along the leafy wall to keep from focusing on the hair-raising breadth of nothingness she could so easily fall into. They had barely made it halfway when she stiffened with shock. A familiar protrusion in the wall, hidden beneath the dense shrubbery. She swept aside the leaves to find the ridged remains of an insectoid creature with a segmented tail, suspended in rock. If she hadn't encountered the same thing behind the waterfall, she would have assumed it to be a fossil . . . but now she knew otherwise.

Yet unlike at the waterfall, there seemed to be more than one locked in these walls.

"What's wrong?" Gabriel glanced over his shoulder, clearly sensing her unease.

Shyaree shuffled away from the verdant wall, yet she couldn't move beyond the step she was on or risk toppling into the fathomless gorge.

Gabriel's face turned grim as she explained her realization.

"Whatever you do, do not touch them, especially not with the hand where you've cut your finger." It might not have been her blood that had awakened the cragalith by the waterfall, and her bloodstained hands over the pupae at the plateau that had caused them to hatch, but she wasn't taking any chances here. There would be no escape should these reanimate while they were trapped along the steps.

After an age, they made it to the bottom of the gorge unscathed.

The air was thicker here. Colder. Another shudder snaked through her, but not from the chill. The light seemed to have followed them down, muted but pervasive in its glowing reach, bathing the grotto in a near-holy transcendence. Yet a conflicting eldritch tranquility filled the air. As though they had found the place where a sliver of heaven met a piece of the five hells.

Gabriel stepped off the stairs and pushed forward.

Shyaree could barely walk. Knee-high thicket carpeted the ground in a rude profusion of leaves of all shapes and sizes, curling tendrils and sprigs of orchids dangling like tiny bells.

Thurin's wrath, she had expected something more . . . An ossuary, perhaps. A crypt or maybe even a catacomb. But a gully replete with ferns and flowers? How—

"Do you see that, wildcat?"

At Gabriel's low and halting query, Shyaree glanced up and gasped.

Clearly there was nothing wrong with her expectations. Not twenty paces ahead, the leafage cradled a somber and sepulchral receptacle—a sarcophagus. And an effigy lay over the stone coffin.

"Ozenn's blood . . . " Gabriel took another step forward and—a soft splash.

That was when Shyaree realized the chill creeping through her boots was not only due to the cooler temperature but also from a shallow layer of water rising from the ground. Shyaree batted away the ferns, trying to catch a glimpse of the dirt floor. It was too dim to see clearly, but she sloshed her feet, and the water appeared only one or two thumb lengths deep.

It was enough to give her pause.

"How did the last few verses go again?" Gabriel asked before reciting them without prompting. "The moon's silver must turn to blood, only then will the tomb begin to flood . . . ?"

Shyaree swallowed.

If the ankle-deep waters were an indication of a rising flood, at the very least it appeared to be a slow one. There was unmistakable apprehension in Gabriel's eyes, and Shyaree had just seen firsthand the panic that seized him when he was in water.

She tapped on his shoulder to draw his gaze from the water and back to her. *"Go back and wait on the steps."* She nodded in the direction of the sarcophagus. *"I'll go."*

Gabriel scowled. "No chance, wildcat."

He forged ahead, shoving plants and splashing his way across sacrosanct ground. Firming her lips, Shyaree followed the obstinate bull.

They halted simultaneously.

Another gasp escaped her lips while a chill slithered down her spine to meet the cold of the water seeping through her damp boots. What Shyaree had assumed to be a stone figurine atop the sarcophagus was no effigy, but a real body.

Drawing up close, she noticed the rise and fall of the woman's chest. Thurin's wrath, it was truly *her*—Mekari the Unholy One—locked in eternal slumber.

And gods above, she was stunning.

The pictorial representation of the necromancer did not do her justice. Apart from the savage scar along her forehead, the image had captured none of her likeness.

The necromancer resembled a sleeping doll, her eyelashes sweeping crescents over skin the shade of warm honey that was accented by the dark jade of her gown. Her figure was full and lush, and her mane was a mass of tumbling curls that cascaded down the stone coffin with a playfulness suited neither to her sober expression nor her reputation.

Shyaree tensed as her gaze caught the gilded details embroidered into the necromancer's gown. Serpenti. Only her mother's clan wore the undulating waves of the sea along the hems of their garments. The lore told of Mekari as a shaman with an affinity for the dark arts but never specified the necromancer's clan.

Mekari the Unholy One was apparently an ancestor on her mother's side.

"The water is rising," Gabriel said through gritted teeth.

The cold surge had crept close to her calves. Gods above, where was all this water coming from?

The guildmaster slipped a knife from his holster belt, but Shyaree stayed his hand.

"We need to bleed her, wildcat. Isn't that what we're here for?" he asked with a callousness that demonstrated his ruthlessness untempered by fear. There was something wildly heinous and heretical about wielding a knife over a sleeping woman, especially one so ancient she had shaped the legends and lore. But Gabriel was right.

Of all the verses in her mother's instruction, this was the most straightforward.

Draw from the vein of the one twice blessed,

Only then will the cursed find rest.

Water swirled up to Shyaree's knees, effectively drowning out her hesitation. *"Give me the knife."*

Gabriel frowned, but he relinquished his knife without protest.

She refused to let him commit sacrilege in her stead.

She turned the necromancer's arm to show her wrist. Mekari's skin was warm to the touch, and that made Shyaree's intent even more repugnant. Pale, silvery scars ran along her inner wrist, as though she'd been cut many times over. Unease rose up Shyaree's throat as another notion hit her. Her own mother had once done this. Shyaree was not the first to draw from Mekari's veins, and she would likely not be the last.

Gabriel fished an empty vial from his rucksack, uncorking it with a soft pop that sounded almost deafening.

"I am sorry," Shyaree signed before making a neat incision. Perhaps it was the dimness of their surroundings, but the sluggish dribble from the necromancer's wrist was so dark it appeared near black. Shyaree had positioned the vial to best capture the blood, but still, a stray droplet hit the stone.

An ominous quake shook the ground.

For one blood-curdling moment, Shyaree wondered if the necromancer had awoken. But a frantic glance at Mekari's face showed no visible change to her endless slumber. Yet . . .

Crack . . . Crack . . . Crack . . .

The sound of breaking stone—the last time Shyaree had heard this, a cragalith had burst from the rocks behind the waterfall. She glanced over to the guildmaster, but Gabriel appeared more concerned about the water than anything else. The cracking seemed to have quickened the flood, because the water swirling about their legs now surged with an alarming speed, submerging the leafy foliage to reach her thighs.

Her vial was only half filled, but it would have to be enough. She corked the little glass bottle and gave it to Gabriel to secure in a pocket beneath his leather cuirass.

Thurin's wrath, the water was at her hips.

"Come." He grabbed Shyaree by the hand and ushered her toward the stone steps. "Let's go before this place fills up."

Shyaree cast the sleeping necromancer one final glance. What would happen to Mekari in the flood? She didn't even have time to stop the bleeding—the wound on the necromancer's arm continued to trickle into a blasphemous black stain on the stone—but Gabriel pulled her along, unyielding and insistent. Shyaree barely managed a hasty *thank-you* before she turned and fled. Or at least, she tried.

The foliage had been a deterrent, but now, coupled with the rising flood, it was almost impossible to navigate back to the steps.

Craaack . . . cracckkk . . . CRACK!

A cloud of debris rained from above, thick enough to irritate her eyes and disrupt her vision. She batted the air, coughing from a dusty inhalation. She would have stumbled without Gabriel's iron grip over her forearm.

"Hurry!" he yelled, half towing, half dragging her against the current.

A tremendous crash at her back.

She whipped around to see chunks of rock splashing into water. The flood had completely swallowed the necromancer and her altar and— Gods above. No.

Cragalith.

It was tall enough that it stood above the flood, its spindly legs adding to the chaos of the churning waters. More cracking ensued. A maddening splash. The distinctive carapace of another cragalith rising from the waters. This one released a high-pitched wail—a near-deafening sound within the spherical confines of the grotto—as it shook itself like a wet dog.

"Go!" Gabriel shoved her ahead of him. The stairs were just ahead. "Go! I'm right behind you!"

Shyaree didn't contest him. She sprinted up the steps.

An unearthly screech told her one of the creatures had probably noticed them. The ground trembled. Water crashed like waves from the creature's bellowing charge, the flood roiling like the sea in a thunderstorm.

She didn't turn back.

Firelight from the mausoleum remained painfully far, beckoning her from the top of a thousand steps like a flickering firefly. Sanctuary. She ran. Faster, faster, faster! Debris continued to hail all around, peppering the stairs with grainy bits that seemed designed to slow her steps. Stone shuddered beneath her soles.

Shyaree slipped, but strong hands steadied her from behind.

"Keep going, wildcat. Don't lo—"

Craaack!

A segmented tail lashed from the wall. It slammed into her side, shoving her from Gabriel's grip. He caught her by the arm just before she would have toppled off the narrow steps. The cragalith burst through in a smattering of rock. Gabriel's hold loosened.

Shyaree flailed.

She didn't even realize she'd fallen until she hit the water.

Pain radiated all over the back of his skull. Gabriel shook his head, trying to clear the disconcertion. He had tumbled down a series of steps. A cragalith had burst from the wall, crashed into Shyaree, and ripped her right from his hand.

Fuck! Gabriel glanced down into the flood where she had fallen. "Shyaree!"

The maelstrom far below gave him no response. He could no longer see the green, or even a single cragalith, much less her. It was nothing but an all-consuming watery grave that surged higher and higher with each breath, and Shyaree was in it . . .

His wildcat was *in* it.

Gabriel kicked off his boots and leapt from the steps.

Cold sliced into him like knives. A familiar, insidious panic reared up to seize his throat and clawed furrows beneath his rib cage. He was in the water. Ozenn's blood, he was in the water *again*. Burning lungs, rending jaws, unending pain. No. No. No . . .

He broke the choppy surface with a gasp. Water whirled around him, turbulence dragging at his feet. *Breathe!*

He treaded water, turning around frantically. *Breathe . . . Breathe . . .*

Shyaree was still in the water. He'd never seen her break the surface. How much time did she have left?

Drawing a deep breath, he forced himself to dive again.

Shafts of light penetrated the surface, but still his eyes struggled for sight. How could he find her when he could barely see — His shadowmark.

She still bore his shadowmark.

He tried to relax, to open his senses and call upon his phantasma, only to feel blockage. His ability to use magic was still restrained. Damn it! Distress compounded his need for breath. He kicked up to the surface again.

Every breath he drew only reminded him of breaths *she* was not drawing.

He squeezed his eyes shut in a desperate attempt to access magic.

Almighty Ozenn, please . . . He might not be able to use magic, but he could still *sense* his shadowmark—a piece of his own shadow. He could feel it like a faint magnetic pull whenever he was near. Taking in another centering breath, he dove again.

Random pieces of foliage swirled around. Something large drifted close enough to knock against him. Cragalith. The creature floundered, its six legs kicking furiously, but it appeared too heavy to swim.

A few more kicks took Gabriel lower.

He spotted another cragalith thrashing near the bottom like a giant overturned crab.

Gabriel's chest burned, but he forced himself lower, hoping to sense his shadowmark through proximity. But the lower he went, the stronger the undercurrent.

Yet another upended cragalith. Spidery legs undulated as though in the throes of impending death . . . then he felt it. His shadowmark. His eyes snagged on slender arms pounding futile fists against the carapace of the overturned insect. He propelled himself deeper. She was trapped with one foot wedged beneath the creature's torso. Her eyes widened at his presence. She reached for him, but her movements were alarmingly sluggish. She was losing air.

Gabriel swam close, fighting the current to shove at the part that was weighing down her leg. No give. He had to lift—

A spray of bubbles escaped her nostrils.

No, no, no!

Gabriel swam around, caught her face in his hands, and molded his lips to hers in sheer desperation. He could not —*would not*—watch her drown. He exhaled into her mouth, sharing air until his own lungs burned. He squeezed her arms, allowing her time to prepare before he pulled away.

"Hang on," he signed before he swam up, seeking the surface to fill his lungs.

The surface seemed farther than before, which meant the flood was still rising. When he finally broke the waters, he sucked in greedy gulps of air before diving back into the depths.

Just as it took him longer to surface, it took him longer to return.

The moment he reached her, he wasted no time sealing his mouth against hers and repeating the process. She gripped him tightly, her nails digging into his skin, and he was glad for it. He could barely see beyond a few handspans ahead now. The water had flooded so high above and had grown progressively murkier. When he had given her all he could, he slipped both hands beneath the creature's lower end and lifted. The water buoyed the cragalith, making it lighter.

Shyaree still struggled to free herself. Her foot wasn't just trapped beneath the carapace but caught in a web of foliage. His lungs protested for air; his muscles strained from effort. After what seemed like an eternity, Shyaree wriggled free.

Gabriel released his load and reached for her arm.

She shook her head, clutching at her throat as another spray of bubbles escaped her lips and nostrils. His own chest scorched with a familiar burn. He dragged her up by her forearm, kicking his legs furiously as he swam against the invisible flow of relentless water. It was hard enough to swim vertically on his own, but with another body in tow, the current was a rambunctious child, seemingly intent on tearing Shyaree from his grasp.

The surface seemed unreachable—

They broke through it.

Shyaree coughed out water. She sputtered and wheezed, and her gasping breaths were sweet, sweet music to his ears . . . until he noticed her flailing. Trying to keep herself afloat. He drew her arms over his shoulders. She whimpered, clinging to him like a barnacle to a ship's hull.

"Are you hurt?" he asked roughly. "Shyaree?"

She only nodded, and he wasn't sure if that was a response to his query or her body shuddering from the cold.

"I'll get us out of here, wildcat, I promise," he said just before he realized the stone steps along the wall were . . . gone? Not gone. Submerged.

The flood had risen well beyond the entrance to the mausoleum. In fact, they were so high up, Gabriel could see the tiny leaves growing along the scraggly domed ceiling of the grotto. They needed to dive *down* and search for the damned entrance before the entire place flooded to the brim.

He told her as much. "Take a deep breath, and hang on to me, all right?"

She nodded.

If swimming up was hard, swimming down and searching for a particular section of the wall was even harder. Weak light penetrating from the dome was the single godsend in helping him navigate the stygian waters.

Still, he couldn't find the exit.

He swam what seemed like from wall to wall, towing Shyaree, who swam lethargically beside him, but they couldn't see, much less find, the stone steps leading to the mausoleum. Ozenn's blood, the mausoleum had to be flooded at this point. Even the glow of firelight from the braziers was gone.

Shyaree squeezed his hand urgently. She needed air.

He kicked back up, and to his shock, they resurfaced a few handspans from the ceiling. He could practically reach up to palm the unpolished stone and the tendrils of roots and vines hanging from it. The flood was persistent. Soon they would be completely underwater.

His head bumped the ceiling.

Water rose steadily to their neck level . . . then it sloshed up to his lower jaw. He angled his head sideways, and Shyaree did the same. The terror in her storm-gray eyes was so palpable that it took him back to the moment in the forest when they were crouched behind the rock, hiding from the Silverbeaks . . .

"Let me drink from you." Her blood had heightened his magical abilities the last time.

It could work to overcome whatever was blocking him now. It had to.

He had never created a portal in water. He wasn't even sure if he could. He definitely couldn't get them out of this realm. But somewhere . . . Anywhere but here. He *had* to.

There was only a small pocket of air left.

Her breaths were ragged, but she tilted her head back without question, baring her neck, trusting him implicitly.

Gabriel latched his lips onto her throat, where her pulse beat against her soft skin. The rising waters made it near impossible for him to steady himself while treading water to keep them both afloat.

He sunk his teeth into her skin, drawing in one mouthful of blood before water engulfed them completely.

Chapter 22

Air sliced into her lungs, forcing her to breathe.

Shyaree coughed, water dribbling from the corners of her mouth. Strong arms steadied her into a semiupright position, soothing her back with firm strokes while a husky stream of Faerian filled her ears, every syllable shaped by scare, each word stiff with worry.

She drew back unsteadily, staring into eyes of glistening amethyst.

A crescent moon hung high in the dark sky, a glowing grin applauding her consciousness, while a cool night breeze caressed her damp skin like an icy kiss. She blinked. She was no longer in the flooded grotto but huddled in a muddy puddle . . . beside a riverbank. The same one near the waterfall where she'd met her first cragalith. The river burbled lazily, rippling past small moss-riddled rocks in shimmering shades of slate.

Gabriel brushed sodden strands from her face, his own face twisted with dread so ill-suited to him that he was almost unrecognizable.

"Are you all right?" he asked in a fear-roughened voice. "How's your leg?"

He was soaked to the bone. Droplets clung to long lashes, and rivulets ran from silver-spun strands, while bruises darkened one side of his cheek. Yet he still looked like an unearthly angel. One who had just saved her life. Again.

She threw herself into his arms with a sob.

"Are you hurting?" Panic softened his tone and tightened his hold. "Wildcat, where does it hurt?"

She shuddered uncontrollably, burying her face into his chest while she clutched his wet shirtfront, the buckles on his baldric jabbing into her skin. She couldn't believe he'd jumped in after her. Gods above, she couldn't believe he had managed to get them out *alive.*

She pulled back to sign, *"How?"*

"Your blood . . . I managed to make a portal." He brushed his lips to her cheek as though to kiss away her tears before he repeated with more urgency, "Are you hurting, wildcat?"

She blew out a shaky exhale and twisted her foot gingerly. Pain protested down to her knees, but nothing felt broken. She could move her ankles, feel her toes. The thick undergrowth had served as a barrier that prevented her foot from being crushed.

"I'm sorry . . . I know the first two items weren't easy to find, but this time I nearly got us both killed."

Gabriel slid a hand into his vest and pulled out the corked vial.

Shyaree released an incredulous breath.

"But now you have everything you need for your elixir," he said quietly, placing the little bottle in her hands and closing her fingers around it. "We did it, Shyaree . . . *you* did it."

She shook the vial, swirling its crimson contents before clutching it to her chest, overwhelmed with relief. She looked up to a crooked curve on his lips. She had always found Gabriel's smirks arrogant and aggravating and . . . grudgingly, attractive. But now, gazing into his grin, her heart tumbled like a wild, giddy thing.

"*Thank you,*" she signed, and placed her palm over his chest, as though she could press gratitude into his skin. "*Thank you for everything.*"

His grin dampened. "No thanks necessary, wildcat. All part of the bargain." His voice was lighthearted, almost dry, but she didn't miss the bobbing of his throat.

Perhaps it was the near encounter with death, or the fact that she finally had everything she wanted for the elixir, but she couldn't seem to keep her hands still. "*Is it really* just *part of the bargain?*"

A snide part of her cringed at the naivety of her query. Wasn't it obvious? Gabriel had clearly jumped in after her for the sake of her blood . . . except she'd seen the panic that had seized him in the lagoon. Whether he admitted it or not, he feared water. She could no longer believe he was protecting her solely on the back of their bargain. Not after everything else that had happened.

No matter his claims, Gabriel *cared* for her. She saw it in the gravity of his gazes, felt it in every tender touch, heard it in the tenor of his voice . . .

"You named your price, and I just paid it."

Or she was just a fool, trying to romanticize a cutthroat who was literally out for blood. A cutthroat who continued to gently comb her dripping tresses with his fingers as though he could not seem to stop touching her.

She gnawed on her lower lip. "*Was my blood the only reason you jumped in after me?*"

He retracted his hand from her hair, his fingers curling. "What other reason could there be?"

"I didn't think you were both a liar and a hypocrite."

He blinked. "What do you mean?"

"Back in the Den, you told me not to lie to myself. Are you lying to me now or just to yourself?"

He stared at her, his eyes darkening with an intensity that caused her blood to flow through her veins in hard, heated pulses. A small eternity passed before he reanimated with a low growl. "Then tell me the truth, wildcat. Would you have reacted the same with any male?" He caged her on the ground between his hands. "Would you have allowed Kai or Hector or any other man who happened to be there to touch you just because you're close to heat?"

Her heart pounded a merciless beat, but she refused to yield. *"Would you have jumped in after me if you didn't need my blood for the draga morli?"*

A muscle ticced in his jaw. He pulled away from her abruptly, turning to glare at the river as though he found its babbling offensive.

Shyaree lowered her gaze and wrapped her arms around her knees, unreasonably chafed by his withdrawal. Did she think she could get a straightforward answer from him? Foolish. It was silly and stupid and—

"I would have shorn off my fangs for the prophecy to be wrong," he said quietly. "A kidney, a lung, a limb . . . I would have given anything if it meant your blood weren't the key to that godsdamned dagger."

Shyaree frowned. The hairs on her skin tingled from the sheer weight of his tone. *"I'm not looking forward to runes being cut into my back, but honestly, I'll be fine. You know I heal quickly."* If she was honest, she *wanted* to do it for him. A little blood and a gory flesh wound seemed like a small price after everything he'd done for her.

"I know. But I would have preferred to keep you in your clan, in your realm, where you belong."

His words stung, and her fingers curled. *"I never felt like I belonged."*

The tiniest smile shadowed his lips. "Me neither."

She frowned. *"How could you possibly not?"* He was Gabriel Blacksage, guildmaster of the Red Knights, with magic oozing from his pores. He was the primus of his pack. How could a man like him possibly feel out of place?

His eyes met hers in a haunted glance. "Because my whole life has been a lie." He spoke so quietly that she wondered if he meant for her to hear at all. He parted his lips, but the words seemed stuck in his throat until he finally shook his head. "I'm tired of the lies, Shyaree." He drew in a deep breath, seeming to bolster himself. "I jumped in after you for *you*. Not your blood. I . . . I would have jumped in for you, even if you weren't the blood sacrifice."

Shyaree held his stare. Something in her chest swelled so much it was almost painful. It wasn't until he ran a thumb over her cheek that she realized fresh tears were sliding from the corners of her eyes.

"Please don't . . . "

"I have never allowed a male to kiss me. Not even in heat."

Her admission hung between them like a pall.

He leaned forward to pull her into his arms before he lowered his head to press his lips against hers. Soft, slow, and indescribably sweet, he kissed her as though to learn the contours of her lips and commit them to memory. Then he pushed deeper into her mouth, wrenching a reedy moan from her throat. A shiver skated down her spine. Gods above, she felt this kiss like the pulse of the earth pounding in her core. They were both drenched, and a small breeze continued to play in the air, but she felt none of the cold. Her blood simmered with molten heat, and need coiled in her lower abdomen.

A whimpering plea escaped her lips, and she raked fingers down his back, over his clothes. She wanted them gone. She wanted to touch him, skin to skin, and press herself into him. She wanted *him*.

"Patience, wildcat." He grinned, one hand snaking between her thighs. "Let me—"

He jerked back with an abrupt hiss, slapping at his nape. "What . . . ?"

He shoved her to the ground. Shyaree fell onto her back. Pebbles dug into her skin, and confusion sluiced through her veins at the red-tipped dart protruding from his neck. He covered her body with his while another whittled through the air, narrowly missing his back. Gabriel rolled off her, alarmingly sluggish. His breath rattled against her cheek with an urgency that belied the slur of his voice. "*Run.*"

She recognized the dart—one her clan laced with huntersbane.

"Please." Gabriel pushed her, but his shove was no more than a weak brush. He could no longer seem to speak without his breaths colliding into his words. "R-run."

She scanned the silhouette of bushes and trees, crouched low as she searched for the dart blower. A familiar scent was all she sensed before a boorish hand dragged her to her feet, then gave her a bruising shake.

"You are a disgrace."

Hesok. Flanked by two other clan warriors, her forsaken groom glared down at her. Disdain dripped from his voice like tar. "How could you let him touch you? A damned fae? How dare you give away what is mine?"

A weak growl sounded at her back.

Gabriel had somehow managed to peel himself off the

ground. He lumbered toward Hesok, fists swinging, but he didn't even come close. One of the clan warriors, Palik, who she recognized by his head bald as the moon, seized Gabriel by the throat and pitched him to the ground. Shyaree lurched to her feet, but heavy hands shoved her back to her knees and kept pressure on her shoulder. She twisted back with a glare at the sinewy male—Joyoh, one of the clan's best hunters and Hesok's closest confidant.

Hesok kept a foot planted on Gabriel's back and jerked his head back by a fistful of hair. "How dare you touch what is mine?"

Gabriel's garbled retort held an unmistakable sneer. "N-not yours, coward."

Shyaree didn't have a chance to flinch before Hesok ground Gabriel's head face-first into the gravel.

"Enough!" Another male stepped from the shadows, this one with dark hair, pointed ears, and a distinguishing dagger tattooed across his cheekbone. "Release him, and keep to our agreement, warrior. Take your woman and leave."

Shyaree hissed. Of course Hesok would have had help from a portal maker. The pantherai clan was leagues from Thurin's Mountain. How else could they have traveled here in a handful of weeks? It would have taken them at least two full moons by foot.

"Arkas." Gabriel spat the name like an insult.

The second-in-command had the cheek to look pained as he retorted in Faerian. Arkas's gaze flitted to Shyaree briefly before darting away, as though it couldn't meet hers.

Gabriel pushed from the ground with knife-edged words in their mother tongue that had the Red Knight flinching. But Arkas never got a chance to respond. A dart struck him squarely in the chest. Followed quickly by two more.

"I've always detested the look of that one," Joyoh muttered, sticking his dart blower into the waistband of his leathers while Palik snickered.

Arkas staggered, heaving stuttering breaths as he slumped to his knees. While everyone's attention was fixed upon the traitorous fae, Shyaree reached discreetly for a blade in her holster belt.

Hesok sauntered over to Arkas and steadied him by the nape as though he were no more than a newborn cub. "Thank you for bringing us to my bride, but we are done here." Then the warrior nodded at his men. "End them both. Their presence stains our realm. Despicable, double-crossing creatures."

Not if she could help it.

Shyaree shoved off Joyoh's grip with a brutal slash that caught his forearm.

"Thurin's wrath!" Joyoh stumbled back.

Shyaree didn't follow up with an attack on the underling. She lunged for Hesok. Too slow. The warrior pivoted from her with ease and delivered a kick to her back that sent her crashing to the ground. Gravel scraped her skin raw, but she turned—

Hesok seized her by the wrist. Twisted.

Dimly she heard Gabriel's outraged growl as she hissed in pain, but that was all it took for Hesok to confiscate her blade. He waved the weapon at her with a disapproving shake of his head before his gaze snagged on the corked vial that must have dropped by accident.

"What in Thurin's wrath is this?"

Shyaree scrambled for it, but Joyoh jerked her back by the forearm with a punishing shake that rattled her teeth. "Stupid whore," he said with a jeer. "I'll take immense pleasure in watching your discipline before the Great Kilinjiri!"

Hesok inspected the vial and met Shyaree's gaze with a smirk before he moved closer to the river's edge, uncorked it, and tossed it—straight into the water.

Shyaree sank her teeth into Joyoh's uninjured arm, drawing a yelp. His grip loosened enough for her to charge, but Palik seized her in turn. It was too late anyway. Shyaree dropped to her knees, watching helplessly as Mekari's blood dispersed into the water.

Hesok laughed. "Did you actually think I was going to allow you to treat Reiken?" He fished the vial from the river, ambled over to drop the vessel so it landed at her feet with a dull clink. "Your brother deserves what he got, and if the curse claims him, then good riddance. The clan is better off without him."

Shyaree picked up the vial with trembling hands.

It was washed clean.

Not a single drop of blood remained.

She lurched up, and her knuckles connected with Hesok's nose with a sharp crack. A growl was all she heard before pain punched the side of her face. Her head snapped back. Dizzying white spots exploded across her vision to accompany the burn of her cheekbone and the taste of iron teasing her tongue.

Gabriel went berserk. He revived with a viciousness that made Shyaree wonder if the dart had been laced with hunters-bane after all. It was impossible for him to be conscious, much less combative. A single shot of the dart was often enough to immobilize a full-grown male, yet Gabriel fought like a rabid wolf. Snarling and snapping, he buried a merciless dagger in Palik's gut before barreling straight for Hesok. They crashed to the ground with Gabriel on top bearing down with the knife.

In her periphery, Joyoh moved to intervene. Shyaree snatched up the fallen knife and intercepted him.

"You'll be tied to the post and paddled raw!" Joyoh retorted, as though the threat of punishment were enough to scare her into submission.

She flipped him a derogatory finger.

"Don't you fucking touch her!" Gabriel shouted, and Shyaree wasn't sure if he was cautioning Joyoh or castigating Hesok.

Fury seemed to lend her guildmaster disproportionate strength, because the dagger sank lower and lower, until true fear flashed in Hesok's gaze. The warrior changed, his clothes disintegrating as his body shifted in a swift and seamless wave of rippling sinew and gleaming pelt. Larger than a normal panther, the pantherai bucked Gabriel off with ease. Hesok snapped his jaws to showcase unforgiving canines dripping with malice. Gabriel hissed in response, baring his own sleek and sharpened fangs.

They collided in a grappling heap of muscle and fur.

A yelp of pain distracted her enough that Joyoh disarmed her and punched her to the ground with a force that emptied her lungs. Blood coated her tongue. She glanced up to see the pantherai circling Gabriel, who had staggered up but seemed unable to stand. He swayed on his knees like a man too deep in his cups.

Joyoh slunk to his back and grabbed him in a chokehold. Shoved him to his knees.

True horror speared her heart when silver glinted in Joyoh's hand and she felt the missing blade in her own. He'd stolen her weapon. She lurched to her feet, a whimpering cry on her lips. Too late.

Joyoh buried it between Gabriel's ribs and kicked him to the gravel.

The pantherai growled its approval before shifting back to his two-legged form, mindless malevolence contorting his features into those of a true monster. He grabbed a fistful of Gabriel's hair and slammed his head into the stones.

Repeatedly.

Shyaree wasn't aware she'd moved until Joyoh wrapped his

arms around both her arms and midsection to immobilize her. Discordant, broken sounds escaped her throat. Nothing loud enough to drown out the sickening crunch of bone and the pulpy pound of wet flesh against hard stone. Gabriel didn't make a sound. In fact, he was no longer resistant.

When Hesok finally slowed, Joyoh leaned so close that his fetid breath wafted into her nostrils. "No one messes with our clan and gets away with it," he murmured with a spiteful chuckle before he released her. Shyaree barely heard him.

She scrambled to Gabriel's side.

Her guildmaster lay in a motionless heap on the ground. The sharp scent of blood saturated the air. A sob leaked from her lips. She turned him around, and another sob choked in her throat. His forehead was a mangled mess, his quicksilver hair matted with an ugly red. His skin was still warm. So warm. Yet something inside her withered—a part of her already knew he was gone without returning the part of her he'd stolen. Very gingerly, she lowered her ear over his chest.

Quiet had never been more deafening.

No. No. No . . . Something inside her convulsed.

"I would have left his body here to rot, you know," Hesok said conversationally as he lowered himself to his haunches. He was unclothed and, like all males after a shift of forms, semi-erect. She had never been more repulsed by nudity.

"But I see you're already missing him, so we'll take his head with us." Hesok strode to where Palik lay panting with undisguised pain as his body tried to heal from the wound inflicted by Gabriel's knife. Hesok picked up the bloody weapon and casually sharpened the blade against a river stone. The blade wailed with each scrape, as though it, too, mourned the death of its owner. "We'll hang it in the Great Kilinjiri so everyone will know what happens to those who seek to claim what is mine." Rough hands wrenched her head back so she could meet his rancorous gaze. "So *you'll* never forget what happens when you disobey me, my darling bride."

Sudden hysteria had her laughing even as hot tears spilled down her cheeks. *Darling.* Gabriel had called her darling. And now she would never hear the word spoken in his husky baritone. She laughed so uncontrollably that cracks split across her skin, as though she were literally coming apart at the seams.

Hesok retreated from her with a stumbling step.

Shyaree clawed at her skin as pain scorched every fiber of her being . . . or perhaps that was simply rage. Something cracked inside her. Bones snapped. Her organs twisted, rearranging themselves until her body became a grotesque mass of writhing flesh in a distorted frame. For the first time since her father's death, a shriek rose from her core and tore free from her throat.

Chapter 23

Bubbles escaped his mouth, carrying along with them the echoes of his tormented screams . . . *Please, let it end. Gods, please let it stop.* His prayers went unanswered. Every time he opened his eyes, skeletal hands dragged him lower into the watery depths of darkness. Gabriel thrashed violently, but they clawed at his arms, tore at his ankles. Sharp teeth ripped into his calves, rending his flesh, but the pain was nothing compared to the frigid waters scorching his lungs.

It *burned.* He willed for stupor, for the mercy of oblivion . . . but it never came.

Gods, *why* wouldn't it come?

A gasping breath sliced through him.

Gabriel jolted awake, his skin clammy and his heart racing so hard it could have cracked his ribs. For a moment he simply breathed, drawing in heaving gasps of air to convince his body that he wasn't back in that infernal lake, stuck in a never-ending nightmare. There were no sirens gnawing on his flesh while he suffered endless drowning. No water burning in his lungs while death denied him.

Gabriel lifted his head, and the world swayed. He groaned. His temples throbbed. For one dazed moment, he did not comprehend the sight before him. It was dark, the moon nothing but a small wedge peeking from between the clouds, but his eyes finally adjusted.

Bodies scattered around him like windblown leaves. And blood. So much blood. The rocks beneath him were stained black, while dark splotches puddled around him . . . as though a wayward child had taken a bucket of paint and splashed it everywhere. Sudden awareness caused adrenaline to spike in his blood and shortened his breaths.

"Shyaree?" Panic speared his chest when he couldn't find her. "Shyaree!"

Four lay on the ground; none of them were her. Gabriel stumbled to the one farthest from him. Arkas, the traitorous bastard. There were no open wounds on him save the three feathered darts protruding from his chest. Gabriel tested his pulse, and despite the bitterness of the betrayal, felt a spurt of relief at the weak heartbeat.

He turned to inspect Shyaree's clansmen. They weren't so lucky. They were covered in vicious claw marks and bite wounds. The whoreson he recognized as Hesok lay on his back, his eyes wide open, his mouth frozen in an endless scream. His jugular was torn so badly that his head was almost detached . . .

Gabriel pushed to his feet, scanning the area. Oval-shaped stones clacked beneath his boots as he lumbered about in broken fear, a single name rolling over and over in his mind. Shyaree . . . Shyaree . . . Shyaree . . .

He found her farther upstream, lying on her side by the river's edge, curled in a fetal position. Shock slammed into him like a vicious cudgel to his skull.

Not only was she stripped bare, but her naked body was painted with . . . scales. Bronze scales blushed her cheekbones, scalloped over her shoulders, and dusted beneath her collarbone. The steady rise and fall of her chest eased the tightness within his own, but she remained unmoving as he took her in his arms. Unconscious. But those weren't the only reasons his breath continued to stall.

Her rounded ears had disappeared from the sides of her face, replaced by two furry tufts sticking out from her hair. Panther ears. While a smattering of scales ran down along the sides of her arms, outlining her in a sheen of bronze, her hands were delicately furred and her nails perfectly tipped with sharp black claws.

Gabriel's gaze roamed the length of her, barely able to believe his eyes. Scales freckled between her cleavage and kissed down her navel to outline the flare of her hips . . . Just like her hands, both her feet were furred and clawed. After he'd processed the astonishing changes to her body did he notice the bruises and the cuts. The blood. It speckled all over her face and smeared over her mouth and jaw. The sight sickened him.

Once again, he had failed to protect her.

He lifted her from the ground and hugged her to his chest, allowing himself one moment to soak in her presence and calm his tattered nerves. Despite the scales patterning her body, she was so warm in his arms. So soft. It was only then that he noticed the tail protruding from the base of her spine like a furry black whip. Another breath left his lips, followed by a shaky laugh. She had told him polymorphism made her a monster . . .

Gabriel wondered if she had ever seen herself in the mirror.

Anguish crashed through her consciousness like a basketful of stones. A whimper welled up to her lips. Her limbs felt stiff, her muscles sore, but . . . she lay on something soft, shrouded in a masculine scent that was both familiar and comforting.

Shyaree pushed up with a gasp.

She was back in *his* room . . . wrapped in his bathrobe and sleeping on his bed.

A dream?

"You're awake." Her dream leaned by the bedpost, towel in hand, wearing a worn pair of pants, damp hair, and the crooked smile she loved so very much. Her vision blurred.

His smile faded; the towel fell from his hands. "How do you feel, darling?"

Darling.

A sob surged through her lips. She shoved from the bed and threw herself into his arms. Her imagination had conjured him to perfect detail, down to the comforting feel of his strong arms and the steady beat of his heart in her ear. She clung to him, relishing his warmth and drawing deep breaths of his scent.

"Look at me," he commanded. "Tell me how you feel. Show me where it hurts."

She only clung to him harder. She didn't want to open her eyes. She didn't want to move. She didn't want to acknowledge reality or process the horror that had just occurred. She only wanted to stay in the safety of his arms and pretend everything had simply been a nightmare—she hadn't lost him. She hadn't lost Mekari's blood and failed her twin. She hadn't changed. She hadn't killed. She wasn't a monster.

But when Gabriel pried himself from her latching grip, she was forced to open her eyes. He was still there. She blinked, and he was still there. She reached for him again and froze at the sight of her own fingers. Her *hands.*

They were not hers. These fingers were hideously furred. Fleshy paw pads lined the palms, black pelt coated the knuckles, and sharp-tipped *claws* replaced her nails.

She lurched away from him, inadvertently falling back onto the bed.

"Shyaree, it's all right." He settled beside her on the mattress and pulled her close, rubbing soothing circles down her back, his voice calm and steady. Tender. As though he weren't comforting an abomination who'd just massacred three grown males. Gods above, she could still taste the hot tang of Hesok's blood on her tongue. She shoved him away, wiping the back of her hand frenetically over her lips.

"Shyaree." He reached for her again, smelling of clean skin and virile male. "Wildcat . . . "

"Stay away from me!"

His jaw tightened. "It's over, Shyaree. They are gone."

"Don't touch me! Don't look at me!" She backed away from him when he continued to reach for her. *"I am a monster."* She buried her face into her padded palms only to feel scales on her cheeks. She sobbed.

"No, you're not." Quiet words laced with unmistakable anger.

"Just look at me." She could barely see his face past the tears blurring her vision.

"You're *not* a monster. You're Shyaree . . . and you are the most beautiful woman I've ever seen in my life."

He was either deranged or this was truly a dream, conjured by her fractured psyche.

"You're not even real." Her tears fell harder, her shoulders shaking uncontrollably. *"You're not real. You're not even supposed to be* alive*!"*

She had watched him *die.*

"Shhh . . . " He captured her face and pressed his mouth against hers with such tenderness that the cracks in her heart fractured wider. His lips were firm and soft, solid and warm. The kiss was nothing like any of the ones they'd shared in the past. This was gentle but insistent, tender and fierce. It warmed her to her core, melting away her fears to replace them with a heated simmer in her blood.

He pulled away, his breath ragged while he wiped all traces of tears from her cheeks with one callused thumb. "Does that feel like a kiss from a dead man?"

"I watched Joyoh knife you! I watched Hesok smash your head over and over into stone."

The crooked smile returned in full glory. He pulled her palm over his chest—to the spot that should have been wounded, where the knife had punched through his leather cuirass and tunic. But her claw-tipped finger only traced hard muscle with the soft covering of hair and smooth, unblemished skin. She stared. There was not even a scar. She knew the fae could sleep to heal, but there was no way his body could regenerate that quickly.

"How? I heard the stillness in your chest." It was the moment her sanity and self-control had shattered and her inner beast had torn through. *"How are you still alive?"*

Instead of answering her question, he wrapped his hand over her distorted one and threaded their fingers together without an ounce of disgust at her deformity. Then he pressed his cheek to her temple, holding her as though he not only wanted to but *needed* to.

"Have you ever wondered why I never showed up the day you were due to leave Amereen Castle?"

Chapter 24

One year ago
Duskhall Castle, Fae Realm

Gabriel waited upon the crenate slate roof for his mark to make an appearance.

Perched on the curved nook of the peninsula overlooking the Wandering Sea, Duskhall was a glistening fortress cradled by a proud redwood forest. The stronghold soared into the sky in a charming amalgamation of curving balconies and puffing chimneys, crowned by stocky turrets and slender watchtowers. But Gabriel was only interested in the tower jutting from the outer fringe. Singular and almost lonely, the tower faced the crashing waves like a solemn sentinel overlooking an endless sea.

Tonight, he would finally discover what lay within those impenetrable walls.

Tomorrow, he would give Declan a full report before he

sent Shyaree back to her home realm. The thought of the wild-cat's departure from Amereen slapped him like another bracing gust of wind.

Well, it didn't have to be goodbye.

He could convince the archmage to delay her leave. After all, Evangeline had just come into her magic. Surely she would benefit from more practice sessions with Shyaree, which would give Gabriel more time . . . for *what* exactly? Five blazing hells, the wildcat didn't belong in Amereen, and she certainly didn't belong in his thoughts.

His wayward emotions caused a disgruntled shake that ruffled his feathers, both figuratively and literally. He did not have time for this. Tomorrow, he would send her home as planned—and that would be the end of it.

He spread his wings and glided into the air, seeking to work off his agitation. He circled the castle grounds until he noticed an opportunity—an open window in the servant's quarters. He would wait for his mark within. He swooped in and incited a small scream.

"Oh, what did I say about leaving the shutters open, ye old codger!" A maid brandished a feather duster in his direction. "You've let in another one of those pesky birds!"

"Only because you burned those eggs and smoked up the kitchen!"

Gabriel chuckled. The sound escaped his bird form in a warble as he flitted from the room and into a narrow hallway. He winged around the corner and landed on the mantle of an empty fireplace beside a bookshelf. One of the many unused parlors in the castle. Gabriel had been infiltrating Duskhall Castle for months now, with none the wiser as to his true presence. No one suspected a spy in the form of a woodland sparrow.

Most of his kind could never possess anything smaller than

a crow. Partly because of the vast amount of magic required to maintain shadowform, much less a condensed one to fit a smaller host. And partly because nonpredatory birds tended to be timid by nature, which made them less likely to survive a possession without suffering a literal heart failure—not only detrimental to the host but also to the Unseelie possessing it.

But Gabriel had spent painstaking days nurturing this innocuous little sparrow with its dull-gray face and plain chestnut striations. A hatchling that had fallen from its nest and been hand raised, it trusted him implicitly. Even so, he kept their sessions as short as possible. The sparrow's heart already labored as though it had flown across the continent instead of a few circles around the keep. Even if it did not succumb to heart seizure, it would likely expire from exhaustion at carrying Gabriel's heavy shadowform within its tiny body.

He wouldn't let it come to that.

Gabriel had been monitoring his mark for weeks now, and the Unseelie prince was nothing if not punctual.

Declan had tasked him with espionage the day Evangeline had imprisoned the mad king Zephyr in a Soul Tree tucked somewhere in the mage realm. After weeks of tracking the prince, Gabriel had discovered nothing extraordinary. Zion's comings and goings were remarkably uneventful and painfully predictable, except for his regular visits to the one room Gabriel could never enter in Duskhall Castle.

The room in the high tower, mysteriously warded by magic.

Tonight, Gabriel would find out once and for all what lay hidden behind that weighty brass door that merited a contingent of operational staff here without a live-in lord or lady. Given that Duskhall had once served as Zephyr's second fortified settlement, the castle's continued upkeep and even Zion's frequent visits might not be particularly brow raising . . . except the prince was certainly not tending to simple administerial duties in his father's absence. Not when he arrived at Duskhall bearing gifts—canvases, brushes, books, and sometimes food.

Gabriel flew close to the ceiling, landed on the wooden beams just above the warded door, and bided in anticipation. Cloistered between dust and cobwebs, his host shivered.

Sky. Flight. The sparrow's yearning pressed into him with nervous agitation. Gabriel wasn't sure how much longer he could push his own agenda and bend the bird's will to his.

Calm . . . Gabriel projected.

Footsteps sounded. Finally.

Bearing a platter of seasonal fruit, Zion unlocked the door with a soft surge of shadowmagic. The moment the door opened, Gabriel flitted in, keeping to the ceiling. He flew atop a four-poster bed and perched at the very edge of the tasseled canopy. He was in a bedchamber. Shelves filled with books, a writing desk, a wardrobe, dressers, and another door that must lead to a latrine and a bath chamber. The occupant was a silver-haired maiden who sat by the desk, her nose buried in the pages of a book. Ozenn's blood, was this simply where Zion kept an unwilling paramour?

"I brought you some of your favorites," the prince said, but he received no response.

When the maiden finally looked up from her book, Gabriel nearly toppled off his perch.

Impossible. The bird's vision must be impaired.

"The nectarines are sweet." Zion slid the platter onto the desk. "Why don't you try some?"

The maiden lowered her book to the desk, picked up the plate, and hurled it at the prince.

He must have anticipated her reaction, because Zion shifted smoothly out of the way. The plate smashed harmlessly to the ground, fruit rolling over weathered floorboards.

"Starving hurts no one but you," the prince retorted calmly.

The maiden lifted her hands and signed, *"Then perhaps you should stop visiting. The sight of your face is enough to sour my appetite."*

Zion chuckled. "Ah, Io, what am I going to do with you?"

The sparrow fluttered its wings restlessly, flapping with enough ferocity to draw attention. Gabriel wasn't sure if it was his shock feeding the bird's anxiety or the fact that his feathered host had reached its capacity to bear his shadowform, but it flew from the canopy and landed on the dresser.

Calm . . . Calm . . . Calm . . .

How could he calm the creature when a furious part of him itched to seep from the bird and rend his sister's captor to shreds?

"How is there a bird in your room?" Zion asked.

Gabriel couldn't see Iolanthe's response—he was too busy trying to keep his host under control.

Whatever she responded caused Zion's voice to tighten with speculation. "What? And you're keeping it?"

Iolanthe strode toward the sole window in the room. She opened the curtains and unlocked the latch. Half driven by the sparrow's natural instincts and half by his own discomposure, Gabriel shot through the opening. The cool night air eased his host, but it did nothing to soothe him. Disbelief and disconcertion slashed at him like unforgiving whips.

How could Iolanthe be here?

How could she be *alive?*

Ozenn's blood . . . had Iolanthe been living in Duskhall this whole time?

Mirroring his emotions, the sparrow released an angry chirrup as he winged back toward Duskhall Castle. This time, he swooped into a different secluded hallway. When Gabriel's shadowform finally diffused from his host, the sparrow lay on the ground, its fragile breast palpitating furiously. Gabriel picked up his tiny friend, stroked its palpitating body in thanks before placing it by an open window to aid its escape once it caught its breath.

Then he stalked to the wrought-iron door at the end of the hallway.

Just like Iolanthe's chamber, this door was locked. But unlike the tower, it was not magically warded.

Gabriel picked the lock easily, slipped in, relocked the door from the inside, and waited. Zion usually spent no more than twenty minutes in Iolanthe's room before coming into this office. And just like clockwork, footsteps approached.

The door swung open.

Before Zion had a chance to react, Gabriel grabbed the prince by the collar and pinned him to the wall, pressing a blade to his jugular.

If Zion was surprised, he did not show it. Instead, the bastard only smiled as though he'd been expecting Gabriel. "You don't want me dead, guildmaster. I'm the only champion she has left in this godsforsaken place."

Gabriel growled and shoved the prince harder into the wall, digging the blade into his throat. "How is Iolanthe here? How . . . How is she even alive?"

Zion chuckled, and the movement only caused Gabriel's blade to dig harder into his skin. A thin line of scarlet welled, slipped down his throat. "Have you truly forgotten everything from your time in the palace?"

Unwanted memories blotched his consciousness like a splatter of sludge.

A shudder snaked down his spine, the dank dungeon air seeming to seep from the dark crevices of his mind to chill the room. The clank of chains echoed in his ears, as sharp as the edges of the metal bands that had once chafed his ankles. Bile rose at the phantom taste of bloody liquor forced down his throat and the burn of fangs sinking into his flesh while he struggled. Gabriel gritted his teeth, but still he heard the king's nauseating groan of satisfaction while drinking deep from his veins . . . But no recollection caused his heart to pound harder than the memory of Ichor Lake.

No.

"I escaped," Gabriel snapped, but the words sounded unconvincing even to his own ears. He had watched Iolanthe die, yet his sister was here.

Zion curled his lips. "Did you really?"

"I. Got. Out."

"Fool. You got away because *he* allowed you to. And he allowed you to because he'd succeeded in leaving a part of himself *in* you—just like he did to the rest of us."

Gabriel recoiled. "That's impossible."

Zion smirked, seemingly unperturbed by the blade slicing ever deeper into his throat or the blood trickling into his collar. "You have no idea, do you? Haven't you wondered how Zephyr managed to survive even though the archmage burned his body to a crisp?"

When Gabriel offered no response, Zion laughed darkly. "He lives because *we* live."

"You are deranged."

"Perhaps, but at least I'm not in denial."

Gabriel snarled. "It's impossible. The draga sul was with the Echelon of Archmages the whole time, and the draga morli was never found." A fact that gave him much comfort. "Your father couldn't have achieved Deathlessness. Not without both those daggers."

A tightening of Zion's lips. "Zephyr isn't my father. And he isn't truly Deathless, is he? He lives on, yet his body was not immune to ravages."

Gabriel shook his head. "The dark arts. Who knows what

he's dug up from the necromancer's scrolls and ancient practices—"

"Zephyr lives because he left pieces of his soul in *us.* His anchors. I do not know how many anchors he acquired, but the ones I've ascertained so far are Iolanthe, Zenaidus, myself, and *you.*"

Gabriel grated his teeth, itching to gouge the prince's eyes from their sockets if only to tear out the terrifying truth reflected in those lavender pupils. "Do you expect me to believe Zephyr has done to his own sons what he did to me?"

Zion scoffed. "Did you think you were special? You weren't the only one he blooded, Blacksage. You weren't even the first . . . Iolanthe was his first experiment, if you will."

For a moment Gabriel couldn't speak. He couldn't do anything but clench a hand around Zion's lying throat and tighten his other hand around the blade while rage consumed his innards like an insatiable wildfire. He squeezed until his hands trembled with effort while Zion gasped like a dying trout and clawed at his grip.

"Don't you think I would have realized if I were made an anchor to his black soul?" Gabriel growled and loosened his hold. "Don't you think I'd have known if I were . . . tainted?"

The lunatic laughed even as he wheezed, as though Gabriel's aggression exhilarated him. "I never knew, either. I've lived five centuries since the last time he . . . " The prince swallowed, showing the first hint of discomfort. "Five centuries not knowing what he had done to me until I saw him come back to life with my own eyes. I butchered him—*her* . . . he was hiding in that magess called Vera, and I butchered her myself, Blacksage. All but turned her to raw meat! And still, the whoreson rose from her body. And Declan? The archmage burned what was left of Zephyr's walking corpse . . . and still the devil survived. That was when I finally realized." A bark of near-hysterical laughter. "All those years of blooding weren't just for his sick pleasures."

The wildfire raging within turned to ice. So cold, it was almost like Gabriel was back in the nightmarish depths of Ichor Lake, praying for a death that never came. His gorge rose with sudden sickness.

He released the prince and took an involuntary step back. "It can't be true. He couldn't have— He couldn't—"

"Use your head and *think*, Blacksage. How else do you think Io survived? She is undying, just like the rest of us! The soulbond works both ways. So long as Zephyr draws breath, we cannot die. And while we live, he cannot end."

Gabriel slammed Zion back against the wall. "That. Is. Fucking. Impossible!"

Zion's lips twisted with another ugly laugh. "Let's test the theory, shall we?"

The prince struck out, and Gabriel drove the knife through his neck without mercy. His blade sank deep, not stopping until it hit the hardness of bone. The maniacal grin never left the prince's lips even as crimson dribbled from the corners of his mouth and the zealous light in his eyes dimmed. Zion sagged to the ground like a marionette with cut strings. A crimson puddle grew on the floorboards.

Gabriel hissed, fingers clenching and unclenching around the hilt of his blade. He dragged in another flustered breath and lowered to his knees. Pressed two fingers to the side of Zion's throat. No pulse.

Undying, his ass!

Yet he waited several moments and tested the man's pulse again. Zion was dead, and Gabriel was a fool. Did he truly expect the prince to rise from the dead? Zion was deranged, and that was all there was to it. Zephyr wasn't Deathless or undying or whatever it was the prince claimed. Gabriel wasn't an anchor. There had to be a straightforward explanation to Zephyr's state—and Gabriel would wager his fangs that he'd find the answers in the necromancer's scrolls.

His breath hitched. *Of course.*

He stepped away from the body and surveyed the office with fresh eyes, his gaze snagging on the books and manuscripts on the table. After every visit to Iolanthe's tower, Zion had holed himself up in this chamber and pored over scrolls.

Scrolls that had once belonged to Zephyr.

Gabriel would find them, take them for himself, and study them. There had to be an explanation to Zephyr's undying state. There *had* to be. Then he would devise a plan to free his sister from the wretched tower, bring her home, and—

Awareness tingled at the back of his neck.

Gabriel whipped around just as something sharp punched into his chest. He expelled a stuttering breath, too stunned by the grinning madman to react. A knife thrust skewered the beating organ within his ribcage.

Zion's chuckle was all he heard before his vision faded . . .

And he woke, sprawled in a puddle of his own blood.

He shoved up to his knees with a jolt of shock. His lungs pulled in painful gasps. He was still in Zion's office, and the prince who should have been dead lounged behind his desk, wearing a collar of dried blood around his otherwise unblemished throat as he regarded Gabriel with a small smirk. "Believe me now, Blacksage?"

Chapter 25

"I never made it to Amereen the next morning . . . ," Gabriel finished softly. "Because I couldn't accept the truth of what I was . . . and I couldn't bring myself to face Declan and Evie."

Gabriel swallowed the same knot of shame that rose every time he thought of the archmage he had long considered a vinaro—a brother of different blood. Gabriel had been racked with such ignominy that he had not set foot in Amereen since that night, no matter the times Declan had called for him telepathically.

How could he face the archmage, or worse, Evangeline, knowing what she had suffered because of Zephyr when Gabriel's every breath contributed to the mad king's undying state? The king might be trapped in a Soul Tree, but his heinous reign prevailed, perpetuated by his firstborn spawn —Zenaidus.

And the new Winter Court king did not appear content to stand idle in the face of his father's continued absence. Zion had evidence of his brother's indoctrination into Zephyr's original plans for the invasion of the mage realm and the destruction of the Echelon of Archmages. Since Zenaidus's coronation, not only had the Silverbeaks grown bolder, but the slave-trade cartel continued to flourish—every transaction contributing to the expansion of Zephyr's demon menagerie concealed by an army of animati shieldmakers.

Zenaidus was truly his father's son.

An undying abomination at the helm.

Zephyr's legacy was a self-devouring serpent, a vicious cycle that would destroy everything in its path while it swallowed its own tail. The only way to end the cycle was to cut off the serpent's head—Zephyr needed to die.

A snap of Shyaree's fingers pulled Gabriel from his dark musings.

"I do not believe they would think any less of you," Shyaree signed from the edge of the bed. It was the only time she had moved to communicate since Gabriel had begun his recounting, and it took him a slow blink before he understood her reference.

"Perhaps not," Gabriel muttered. "But if I told Evie and Declan the truth of what I am, I would put them—especially the archmage—in an uncomfortable position, to say the least."

Gabriel had seen firsthand the archmage's desire to destroy the danger Zephyr posed to Evangeline. The gods knew Gabriel had lusted for Zephyr's blood just as much . . . How could he admit that his life had been tied to Zephyr's unending one this whole time?

Gabriel shook his head with a dark, humorless laugh.

Perhaps if it were his life alone, the truth would have been easier to accept and divulge, but Iolanthe was also involved. And when push came to shove, Declan would have no qualms annihilating all who contributed to the threat against his mate. As he should. But Gabriel would do everything within his power to keep his sister from that path of destruction.

Another snap of Shyaree's fingers. *"I do not understand."* Her brows furrowed with wary confusion. *"You hurt just like any other. If you are undying, then why did it take you so long to recover from your injuries?"*

"Apparently all wounds are mine to bear unless they're fatal." That was why he had never suspected he had been altered in any way after his escape from the Winter Court Palace. He'd had to recover from every little cut, scratch, and blister just the same . . .

Tension stiffened his frame. That was not the truth.

Deep down, hadn't he always suspected something was *wrong* since the day he'd survived Ichor Lake? Hadn't he always wondered why death had eluded him despite the live rending of his body?

"How did he make you undying?"

Gabriel forced himself to meet her gaze. Bitterness coated his tongue like ash.

"You don't need to tell me if you don't want to," she added quickly, handling him and his emotions with such care even though her body remained half-changed and her own emotions must be in turmoil. Almost as though she were stubbornly trying to distract herself with him and his dismal past. He was happy to be of service.

"Before Mekari made the draga sul and draga morli, she attempted numerous blood rites to raise her lover from the netherworld." And Zephyr had been desperate and demented enough to experiment with each one, trying to perfect processes the necromancer had proven to be flawed. "According to the texts at Duskhall, *umbralis sanguinem* was one of her many failed attempts. I believe it's the closest to the one Zephyr performed on me."

Shyaree's nose wrinkled. *"Zephyr tried to recreate Mekari's failures?"*

A hollow laugh rattled in Gabriel's throat. "I suppose he thought he could succeed where she had failed. I suppose he did. Somewhat."

Most of Gabriel's memories from those days were nothing but a drunken haze, distorted by the forced consumption of a foul liquor mixed with blood. "If I refused, the guards would pour the liquor down my throat, forcing me to drink until I was intoxicated. Only then would a dark acolyte enter my cell to carve the necromancer's runes into my back."

Shyaree paled. *"They carved into your skin?"*

"I barely remember the pain from the blade, but I'll never forget the feel of Zephyr's fangs in my throat."

He had struggled so much each time Zephyr had torn through his neck with regularity. In an intimate setting, fae couples shared magic by drinking from each other. An act that could also take a darker turn into bloodlust. It had made Zephyr's *visits* even more repulsive, because even as a young boy, he'd understood the king had drawn erotic pleasure from the taste of his blood.

Gabriel wasn't sure if Shyaree was disgusted or outraged, but a shudder racked her frame. "Enough of this," he murmured. "You need a bath. It'll make you feel better."

She hesitated but allowed him to lead her from the bed. She froze at the threshold of his bath chamber. Gabriel followed her gaze to the mirror, where she stared at her reflection, as though paralyzed by the image of her new form.

He scooped her up in his arms, startling her into a gasp. Despite her squirming protests, he carried her inside and set her down upon the changing bench with her back to the mirror, all while squelching the urge to stroke her adorably tufted ears. As though sensing his scrutiny, they flattened.

She lifted her feet from the floor, tucked her knees into her chest, and wrapped her arms around them in an attempt to hide her body under the bathrobe while her long black tail coiled protectively over her ankles.

Gabriel bit down on his inner lip to stifle a smile. He was not sure she would appreciate his thoughts on her current appearance, so he focused on filling the copper tub instead.

As the spigot spouted water, Gabriel went over to a woven basket by the wall and picked up magma stones sourced from Mount Chaos. Pulling magic from the shadows in his vicinity, he channeled it into the stones. Once they began to warm, he placed them in the tub. Personally, he would have stopped with three, but his wildcat enjoyed soaking in ridiculously hot waters, so he added two more. As they waited for the tub to fill and the water to warm, Gabriel leaned against the wall and cleared his throat.

"Do you want to talk about what happened by the river?"

Her lower lip quivered, but she unwound her arms only to sign, *"I'd rather you tell me more about your past. How did you end up in the dungeon in the first place?"*

Gabriel regarded her for a long moment before conceding with a nod. He had never told anyone of his time in the palace dungeon. He never wanted to dwell on the darkest parts of his history, but if she wanted them . . . he would face them.

"Most believe the death of Zephyr's queen, Seraphina, to be the catalyst for the Winter War, but the war began the moment Seraphina delivered her first stillborn." To assuage his queen's dire spirits, Zephyr had demanded a girl child of noble blood to replace the daughter Seraphina had lost. "They took my sister."

Even after all these years, a fresh flicker of rage ignited beneath his breastbone as he spoke those words aloud. His parents hadn't had any choice but to forfeit their daughter or be charged with treason, but as a boy, he had failed to see their reasons.

"I tried to get her back." He had portaled near the Winter Palace and snuck through the palace gates in the guise of a stable boy. He had always been impulsive, but that time his recklessness cost him more than he could afford. When he was caught, the king seemed so impressed by his portal-making abilities that Zephyr decided to *keep* him. Not the way Iolanthe was kept as a daughter.

Gabriel was locked in the bowels of the palace—a dungeon warded with magic that prevented him from portaling out.

"There was another boy in the dungeon with me, but whatever Zephyr tried on him failed, because he died not long after."

That boy had been the lucky one.

Zephyr continued his *experiments* long after Gabriel's cellmate had departed, until one day, it got worse.

Gabriel could almost feel the guards' rough handling as they ripped the shackles from his scabbed and skinny ankles. He had shivered uncontrollably, his body craving the blood liquor that had turned into a repulsive addiction. He remembered begging for it, begging for stupor, but the guards had paid him no heed as they dragged him from the dungeon.

The king had waited for him by the edge of a black mirror lake, hands clasped casually behind his back. Zephyr's long-ago voice echoed in his mind like a ghostly undercurrent rippling beneath the water's deceptively flat surface. "Tell me, my boy . . . can you swim?"

Ugly memories surfaced, the ones he kept tightly locked in the darkest recesses of his mind. The scalding of his lungs as he drowned. Bird-boned fingers clawing from the depths of the lake . . .

The sound of clapping jerked him from the past and back to the present.

Shyaree stared at him with a questioning gaze, her eyes brimming with concern.

Gabriel jerked away from the bath. His proximity to a simple tub of water was enough to hasten the rapid pound in his chest. He drew in a deep, centering breath, and gave her an abridged account of what happened at Ichor Lake, but he could not bring himself to speak of the suffocating terror. The torture of endless drowning. Or the sirens' relentless tearing at his flesh.

"They tossed me back into the dungeons, but the blood rite ceased. The guards stopped forcing the blood-laced liquor on me, the acolytes stopped coming, and so did Zephyr." It should have been a mercy, but the grueling effects of alcohol withdrawal had been bad enough to rival the torture of Ichor Lake.

"I lost all indication of time, until one day, Arkas and Iolanthe stole into the dungeons. Seelie soldiers infiltrated the Winter Palace, and Arkas used that opportunity to sneak into the palace in search of me."

Arkas had always taken his role as housecarl for the Blacksage family very seriously and had timed his rescue with the Seelie invasion. Chaos had created the perfect chance for escape, but fate had different plans. Arkas had always blamed himself for what happened next, but Gabriel knew better.

He had been the one to blame.

Had they not sought to free him, Arkas might have succeeded in freeing Iolanthe that day . . . but they would never know, because palace guards had foiled their escape.

Gabriel had been too slow to run, his body weak from captivity. Arkas and Iolanthe had fought to protect *him*, but they were only children, no match for tenacious guards trying to reinstate order. Gabriel had been pinned to the marble floor when the sharp end of a stray sword slashed Iolanthe in the abdomen.

He would never forget how blood had seeped over her pale-pink dress like a devouring rot, or how her eyes had rounded with shock before her small body crumpled.

"Somehow, Arkas managed to shove the guard off me and drag me through his portal, but we couldn't take Iolanthe with us . . . I should never have left her behind." His voice cracked, brittle and bitter to his own ears. "Zephyr had her warded in the tower. I believe he's bound the largest part, or maybe the most fragile part of his soul in her."

At Shyaree's scrunched brows, Gabriel continued, "Mind, physicality, ability, spirit, and heart. According to the necromancer's texts, those are the five parts to every soul. In order to achieve Deathlessness, Zephyr would have to carve out a piece from each part and replace it with pieces from his anchor to create soulbonds."

A horrified stare. *"Which part did he put in you?"*

"I'm not sure." But he could guess. Gabriel had lost his ability to create blackfire since his time in the dungeons. "I'd wager it was an ability that he took from me . . . but it doesn't matter. I need to cleave the soulbond. I need to cut out what he's put *inside* me. I need . . . " He clenched his fingers. "I need to do the same for Iolanthe. It's the least I can do after all these years."

His little sister had tried to free him, and he had left her to suffer a lifetime of imprisonment. Gabriel squeezed his eyes shut, pounding a fist to his forehead as though he could beat the regret from his past.

A protesting squeak of the spigot reopened his eyes.

Shyaree had left her seat by the bench to turn off the faucet. The bathtub was so full it was one splash from spilling over.

She straightened to face him. If his tale horrified her, she did not show it. *"Why do you speak as though it were your fault that an accident happened?"*

"An accident?" Gabriel slammed a hand against the rim of

the tub. Water sloshed to the floor. "Iolanthe's apparent death would not have occurred had I not been there! The rest of my family would not have perished had I not snuck into the palace in the first place!"

When Gabriel and Arkas had returned to Evenmere, it was only to learn of the devastation of the Blacksage family. His father had stormed the Winter Court Palace at Gabriel's disappearance and demanded his son's return only to be slain in cold blood. Zephyr had claimed treason. Then the iniquitous king had sent slave traders to their lands.

Gabriel's elder brother had died defending their mother and sisters, but Grayson hadn't been able to stop the slave traders from doing their worst.

Gabriel tightened his grip until his knuckles turned white as he sneered at his distorted reflection in the water. His entire family had paid for *his* folly when he alone deserved to die.

It was sheer irony that he had returned, immune to death.

A gentle touch rested upon his back, and Gabriel blinked from the tears blurring his vision. "Do *not* tell me how it's not my fault."

Arkas had done plenty of that over the years, but nothing anyone could say would erase the fact that Gabriel had led death to his family's door. He hit the tub's edge again with enough force to send water onto the slate tiles.

"Do you know what it feels like to look at yourself in the mirror every day only to see the face that has brought about your family's demise?"

Shyaree cupped his face. Her clawed fingers rested in sharp points over his cheek as she sought his attention. But she did not tell him that it was not his fault. She did not try to erase his sins. Instead, her eyes connected with his in a weighty, solemn glance.

"I do understand."

Three simple words and the crushing burden over his chest, while no less heavy, suddenly seemed more bearable. He drew her into his arms and buried his face in the crook of her neck, breathing in the heady scent of her as she stroked soothing hands down his back. This woman, who sought to comfort him when she doubtlessly needed comfort herself.

Gabriel kissed her.

She tasted like a fresh spring after a long drought, and he drank her in like a man dying of thirst. A breathy sigh seeped from her lips into his before she kissed him back with a fervor that pulled a groan from his throat.

Gods, her canines were sharp like fangs.

The notion was so arousing it hardened him to the point of pain, but he managed to keep his control . . . until she produced a purr-like sound that stripped him of all sanity. He delved deeper into her mouth, taking everything she had to give. Solace. Solidarity.

Sweet, sweet oblivion.

His hand roamed beneath her bathrobe to assuage his need for touch, palming her breasts, then his fingers flirted with the deliciously hardened peaks. She arched into him, spurring him on with another breathy purr. His hands wandered lower to cup her rear, inadvertently glancing at the furry end of her tail.

She stiffened like a cat with a yanked tail.

He reluctantly relegated his hands to her hips before rooting for another kiss, but she barred him with one hand to his chest. She stepped away, stiffly drawing her robe back in place as though she hadn't rubbed herself against him just moments ago.

Gabriel reached for her. "I won't touch you there if you don't like it, Shyaree, but please don't pull away from me."

For reasons he could not explain, her rejection so soon after he had just bared the ugliness of his past cut like a knife between his ribs.

She shook her head and shrank further from him. *"I'm sorry. I don't know what I was thinking. We shouldn't be kissing. I am between forms, and I could be . . . "* She cringed. *"I could be venomous."*

He smiled wryly. "You know you couldn't kill me even if you tried."

She kept her head lowered. *"It doesn't matter. I don't want you to see or touch me when I am like this. I feel . . . hideous."*

Gabriel snorted. "Who do you think found you by the river? There's nothing I haven't already seen, darling."

Color darkened her cheeks, and to Gabriel's unending fascination, the scales along her cheekbones *shimmered* as if flecks of glistening gemstones lay beneath her skin. He leaned forward like a man in a thrall, needing to trace his lips against those iridescent scales, but she squirmed and scurried away, wrapping her arms around her chest as though to disappear into herself.

He could not stop the growl from exiting his throat. "You being stuck between forms doesn't make you any less attractive to me."

She stared at him with incredulous eyes while her hands jerked at her sides like a puppet with pulled strings. She tugged at her furry feline ears with offensive disdain. *"This is attractive to you?"* She pointed to the scales on her cheeks and waved her hands at him as though he might have somehow missed her claws. *"And these? You think the snake skin, patchy fur, and these horrendous black claws are* attractive?"

"Do you remember the first time we met, wildcat?" he demanded. "Do you know what I felt when I first saw you?"

Her brows furrowed and she gave a slow, cautious shake of her head.

"Hate," he said, and watched her flinch.

All of a sudden, he itched with an irrational urge to portal away, to spare himself from more vulnerability . . . but he would rather be damned to an eternity in Ichor Lake than allow her to dwell in another moment of misconception.

"I hated you, wildcat." He wet his lips with a nervousness he rarely felt. "From the very first moment I laid eyes on you, I hated you because you made me *want* . . . with such intensity that it frightened me."

Chapter 26

Incredulity hammered in her chest. Shyaree stepped back from him as though to displace her disbelief with distance. She searched his face, looking for falsity, evidence his declaration was nothing more than a charitable platitude.

"I don't want your lies. I don't need your pity."

His mouth was a sober line slashing across his face. "I haven't given you either."

Her fingers itched to hurl out questions to gauge his sincerity, but she only managed a skeptical shake of her head. How could she ever have inspired want in a man, especially one so cavalier, when she had failed to inspire acceptance in her own people?

As if he heard the cynical ruminations of her mind, he bridged the distance between them to catch and cradle her face in his hands. He held her gaze with such earnestness shining from his violet depths that her wits scattered like ash in the wind.

In that moment, all she wanted was to fall into him.

He seemed to sense her desire, because he lowered his head to merge their lips and slipped his tongue into her mouth in a slow and sensual supplication. She sighed into him, wanting to fill every void and crevice that separated them . . . until her claws inadvertently caught his skin. He jerked, but he didn't push her away. He didn't pull back. He continued to plunder her mouth, showing absolutely no care or concern for the venom she could excrete. If anything, he held her even tighter, seeming to sense her urge to bolt.

Balling up her hands to keep her claws covered, she shoved at him with her fists. It was like shoving against a deeply rooted Kilinjiri. It wasn't until she clasped an urgent hand to his cheek that he reluctantly released her lips.

She extricated herself from his arms. *"We can't do this."*

He blinked, his eyes still glazed from ardor. "Why not?"

"You don't mean that." She gestured between them. *"You don't mean this."*

Gabriel was a complex man with a convoluted past and, intuition told her, an even more complicated heart. She would do well to guard her own.

His voice was hoarse. "After all this, you still don't believe me?"

No. The kiss had been a momentary lapse of logic. The notion of Gabriel Blacksage wanting her—*pining* for her—from the very beginning was so preposterous, so utterly absurd that it could not be anything short of a jest. A lie. Every male in her clan had either avoided her like the plague or treated her with passive indifference, but . . . she fidgeted with her hands.

Gabriel had never evaded nor ignored her.

If anything, he had gone out of his way to spar with her in every possible way: through body language, verbal communication, or Handspeak. Her pulse hastened with a sudden realization—his grasp of her mother tongue had improved to startling fluency since the time they'd met.

"*We never got along,*" she added hastily as a reminder, not just for him, but for herself. "*We disliked each other from the beginning.*"

"You disliked me, hmm?" A caustic bark of laughter. "Well, I wouldn't reduce my feelings for you to something so lukewarm. Make no mistake, wildcat. I meant what I said before. I resented you with every fiber of my being. I despised you. I hated the irrepressible want you made me feel. Hated how my eyes were always drawn to you. I didn't want to look at you. I didn't want to be around you. I certainly didn't want to know you, because I feared if I did, you'd make me fucking obsessed." He shook his head with a sardonic laugh. "Then Declan asked me to be your interpreter . . . that bastard."

She took a wary step back until her spine hit the wall. Backing away proved a mistake. It only seemed to trigger his predatory instincts. He caged her between his arms, staring at her steadily like a wolf on the verge of pouncing.

"I thought if I found things to hate about you, I would be safe from your wiles. I didn't want to be your friend, so I gave you every opportunity to *dislike* me. I didn't want to see your smiles, so I worked for your scorn. I didn't want your trust, so I made sure you saw the worst of me. I collected your ire like pearls, and I wore your contempt like a crown." Gabriel shook his head and closed his eyes for a moment. "But the more I looked for things about you to hate . . . the more I found to *want.*"

Something fluttered in her stomach like the brush of tiny, spirited wings, yet years of ingrained insecurity shook her head. "*How could you want me now after seeing what I am capable of with a single bite?*" She pointed to herself in a sweeping gesture. "*How could you want me when I look like this?*"

He hissed. "You just don't get it, do you?"

That was her only warning before his lips descended to hers.

He was not fierce or forceful, but gentle and lingering. He kissed her as though trying to coax truth into her, to convince her with his lips where his words had failed. His hands delved beneath her robe once again to caress her back, stroking strong and sure down her spine without shying from the horrendous protrusion that was her tail.

Racked by both agonizing arousal and debilitating self-consciousness, she angled her rear from his touch, tucking her tail between her legs.

He sighed. "You have nothing to be ashamed of, Shyaree."

Her heart swelled even as she searched his gaze. She doubted him as much as she wanted to believe him. She wanted him to stop just as much as she wanted him to keep going. She wanted escape as much as she wanted to drown in him. She was a molten paradox of unbearable desire and numbing fear . . . waiting . . . just waiting for the moment he would realize she was no prize. So when he drew her bathrobe from her shoulders, she allowed it to pool at her feet, expecting flashes of disgust or disdain to flicker over his face.

She found none.

Instead, a baffling hunger clouded his eyes as his gaze roamed her naked body, as though her polymorphic form were not only pleasing to him but provocative. Arousing.

He spun her around to face the mirror.

Her tail flicked like an awkward whip. The view of her own nude body and his magnificently muscled form framing her back was both titillating and confronting.

She shifted her sight to the ground.

He lifted her chin, gentle but insistent, redirecting her sight to their reflection. "How can you be embarrassed about yourself? Do you see what I see? Gods, just look at you . . . " His voice had lowered to a dark octave as he held her gaze in the mirror. "You are so beautiful, darling . . . you make me ache." He pressed the evidence of his desire into her back. The iron-hard bulge caused her breath to hitch.

She squirmed, but he held her in place by clamping one large hand over her throat and kissing along the curve of her neck. He grazed her sensitive skin with his tongue and teeth while his hand swept over her ribs to her cleavage and splayed possessive fingers over her chest. And in that moment, framed by the misty mirror and cradled in his concupiscent embrace, she felt . . . flawless. Desirable. Beautiful.

A moan rose from her throat, then fresh dampness formed between her legs.

Suddenly the sight of their entwined bodies in the mirror aroused her beyond reason.

She tried to turn around, needing to kiss him the way he was kissing her, to touch him the way he was touching her, but he refused to loosen the hand around her throat.

He kept her in place, keeping their gazes locked through their reflection as he reached for her feline ears. He caressed the furry tips until they twitched. "Beautiful," he whispered, before kissing them both with a soft chuckle. Then he ran one knuckle along the scales on her cheekbones. "Fascinating," he murmured, sparking a new wave of arousal in her core as he replaced his knuckle with his lips. "They look like tiny stars on your skin."

She whimpered, imploring him with her eyes.

A dark, carnal smile graced his face before he finally allowed her to turn. But he did not give her a chance to touch him. He lowered his head to her breasts, breathing the word "perfect," just before he drew one hardened peak into his mouth. He worshipped each breast with equal, meticulous fervor, toying with them with his tongue until she arched into his face shamelessly, gasping with need. When she was certain she was about to go mad, he released her breasts only to reach for her wrists.

Tension returned to her lust-softened limbs.

She could allow herself to believe the pretty words he whispered about her breasts, her panther ears, and her scales . . . but her furred hands? Ghastly. She tried to pull away, but he held her firmly, refusing to free her until he'd kissed each and every pelt-covered knuckle with perplexing ardor.

"So soft." He rubbed the ends of her hideous black claws. "Yet so sharp." He grinned. "Sexy."

His praises spelled her ruin.

Her fingers and thighs clenched in tandem, but he seemed determined to demolish her, because he locked their lips together once more in another soul-stealing kiss before whispering, "You . . . are . . . perfection, Shyaree."

She puddled in his arms.

She was so drunk by his appraisal that she did not realize his hands had snaked down to her rear until he was fondling her tail. No one had ever touched her like this, in this form—she'd had no idea her tail was a highly erogenous area. Every squeeze and stroke of his callused hand sparked arousal up her spine.

"Everything about your current form is just . . . " He groaned into her skin and pressed against her. The insistent bulge in his pants had grown even larger. "Gods, I want to turn you around, spread you over this bench, and fuck you boneless."

"Do it," she signed, emboldened by his desire and the urgent need pulsing between her legs. She was in heat—no question about it. And she no longer wanted to endure it alone. *"Now."*

He paused, as though taken aback. "Really?"

A ridiculous question. Desire was practically dripping down her thighs. She could only nod, but he didn't seem satisfied with her response. He curled a large hand around her throat and squeezed with a firmness just shy of impeding her breath. She wasn't sure if he was trying to dominate or intimidate, but his rough handling only made excitement prickle over her skin. "Tell me, wildcat. Tell me you want me."

"I want you."

His hold loosened only to squeeze again with possessive demand. "My name," he said, staring down at her with rapt anticipation. "I want to see you sign my name."

She lifted her hands with teasing slowness, feeling like a goddess weaving the thread of life as she formed his name with her hands. *"Gabriel. I want you. Only you."*

His eyes darkened, and he gave a lusty growl just before he pounced.

He locked their lips together, plundering her mouth like an intoxicating promise of what was to come while his hands caressed until broken sounds leaked from her. She didn't even know when he had shed his pants, but one moment they were kissing, and the next, the unyielding length of his arousal twitched at her abdomen.

He rumbled at her wide-eyed, open-mouthed assessment and crushed her back against the tiled wall. "Keep looking at me like that, darling, and you'll get it faster than you want it."

He lifted her by her rear, draping her legs over his hips as he rubbed himself teasingly against the cleft of her entrance. A breathy whimper sounded, and it took her a slow moment to realize it came from her.

"Purring for me already?" He grinned, and his voice oozed with male approval.

She would have been mortified, but she was well past caring. She lifted her chin, all but begging for his lips. He obliged. Heartily. Gabriel kissed like a starving man trying to suck out her soul and consume it whole . . . then he pulled back unceremoniously.

She protested with a whine, feeling his sudden distance like an absence of air.

He set her down on the bench with a gleam in his eyes. "Do not deny me this time."

Before she could process his words, he dropped to his knees, spread her legs, and hooked them over his shoulders with deft hands. Her thighs clenched reflexively only to clamp the sides of his head while heat pinched her cheeks at her scandalous position . . . but she couldn't look away.

Wearing a heart-stoppingly roguish grin, he held her gaze while he ran a slow, wicked tongue over the seam of her sex. A gasp shot from her throat just as a groan exited his. "Gods, your taste . . . " The rapture on his face set fire to her veins.

He returned for another torturously slow lick. She bit her bottom lip in a half-hearted attempt to stifle the undignified noises escaping her. Gods above, all she wanted was to roll her hips into his face and beg for more. More . . . More . . . Instead, she kept herself valiantly seated upon the bench, curling both hands to keep her claws covered while he lapped between her thighs like a man with all the patience in the world. Each unhurried swirl of his tongue brought her a little closer to ecstasy, and just as she was at the cusp of shattering, the bastard halted.

She snarled.

Not the least perturbed, he licked his glistening lips with a smoldering smirk. "Tell me again, darling . . . tell me you want me, Shyaree," he demanded, as though her affirmations did to him what his praises did to her.

She did not argue, signing the words swiftly. Impatiently.

His rumbling chuckle jolted through her core. "Good girl . . . " He lowered his head once more, rewarding her with his wicked tongue *and* his wondrous fingers. He had barely started before the climax shot through her with an intensity to liquify her bones.

She slumped helplessly against the wall, legs still dangling over his shoulders. Thurin's wrath . . . Dreamy and dazed with bliss, she did not even realize he had flipped her around until her palms and knees hit the bench. The stone felt icy to her lust-heated skin. Only when he shoved a leg between her knees did she realize what he intended.

"I told you I'd spread you out on this bench and fuck you boneless, or have you forgotten?" The vulgarity of his words only thrilled her, while fresh anticipation tingled deep in her bones as he positioned her rear with a rough stroke along her tail. Yes, yes, yes . . . He nudged into the seam of her entrance, and the breath left her lungs.

Her body tensed. Despite the eagerness of her damp flesh, he was large enough that his invasion bordered on pain. He did not seem to notice. His hips pistoned with another shallow pump that drove him a little deeper.

She winced. Gods above, he was . . . enormous.

He groaned. "Gods, you are . . . exquisite."

Another roll of his hips, and her eyes watered. But before she could express her discomfort, he slammed into her with an overeager thrust that wrung a breathless scream from her throat.

He froze at her back. "Shyaree?"

She whimpered. He muttered a curse and began retreating, but she held him in place, clenching and unclenching her muscles, trying to accustom herself to his size.

"Why didn't you tell me?" he growled. "Fuck, I'm such an idiot."

She did not think her inexperience made the act any less pleasurable for him . . . but she could not know for certain.

Arranged couples often mated long before husungai, but Hesok had avoided touching her. She tried to catch a glimpse of Gabriel's expression over her shoulder, but he did not give her a chance to turn around. He was already rubbing hands down her spine, planting kisses along her shoulder, massaging her hips as though to relieve her. "I'm so sorry, Shyaree . . . I should have asked."

More kisses rained on her back. She squirmed with renewed need. In a few drawn-out breaths, she wriggled her rear restlessly, seeking more friction. Her heat was relentless. He seemed to understand, because he rolled his hips in measured pumps, slowly but surely sliding back into the clasp of her core. "That's it, darling . . . " He grunted. "Just a little more . . . "

The initial pain gave way to pleasure, and she angled her hips, greedy for every breath-stealing inch of him. When he sheathed himself to the hilt, her name tumbled from his lips like a choked prayer.

"Good girl. You take me so well . . . "

His praises ignited almost as much pleasure as the feel of him stretching inside her.

He placed a hand over her nape and shoved her lower until her cheek kissed the bench. Then he lifted her hips higher and spread her legs farther apart. Gods above, the new position took him impossibly deeper, and he was hitting places she'd never known existed in her body. All she could do was cling to the bench, scraping her claws into the stone while she took every toe-curling thrust. More unseemly noises wormed up her throat.

He used her with such vigor that the top of her head collided with the wall.

She barely noticed the knock, but he drew her up from the bench with a muttered curse, withdrawing from her sheath.

"Damn it . . . need to stop hurting you."

She huffed. Gods help her, if he stopped now, she was most certainly going to hurt *him.*

He spun her around, wisely pacifying her with a devouring kiss before shoving her back into the wall. He lifted her bottom, guiding her legs around his hips like a man who had done this a thousand times before—the inkling made her hiss. But her agitation dissolved the moment he found his way back into her in one mind-blanking plunge.

She barely remembered to guard her claws before he began pounding her mercilessly into the wall, claiming her to a ruthless and relentless tempo that stoked her heat to a raging inferno capable of consuming them both. Her head lolled from side to side; her mouth gasped the silent shape of his name as she begged for the release only he could give.

She came with a breathless cry, with her head arched back while she spasmed around him in a wave of liquid heat. When she regained her faculties, she was winded, limp, and blissfully euphoric, but still, he showed no signs of slowing. If anything, her unraveling had only seemed to spur him into a frenzy.

She ran a hand down his powerful back, marveling at the bunching and flexing muscles, seemingly tireless as he attempted to grind her into the wall.

A harsh litany of Faerian escaped him. She did not understand the ragged words, but the rapture in his tone was enough to undo her.

"Fuck, Shyaree . . . I—" With a lusty growl, he dragged her head back by a fistful of hair to expose her throat. She sucked in a single, shuddering breath before shadows slithered over her sight like a silken blindfold.

Sharp fangs sank into her neck.

The unexpected jolt of pain and the feel of him drawing from her throat sent her hurtling anew into an abyss of pleasure. This time, she shattered so violently that pinpricks of white splintered across her vision like falling stars streaking across the darkest night.

He came with his lips still fused to her neck, his deep-throated growl vibrating into every fiber of her being. Uncontrollable shivers racked her frame, but it wasn't until she opened her eyes that she realized she wasn't just trembling from the aftershocks of pleasure . . . but the actual cold.

A brisk wind whispered against her sweat-slicked skin.

She was no longer vertically pinned to the unforgiving wall of Gabriel's bath chamber, but crushed beneath him, staring over his shoulder into a star-studded sky. Her back pressed into an uneven and scratchy plane. A dazed glance around showed they were lying upon an open field laden with rustling grasses and waving wildflowers.

Still drowsy with pleasure but unnerved from the sudden change of environment, she patted his back in alarm. Gabriel rolled off her with a reluctant grunt. He glanced up, and the ensuing lines pinching his forehead told her he was equally befuddled.

"What in Ozenn's blood . . . ?"

He pushed to his knees. Despite her disorientation, her mouth dried at the sight of his semierect form, but somehow she managed to control her limbs.

"What happened? How are we here?"

He speared a hand through his moon-kissed hair, ruffling the already disheveled strands. "I must have portaled us here."

She stared at him in bafflement until a flush darkened the tips of his ears. *"Why? Where is this place?"*

"I . . . " He blew out a sheepish breath. "It was an accident."

Accident? Before she could make sense of his words, he distracted her with a wandering gaze over her nude form—not in lust, but wonderment. "Darling . . . you've changed."

She glanced down at herself. Only then did she notice her

missing claws. Her furless forearms. She ran her tongue over her teeth and felt blunt canines.

She blinked up at him in surprise.

"I felt it happen while I was drinking from you." He scooped her up from the ground, tenderly picking a piece of grass from her hair before nuzzling into her neck. He lapped at her throat as though to soothe the spot he had bitten. "The taste of your blood and the feel of you coming around me . . . I just lost control." He looked almost abashed, his ears angling with chagrin. "This is where I sometimes come to sketch."

She twisted from his embrace with the intent of finagling more information about their new surroundings but winced at the soreness between her thighs.

He noticed immediately. "Are you all right? Did I hurt you?" He tightened his arms around her. "Did I scare you with the bite? I didn't mean—"

She pressed her lips against his to hush him. She'd *changed*, and for once, it hadn't hurt. In fact, she hadn't even felt it. She wrapped her arms around him to show him she didn't mind his roughness or his bite. In fact, she was thrilled. She wasn't sure what blooding meant to the fae, but a bite in the neck was a part of husungai. Only mates bit each other in the throat during mating . . . Could it be the same for the fae?

Did Gabriel think of her as a . . . mate?

A conflagration of wings fluttered in her stomach. While she mustered the gumption to question his bite, he formed a portal and took them back to his bedchamber. He placed her on the bed, crawled in after her, and began planting soft kisses wherever he found skin.

"Did I hurt you, wildcat?" he repeated while he rubbed her crown where it had hit the wall with one hand and cupped between her legs with another. "I can be such a brute."

She wriggled against him, chewing her bottom lip with a

small smile. *"I think I may be developing a taste for brutish behavior . . . "*

His lips curved in a soul-stealing grin as he climbed on top of her. A finger slipped into the cove between her thighs still damp and quivering from his use, igniting a wave of renewed anticipation over her skin. He dropped his head, fusing his lips to hers while she clenched her muscles against his finger, drawing him deeper into her clasp, when an intrusive rap halted them both.

"Gabe?" Malakai's muted voice carried through the bedchamber door, followed by a stream of Faerian. Gabriel pulled away from her lips, grating out a harsh reply with enough irritation to mirror her own impatience.

There was a pause before the Red Knight retorted with more Faerian, ending distinctly with the name "Arkas."

Chapter 27

Gabriel sidestepped a creaky stair as he made his way to the lowest level of the Blacksage Manor. It reeked of mildew, rust, and death.

He had established the Red Guild on the back of assassination and espionage services, but he had done little to restrict other periphery offerings. Apart from the slave-trade cartel and any involvement that might pose a conflict of interest to the guild's existing allies, everything was fair game. Physical and mental torture, information extraction, incarceration, and lengthy executions were all in a Red Knight's repertoire, so long as their patrons had the coin to fund it. And the dark deeds were often performed in the sprawling space that had once served as an innocuous wine cellar. While casks of wine and barrels of mead continued to occupy it, the cellar was also outfitted with iron cages, metal hinges, wall manacles, and other unsavory tools and devices to break flesh and bone as well as spirits.

The imperturbable Caspian typically manned the torture chamber, and he meted out the grisliest acts with nary a blink of an eye. But today even the guild's finest torturemaster sounded discomfited.

" . . . doesn't mean you had the right to do what you did!" Caspian's reprimand floated up the stairs. "Ozenn's blood, Arkas. It's a wonder he brought you back at all!"

Chains rattled against stone, then came Arkas's heated protest. "What else could I have done? They said she was in heat! She could have changed into that abomination at any moment! She was—"

"The one who saved your life," Gabriel interjected as he stepped into the musty chamber with a calm that belied the maelstrom churning in his chest. Hesok and his men had slaughtered him, or thought they had, and would have done the same to Arkas had Shyaree not changed and attacked them.

Arkas sat on the ground, both hands propped over his knees, one ankle shackled to the stone wall. The shackles wouldn't have contained someone with the ability to vaporize, but Arkas did not possess that skill. He was a master with black-fire and portalmaking, but little else. He narrowed his gaze at Gabriel's entry, not the least remorseful. "She was the one who endangered us in the first place."

Gabriel started forward with a snarl.

Caspian barred him, both hands raised in a placating gesture. "Arkas has overstepped his bounds, but surely you're not going to let some animati woman come between—"

Gabriel's glower silenced him. Caspian tightened his lips, lowered his hands, and retreated to hover by the door.

Without another word, Gabriel plowed a fist into his cousin's face. Blood welled from a crack on his lower lip, but Arkas merely lifted his chin to meet Gabriel's eyes with an unre-pentance that sharpened his fangs.

"Why did you do it?" Gabriel hissed. "Why would you betray me?"

"I was trying to protect you!"

"Horseshit!" Gabriel's fist collided with his former second's gut. Arkas doubled over and grunted. "Do you have so little respect for me that you've forgotten who I am? I don't need your fucking protection!"

"Respect?" Arkas spat out a mouthful of blood, his split lip curling. "Did you show me or the guild any respect by keeping your little secrets?"

Gabriel clenched and unclenched his fingers, fists trembling with rage. "Don't bring the guild into this. It has nothing to do with the guild and everything to do with your personal vendetta against Shyaree!"

"It has everything to do with the guild! You've been remiss in your duties. Disappearing for days . . . and for what? An abomination who has you believing Iolanthe is somehow alive?"

Gabriel hissed. "Iolanthe *is* alive. I've kept it a secret because I knew exactly how you'd react—irrationally! And you've just proven me right."

Arkas stared hard at him before shaking his head. His response came out measured. Wary. "I went to Duskhall Castle, Gabe. I checked the tower. There was no one there. No servants. No lonely girl locked up. The place is *deserted* . . . as it has been since the day Zephyr went missing from the battle with the archmage."

Gabriel frowned. "What are you talking about? I know what I saw! Iolanthe—"

Arkas looked at him with such concern and conviction that a miasma of bewilderment crept into Gabriel's chest. "You haven't been acting like yourself since a year ago. The constant disappearances . . . the drinking." He paused, as if choosing his next words carefully. "I don't know what's happened, but I think you're . . . confused. I know you miss her deeply and you blame yourself for what happened . . . but whatever you're doing to help that animati female on that godsforsaken mountain isn't going to bring your sister back. Shyaree is clearly using you. I wouldn't be surprised if she's been conspiring with Zion."

Gabriel took a step back. "That is preposterous! Duskhall is running at full staff. I know what I saw."

Arkas only stared, the furrows between his brows further compounding Gabriel's fury. Worse, Caspian was beginning to look at him with the same shade of concern—as though Gabriel had suddenly become a madman.

"I've been watching Zion and his comings and goings at Duskhall for an entire year. Iolanthe has been held captive in that tower. Whether you believe it or not, Zephyr had done things to her. Experiments . . . " Gabriel shook his head, unable to articulate Zephyr's experiments had also been performed on himself. "As I said before, the prophecy states that Shyaree is the key to the draga morli. Iolanthe's freedom. And you nearly killed her with your deceit."

Arkas's lips flattened to a seam before he snapped. "What is this prophecy? Why haven't we heard of it until now?"

Gabriel ground his molars. "I didn't share it because it's none of your fucking business, Arkas! You help me run the guild, not my personal life!"

"Are you even listening to yourself, Gabe? This all started a year ago when you began spying on Zion! The same day you told me to take Shyaree home from the mage realm . . . Don't you think the timings are too much of a coincidence? I've never—"

"You betrayed me," Gabriel said flatly. Nothing Arkas said could justify the treachery or turn back time. Nothing could restore the broken faith between them. "Shyaree has done nothing to you, but you've hurt her again and again with your unfounded fears. And for what?"

Arkas flinched. "I've failed you and your family over and over. I can't let that happen again."

"What in Ozenn's blood are you talking about?"

"I was born to *protect* you and your family, Gabe. The Blacksages are my wards. I've already failed with Iolanthe. She died under my watch. And Rebekah's deceit nearly got you killed! Did you think I'd stand by and watch history repeat itself?"

"Rebekah?" Humorless laughter escaped Gabriel's throat. His last serious lover had been the Den's housekeeper before she'd showed him she was inclined to do more on the bed than change his sheets. Gabriel had been content with her. Happy, even. Had she chosen him for a mate, he would have accepted. Rebekah was as dainty as a bouquet of freshly picked spring flowers and just as sweet. Never had she contested or challenged him in any way. Never had she defied and driven him to the brink of his sanity, caused him to lose control of his magic . . .

"Shyaree is *nothing* like Rebekah," Gabriel said.

Rebekah had used him for safety and shelter, coaxed him into a false sense of security before betraying him with a Silverbeak. She had let her lover into the Den. The ambush would have cost Gabriel his life had he not been undying. Rebekah had no qualms about betraying him . . . while his wildcat wouldn't leave him even to save her own life.

"No, she isn't," Arkas agreed with a snide sneer. "Shyaree is far, *far* more insidious. Rebekah may have broken your trust, but that animati female could have been your end."

Gabriel stared at the other man with undisguised disgust. "You have no understanding of who and what she is! You have no right to judge her . . . No right to try to take her from me."

Rage simmered to a boil. "You have no fucking idea what you've done."

He held a knife to Arkas's throat before his cousin could utter a response.

Caspian moved forward in his periphery.

Gabriel narrowed his eyes. "If you have a problem with how I run this guild, then you should leave it. Now."

Caspian's jaw worked, but he stormed from the cellar without another word. No Red Knight would dispute or defend deceit—not even for one of their own.

Gabriel trailed the tip of the knife along the curve of the traitor's throat. "I'm sure you recall what happened to Rebekah . . ."

Arkas's only reaction was a visible swallow.

Gabriel ran the knife down the other man's pectoral, positioned it exactly where a single shove upwards with moderate force would slide the blade between the ribs to puncture the beating heart beneath. The thought of plunging the knife into a man he'd regarded as a vinaro caused a physical pang in his chest . . . but how could he forgive such mutiny? He dug the blade a little deeper into flesh until blood trickled.

"Now," he said in a quiet voice that belied the insidious anger thrumming within his veins. "What do you think I'll do to you?"

Gabriel returned to find his bed empty of Shyaree. A quick survey of the bath chamber and his heart nearly ratcheted from his chest. She lay in a trembling heap on the ground, her bathrobe discarded, while blood stained the rim of the tub and swirled on the floor.

"Shyaree!" He rushed to her side and picked her up, noting

the blood on her fingers—her claws. The scales had returned to her skin, along with her feline ears, but her tail was noticeably missing, and so was the pelt that had coated her knuckles. In fact, a lot more scales covered her body this time, swaths of glistening mosaic pieces patterning her torso and hips.

"What happened? Why have you changed again?"

Her body trembled like a leaf blown by the wind. She whimpered before crawling to him and burying her face in his chest with a muffled sob.

"What happened, Shyaree? Why is there so much blood?" he demanded again even as a slew of sickening thoughts assailed him—visions of his own men breaking in to attack her under his own roof. "Did someone come in here? Did they hurt you?"

She pulled away from his chest to shake her head while a sobbing hiccup escaped her lips. She lifted shaking hands but made no discernible signs. She seemed too overwhelmed to handspeak.

Ignoring his own rampaging emotions, he stayed on the ground and held her, whispering soft reassurances into her ear. After what felt like an age, she finally pulled away to sign.

"I tried to change . . . I thought if I could shift into my human form without pain, perhaps I could change into my pantherai." Her face crumpled again. *"I thought I could do it, but I can't . . . It hurt."* Fresh tears streamed down her face as she gestured down at her leg. Only then did he realize two of the toes on her right foot were missing . . . A foot that was contorted as though it couldn't quite decide if it wanted to be a human foot or a panther paw. He inspected her left foot where her five toes remained pristine, tipped with perfectly curved claws.

Now he was beginning to understand the full breadth of her fears of polymorphism—every change was fluid. Indeterminate. She had no control over the morphing of her body.

"Dapa was right," she signed tearfully. *"I should never succumb to it—I should never even try."*

Gabriel gently stroked the damp tendrils from her face. He didn't ask if she had attempted to shift back to her human form. Of course she had.

"Shyaree . . . " He pulled her close for a kiss. "You changed back before, and you can do it again." In an attempt at levity, he pulled on a suggestive smirk as he raised a brow. "I'll be happy to help you."

A small smile ghosted over her lips, but tears continued to well.

"What else bothers you, darling?"

She shook her head, squeezing her eyes shut. It would have been easy to take her disinclination to further express herself at face value, but he knew there was more eating at her. And whatever chewed at her consumed him.

"Are you hurting?" He caressed her arm. "Where does it hurt?"

A listless shake of her head.

"Are you worried about Arkas?" He swallowed. "He won't come near you again."

Gabriel hadn't been able to bring himself to mete out death, but he had left the traitor bruised and bloodied in the cellar. Arkas had to be dealt with—but he refused to do it with anger churning in his heart.

Small frown lines furrowed her brow as though she'd already forgotten about the second-in-command.

"Is it about . . . Hesok? And Mekari's blood?" he prodded gently.

The tensing of her jaw told him he was right. Her fingers curled before she finally conceded. *"I failed Reiken. The curse will eventually turn him rogue. I have doomed them all. My mother. Father. Reiken's brides, and now my brother. My whole family."* She didn't bother hiding her sobs this time, and her shoulders shook. *"I killed Hesok and his warriors . . . the clan will have my head for that."*

"Not if I can help it," Gabriel murmured roughly into her hair as he held her trembling frame close. He kissed away the offending tears, anxious to dry them. "Everything will be all right. Everything will be all right," he repeated again and again as he stroked her back until he was no longer sure if he was placating her . . . or himself.

Another bout of torrid lovemaking was all his wildcat needed to shift back into her human form. It must have been painless, because she didn't seem to notice her own change, and Gabriel didn't mention it. She seemed utterly spent. He didn't have to cuddle her long before she fell into slumber. Then he slid out of bed, pulled on his clothes, gathered his supplies, and stepped through a portal into darkness and the stench of guano. He immediately stooped to his knees in anticipation of startled bats.

He was *not* taking another dunk in the lagoon.

He had come prepared this time, with an oil lamp in his hand and climbing equipment strapped to his back. As he'd expected, a high-pitched chittering sounded at his sudden presence, followed by a rush of wings as the bats were triggered to flight. He held his lamp up to the walls, searching for brass braziers, but found none. Instead of smooth walls, he found rough and unpolished rock. The hairs on his skin prickled as he surveyed his surroundings.

This was not the mausoleum.

There was nothing etched into the walls—no stone lintels or ornate entablature. No intricately carved friezes, no engraving or inscription on the walls. Nothing. He was standing in a natural cavern, with rock protrusions dripping from the ceiling and stalagmites where columns once stood. He followed the curved walls, searching for the seven passageways, but in vain.

Frustrated, he cast another portal, picturing the necromancer in her enchanted eternal sleep upon the stone altar. If he portaled himself straight into a flooded grotto, so be it . . . Only he stepped back into the same spot. Gabriel held his lamp up, taking in the unremarkable cave with the heavy weight of disappointment crushing his chest. The inscription upon the barrier flashed across his mind: *The moon only shines once into the same grove.*

Finally, he understood what that meant—no one found Mekari's tomb twice.

Ozenn's blood. He had failed her in every *possible* way . . .

Gabriel sagged to the ground, and in that moment, he was exactly where he deserved to be—shrouded in darkness, defecation, and desolation—as he stared listlessly at the lamplight flickering in the darkness.

Then his lips parted—a sudden epiphany.

"Why didn't you tell me this sooner?" The archmage of Amereen wore no discernible expression, but his voice dripped with ice and ire.

Despite the flames crackling in the marble fireplace, the archmage's office felt unseasonably cool. The temperature had taken a progressive nosedive since the start of Gabriel's explanation, as though he had brought winter along with his tale.

Gabriel tightened his lips. "And what could you have done?"

"You could have brought Reiken here to begin with. Evangeline may be able to help with his . . . condition."

"Even a Jilintree doesn't have the power to break a curse. There was nothing Evangeline or you could have done to help Shyaree on her quest . . . " He rubbed frustrated fingers between his brows. "Is a little blood really too much to ask?"

Declan Thorne might not have been blessed by the god of death and the goddess of life, but he was the only person in known history to have fallen into Arksana, the heart of the goddess of light, *twice*—and survive. The mages believed every ascension was a blessing from Railea herself, and Gabriel was desperate enough to give Shyaree the next best possible alternative to Mekari's blood.

A brief pause. Viridian eyes skated over him like a wash of frost. "You think you can march in here, interrupt my day, and demand my blood when you've avoided me for a full turn of the sun? You ignored all my calls, Gabriel."

Gabriel met Declan's icy irritation with blistering scorn. "It may surprise you, Lord Archmage, but I have other things to do than pander to your every whim. Besides, I've sent Arkas to you every time."

"Your second-in-command is a fine portal maker and spymaster . . . " The archmage shifted near imperceptibly in his seat. "But he isn't your replacement."

A lump formed in Gabriel's throat. "Missed me, did you?"

The bastard didn't even blink. "About as much as a horse misses the fly buzzing around his ears."

Gabriel's lips twisted. "Yet here you are, making a mountain out of the molehill of my absence."

The temperature in the room grew impossibly cooler.

Gabriel sighed. Vaguely he wondered if his wildcat had

awoken, if she was searching for him. He should have left her a note. He glanced at the archmage's implacable countenance and tensed his jaw. He would have gotten to his knees and begged, but pleading would annoy the archmage more than persuade him. No, Declan Thorne was most comfortable dealing in transactions and bargains.

"What can I offer you in exchange for a vial of your blood?"

Declan leaned back in his seat, studying him for a long moment before he asked, "What are you really after, Gabriel? We both know you care nothing for Reiken or the animati. And as memory serves . . . " The hint of an utterly uncharacteristic and insufferable smirk touched his lips. "You did not particularly get along with Shyaree. What changed?"

Gabriel scowled. "When did you become so nosy?"

Declan arched a discerning brow, and Gabriel heaved out an exhale. "She has been warming my bed. Does that make my motivations more believable to you?"

If the archmage was surprised, he did not show it. "Is that the reason you were so . . . preoccupied last year?"

"So you *do* miss me."

Gabriel could have sworn the bastard rolled his eyes before insisting, "If you want my blood, then tell me, why are you helping her or her brother?"

Gabriel glanced to the fireplace. Evangeline was certainly a bad influence on the archmage. Before her, the archmage would never have been interested in his personal affairs with a *woman*. "I . . . "

Why was the question so hard to answer?

He wanted to help Shyaree create her curse-breaking elixir, but it was no longer for the sole reason of fulfilling a bargain. No, the answer was far more complicated and strangely simple: He wanted to see her happy. He wanted the spark back in her eyes. He wanted—needed—to give her hope . . .

Only to snuff it all out on the impending night of the blood moon.

Sickness spread over his innards like grease, and for one harrowing moment, Gabriel wanted to reveal the true extent of his motivations to the man he had long regarded as a vinaro. Declan would not condone his search for the draga morli, while Evangeline would balk at the prophecy and Shyaree's role as the blood sacrifice. Perhaps Evie would be angered enough to entomb him in a Soul Tree the way she had Zephyr . . .

Then Shyaree would be safe.

But Iolanthe would forever be imprisoned. Zephyr would continue to live, and the Balvaris reign would persist. Nothing would ever change.

"I don't want to see all our effort from the past few weeks go to waste," Gabriel said finally.

Emerald eyes pinned him in place, and Gabriel was suddenly aware that the archmage could scour his mind telepathically for the truth if he wanted. Instead, Declan murmured, "Shyaree . . . she is well?"

"She is *safe.*" For now.

The archmage nodded. "This is the first I've heard of the curse-breaking elixir. I do not know if my blood is a fit substitute for the necromancer's, but if you think there is a chance"—Declan unrolled his shirtsleeve to reveal a forearm etched with golden glyphs and stretched it over the table—"then you will have it."

Wordlessly, Gabriel handed the archmage a blade and the empty vial.

The archmage cut himself and filled the vial without dripping a single drop on the table. His skin was already sealed by the time he handed Gabriel the stoppered vial. No creature in the five realms healed as quickly as an archmage.

Gabriel clutched it and spoke past a throat thick with emotion. "Thank you."

He pushed from his seat, but before he could take his leave, the archmage asked, "Do you remember the time you confronted me about confining Evangeline to the castle?"

Gabriel narrowed his eyes at the recollection. "What about it?"

He had gone fist to fist with the archmage, and while he had given as good as he'd gotten, he'd ended up in the castle's infirmary for *weeks*, while the bastard had pretty much healed from his wounds the same day.

An infinitesimal smile on Declan's lips, but his words were wholly unexpected. "I allowed my insecurities to dictate my actions, and it nearly cost me Evangeline. You were right, you know. The truth hurts." Wryness bled into his words. "Facing it hurt even more, but it was worth it."

Gabriel could only nod.

He understood what Declan was alluding to, but Gabriel's truth wouldn't set him free. No. His truth demanded her blood and her sacrifice. His truth was as dark and deviant and twisted as his irredeemable soul. Facing it wouldn't just hurt—it would destroy him.

Chapter 28

"How did the two of you get a Tribe elder's permission in the first place?" Dapa Jetossi asked, hovering over Shyaree with circumspection shining in his eyes.

His gaze darted every so often to her guildmaster, who stood by the window of her brother's hut, casually looking outside. Gabriel gave no visible indication of hearing Dapa Jetossi's query, much less intention to respond. He had been largely silent since the moment they'd arrived at her clan, allowing her to handspeak to her people and even to explain her disappearance and his forbidding presence. He intervened only when her clansmen had attempted to herd her from his sight, which had proven to be a very bad idea.

Gabriel had almost severed the arm of a warrior who'd tried to keep him outside the shieldmaker's walls while they took Shyaree into Reiken's hut. He insisted on keeping close to her side, which was not only reassuring, but heartening. He was clearly intent on keeping her safe. Of course, he needed her safe for the sake of her blood. But a part of her now believed his protection went beyond the terms of their bargain.

When Gabriel had first abducted her, all she'd wanted was to escape and return home. And now that she was finally back, she was not eager to stay. Could things have changed for him as well?

Shyaree took her time pouring another dribble of elixir into her twin's lax mouth before she carefully set the jar on the ground and responded.

"We didn't need an elder's permission to pass the wall. Gabriel is a portal maker."

Dapa Jetossi looked aghast. "You went up Thurin's Mountain . . . unauthorized?"

Shyaree could only shrug. *"At least now I have the curse-breaking elixir."*

Or at least, she hoped she did.

Gabriel had returned last night with a vial of the archmage's blood to replace the necromancer's. While Shyaree remained skeptical, she was enlivened given Mekari's tomb was no longer accessible to them. At this point, she was desperate enough to try anything, and Gabriel's rationale made sense.

The archmage had survived ascension twice—and what was a mage's ascension if not a blessing from Railea? According to lore, Arksana was the mage realm's version of Thurin's Mountain.

"If the Tribe Elders find out about your illicit entry into Thurin's Mountain, our clan will be shamed!"

"As shamed as we would be without a primus?" Shyaree countered.

Dapa Jetossi shook his head, but he said nothing else as he watched Shyaree feed a little more of the elixir into Reiken's unconscious form. Apparently, her brother's episodes had escalated, and he had been kept sedated with huntersbane for days now. Shyaree hoped she hadn't returned too late . . . and she prayed to Thurin the elixir would work. Her mother's song had given no instructions for the concoction, and Shyaree could only prepare it the way she'd been taught to do every other elixir. Through the distillation of the ingredients down to their essences.

"Hesok, Joyoh, and Palik went in search of you," Dapa Jetossi murmured after a long silence.

Shyaree tensed, but she did not glance up from her task. She kept her hands steady as she fed small sips down Reiken's throat.

"Did you come across them on the Mountain?"

Shyaree shook her head, and the clan elder sighed.

"They have been gone for a few days now."

"Thurin's Mountain is fraught with danger. Perhaps they encountered some trouble on the way up," Gabriel said coolly without glancing over.

His interjection in fluent Animatish only served to tighten Dapa Jetossi's lips. The clan elder crouched beside Shyaree, pitching his voice to her ears.

"You have committed a great folly, daughter of Baleen."

Shyaree glanced up with a frown. *"I am only trying to save my brother, who happens to be your primus."*

The clan elder shook his head again, censure oozing from every line of his time-weathered face. "The fae will not make you a good lifemate."

The jar of elixir nearly dropped from her hand.

Dapa Jetossi sniffed, his lips curling. "It is obvious you are in heat. And I can smell him all over you." Because he was not wrong, an entirely different kind of heat washed over Shyaree's cheeks.

"Hesok will not forgive and forget this betrayal easily," he added.

"What I choose to do is none of Hesok's business," she signed. *"If you forgot, I have forsaken him."*

"Foolish girl. You are animati. Do you think the fae will keep you by his side forever? One day you will find yourself abandoned, and you will regret forsaking the warrior who should have been your lifemate for the likes of"—a leery glance in Gabriel's direction—"that."

Shyaree pinched her lips together, but she gave no response.

She had no regrets about forsaking Hesok—or leaving him to rot somewhere on Thurin's Mountain—but she could not ignore the niggling truth in the rest of Dapa Jetossi's words. She was animati, and Gabriel was fae.

He could portal out of her life as easily as he'd portaled into it.

Gabriel might be eager to comply with her every wish in bed so far . . . but how long would that last? A sinking sensation filled her gut. She had exactly seven more days till the blood moon. Seven more days until their bargain ended and he no longer needed her.

So when she was done feeding her twin the elixir, she turned to Gabriel, needing to be in his arms for as much of the next seven days as possible.

"Did it work?" Gabriel asked.

"We won't know until some time has passed, but at the very least, his skin is no longer scalding. Will you bring me back in a couple of days to check on him?"

An unreadable emotion flitted across his expression, but he nodded. "Should we go home now?"

Home. Shyaree swallowed the unwarranted surge of giddiness at his choice of words.

She fidgeted with her fingers before signing on a whim. *"Do you have time to take me someplace else?"*

Water flirted with her toes.

Shyaree encouraged the waves, splashing with her feet as she relished the sensation of wet sand shifting beneath her. She drew in a greedy breath to fill her lungs with as much brine-laced air as they could contain, wishing she could hold on to this moment forever.

She exhaled slowly, reluctantly, and sighed. The Aesagi Sea that bordered her mother's village was exactly as her dapa had described. Vast and unending, it stretched into a resplendent sheet of turquoise and teal, glimmering all the way to the end of the world. What would it be like to swim to the lip, where the sky kissed the sea?

She meandered forward, enchanted by the sighing waves.

Could one truly cross the curtain of the Abyss and enter the next realm? Or would one fall off the edge of the horizon?

Wrapped in wondering, Shyaree missed the mischievous swell of the sea. The waves lapped at her ankles, seeping up the hem of her pants. She gasped at the cold. She danced a little jig until a chuckle sounded at her back, washing a wave of desire down her spine.

She whirled to face her guildmaster, who hovered just shy of the shoreline, firmly planted where the waves were one lick away from his feet, watching her with avid eyes. She beckoned him over.

"I prefer to keep my feet dry, wildcat." He narrowed his eyes at the rolling wavelets as though daring them to blaspheme his boots. He never had told her the full details of Ichor Lake. But whatever the mad king had done to him there had to be traumatizing.

Shyaree strolled back to him until they were toe to toe.

Emboldened by the fact that there was no one around, she

stepped out of her pants with a coquettish smile. *"Are you sure, guildmaster? Because I'm going for a swim."*

His throat worked, but his lips remained sealed.

She didn't press him again.

She slowly unbuttoned her tunic and dropped it to the sand. Then she peeled off her undergarments. When she wore nothing but her skin, she shook out her hair, turned around, and sauntered back into the sea.

She only had seven days left with this man.

Every night while he pounded her into the mattress, he whispered Faerian into her ears—melodic, husky words wrapped in passion that tingled down her spine. Incomprehensible words. He worshipped her body, gave her indescribable pleasure, and groaned her name every time he came . . . yet he made no promises for the future. No declarations of love.

He knew she was in heat. He was only indulging her while their bargain lasted.

She had no illusions of what would happen after the night of the blood moon. The moment he got the draga morli, he would send her home. She had no place in the Den, no place in his life. Perhaps it was a selfish urge borne of pride, but she wanted to leave him with a memory he would cherish when she was no longer in his bed.

And if it was a positive one to counteract his fear of the water—all the better.

She was waist-deep in the clear, crystalline sea when she turned back. She chuckled. Gabriel paced the shoreline like a surly wolf who very much wanted what he saw but couldn't quite get past the barrier of the waves.

She was wading back toward him in hopes of coaxing him in when he did something extraordinary. He unbuckled his baldric. He flung the leather sheath to the shore before shrugging out of his shirt to reveal mouthwatering slabs of muscle.

Then he unbuckled his belt.

When he finally shed his pants, her mouth had gone dry, and it took every iota of her self-control not to wade from the waters and wrap herself around his magnificent form.

Instead, she stayed where she was, stretched out a hand, and waited for his approach.

Gabriel had never experienced jealousy of an inanimate entity before. Now he was not only leery of the waves, but envious of their watery embrace of Shyaree's nude and nubile form.

Spurred by a need to touch her, he shed his clothes and managed a small step forward. Then another. Foamy seawater swirled at his ankles as though testing the taste of his skin. His pulse quickened, and it wasn't for ardent reasons. But the sea seemed to sense his hesitation, because every surge grew milder, almost like the sea was calming itself to lure him in. He swept his gaze over the shimmering expanse, and his heart tightened involuntarily as he searched for insidious shadows that might lurk beneath. Nothing but clear water and warm sand and . . . Shyaree.

He focused on her, and the tightness began to ease.

She bobbed less than ten paces away, and he ventured further despite the incessant gnawing beneath his breastbone, enthralled like a sailor by a siren's song. Except Shyaree was no sinister flesh-eating creature, nor did she sing. Her beaming smile worked as her bait; her delight at his every step was all the encouragement he needed.

When he finally reached her hand, she grinned and rewarded him by pulling close and wrapping her arms around his shoulders. Gabriel sighed and buried his face into her hair, still trying to control his ragged breaths while his heart frantically battered his ribs.

Frantic, but not panicked.

She beamed up at him. *"See?"* She gestured at the waves. *"It's not so bad, is it?"*

He glanced down, his throat bobbing before he said, "Only because you're in it."

She cocked her head with a wry smile. *"So all you need is a naked female to overcome your fear of water?"*

A strained chuckle escaped before he swept her even closer, until her legs parted and cradled his hips. "You are what I need to overcome my fear of not drowning."

She was too close to him to handspeak, but she didn't need to sign for him to read the query in her eyes.

"Do you know what's worse than death, wildcat? It's not being able to die when you desperately want to."

Drowning in your own blood while simultaneously having your flesh torn from your bones was nowhere near as agonizing as waiting for the oblivion of death that never came. Zephyr had shoved him into the siren-infested lake—not out of capricious cruelty or senseless malice, but as a test of his immortality.

As a boy, he had never comprehended how he had survived the lake allegedly used to dispose of Winter Court prisoners. He had believed himself lucky, and after some time, he'd even believed that Zephyr had fished him out and shown him some small mercy. He remembered waking up in the dungeon covered in grisly gaping wounds that eventually grew inflamed with infection, yet death never came for him . . . Never had he considered that he'd died a myriad of deaths. Or maybe he'd never wanted to consider the possibility.

Until the day Zion had showed him the truth.

Shyaree shuddered against him, caressing his back in soothing circles. He lowered his head and sought her lips. She did not deny him. She gave herself freely, and he devoured her greedily. Selfishly.

"I love the way you feel against me, wildcat." He rubbed between her thighs, relishing the heat emanating from her core despite the coolness of the sea. He licked along her throat, tasting the sweetness of her skin mingled with salt. He groaned, and his fangs sharpened in anticipation. "I love the way you smell and the way you taste . . . and gods, I love the little sounds you make when I'm inside you."

Her fingers dug into his arms in a silent demand, asking for more . . . giving him more.

"I love you, Shyaree," he whispered into her ear just before he plunged into her in a single hard stroke. He repeated the words over and over in tandem with every stroke until she clenched and convulsed against him. When he finally emptied into her, she smiled up at him dreamily, drawing idle strokes down his spine as though his confessions had swept past her, no more lasting than the waves around them. Of course, they had.

He had spoken only in Faerian.

Chapter 29

Gabriel winged across the horizon, past the yawning sun slowly but surely sinking. Retreating light penetrated the overcast sky like gilded pins spearing the Winter Court Palace. The Unseelie fortress gleamed in shades of silver, ivory, and muted grays, while Ichor Lake was a crescent-shaped mirror cradling the south end—not a single ripple disturbed its glistening black surface.

Gabriel detested going anywhere remotely close to the southern end of the Winter Court demesne and that insidious lake, but it had to be done.

The prince did not reside in the palace but in Whitebone Manor.

Gabriel flew over the stables and training yards and swooped past long-dehydrated gardens and dead orchards until he landed atop the balustrade of a curved balcony. The doors remained blessedly open, as though the prince were expecting him.

Gabriel vaporized from his host before slinking into the room.

A man in a flowing robe stood facing a bookshelf. Gabriel jerked him around. Pinned him with the sharp end of his sword before the man could scream.

The hooded figure gasped, eyes widening at the red sash tied around Gabriel's bicep. "Oh gods . . . please don't hurt me!"

Gabriel's eyes narrowed. Damn it. "Who are you? And what are you doing in Zion's private quarters?"

"I-I . . . I . . . am M-Matthias, the p-prince's steward."

Unfortunate. Gabriel could not have the steward running out, sounding the alarm of an intruder. Matthias would have to be silenced. But first . . .

"Where is he?" Gabriel asked. "Your prince."

"Right here," replied a voice at his back, smooth like a silken shadow. "Be at ease, Matthias. The guildmaster is a friend."

The stuttering steward's gaze widened even more. "B-but he's a Red Knight, m-m-milord."

Zion smiled. "I'm well aware."

"A-an enemy to the Crown . . . "

The prince emitted a congenial chuckle. "Ah, Matthias, Matthias . . . Why don't you let me worry about that while you bring us some wine?"

The steward nodded anxiously, dislodging books as he scurried from the room.

Gabriel started forward. He could not permit the steward to scamper off. Matthias was more likely to return with a contingent of guards than a bottle of wine, and that would make for a messy escape.

But before he acted upon that train of thought, Zion intercepted his steward.

For a moment, it appeared as though the prince had

reached out to draw the man into a friendly and reassuring embrace—until Matthias gave a wet gurgle.

The steward staggered to his knees, one hand cupping the small blade that had infiltrated his gut, the other grasping air as he reached for the doorknob. Zion shook his head with a tsk before he crouched to the ground only to murmur words loud enough for Gabriel's ears. "I did tell you never to question me. It is so tiresome to repeat myself."

The prince yanked the blade from the man's gut only to plunge it into his lung. It wasn't long enough to do more than puncture the organ, which meant Matthias would be suffocating in his own blood long before death crept up on him.

One edge of Gabriel's lip lifted in disgust. He would have killed Matthias in cold blood and not suffered a smudge to his conscience, so he was not usually one to judge. Every man answered to Ozenn at the end, but as someone who usually aimed for the perfection of a swift and clean job, he found Zion's gratuitous violence—and the resulting mess—repulsive.

While the steward struggled with his death throes, the prince rose lazily to his feet, wiping his hands on a kerchief he produced from his pocket, and shot Gabriel a mild smile. "So . . . what brings you here, guildmaster?"

"Enough with the games. Where is my sister?"

Zion's brows rose as he sauntered to the seat behind the desk. "The last time I checked, Iolanthe was exactly where she has been for the last two hundred years."

"There was no one in Duskhall Castle. Not a single servant remained."

With Arkas's claims niggling at the back of his mind, Gabriel had portaled to Duskhall once his wildcat had fallen asleep only to find the castle devoid of all staff. Even the cook's ginger cat no longer lingered in the kitchen. The tower itself remained magically warded, its windows curtained shut, but there was nothing to indicate Iolanthe's presence. Arkas had spoken the truth—Duskhall *was* deserted.

Zion smirked as he reclined in his seat, crossing his booted feet over the edge of the desk. "Come on, Blacksage . . . the blood moon is less than two days away. Did you think I'd allow an entire staff to linger? People who are loyal to Zephyr, and by extension, my dearest half brother, Zenaidus, to witness the sacrifice? Or Iolanthe's escape?"

The sacrifice. Words spoken with such nonchalance, as though Shyaree were nothing but a vessel. A replaceable fixture with no greater purpose in life than to fulfill the prophecy. A concoction of tightly suppressed emotions—anger, self-loathing, guilt, fear—swelled in his gut like painful abscesses in desperate need of lancing. Gabriel clenched his teeth until blood hit his tongue and pain radiated along his jaw, but the prince prattled on, completely oblivious to his internal turmoil.

"Zenaidus would have my hide and tan it for the saddle of his roan should he know of your sister's impending escape. He always fancied her, you know?" A wry snort. "Hence I disbanded the servants weeks ago. But don't worry, I've left two in the vicinity with the sole duty of tending to Iolanthe."

Gabriel forced his fingers to unfist. Forced himself to nod. It was a logical reason. Yet . . . something about the prince's placid smile grated.

"Iolanthe remains in the tower?"

"She has no means to escape." Zion snorted. "Not even through death. Well, at least not without the necromancer's daggers." While the draga sul and draga morli were best known for their use in raising the dead, the daggers were also talismans with enough power to tear down magical wards.

"And the seer's blood," Gabriel added sharply. "Have you procured it?"

According to the necromancer's texts, prophetic blood was

a requirement for every rite involving the draga morli and draga sul. Unfortunately, the last known seer of the five realms, a Seelie prophet named Elias, had long ago perished in the Winter War—but not without preserving a portion of his blood. Blood only Zion had access to.

And that made the bastard prince indispensable to Gabriel's goals.

"Just make sure you have the draga sul and the sacrifice ready on the blood moon," Zion said with a glib wave of his hand. "I'll take care of the rest."

Acid burned through Gabriel's veins at the offhand mention of the *sacrifice,* but he forced himself to calm. His gaze flickered over to Matthias's body. "These servants of yours left at Duskhall—how do you know if they can be trusted?"

"They are loyal. I assure you, they will see to Io's every need . . . Do *you* have everything we need, guildmaster?"

"You let me worry about that." Gabriel was already prowling to the balcony doors, but he halted. Turned. "I will perform the sacrifice myself."

It was a wonder his voice came out even. Cold and unfeeling. As though the sacrifice weren't now sleeping in *his* bed, sated by his lovemaking from mere hours ago. As though his gut weren't infested with maggots eating him alive.

Zion inclined his head with a smile. "Of course. I will keep to the terms of our agreement, Blacksage. You can trust me."

"Can I?" Gabriel's lips curled as his gaze swept over the dead steward lying in the pool of his own blood.

Zion laughed again. "Think about it. You need the draga morli to break the ward on the tower and to cleave both yourself and your sister from Zephyr's black soul . . . so you can ultimately put an end to him. And all I want is an opportunity to butcher the bastard the way he did my mother. The way I see it, we are fighting the same battle—from opposite ends." The prince drummed idle fingers on the desk, not the least perturbed by the growing puddle staining the woven carpet. "You know what they say . . . the enemy of my enemy is my friend." Lavender eyes gleamed. "And I say we're the best of friends."

Chapter 30

Dawn seeped from beneath the thick curtains to suffuse the room with soft light.

Shyaree lay within Gabriel's arms, listening to the rise and fall of their quiet breaths while she stared languidly at the dust motes twirling in the air. She had been awake for a while, but she was reluctant to move, unwilling to disrupt the tranquil serenity. If she could seize time, she would stay in this moment forever—cradled in his arms like a woman cherished . . . A woman *loved.*

He never did say the words, but she felt it in every tender touch and heard it in every husky murmur. His sword-callused hands would gentle every time he brushed the hair from her face or held her still while he kissed the breath from her lungs. His voice would soften even when he teased her to exasperation. And somewhere along the way, the moniker *wildcat* no longer sounded like a mockery but an endearment sweeter than any other. She saw it in the way he watched her every gesture, as though her signing were not just a form of communication, but a captivating dance he loathed to miss for a single blink.

She was happier than she had ever thought possible, and more fearful than ever before. Today marked the end of their bargain: the night of the blood moon. Tonight, Gabriel would take her to a place called Duskhall where he would lay her upon an altar and carve twelve runes down her spine.

Ironically, it was no longer the ritual she feared, but its aftermath.

She could bear the pain of twelve runes cut into her skin—but how could she bear the moment it all ended? When he got what he wanted?

Gabriel would not only use the draga morli to free his sister. He would also use it to cleave himself from the mad king Zephyr—the soulbond that kept him undying. While she understood how much it galled her guildmaster to be bound to a madman who had once tortured him and destroyed his family . . . she was ultimately a selfish creature.

If Gabriel were no longer undying, he would be vulnerable to her venom. And perhaps that was the reason he had never uttered a single word of love and said nothing of his plans for the future beyond the blood moon—they could not stay together. Not indefinitely.

Something inside her shriveled.

Gabriel must have sensed her wakefulness because he pulled her closer until his hardness prodded suggestively against her. Usually, he would roll her to her back and kiss her until she was wet and wanting before burying himself in her. It had been a delightful way to start the morning, but this morning he did none of those things. He simply held her.

Shyaree sighed and shifted to face him.

His eyes were the darkest amethysts lined by shadows, gazing back at her as though to commit her face to memory. "Are you scared, wildcat?"

She pushed up to her elbows. *"Of what?"*

"Tonight."

Tonight. The ritual. He was not asking about her fears of tomorrow.

She shook her head. "I am not afraid of a little blood or pain."

He did not appear convinced, but he said nothing, staring at her with an uncanny quiet. She stroked fingers into his disheveled silvery strands. She leaned over and kissed him slowly, leisurely, deeply. No matter what came tomorrow, in this one moment, he was still hers.

"I'm sorry," he whispered, his voice thick with emotion. "I'm sorry, Shyaree. I wish to the gods the prophecy were wrong, but—"

She shushed him with another kiss. *"I've cut myself more times than I can count. Many rituals of my people involve blood . . . I do not fear it. I will keep to our bargain."* She kissed him again. *"I know what the draga morli means to you . . . "* Freedom. Freedom for his sister. Freedom from a soulbond he'd never asked for. Freedom that would make loving her a lethal pursuit. *"And I want you to have it."*

His throat worked compulsively, and a sheen glistened in his eyes, but he said nothing. Instead, his hands roamed to the backs of her thighs, coaxing her atop him so she sat astride him. Her heat had ended days ago, yet her body continued to yearn for every opportunity to couple with his. Unnerving truth dawned on her—it was not lust. It never had been.

Gabriel ran tender hands over her body, possessive hands that halted her ruminations and blanked her thoughts.

He played her like his favorite instrument, tuning her body and stoking her arousal with his fingers until she made all the embarrassing needy sounds to his satisfaction. Impatient, she tried to take him from the top.

The knave checked her with a teasing chuckle. "Patience, my darling wildcat . . . "

She'd show him patience.

She gyrated against him, making sure he felt every glide of her hips, until he cursed and gripped her thighs to keep her still before thrusting up and into her. When he was fully sheathed, ragged Faerian that had become a familiar serenade flowed from his lips. He gazed up at her as though she were a goddess in the flesh who deigned to grace his bed. This was a powerful position—and a dangerous one.

It allowed her to use her hands if she wanted, and the gesture for *I love you* was at the tips of her fingers.

Shyaree lowered her hands and busied herself with the spectacular planes of his body before she could succumb to foolishness. She wouldn't—couldn't—sign those words. Not when she knew well what tomorrow would bring.

It wouldn't be fair to him—or herself.

The Prophecy

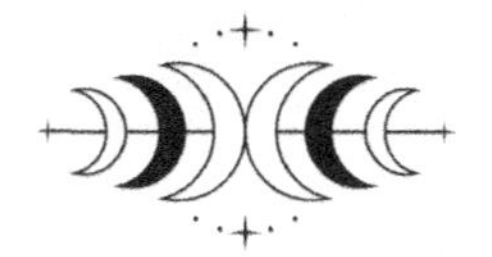

Seelie and Unseelie, two parts of a whole,
destroy one, and to the other woe.
Without light, there can be no shadow,
winter will reign, and darkness will follow.
Thousands slaughtered in vengeful creed,
thousands more sold in the name of greed.

A single summer seed to return a Seelie clan,
a starflower sewn into a foreign land.
To bridge the abyss and brave a sea of fire,
strength to heal and blossom amid treachery most dire.
Railea's mightiest to kneel before her bloom,
an Unseelie king be brought to doom.

The necromancer's dagger falls to a guardian,
a cursed twin at the brink of desperation.
His voiceless sister's blood sings of untouched power,
twelve runes carved on her spine at the blood moon's hour.

Two hearts to break while one ceases,
the necromancer's lost dagger her death releases.

Chapter 31

Redwood Forest, Courtyard of Duskhall Castle

"It's a sacrificial rite, not a damned execution!" Gabriel clenched his fists, on the cusp of throttling the overzealous prince.

A wooden platform, reminiscent of an executioner's scaffold, occupied the middle of the open courtyard. Instead of a chopping block or a hanging gallows, there was a crossbeam equipped with manacles on both sides designed to keep the occupant kneeling with her arms outstretched. Flanking the wooden framework were two grim-faced heretics—devotees of Draedyn, recognizable by the symbol of death tattooed across their foreheads. Zion had obviously gone to extreme lengths to keep this night's events covert, because there was no one else present. No guards, no servants. Just the prince, two priests, the betrayer, and his blood sacrifice.

Gabriel wanted to snarl, to rage, to *kill*. He lusted for

blood, and it wasn't his wildcat's. Yet he managed to keep his boots rooted upon the granite tiles and his hands from Zion's throat.

The lunar eclipse had begun.

The dreaded hour of the blood moon was upon them, made all the more harrowing by the prince's grisly setup.

"We only have one chance, Blacksage." Zion paced the length of the platform, assessing the crossbeam. "The shackles are necessary to keep her from bolting partway and ruining the ritual."

His wildcat might not understand Faerian, but she narrowed her eyes at the prince and his priests in open distaste. *"I do not need to be bound."* She implored Gabriel with her eyes. *"I won't struggle."*

"Twelve runes imparted by a blade isn't something one would take lying down, Blacksage." The prince spoke over her hand signals. "You of all people should understand."

Memories of the acolytes carving runes into his back were a phantom burn across his skin, and the fact that he would soon be wielding a knife over Shyaree in the same fashion made him physically ill. Gabriel shook his head. "She's stronger than you think."

The prince snorted. "It doesn't matter what I think. It doesn't matter what she wants. What matters is that we get it *done* if we hope to be free of Zephyr." Zion narrowed his gaze. "Did you bring it? The draga sul?"

Even though they still conversed in Faerian, Gabriel stiffened at the mention of the soul catcher. A glimpse at Shyaree's face showed his wildcat was too disturbed by the notion of being bound to the wooden crossbeam to have caught the dagger's mention. He had a sudden, hysterical urge to laugh.

Why did it matter if she found out he had stolen the dagger from her brother's hut? Gabriel was already betraying her in the worst possible way. Stealing from her brother was a far cry from sacrificing her life.

"I have it," Gabriel said crisply. The draga sul was inconspicuously sheathed in his right boot. "Did you bring the seer's blood?"

A seer's blood. The final piece of the necromancer's trifecta for raising the dead—or breaking a magical ward.

Zion nodded, absently patting the front pocket of his coat. "Of course I did. Iolanthe will be free from that tower tonight." Anticipation gleamed in his gaze. "We'll *all* be free. At last."

Gabriel had been obsessed with Iolanthe's freedom ever since he'd learned of her imprisonment. And now, instead of gladness, the weight in his chest compounded, as if his heart were turning to stone. The sickness in his gut intensified to actual physical pain, as though his flesh were rotting from the inside.

"We only have a little over two hours to complete the ritual before the eclipse fades and the blood moon recedes. Let's begin." Zion beckoned the priests, who stepped up to Shyaree.

His wildcat snarled, head shaking.

It took Gabriel every iota of willpower to ignore his instincts to maim while the priests seized her arms and dragged her up the short steps to the elevated platform. He clenched his teeth, the taste of his own blood coating his tongue as the priests shoved her to her knees. Something akin to acid burned through his veins as he did nothing but watch while they stretched out her arms and shackled her wrists.

He would never forget the wounded shock on her face when she finally realized he was not going to do anything to intervene. Shyaree stopped struggling. She stared at him with enough hurt in her eyes to bore lesions into his soul.

Still, Gabriel held himself in place.

Shyaree was the prophesied blood sacrifice. A seer's foresight could not be contradicted or evaded. Her fate was sealed by the gods.

Her detainers stepped back with a reverent bow while Zion inspected the manacles on her wrists. With a hum of approval, the prince pulled a ceremonial knife from its sheath at his belt and held it up. "It's time. Do you still wish to do this, or shall I?"

Wordlessly, jerkily, Gabriel moved up the platform, holding her gaze as he allowed this moment to sear into his memory. Shyaree on her knees, arms outstretched and bound like a heretical offering. A moment he'd orchestrated. Gabriel would not allow another to commit this desecration on his behalf. No.

He owed it to her to feel her pain.

He owed it to her to remember every instant. To feel every cut and relive it in every waking moment the rest of his wretched life.

He took the ceremonial knife from the prince and tested the edge. Sharp enough to split hairs. Good. He would make it swift, at least.

With her arms bound, she couldn't handspeak even if she wanted, but she seemed content to keep her silence. Fingers curled, lips sewn tight. Hurt swirling in the depths of her eyes. She no longer looked at him but up at the cloudless night sky, where the full moon glared down at him like an unforgiving red eye.

Gabriel walked to her back to undo the laces of her dress to reveal her smooth back. He'd had her put this on earlier, for exactly this purpose, driven as much by an irrational urge to soothe his need to keep her covered before the prince as to spare her the indignity of disrobing should she wear a regular shirt.

Gabriel leaned down to brush his lips over hers in a silent apology before whispering into her ear. "Forgive me, Shyaree . . . "

He lifted the knife.

The blade glinted a mocking and malicious silver—hungry for blood.

Hungry for sacrifice.

The stone that was his heart cracked.

"I should never have let them touch you."

He hurled it at the closest priest. The sharp end sank into the man's eye before he had a chance to blink. Before the heretic hit the ground, Gabriel sent a diken sailing into the other's throat. His marks collapsed—one already dead and the other not far from Ozenn's embrace—before the prince snapped from shock.

"What in the five hells are you doing?" Zion roared with a sudden and distinct drop of the surrounding temperature. A burst of black erupted from the prince's hands like a swarm of locusts, cutting across the wooden platform in streaks of obsidian.

Not blackfire, but frost. Black*frost*.

Gabriel darted away from Shyaree to redirect the prince, narrowly avoiding the cold rush of power. He leapt from the wooden platform, rolling when he hit the granite ground and flattening his back to the wooden edge.

He held himself still despite Shyaree's panicked breaths and the jangle of her shackles as she struggled against them. Her little sounds of distress galled him, but Zion wouldn't hurt his precious blood sacrifice outside the blood ritual. Still, Gabriel couldn't take the risk.

"No hard feelings, *friend* . . . ," Gabriel yelled from his position, calculating the best chance of neutralizing Zion. The half-breed prince was part mage, and Declan had once disclosed that this bastard had the ability to warp. "But I've changed my mind."

From the tread of the prince's boots, Zion remained on the

platform, likely close to Shyaree. Gabriel wouldn't risk hurling his knives where Shyaree might get hurt.

"Changed your mind?" Zion yelled. "You've fucking lost it! The prophet Elias was never wrong! His prophecy cannot be altered—you're only wasting time!"

Gabriel sneered. He might already be damned to the five hells, but he refused to stand by and watch his wildcat bleed out before his eyes. If her fate was indeed set for death beneath the blood moon—then it would be over Gabriel's dead body.

And he was fucking undying.

He bolted up, stomping hard as he ran to the opposite edge of the platform. Away from Shyaree. And from the sound of Zion's footfalls, the prince followed. Gabriel climbed back up onto the platform, hurling three dikens without comment or pause.

Zion deflected the first two with a burst of blackfrost, but the third grazed a red welt across his cheek. He warped, reappearing behind Gabriel in a blink of an eye to seize him in a chokehold.

"Fool!" Zion seethed. "Do you no longer care about Iolanthe? Or that Zephyr has an unending tie to our lives?"

Of course he did. Gabriel cared so much it made him crazed.

But in the moment he'd been about to wield a knife over Shyaree, he'd found greater clarity—the weight of all those factors combined did not surpass that of her life. They didn't even come close.

Gabriel jabbed his elbow into the prince's gut. Zion's chokehold loosened for a fraction of a second, and that was all it took for Gabriel to kick back and flip his opponent over his shoulder. Slam him to the floor, causing the entire platform to shudder.

"We'll find another way to get that dagger," Gabriel said.

Magical loopholes. Untapped sources of power. Something. There *had* to be.

Gabriel would devote the rest of his life to searching for it.

The prince hissed. "Her sacrifice is the only way! We can never be free from Zephyr without the draga morli!"

"There are more ways to kill a dog than hanging." And no better way to demonstrate his example. Gabriel whipped up a knife from his holster belt and sank it into Zion's jugular.

The prince sputtered incomprehensibly, blood and bile dribbling from his mouth, dagger jutting from his throat, loathing in his eyes. Then he sagged. Still.

For now.

Gabriel ripped out the knife and nailed it into the prince's heart for good measure.

That should give him time enough to free Shyaree and portal them home before the undying bastard found his breath again.

He bolted back to Shyaree's side. She jangled her restraints, her eyes filled with shades of trepidation and terror. "I'm sorry, wildcat." He pressed a swift kiss to her lips, not to reassure her but to reassure himself. She was unharmed. "Everything is going to be all right."

Gabriel turned to the dead priests, searching for the key. The moment he unlocked her shackles, she hurtled into his arms. Relief washed over him like rain over dryland.

The day he'd learned of his undying state and Iolanthe's survival had shaken him to his core, muddied his sense of purpose and beliefs. He had been running from his reality for an entire turn of the sun, and he'd almost forgotten the most fundamental part of himself. He might be the guildmaster of a band of ruthless cutthroats, the heir to a dead dukedom, a brother who'd never gotten a chance to make up for his mistakes . . . but somewhere along the way, he had also become *hers.* A man who would slay and sunder all who dared lay a finger on her.

She pushed from his hold to gesture at the dead bodies. *"Why did you kill them? What about the dagger?"* She glanced up at the moon. The lunar eclipse was slowly falling away, leaving only two thirds of the plump moon cloaked in a hazy red sheen.

"I'll find another way," Gabriel said.

If he had found a way to replace Mekari's blood for her curse-breaking elixir, he could find a way to free Iolanthe from the tower and sever Zephyr's soulbond.

Gabriel could do anything, face anything, so long as his heart was intact. And Shyaree didn't just take up residence in his heart. She *was* his heart.

"I'll find another way," he said, hugging her to his chest. "All that matters is that you're safe." He summoned a portal, needing to get her away from this grisly place as soon as possible, but she halted him with an urgent snap of her fingers.

She pushed out of his arms. *"It was never just about collecting my blood, was it?"*

Gabriel swallowed. "I'll explain everything when we get home."

He reached for her again, but she backed away from him. Slowly. Cautiously. As though she finally saw him for who he truly was, and she did not like what she saw.

"This whole time . . . Our bargain. Was it all a lie?"

He shook his head, but he struggled to find the right words. Shame and trepidation and fear. He should never have lied, and now he dreaded her finding out the truth.

He didn't have to wait long, because her gaze darted to the ceremonial knife, still lodged in the dead guard's throat, and he saw the exact moment she pieced it together. *"You were meant to kill me, weren't you?"*

At Gabriel's incriminating silence, tears welled in her eyes.

He could have dealt with rage. He would have preferred for her to shift and snap at him with her sharp claws and venomous canines. But all he got was heart-wrenching dejection. Her gaze searched his face, perhaps trying to see past his black and wretched soul to find pieces of redemption . . . but finding none. He could almost see her heart break from the caving of her shoulders. He could almost hear the pieces shatter from her shredded breaths.

It hurt worse than drowning without means for death.

"I'm sorry," he whispered. Gabriel swallowed convulsively, struggling to find the words so he could fucking make it right. "I should have told you the truth, but—"

"Men just can't be trusted," finished a soft, singsong voice in Faerian.

The new presence emerged from a portal as evanescent as fog in the sun, and Gabriel's breath emptied from his lungs. She smiled, a bittersweet memory.

"Hello, brother dearest."

Chapter 32

An illusion. A conjuration of his guilt, perhaps. Or a manifestation of his mind, which must have finally cracked under the burdens it bore. She could not be real. Except his illusion moved closer in sure-footed steps, the hem of her elaborate imperial-blue gown a soft whisper of silk and muslin against the courtyard's granite tiles.

Waifish as fae women were wont to be, she pinned him with large lilac eyes. Her lips curved with a small, secretive smile that reminded him so much of the impish little girl she once was that he wanted to pick her up, twirl her around, and hug her close.

Gabriel did none of those things.

Instead, he angled his stance to block Shyaree, who radiated enough wary tension to cast them in a shroud. He didn't blame her.

Iolanthe was not alone.

The newly minted king hovered by her side like an overbearing lover, his height further enhanced by her slightness. Unlike his father before him, Zenaidus was elaborate in his appearance. The Winter King wore a traditional robe of royal jade that parted down the middle, each flap embroidered with the symbols of the two fae courts in sweeping curlicues of antique gold. His long mane was more slate than silver, braided in places and fastened with gold clasps to match his crown, while signet rings adorned his fingers. Zenaidus made no attempt to disguise his contempt, eyeing Gabriel and Shyaree as though they were a pair of rats flushed from the sewer, but even the king's unprecedented presence was not half as bewildering as the sound of his sister's voice.

"Iolanthe," Gabriel croaked when he finally found his tongue. "You're speaking."

She chuckled as though his observation were an inanity. "It does seem so, doesn't it?"

Stupefaction shook his head. "How?" Iolanthe had been born with a speech disorder. She was the reason he'd been schooled in Handspeak as a child. He had never heard her utter a word, much less string a full sentence together —until now.

Now, she spoke like a song lark, her Faerian fluent and melodic, even if there was a slight accent to her words.

"Let's just say Zephyr never did have the patience for my signing." Words so sharp they could have carved blood from the air.

Dread pooled in the pit of his stomach. "What did he do to you?"

At the tightening of her lips, Zenaidus shifted with an air of querulous impatience. "Nothing more than improve the quality of her life. Iolanthe was always my father's favorite. Though . . . " A disdainful sniff. "Father did let *you* get away with far too much impertinence. How dare you stand in my presence without acknowledging your king, Blacksage?"

"My king?" The mirthless laughter escaping Gabriel's

throat was as dry as chaff. "You're nothing but a puppet wearing a crown."

Zenaidus's fangs showed sharply. He moved with the threat of a lunge, but Iolanthe secured him firmly by the crook of his elbow before patting a placating hand over his chest. "Calm, my love. Remember your promise . . . "

Gabriel glanced at Shyaree, not liking the way she stared at the Unseelie king with wide, unblinking eyes as though ensorcelled. Zephyr had been a master illusionist, and his firstborn spawn was no different, but Gabriel felt no brush of insidious shadowmagic. Zenaidus was not projecting illusions—or was he? For unfathomable reasons, Iolanthe clung to him like a honeybee drunk on floral nectar, speaking to the pompous fop in the hushed tones of a paramour.

"My brother has always been the rebellious sort . . . " Her jewel-toned gaze narrowed ever so slightly at Shyaree before drifting over the bodies on the ground. "And it seems you haven't changed one bit. Just look at this mess." A derisive roll of her eyes. "You leave carnage behind the way a child leaves crumbs."

"How did you leave the tower?" Gabriel demanded and jabbed a thumb at the glowering king. "Why are you with *him?* Is he forcing you, Io?"

Iolanthe laughed. The peal of her amusement was both girlish and grating at the same time, like shattering glass and a thousand tinkling shards. Fragile, but hard and cutting. "What? Does it seem like I'm unwilling?"

The unlikely couple exchanged a shared smirk. Dread pooled in the pit of his stomach before Iolanthe lowered an affectionate cheek to the king's chest.

"Your sister and I have been officiated by a high priest just this morning. She is my queen, Blacksage."

Queen. His sister, the Unseelie Queen. The moon could

have fallen from the sky, and Gabriel would have been less alarmed. "I watched you for a year—Zion was your only visitor. Your guardian."

"Zion?" Iolanthe extricated herself from the king's side with a delicate sniff. "I've been free to leave the tower for three years now, and the fool still believes me captive." A sneer. "He doesn't even know I can speak. He only sees what he wishes to see, and that makes him such a bore. All he cares about is the precious kingdom and his dreams of"—she rolled her eyes—"rebuilding the fae realm."

As though in response, Zion began to stir. The prince reanimated with a loud wheeze that caused Shyaree to startle. He sucked in ragged breaths, clawing at the blade still lodged in his chest. Before Gabriel could react, Iolanthe hurried over to the wheezing prince, primly holding her skirts to sidestep puddles of blood. She unsheathed the bejeweled sword at the prince's hip with the practiced ease of a seasoned swordswoman.

"A fatal wound may keep one of us down for a few minutes," she said conversationally. "But a decapitated head?"

Gabriel's breath caught in his throat as she brought the sword down in one deft and merciless swing. The poor bastard didn't even have a chance to protest before his head rolled like a melon falling off a cart.

"Ah, that'll take a while . . . " The king shot his bride a wincing smile as though he spoke from experience.

Gabriel was still reeling from the sight of his sweet little sister's unflinching penchant for violence when she cocked her head at him. "Anyway, brother dearest, I believe you owe me a wedding gift." Her gaze settled on Shyaree, who had all but turned to stone behind him. She might not understand their exchange, but his wildcat was perceptive. She must have gleaned enough from their body language to understand that Iolanthe and the king posed a threat, because Shyaree looked ready to bolt.

"Give me the blood sacrifice," Iolanthe said, casually gesturing at Shyaree. "Then we'll part ways. Amiably. And if you'd bothered to heed our emissary, you'd know Zenaidus has even promised to reinstate your dukedom . . . if you comply with the Crown, of course. Duke of Evenmere sounds a lot better than guildmaster of the Red Knights, don't you think?"

Sickness coated his throat like grease while some innate part of him continued to writhe in denial. She was ensorcelled. She had to be. Gabriel caught Shyaree's hand, holding her firmly if only to reassure himself. "Shyaree stays with *me*."

Displeasure twisted Iolanthe's face into an unrecognizable mask. "Be careful, brother. Do not look a gift horse in the mouth."

"This swine you call king is part of the reason our family is gone! Do you know what he's been doing to the realm? Are you so misguided that you think—"

Iolanthe bared her fangs in a hiss. "Shut up! You're not Papa. Nor are you Grayson. Don't act like you've got any right to lecture me on my choices! You're lucky I'm even speaking to you, Gabriel."

Hearing her mention their father and elder brother caused a pang in his chest that dampened his outrage. "I know you've suffered, Io. But this is a mistake. He is a mistake."

"I've made her a queen! I can give her everything her heart desires and more." Zenaidus continued to expound his indignation, but he could well be a twittering bird for all the attention given to him.

"A mistake?" Iolanthe's voice wobbled. Her chest heaved; her hands clenched. "A mistake was you and Arkas running away, leaving me to rot in the palace!"

Gabriel blanched. "I thought you were dead! I would never have left you—"

Iolanthe's eyes flashed with derision. "You thought I was dead? You *thought?* You knew what Zephyr was doing to me, yet you thought I was dead?"

Gabriel could only shake his head, his throat clogged with emotion. "I didn't know what he was doing to me! I never understood any of it until *a year ago.* I had no idea he'd done the same to you . . . or his own sons!"

His outburst incited a squeeze from Shyaree, but Gabriel could not afford to look away from his sister, or the king.

"Ingrate." Zenaidus scoffed. "When I realized Father's experiments had worked, I *begged* to be one of his anchors."

Gabriel snarled. "Do not mistake the inability to die for anything but a curse. Have you ever been in a situation where death would have been a mercy?"

"Of course we have," Iolanthe retorted. "I've killed myself a dozen times in an attempt to escape the tower, only to wake again every single time."

Gabriel squeezed his eyes shut. "If I'd known . . . if I'd known, I would have come for you a long time ago."

"Oh, would you?" She gestured at Shyaree. "It looks like you just had a chance to *free* me, dearest brother, yet you decided not to."

"Shyaree doesn't have to be the answer to our freedom. She doesn't deserve to pay with her life."

"She doesn't deserve to pay?" Iolanthe's voice pitched perilously close to a shriek. "She doesn't deserve to pay, but I do? Did I deserve to be trapped in a tower for two hundred years? Did I deserve to be killed over and over and over as Zephyr perfected his sickening experiments?"

"None of that is her fault! She—"

"Even after you learned the truth of my survival, you chose your whore over me!"

"It doesn't matter." Zenaidus lifted Iolanthe's hand and kissed her knuckles. "Those years are behind you now, my little dove. Once we secure what we need, nothing will stop you from running this kingdom the way you see fit. We will rule. Together. Forever."

With a flourish of his hand, the king snapped his fingers. Four portals opened simultaneously, foggy gateways spewing guards into the courtyard. At least ten from each portal, soldiers dressed in the silver regalia of the Winter Court, armed with shadowbows and swords. The soldiers moved in perfect synchrony to form a half circle, arrows notched and aimed—not at him. At Shyaree.

Gabriel drew his swords while simultaneously trying to keep Shyaree shielded, but the soldiers surrounded them from all sides. Shyaree squeezed his arm with an urgency that spoke of her fear.

"I'm sorry I've wronged you, but Shyaree has nothing to do with this," Gabriel cried in desperation. "She's innocent! Please, Io, listen to me. Come *home* with me. Arkas mourned you. *I* mourned you. There isn't a day I don't miss you or our family . . . please."

Iolanthe's eyes glistened, and for one moment Gabriel saw beneath the harsh veneer of the woman to the little girl who was once his sister.

"You mourned me? You missed me?" A brittle laugh before her lips formed a bitter line. "That's just too bad, because I certainly won't be mourning *you*." She lifted a regal hand. "Kill him, and bring me the blood sacrifice."

The first arrow flew.

Gabriel rolled to the ground, dragging Shyaree with him as the arrow speared the wooden scaffold with a hollow thunk.

He jumped up to a crouch and opened a portal when a pained sound escaped his wildcat. For one spine-chilling moment, he thought she'd been shot, but then he heard the unmistakable crack of bone. Her nails sharpened to claws, scraping furrows into the wood. A breathless rasp in her throat escalated into a thin cry as her spine contorted in a painful arch.

The terrifying whirr of more arrows.

Gabriel darted over her, using his back like a shield. An arrow struck, a jolt of pain. Another thudded into his shoulder, followed by another. The agony searing across his back paled against the horror of his portal diminishing before it could fully coalesce—the arrows were bespelled. Magic dried in his veins like moisture in a drought.

Shyaree was trapped.

All while the full moon smirked, a merciless red stain in the hazy sky.

Chapter 33

Pain was the blinding agony of her existence, an excruciating nightmare fueled by fear and fury. Her bones snapped and disarticulated. Her spine curved while her limbs contracted. Her muscles stretched and pulled, and her innards seemed to liquefy, shifting, resizing, reorganizing themselves to fit a new mold. Her body transformed like clay, except she had trained her whole life to discard malleability. Suppress. Control. Never let it out. She was an intractable cage of living flesh, meant to contain the venomous beast within.

She could no longer do it.

The harder she defied the urge, the stronger her torment.

Vaguely, she heard herself scream as her vocal cords realigned. She heard frantic footsteps. Clashing steel. Men hollering. But change and chaos garbled all her other senses. Her vision was nothing but a mass of indistinct shadows and shapes.

She retreated to the depths of her mind, where she saw herself, a child from so long ago, sobbing for reprieve while the urge to change overcame her. She could almost feel the ghostly blows and the hard crack of her father's knuckles against her flesh. Dapa had begged her time and time again to resist. Her brother and her clansmen had reinforced the notion of her inner beast as a monstrous abomination of wreckage and pain. A creature to be quelled and subdued. A creature to be feared. She had believed them all without question, until . . . Gabriel.

Gabriel had called her wondrous. He had barged into her life and broken down all her barriers and shown her what it was to feel wanted. Desired. Loved. He had kissed and touched every part of her with the rapture of a drunken man, worshipped her body with a lover's wicked intent and toe-curling tenderness. He'd made her believe she was not only beautiful but flawless in all her forms. He had called her perfect.

A man who had lied to her from the very beginning.

Something cracked deep within, and it went beyond the physicality of disjointed bones. Something bled, not from ripping sinew or tearing muscle but from the soft organ that was her heart. It hurt. *Everything* hurt.

Enough!

Perhaps she had hit the pinnacle of her pain, broken past the threshold of grief, but suddenly she didn't care anymore.

Dapa's assertions were no longer relevant.

Her people's contentions no longer applied.

Gabriel's betrayal no longer mattered. If she was fated for death this night, she would meet it as herself. She permitted her bones to shift without struggle, and allowed her muscles to morph without protest. She accepted her existence the way nature intended.

She allowed herself to *be*.

Fur rippled to replace smooth skin. Her spine extended to a lashing tail, and her teeth honed themselves to match her claws. Her vision focused. Her voice returned in a deep-throated roar.

In a moment of suspended animation, the surrounding fae stared as though she were a creature risen from the depths of the five hells. Perhaps she was. She had never changed like this. She had never inhabited a form that took her down to all fours. Venom pooled like saliva in her gums, and strength coiled deep in her muscles, her fury barely leashed. Her tail flicked irritably at the gawking soldiers armed with their notched arrows and gleaming swords.

She lunged, and the soldiers scattered like frenzied ants.

Armor shredded beneath her claws like paper instead of steel. She sank her teeth into flesh, injecting venom with every bite. The king—or so she assumed from the crown on his head—and the woman beside him, Iolanthe—shouted the same words over and over. Whatever they commanded must be for the soldiers to subdue her, not kill her. No arrow pierced her flesh, even though the soldiers were armed with crossbows. No swords cut her even as she tore out throats.

Of course. For as long as the blood moon lorded the sky, they needed her alive for the sacrifice. By the wrath of Thurin, she would kill as many as she could before she allowed them to take her.

A faint voice penetrated the murderous mayhem of her consciousness.

A male voice, the sound of it so familiar, so endearing, so *pained* that she paused and listened.

Gabriel.

His voice was pitched so low she would never have heard it under ordinary circumstances. But in this form, she did. She picked it out distinctly from the cacophony of shouts and commands.

She darted to the source of his voice, the wooden platform.

Her heart seized in her chest.

There he was. Hunched beside the headless corpse, a score

of arrows protruding from his back as though he'd sprouted quills in the time she'd changed.

But that wasn't what made her heart falter.

He was completely slick with blood. It glistened on his skin and covered his lower jaw. Not *his* blood. She could scent the difference. It was the corpse's blood.

Gabriel had been drinking from Zion's dead body.

A shudder wended through her bestial form in conjoined waves of shock and nausea.

"Come here," Gabriel commanded in the thready voice of a man close to unconsciousness.

She should be afraid. She wasn't. She should be angry. Yet she obeyed, nudging him with her snout, a soft whine escaping her throat. He was undying, and still her traitorous heart labored over the sight of his battered form. Why did he drink from the dead?

Shouts reminded her they were not alone.

Soldiers surrounded the scaffold, but for some reason they seemed wary—of her?— because they were not stampeding up the platform.

Gabriel gripped her foreleg, and the glaze of his eyes turned an ominous black. A sting of icy pain dragged through her flesh. His veins blackened beneath his skin like the branches of a rotted tree. She felt the exact moment he ripped his shadow-mark from her flesh.

"Declan and Evie will protect you." Shadows flared in black wisps, like the flimsy flames of a candle flickering in the wind just before her. The beginnings of a portal that was so unlike the effortless ones he usually made. She understood, then, *why* he'd drunk from Zion's corpse and ripped out her shadowmark. He was gathering magic.

The platform trembled from encroaching soldiers, but his portal was not quite formed.

"I love you, Shyaree." He pressed a hasty kiss to her forehead, as though he hadn't just tipped her world with those precious, precious words. Words she no longer knew if she could trust. "Now get ready to run. And don't turn back."

He snagged his swords from the ground and lurched to his feet. With a feral hiss, he charged at the soldiers before they could reach her. They swarmed him just as his portal widened with darker strokes of swirling shadows.

It was the same song and dance they'd played over and over in Thurin's Mountain. He would cast a portal, insist she leave, and she would defy him.

Not this time.

Shyaree was one leap away from sanctuary when the king shouted in thickly accented Animatish from somewhere at her back. "Run, and I promise he'll spend an eternity in torture."

Shyaree turned with a snarl, her tail lashing in agitation.

Iolanthe waved from beside the king, flagging her attention. But unlike the king, she clearly couldn't speak the tongue of Shyaree's people, because Iolanthe spoke through her hands. She was the reason Gabriel was versed in Handspeak, after all. *"Being undying is a gift as much as it is a curse. To suffer repeated death without reprieve . . . trust me, there is no worse torment."*

Gabriel's recount of Ichor Lake surfaced in her mind. He hadn't told her the full details. He didn't need to. She had witnessed his panic when he fell into the lagoon . . . and she finally understood the full breadth of his fear.

It was not water or drowning he feared, but his *inability to die* in it.

Shyaree's heart twisted. She was about to leave him to face his worst fear . . . Gabriel must have known he would face consequences for falling into the hands of the king's soldiers, and he had done it anyway. For her.

A glance showed Gabriel surrounded by soldiers. She could barely see him, but she heard him. He yelled something, his tone frantic, probably urging her to leave. But his words were an incomprehensible wet gurgle. They were slaughtering him.

A shrill whistle drew Shyaree's focus back to the woman. *"If you change back to your human form, no harm will come to him upon your sacrifice."*

"Yes," the king agreed. "I will honor your sacrifice with his freedom."

Conflict warred in her chest. Gabriel had betrayed her. Lied to her from the very beginning . . . yet he had ultimately chosen *her* at the cost of his own freedom. He hadn't deserted her. Could she desert him? Leave him to suffer his greatest fear?

If the prophecy had foretold her death, and if the foretelling was true, she would die tonight regardless.

If the prophecy was false . . . well, she could not hide in Amereen forever. Especially not when Gabriel was being held captive.

Sickness perforated her innards.

Gabriel's portal began to dwindle, yet she stayed exactly where she was—her choice chillingly, startlingly clear.

"There is no running from fate," Iolanthe added with the smile of a woman who knew she had already won. *"One way or another, this night ends with your death. But how my brother suffers? Now, that is your choice."*

Her choice.

Gabriel had been right from the start. She *was* a fool.

She couldn't leave him—not even to save her own life.

The first thing Gabriel noticed as he came to was the pale, pearlescent moon riding high in the sky. The second thing he noticed was the tang of iron saturating the air. The scent of blood.

Shyaree.

He jolted up, only to fall back to the ground. His hands were bound at his back, tethered to the wooden crossbeam—

"No . . . " Chill was an insidious whisper passing through his veins, icing his blood until every fiber of his being constricted with horror. He squeezed his eyes shut to scrub away the sight, but it was a nightmare seared into his brain.

"No! No! No! Gods, no!" Gabriel tore at his bonds, trying to rise to his feet only to slip because the platform was slick with blood.

Her blood.

Shyaree. His beautiful wildcat was back in her human form, bound to the crossbeam with both arms outstretched, knees bent. Strands of silken hair clung to her bare breasts as though to cover her nudity while nauseating rivulets of blood ran down her body like little crimson rivers. Her head dipped, and her eyes were serenely, harrowingly closed.

Gabriel had never truly prayed. He was far from pious. But in that instant, he prayed to the gods, all five of them, that she was merely unconscious . . . that his Shyaree *breathed*.

He could almost hear the gods cackling in his ears.

The lunar eclipse was over. It was over.

Gabriel howled, thrashing against his bonds. He howled until his vision blurred and his voice cracked. Howled until something inside him broke, and still the agony boiled from him in baying bursts. She was gone. His wildcat was gone.

He'd lost her.

A wooden plank groaned from the weight of an approaching figure.

"Look at you," Zenaidus said with a tsk as he crouched beside him. "Pathetic. Your whore didn't make half this ruckus when I cut her flesh." The king snickered. "In fact, she barely made a single sound."

Gabriel lunged as far as his bindings would allow. He managed to headbutt the other man with enough force that the king toppled back with a muffled curse.

Gabriel kept lunging despite the ropes chafing his wrists. "Whoreson!" he roared, his anguish an inferno of rage. "I'll kill you! I'll fucking kill you!"

"Control yourself!" Iolanthe strode into his line of sight, wearing a small smile that was somehow more off-putting than the bloodstains on her skirt. "It isn't Zenaidus's fault she stayed, you know. She had a choice, and she chose to stay"—she leaned close with a whisper that extinguished the fire of his rage—"for you."

His shoulders quaked with torment. He glanced back at Shyaree, but he couldn't see beyond the tears muddling his sight. His foolish, foolish girl. Why had she done it? His life wasn't on the line, and even if it were, it wasn't worth a single breath of hers. Yet here he was, drawing breath when she drew none. Every inhalation was a laceration in his lungs. The gods knew he deserved every single one.

Iolanthe reached out to cup his cheek in a gesture of sisterly affection that only curdled his innards. "There, there . . . it wasn't as bad as it looks. She didn't even cry. And look," she gestured magnanimously at the courtyard, now empty save the bodies. "I even ordered the guards away to preserve her dignity, but I kept you here because I know she wanted you close in her final moments."

She regarded him like a child expecting praise for a good deed.

Gabriel gave her no response, but she did not seem to take offense. In fact, she seemed to relish his tears, feed off the anguish pouring from his soul. He no longer recognized her. Perhaps his little sister *had* passed all those years ago. This was an impersonator wearing her skin. A demoness inhabiting the shell of a girl who once was . . .

"Oh yes, we hoped you'd wake in time to witness it," Zenaidus said snidely, mopping his bloodied nose with a silk kerchief while Iolanthe continued to crouch before him, a spider staring at a fly snared in its web.

"You should have seen the way the dagger manifested from the pool of her blood," the king continued with a spiteful laugh. "It congealed with every cut of the necromancer's rune into her skin, and on her last breath?" The king grinned. "Blood solidified into metal. I've never seen anything quite like it."

Zenaidus tucked his kerchief into his back pocket and fished out a deceptively small dagger with scarlet stones at the hilt. Gabriel didn't need an introduction to know he was looking at the draga morli, the dagger manifested from Shyaree's blood.

Its identical twin was still sheathed in Gabriel's boot.

As Zenaidus approached, the draga sul warmed against Gabriel's skin, seemingly excited by the proximity of its other half.

The king frowned down at the dagger in his hands. "Strange. It warms."

"It's probably lusting for your blood," Gabriel spat the words like acid on his tongue.

Zenaidus curled his lips. "Impertinent fool." He lowered to his haunches, caught a handful of Gabriel's hair, and jerked his head back. "Since you so despise the gift my father gave you, now you shall be free of it."

Zenaidus carved into his neck. Gabriel didn't need to look to know it was the necromancer's rune for *cleave*. The sharp end of the draga morli hissed against his skin like heated metal against a cool source. It wasn't an egregious wound by any means, nor did it hurt more than the pain of Shyaree's death, but the moment the dagger broke his skin, Gabriel heaved. Fluid streamed from his throat. Not blood nor bile but a black tarlike substance that tasted of bitterness and death. He *felt* death. Each and every one of them.

The unending agony of Ichor Lake . . .

The thrust of Zion's blade into his heart . . .

His head cracking against the river stones . . .

The arrows in his back, draining his magic, and the blade that had finally severed his throat . . .

Gabriel had died over and over—and now, with the rune carved into his skin, his body experienced each agony at the *same* time. His muscles locked, and vile sludge poured from his throat like rot purged from his soul. He was so overcome by the myriad sensations of death that he barely noticed Zenaidus jerking his head back by his hair again, exposing his jugular.

"What are you doing? He is already cleaved." Iolanthe's voice was shrill enough to penetrate the fog of Gabriel's torment.

"If he doesn't rise, we'll know it worked," Zenaidus retorted, dragging Gabriel's head higher.

"Isn't it already obvious?"

"Don't tell me you care what happens to him, little dove. He left you to rot for centuries."

Gabriel tried to wrench his head away, but he couldn't move. The black substance had dissolved to slurry still dribbling from the corners of his lips, but his body continued to spasm.

He met Iolanthe's gaze, searching for the sweet little girl who had once sat over his shoulder, legs kicking as she pretended to steer him like a horse. For the girl who had braved soldiers in the Winter Court Palace to break him free. He searched in her eyes for traces of his beloved sister. And for one glistening moment, he might have found her, until Iolanthe dragged her gaze away.

"As you will, my king," Iolanthe said.

Zenaidus snorted, tightening his hold on Gabriel's head, securing him in place. The king raised his arm, draga morli glinting in his grip. Gabriel growled. His fangs sharpened to points. If he was to finally meet death, he would take a piece of the king with him. Hurling an imprecation, Gabriel threw his weight back—

Iolanthe struck out like a viper.

She jammed her elbow into the king's side, tearing the blade away from Gabriel's throat with surprising dexterity. The draga morli flew from the king's hold and clattered on wood.

Fangs flashing, Zenaidus bellowed. "Iolanthe!"

She spun in a swash of whirling skirts to deliver a well-aimed kick to his groin. The king doubled over with a groan.

Gabriel scrambled toward the fallen dagger, twisting his body to pick it up with his bound hands. Grasping it in one hand, he sawed hastily at his bindings. An audible growl drew his attention back to Zenaidus. The king cuffed Iolanthe in the cheek with a force that sent her crashing off the wooden scaffold.

Zenaidus leapt off the platform, disappearing from view, but his bitter words echoed in the courtyard. "Traitorous bitch! I gave you everything! You are nothing without me!"

Iolanthe's response was a muffled hiss.

Gabriel ripped his remaining bindings free. With a feral growl, he lunged from the platform and crashed headfirst into the king. He dragged the whoreson from his sister, pummeling rage-fueled fists into the man's face. Zenaidus cowered, arms shielding his head, and that was all Gabriel needed to jam the necromancer's dagger into his gut. That was to incapacitate. He ripped it free. Now to cleave.

He began carving the rune into the king's neck.

Zenaidus squirmed in his hold like a worm speared on a fishhook, clutching at his gut, heaving tar before the rune was even complete. From the way his body convulsed, Gabriel could only imagine how many false deaths Zenaidus had endured.

Gabriel gripped the draga morli, waiting for the moment of clarity to descend over the king's face before issuing the killing blow. He wanted the wretch to feel his final death, to suffer the pain of the blade as Shyaree must have suffered.

He never got the chance.

Iolanthe jammed a nondescript knife into the king's back while he was still on his knees, vomiting sludge. A king who was no longer undying. Zenaidus sucked in wheezing gasps, black spittle speckling the ground like fungal spores. He craned his neck, staring at his bride, face petrified with disbelieving horror.

Iolanthe only smiled. "Just so you know, my love . . . I *am* queen." She flipped the blade in a practiced move and coolly plunged it into the king's back again.

Gabriel didn't stay to watch.

Draga morli in hand, he darted back onto the wooden scaffold. His stomach revolted once more at the sight of Shyaree's blood-soaked back. Zenaidus had carved all twelve runes along her spine with startling precision. Gabriel's vision blurred, but he hurried over to Zion's headless body.

To his disgust, pulpy threadlike tissue was already growing from the severed neck. The prince's vertebrae jutted, a milky-white bone covered with pink veins. Gabriel searched the prince's coat pockets, knowing Zion had tucked the seer's blood somewhere—

Where was it? He searched for a vial. A bottle. Anything. But all he found was a piece of folded parchment. A roar of frustration surged up his throat. Had the prince played him for a fool? Gabriel pulled out the parchment, unfolding it to skim the time-tattered letter. His eyes widened. Correspondence from the prophet Elias, the last known seer in the five realms, to the late Seelie queen. A letter written in *blood*. The prophet's blood?

Gabriel hurried over to Shyaree, boots sliding over the blood-slicked panels of the platform. His hands trembled as he gingerly plastered the fragile and fraying paper over the twelve stomach-turning runes carved along her scarlet-stained back. It wasn't large enough to cover the entire length, but he set the parchment over the runes of *life* and *breath.*

Fresh blood soaked into the parchment, mingling with the long-dried blood of the seer. Tears blurred his eyes once more, and he had a hysterical urge to laugh. Could he do this? Everything he knew, he'd gleaned from the necromancer's texts and the inscription upon the walls of the mausoleum . . . there was so much that could go wrong.

But not trying was not an option.

Heart pounding, he forced himself to move to her front.

Rustling movement at his back.

Gabriel tensed at Iolanthe's presence. Her cheek sported a bruise from Zenaidus's cuff, but she appeared otherwise fine. *Too* fine to have just slain her king and husband.

"Go on," she murmured, lavender eyes narrowed with undisguised interest at Shyaree's grisly back. "Don't let me stop you."

He wouldn't have. Gabriel bent to pull the draga sul from his boot, and judging by Iolanthe's shocked inhalation, she knew exactly what it was. Of course she did. The daggers were virtually identical in form, if not in function.

Lowering to his knees, he supported Shyaree's limp frame against his front, and cradled her head with a trembling hand. Stroked the hair away from the column of her graceful neck. "Please come back to me," he whispered, and made a small incision at her neck, just below the shell of her ear in the shape of a fishhook. The first cut of the rune of *life.*

He dropped the draga sul, not caring where it fell, and completed the rune with the draga morli. Done. He clasped her against him, waiting for what felt like an eternity while his thoughts turned to a raging maelstrom. Had he misinterpreted the inscription at the mausoleum? Carved the wrong rune? Carved it in the wrong place? Misused the daggers? Whatever it was, he had failed, because Shyaree remained unmoving.

All he'd accomplished was further mutilating her body.

"Hmm . . . " Iolanthe smoothed out her bloodstained skirt, her legs primly crossed as she sat on the edge of the platform. "Well, that's underwhelming."

Desolation sank talons into his chest, triggering a new wave of anguish. His fingers tightened over the hilt of the draga morli until his knuckles trembled. He cupped the back of Shyaree's head, pressing his forehead against hers and . . . felt a breath. He jerked back, staring hard.

Her chest *rose.* And *fell.*

The draga morli clattered from his grip. Shyaree's eyelids remained closed, but her eyes moved rapidly beneath, as though she were merely dreaming. Asleep.

Alive.

His wildcat was alive. If he weren't already on his knees, he would have fallen to them. A sob leaked from his lips. He needed to get her home. Keys. Where was the damned key?

A feminine chuckle. "Looking for these?"

Iolanthe dangled a key before him. "Hand me those daggers, brother, and I'll give you the key to her cuffs."

Gabriel stared. Iolanthe could have picked up both daggers, and he wouldn't have noticed. Instead, she had busied herself with the key. Why? He didn't have time to contemplate her actions, not when his heart was chained and bleeding. He retrieved the daggers from the blood-soaked platform and relinquished them without second thought, earning himself a soft smile. Not the smile of the cold-blooded killer, but one with a semblance of sisterly affection. "I am very pleased to have witnessed the power of these daggers firsthand . . . but how did you know exactly which of the twelve runes to carve into her skin?"

Gabriel shook his head, his tongue tangled, his mind spinning. Had they never embarked on Shyaree's quest for the curse-breaking elixir, he would never have found the mausoleum. He would never have seen the runes or read the inscription upon those walls.

Iolanthe rolled her eyes, seemingly impatient. "It doesn't matter. I will find out eventually." She pressed the key into his hand. "Remember this moment, brother . . . because this will be the *final* favor you'll get from me."

Gabriel shook his head, his tongue untangling. "It's not too late. We can—"

She let out an abrupt, shrill scream. "Guards! *Guards!*"

Gabriel spun for the platform.

"The king! He's hurt the king!" Iolanthe's shrieks evoked a storm of rushing footsteps. "Guards! Save the king!"

Gabriel slotted the key frantically into the fetter to undo the first shackle.

Footsteps intensified. Soldiers pouring into the courtyard. Frenzied shouts rose at the sight of their fallen king. Gabriel pulled threads of magic from the shadows even as the soldiers hollered for him to cease and desist. Their footsteps thundered closer.

Gabriel undid the second shackle. Shyaree sagged into him, free. Alive. But still bleeding. He had to get her to a healer. Not just any healer. One with supernatural ability—*Evangeline*. He needed to get Shyaree to Amereen Castle. Now. He slid his arms beneath her legs, scooped her up, and rushed into his shadows.

Something pierced his portal, striking his back with a fresh jolt of pain.

Another fucking arrow.

It pitched him to his knees in a haze of hurt and panic. Magic slipped from his control like water seeping through his fingers. His shadows unraveled.

His portal imploded in fractures of blinding light.

CHAPTER 34

Gabriel blinked with a groan. Sunlight pierced his irises like tiny shards of glass, but he forced his eyes open. Ozenn's blood. His muscles ached, and his back throbbed, but Shyaree . . .

Her head lolled against his chest, her ashen pallor driving him to his feet.

He cradled her tighter, murmuring reassurances that were more for himself than her. "It'll be all right, darling. You'll be all right . . . " He took one excruciating step forward before he realized he had no idea where they were—his portal had fractured. He glanced around, his heart sinking. This was not Amereen Castle.

There were no neatly manicured lawns, no sandstone walls or white rosebushes. No archmage. No Evangeline. No magical healing.

Instead, woodland crowded at his back. A valley stretched before him into an open field of cropland beside a small village.

He sucked in a harrowed breath. He had no idea where they were. *Fuck!* Gabriel attempted another portal. He pulled from the shadows, willing threads of magic to obey him. Nothing. His body had once again been drained by the damned arrow.

He shut his eyes, drawing in a centering breath. At the very least they were not lost in the Abyss—the amorphous void between realms. He needed to get Shyaree to Evangeline.

Gods, why was she still bleeding?

Blood seeped from her wounds, dribbling from her already battered body. Gabriel latched his mouth to the gash on her nape, drawing in a mouthful of it. Something was different—it no longer hummed with power. Perhaps it had something to do with her death. Or perhaps it was simply because she had changed. She was no longer mahalwei. All the while, the arrow in his back leached whatever magic he did draw from her blood.

Despair weighed like stones in his gut, but desperation whipped him like a spur. He put one foot in front of the other. There *had* to be a way. If there was a village, there could be a healer. He refused to let her die again.

Renewed rage mounted in his chest, driving him forward. He would find a way to revive her once more if she did. He would follow her through the gates of all five hells if he had to, but he refused to lose her again.

He *refused.*

He clung to that mantra, clung to his fury and used it to fuel him one shaky step after the other. The sharp spice of pine resin rose from the needles crushed beneath his boots until he came upon a barn. The sound of laughter.

"Help . . . "

A trio of children playing with a jump rope screamed and scattered at the sight of him.

"Help . . . " Gabriel collapsed, the arrow in his back jarring with fresh pain. He lay on his side, wheezing like a landed fish, still clutching Shyaree in his arms.

"Don't you dare take her," he whispered aloud, both a

threat and prayer to the five gods. "Don't you dare take her without me."

A splash roused him from the fog of stupor. A stinging slap to his cheek woke him fully. Gabriel shook his head, blinking against the water dripping into his eyes.

He lifted his head with a groan. "Shyaree . . . ?"

"Who are you?" asked a gruff voice attached to a burly figure.

"Why have you come here?" asked another voice.

Alarm speared his senses. His weapons were gone. He was stripped down to his skin, wearing only his pants and boots, while his arms were bound behind his back. Again.

Gabriel snarled. "Where's Shyaree?"

He was pressed against a giant oak tree in the middle of wide-ranging farmland, surrounded by four men. Three were tall and strapping, but the fourth was long limbed and lanky, so young he was hardly a man. They all wore work tunics, stained and frayed at the edges. Two of the men carried pitchforks, and the boy held a bucket. None wore a remotely friendly expression.

The ginger-haired one with a bushy beard aimed a pitchfork in his direction. "Answer us, Unseelie!"

Gabriel scrambled to his feet, canines sharpening. "Where is she? What have you done to the woman I was with? Why am I bound?"

In his periphery, a scarecrow smirked at him with one missing eye, standing jauntily over a field of green-leaved crop that seemed to stretch for leagues.

"What have *you* done to her?" Ginger Beard retorted. "She

was cut up bad and barely alive."

Barely alive . . .

Gabriel strained against his bonds. "Return her to me!"

When the men only glared at him, blackfire erupted from his hands, destroying the rope binding his wrists. The men shouted, jumping away from him in shock, but Gabriel was just as stunned. He stared at his hands and the curious black flames dancing over his fingers. Ozenn's blood, he hadn't managed this since his time in the dungeon.

Since Zephyr had ripped it out of him and replaced it with a piece of his soul.

"Calm down." The blond man with a pitchfork held out a palm to placate him. "The woman is fine."

Gabriel's thundering heart refused to slow. He couldn't calm when he couldn't see her. "Where is she?"

Blondie's eyes narrowed. "Who in Chonsea's mercy are you, and how did you find us?"

Gabriel's ears pricked at the man's choice of goddess. Was he in the human realm, then? "You'll get your answers when you bring her to me. I want to see her."

Ginger Beard aimed the pitchfork at Gabriel once more. "You've got a funny way of expressing gratitude, Unseelie, after all the healing Quentin's given you."

It was only then Gabriel realized he was backed into the tree . . . no arrowhead lodged in his flesh, no pain at his back. He rolled his shoulders experimentally and suffered no pain.

His jaw slackened. "How long was I out?"

"It's been one hour or so since sissy found you," supplied the boy, still clutching the bucket.

One hour? What could they have done to help him recover from an arrow wound in the span of a single hour? Only Evangeline could have . . .

Gabriel's eyes widened. They were conversing in his mother

tongue. *Faerian.* But these men did not look fae. There were no purple irises, no pointed ears, no fangs. It was possible they veiled their appearances with magic—even a faeling could accomplish that—yet they didn't *feel* fae. Gabriel sensed no magical aura around them, no affinity for the threads of Ozenn that would have called to his own.

"Who healed me?" he demanded.

There was a long pause before Blondie admitted, "I did."

"Quentin . . . ," protested the unarmed man with unruly brown hair vaguely like a lion's mane. But Quentin only speared his pitchfork into the ground with a shake of his head, silencing all protests. He lanced Gabriel with an assessing glance. "I assume Shyaree is the woman with you?" He jerked a thumb over his shoulder, toward a humble farmhouse with a sloping roof. "She is in the house right now, with my wife. And she's safe. Now we have answered two of your questions. You will answer ours. Fair?"

Gabriel scowled at Ginger Beard, who still held a pitchfork aimed unerringly in his direction as though he were a mindless bull ready to charge at the slightest flash of red, but he nodded. There was a peaceable quality to Quentin's tone, one that coaxed him to a wary calm.

"My name is Gabriel Blacksage. I was on my way to the mage realm when my portal imploded. Who are you?"

He received no response. Fair enough. Gabriel licked his lips. "Thank you for your healing, but Shyaree must be returned to me."

Quentin's eyes flashed. "Do you work for the cartel?"

An incredulous laugh escaped Gabriel's throat. No wonder the men eyed him with such circumspection despite healing him. They thought Gabriel was a slave trader. He shook his head. "I am guildmaster of the Red Knights. I have nothing to do with the cartel, and Shyaree is my . . . " He swallowed. She wasn't his mate, nor was she merely a lover. "She is my heart."

Quentin continued to regard him warily, but the stiff line of his mouth seemed to soften. "Why was her skin mutilated? Who hurt her? And who shot you?"

"We were trying to escape from Winter Court soldiers when I—"

"The Winter Court," Quentin said sharply. "You were running from King Zephyr?"

Gabriel blinked. "Zephyr is gone."

A subtle murmur ran among the men. Lion Head and Ginger Beard shifted uneasily, while Quentin's eyes narrowed. "Zephyr is dead?"

"I didn't say he was dead. I said he was gone." Gabriel swept a narrowed gaze at the men. "You're all Seelie, aren't you?"

Only the Seelie could heal such egregious wounds, leaving his body completely hale, in such a short period of time. The only problem was . . . Evangeline was the *only* one left of her kind. Allegedly, anyway.

Their only response was the tightening of their expressions. "Your portal imploded? And you landed *here*?" Quentin pressed. "Why—"

"Quentin?" interrupted a soft, female voice.

Gabriel turned to the source, and his knees nearly buckled. Standing beside a short woman in a checkered dress was *Shyaree*. No longer covered in blood and grime and the horrors that had been carved into her skin, but a formless dress that barely reached her knees.

When her gaze met his, it welled with tears. In relief or anger, he did not know, but she did not immediately rush to his side.

"Shyaree," Gabriel whispered, stepping forward like a man in a trance only to be herded back by Ginger Beard, who seemed insistent on waving the pronged ends of his pitchfork at Gabriel.

Gabriel scowled. "Keep aiming that at me, and you'll come to regret it."

"Oh yeah?" Ginger Beard sneered, not the least intimidated. "We'll see about that."

Gabriel liked him immediately. A hard roughness to him spoke of a warrior's bearing. They all had it.

"She can't seem to speak, but she insisted on leaving the bed," the brunette woman said. "I figured she was looking for . . . him."

"You should have kept her in the house, Kadie." Quentin stepped into Gabriel's line of sight, blocking his view of Shyaree. "How do I know you won't take your woman and leave?"

Gabriel fisted his hands. "If you're so afraid, why heal me in the first place?"

Quentin tensed, and his tone turned combative. "Have I made a mistake? Should I not have?"

"I won't betray you or your people. You have my word."

"Your word means little given what you are."

Unseelie. They didn't trust him because he was Unseelie.

"I am not an enemy," Gabriel insisted, shifting to keep his sights on Shyaree. She lingered beside Kadie, wearing an unreadable expression that heightened Gabriel's restlessness. Was she angry with him? Something in his gut sank. How could she not be?

Softening his tone, he asked in Animatish, "Are you all right, darling?"

To his alarm, she clenched and unclenched her hands. Tears dribbled down her cheeks.

Her reaction did not go unnoticed by the Seelie. The men bristled, crowding around Gabriel as though he were a slaver in their midst.

"She doesn't look like she *wants* to be your heart," Lion Head said with a curl of his lips. "I know your kind. Unseelie sadists with a taste for a woman's fear."

Gabriel scrubbed a frustrated hand over his face. "You asked why I was headed to the mage realm before my portal imploded. I was trying to take Shyaree to . . . Freya." He would not disclose Evangeline's current name or title until he was certain these men were who he thought they were. "I serve Freya Jilintree."

The men blinked collectively before bursting into laughter. Quentin shook his head. "Do you take us for fools? The Jilintrees are long gone, along with the Summer Court, or we wouldn't be here. And why would Freya be in the *mage* realm?"

"Freya survived," Gabriel insisted, but he refused to give them any further information. "She is the reason Zephyr is gone. You only have to return to the fae realm, and you'll know. The prince Zenaidus has been king for a full sun cycle." And was now dead.

The Seelie men did not receive the news well. Chuckles faded to murmuring frowns. "You blaspheme," Ginger Beard said. "The Jilintrees are all gone . . . had they lived, Queen Katerina would never have fallen."

Gabriel snorted with a roll of his eyes. "Freya was a child during the war. She couldn't have helped even if she hadn't fallen prey to Zephyr's men."

"Liar!" Lion Head cried. "He's a spy. That woman and everything must be a ruse to rouse our sympathy, Quentin. Our location is compromised. We should silence him."

Quentin ripped his pitchfork from the dirt, aiming the three sharp prongs squarely at Gabriel's throat. "Is that why you're here? Have you come with lies to convince us to return?"

Gabriel exhaled. "Look—"

Kadie's shriek and the boy's stuttering alarm diverted their attention.

Shyaree craned her neck. So far sideways it almost looked like her head would dislocate, but in the next heart-stopping breath, she changed.

Gabriel's jaw grew slack. He had never seen her change so painlessly or so *quickly.* Too fast for the eye to follow. One moment she was standing on two feet, and in the next blink she was on all fours, covered in glistening black fur. There were no painful moans, no cracking bones or tearing muscles. She had changed in a single breath—exactly as animati were born to do.

Stormy eyes pinned on Quentin, Shyaree released a warning growl, tail lashing as her sinewy form crouched low, poised for an attack.

Gabriel rocked back on his heels. Shyaree was defending him. After everything he'd done, and everything he'd put her through, she was *still* protecting him.

She humbled him beyond words.

Quentin and Ginger Beard both raised their pitchforks in alarm.

"No!" Gabriel darted forward, planting himself between his wildcat and the Seelie. He would not allow the men to harm her in their ignorance, nor did he want to see them hurt. He pulled threads of magic from the shadows of the overarching oak. Darkness eddied, foggy tendrils of a nascent portal.

Quentin bared his blunt teeth, which sharpened to fangs. Definitely fae. Seelie fae.

"You are not leaving!" Vines speared from the ground, coiling around his ankle and startling Shyaree into a growl.

An uncontrolled arc of blackfire burst from Gabriel's hand, scorching a crescent patch in the ground. He raised his brow, impressed by the intensity of his own magic. He'd been missing out on *that* this whole time? Fuck Zephyr to the five flaming hells.

More vines crept up around his ankles, but they were

smooth and curling tendrils. Meant to deter, not harm. Proof they did not genuinely believe him a Winter Court spy. Gabriel had fought enough Seelie warriors in his conscription days to know their kind were capable of viciousness if they wanted. Nevertheless, he wasn't staying where their pitchforks could end up injuring his wildcat.

Another burst of blackfire dissuaded more vines.

"If you wanted a prisoner, you shouldn't have healed me." Gabriel backed toward his portal, herding Shyaree into it. She could have leapt out of the way at any moment, but she didn't. To his relief, she *allowed* him to herd her into the thick of his shadows.

"The Red Den in Evenmere," Gabriel called before his portal ebbed, knowing Quentin and his men would come. When they were ready.

Chapter 35

They stepped from his shadows onto a riverbank laden with smooth oval stones. Not the river on Thurin's Mountain, but the tributary close to Shyaree's clan.

His wildcat looked around with a faint chuffing sound, clearly recognizing her home territory. She paced a short distance along the river. Her sinewy muscles rippled with each step in sleek, feline grace. Before she could run from him, Gabriel lowered to the ground, his knees kissing unforgiving stones less than three handspans from the river's edge. Surprisingly, he no longer felt the pang of fear being at such proximity to water.

"Shyaree."

She paused her pacing.

Ozenn's blood, she was *magnificent*. Thick, soft fur with darker rosettes hidden like black roses in her gleaming coat. Long, elegant whiskers and a sweeping tail. Beautiful storm-gray eyes that had always spoken to his soul.

"Shyaree," he called again, reaching for her head, wanting to—

A rumbling growl halted him.

He was painfully aware that he was no longer undying. She was in her pantherai form. He'd watched soldiers fall like pins in the courtyard from a single graze of her sharp, venomous teeth. He stretched out his hand anyway. If she chose to snap, he'd die with peace in his heart knowing he'd brought her home. Alive.

She held his gaze for a long, assessing moment before she lowered her head into his palm. Rubbed her face into his hand in a brief, nonaggressive nudge, but it was not affectionate, either. She glanced back at the path to her village.

Gabriel's fingers curled, and he forced his hand back to his lap. "I won't stop you if you wish to go, wildcat . . . but will you allow me one moment? Hear what I have to say?"

She sniffed daintily, tail twitching, but she lowered herself to her haunches.

Overwhelming relief clogged his throat. "I'm sorry." The words tumbled from him in a rush, his voice humiliatingly hoarse. "I'm so sorry. I should never have lied to you. I should never have put you through all that, but I did, and I hate myself for it. I was so desperate to free my sister, to free myself from Zephyr's soulbond, that I thought I was willing to pay any price, even at the expense of my own conscience and my heart. But I was a fool." He paused to scrub at the tears coursing down his cheek. "Perhaps I could have cut out my conscience, but I would rather cut out my own heart than see you come to any harm. I'm sorry I ever thought I *could* cause you harm. I'm sorry I ever thought your life was worth the price. I . . . " He couldn't continue because sobs racked him.

It took him several breaths to compose himself. He opened his mouth to say more, to explain his reasons, but lowered his head. He would not feed her worthless excuses.

"I know I don't deserve to ask your forgiveness"—the gods

knew he didn't fucking deserve *her*—"but I'm going to beg for it anyway."

His only response was a slow blink of her eyes and a languorous flick of her tail.

Gabriel shuffled closer on his knees, wishing she would change back to her two-legged form and handspeak with him. Rail at him. Slap him. Bite him. She did none of that.

She observed him regally, like a queen at a hearing, withholding her judgment.

Gabriel hung his head, awaiting his sentence. It did not seem forthcoming. "What can I say to make you forgive me? What can I do to make it up to you? You only have to name it, and I will do anything you ask."

If she asked for his blood, he would cut open his veins and pour it at her feet.

If she asked for the moon, he would find a way to grow wings.

If she asked for his life, he would bare his jugular for her teeth.

If only.

She asked him for nothing. She continued to regard him with solemn eyes and gut-wrenching silence. His heart sank, misery precipitating deep in his marrow. "Do you need time? I can wait. I will wait however long you need. Shyaree . . . please." Gabriel shuffled further forward until his knees bumped into her soft paws. "Please don't leave me."

The bone-chilling memory of her strung up, bloodied and lifeless, on the wooden crossbeam flashed in his mind's eye. Tears obscured his sight once more. "If I could turn back time, I would never—" He shuddered and reached for her again, needing to feel her, to reassure himself that she was indeed here. Alive.

She released a soft chuffing sound, but she didn't back away from him.

Relief was a tidal wave flooding through him. Sucking in a tremulous breath, he lowered his head and buried his face in her flank, relishing the feel of her warmth, drawing in the familiar sweetness of her scent. "I'm so sorry, Shyaree. Darling. Gods, I'm so sorry . . . "

He pulled away once he regained his composure, rubbing his eyes with the back of his hand before he could further humiliate himself by soaking her fur. But she seemed content to remain despite his incoherent blathering. Hope fluttered in his chest like the wings of a newborn sparrow. She must still care for him, because she had defended him from the Seelie men. His wildcat with her sharp claws and her soft, soft heart.

Something else occurred to him, torment squeezing in his chest.

"Why did you do it? Why didn't you use my portal back at Duskhall?" His voice thickened. "Why would you allow yourself to be sacrificed?"

Her heart constricted; a storm raged beneath her breastbone, but her pantherai merely displayed it through a flick of her tail. Shyaree had conceded to her sacrifice for the same reason Gabriel had killed Zion and those priests at the very last moment, the same reason he'd leapt toward his enemies while urging her through his portal—or at least, she *hoped* his motives were the same.

She loved him.

She loved him so much that the thought of him being tortured, even for a single moment, was so abhorrent she would give anything to avoid it.

Even her life.

Perhaps it was foolish, but she didn't really have a choice. She couldn't stop loving him any more than she could keep the sun from rising. Her heart belonged to him so wholly and irrevocably that even now she ached to change into her two-legged form to draw him into her arms and hold him. To demand the answers she so desperately needed, yet so anxiously feared. Back at Duskhall, he'd said he loved her, but he'd been about to die. Had he said it, had he done everything to stop her sacrifice out of love . . . or a guilty conscience?

Gabriel could have taken her to anywhere in the five realms, but he'd brought her *here.* To the very spot where he'd abducted her—he was clearly ready to let her go.

Her human body was not only her most vulnerable state, but it was also the form most susceptible to Gabriel. She would not be able to part ways with him with her head held high and her eyes dry. At the very least, her pantherai allowed her to conceal heartache beneath fur and fangs.

"I told you never to risk your life for mine. I'm not worth it, you know," Gabriel continued, and despite the torment in his tone, she caught the edge of mild exasperation. "Why won't you ever listen to me, wildcat?"

Irritation rippled over her skin.

Why did her choice matter? Clearly he had stopped her sacrifice in time. She had fainted somewhere after the king started carving the eighth rune into her back. Maybe it was the seventh. She couldn't be sure. But her guildmaster must have broken free and saved them both. How else could they have escaped?

"When I lost you"—his throat worked—"it broke something inside me, Shyaree. I can't . . . I can't ever see you like that again."

Lost her? What in Thurin's wrath was the man talking

about? A rumble of annoyance surfaced at her inability to communicate. She nosed into his palm, chuffing her confusion. But Gabriel must have mistaken her gesture as a request for head pats because he stroked her crown, even scratching behind her ears.

Pleasure hummed in her chest even as annoyance ratcheted in her heart. Thurin's wrath. She wasn't getting closer to any answers in this form.

Gathering her courage, Shyaree changed.

She expected agony, but it never came. A single slow blink, and her body changed as easily as a deep exhale. She glanced down at herself, checking for signs of polymorphism, but there were no missing fingers or toes, no fur or scales. She was—

Gabriel dragged her into his arms like an overzealous child with his favorite doll. "Shyaree," he whispered roughly into her hair. "Darling."

She shivered in his hold, acutely aware of her nudity and his lack of a shirt. They were pressed skin to skin, and this body reacted in ways her pantherai hadn't. She pushed away in a weak attempt to create distance, and he reluctantly released her. Only then did she notice the faint mark on the column of his throat. A scar.

"What is that?" She traced it with her finger.

"The rune for *cleave*. Zenaidus severed my soulbond to his father."

Shyaree's lips parted as she processed the ramifications of his words. *"You are no longer undying?"*

He shook his head.

"How did that happen without the draga morli?"

Gabriel looked at her strangely. "Zenaidus used the draga morli. Darling, you . . . died. You fulfilled the prophecy." He reached for her, and when she didn't resist, he pulled her into his arms once more. "You have no idea, do you?"

She could only stare. He brushed her hair from her neck and traced a spot just below her earlobe. "Can you feel this? I cut this into your skin . . . to raise you."

Kadie, the woman who had healed her in the farmhouse, must have done a remarkable job, because all she felt was smooth skin. She pushed away from Gabriel again to sign her alarm. *"You raised me? From the dead?"*

Amethyst eyes tracked her face with unconcealed anguish. "I couldn't let you go. Shyaree. Wildcat. Darling . . . I love you. Had I failed, I would have followed you."

Shyaree sucked in a shuddering breath, and he misunderstood her reaction. "I would have followed you through all the five gates of hell and wrestled the fates to find you, Shyaree."

She shook her head. *"You love me?"*

He bridged the distance between them, shattering every safeguard of her heart with a simple whisper. "So much." His lips met hers in a drugging kiss and demolished all lingering doubts in her mind until they crumbled to ash at his feet. "I love you so much it scares me. I've loved you for a long time, Shyaree. I was just never brave enough to admit it."

Chapter 36

One moon later

The sun dipped close to the horizon, painting streaks of orange, gold and reds in the castle's backdrop. A low-hanging branch slapped his face. Gabriel muttered a low curse as he wrestled the unruly branch into submission and harvested a luscious cluster of kovi from its shoots. Just a few more to fill his sack before he headed home.

Heady anticipation hummed in his chest.

He had taken to portaling Shyaree to a new location each day. A once-prosaic activity now filled him with giddiness. His wildcat made the most mundane of places—even a common pasture of roaming cows—seem like a new experience. She was always curious, though it was not her inquisitive nature that made everything seem like an adventure, but her unfettered excitement. She relished discovering new places, while he relished watching her face light up with the same zeal to a sugared plum and a public outhouse.

Would she light up at his surprise later?

A bout of nervousness coiled in his gut. He wasn't taking her out of the Den today, but to the one place in his manor that she was not yet privy to—a part of him he had yet to bare . . . but what if she didn't like it?

Gabriel frowned at himself. Why wouldn't she?

Shyaree had already seen the darkest and ugliest part of him, but she accepted him anyway. More than accepted. She had forgiven him. And she had spent the last weeks showing him *exactly* how sweet and forgiving she could be.

A beam spread across his face at nothing in particular. He had always assumed he would eventually rot in the five hells . . . but it seemed the gods had deigned to give him a second chance. Cleaved from Zephyr's soulbond, he was finally free to live his life for himself. And he would spend the rest of it cherishing her.

The tension between his shoulders eased, and he resumed raiding the branch. He had contemplated his surprise for days now. She would like it. He was certain. Well, *almost* certain. And if she didn't . . . he would make up for it. In bed.

Now with *that*, he was confident.

A whistle started from his lips. He had to appear a jaunty fool perched on the ladder against the kovi tree, but luckily there was no one around to witness his—

"You are becoming rather predictable, Blacksage."

Just two paces away stood the archmage of Amereen, seemingly materialized from thin air. He probably had. Declan regarded him with narrowed eyes and crossed arms as though he'd caught Gabriel red-handed in the middle of a felonious crime.

Gabriel flattened his lips before plucking another bunch of kovi off the branch. "Oh? How so?"

Declan nodded at Gabriel's half-filled burlap sack beside his discarded baldric and swords. "Coming here every week. Stealing my berries."

"Stealing?" Gabriel cocked an indignant brow. "Evie said I was welcome to as many as I wanted."

A welcome he was grateful for considering the berries grown from Evie's magic yielded significantly superior fruit.

The archmage stalked over and rudely helped himself to a handful of Gabriel's harvest.

"That may be so, but my little fire was probably unaware that you'd abuse her welcome." He leaned a shoulder against the trunk and popped a berry into his mouth.

"Evie was the one who insisted Shyaree get whatever she might want or need from the castle." It was unfortunate that kovi only grew in the mage realm, or Gabriel would have long since planted a grove in his own backyard. He selected another bunch and gently deposited the cluster into the sack so as not to damage them. His wildcat wasn't picky, but she much preferred overripe berries—which bruised easily if he wasn't careful.

Declan chewed thoughtfully, lips curving into a slow smile. "Hmm. So you've been giving Shyaree everything she needs?"

Gabriel frowned, increasingly disturbed. This was all Evangeline's doing. Before that girl entered the archmage's life, he couldn't recall the last time Declan had cracked a smile. But now? Declan Thorne, one of the eight supreme rulers of the mage realm, seemed to have nothing better to do with his time than wander about in the orchard, needling him over a handful of berries.

"Where is Evie?" Gabriel asked wryly.

"In Mailin's chambers. Fawning over the little one."

A slow turn of his mind supplied a memory of cherubic cheeks and a gurgling laugh. Waylen An Jin Teranos. Killian's boy. Gabriel snickered. "You were passed over for a baby?"

Another bunch of kovi levitated from the sack straight into the archmage's open palm. Declan shrugged coolly. "At least I'm not wearing berry juice on my face."

Gabriel scrubbed his face with the back of his hand, muttering a low curse. Damned overripe berries. He hopped off the ladder and tied his sack before the bastard could tax any more of his harvest.

"I would keep you company." Gabriel smirked. "But my wildcat is waiting. Tell Evie and Mailin I said hi, won't you?" He strapped on his holster belt and baldric.

"Gabriel." The archmage's tone was devoid of the teasing banter from just a moment ago. This tone Gabriel knew well. He sighed. He should have known the archmage was never one to amble about without an agenda.

"Evangeline recalls a Quentin among her father's men," Declan said. "I wish to meet him."

Gabriel had gathered his nerve and divulged the truth. The *full* truth. As he'd anticipated, the archmage had descended into a frosty rage . . . but remarkably, not for the reasons Gabriel had expected. Declan's greatest point of contention was not Gabriel's inadvertent involvement in Zephyr's undying state, but the fact that he hadn't shared it earlier.

It had been a humbling and heartening notion.

"I do not think they would welcome strangers. Much less an archmage."

Frown lines wrinkled Declan's brow. "I will not hurt Evangeline's people."

"I will not betray their location." Gabriel secured his baldric and picked up his sack. "But should they ever come by the Den, I'll send word."

As unaccustomed to denial as he might have been, the archmage acceded with a nod before he launched into the next query with the bluntness of a hammer. "And what of your sister? Have you heard more since she was crowned queen regent?"

A pang struck Gabriel's chest. After all that had transpired, he still struggled to believe his sister had married that whoreson. He struggled reconciling the memory of his sweet baby sister with the woman she had become. He struggled . . . but he would accept it. They all made their own choices. Iolanthe had made hers.

"Iolanthe has made no overt move since her crowning, although Zion remains, allegedly, missing." Gabriel wasn't sure if his sister had ended that bastard . . . or if Zion had somehow escaped, however unlikely that possibility may be.

Unease glinted in emerald eyes. Clearly, Iolanthe as queen regent on the Winter Court throne *and* in possession of the draga sul and the draga morli disquieted the archmage as much as it did him.

"Evangeline and I have recently visited Nathaniel. She inspected the Soul Tree, and Zephyr remains entombed." A grim smile. "But the tree suffered the loss of several branches. According to Nathaniel, the leaves shriveled and the branches blackened before turning to ash."

Gabriel snorted. "I hope Zephyr felt every moment."

And he hoped it was excruciating.

The archmage chuckled as the shadows of Gabriel's portal spun to life. He was about to step through when Declan spoke his name again.

Gabriel turned back with an inquiring brow.

"You are always welcome here. Don't forget that."

Shyaree set the platter before the man who had catalyzed her first change, motioning for him to eat. Arkas only returned her guarded gaze with a stiff-lipped glower. Sweat and blood and grime—he was covered in it. Stank of it. But still, the traitor managed to appear rigidly affronted by her presence.

Gabriel had never released his former second-in-command from the cellar. Nor had he meted out punishment. Perhaps Arkas's continued imprisonment could be considered a punishment, but Shyaree knew her guildmaster. Had it been any other, Gabriel would have long since slain the traitor without losing a wink of sleep.

She would have been happy to forget his existence, but Arkas meant more to Gabriel than he cared to admit. The blackguard was not only his cousin but the one who had once rescued him from the dungeons of the Winter Court. Years of companionship and brotherhood bound them together, not so easily severed by Arkas's erroneous actions.

So here she was—making a reluctant attempt to overcome Arkas's prejudices against her because he meant something to her guildmaster.

"I'd rather starve to death," Arkas muttered, words clearly for her ears as he spoke the tongue of her people, turning his nose from the platter.

Shyaree sneered. Hopefully sooner rather than later.

"Don't be an ass," Caspian said with a scowl at the shackled scoundrel, exasperation heightening his tone. "Eat. Or I'll shove it down your throat."

Caspian had replied in Animatish even when he hadn't needed to. It was a subtle gesture, one that warmed beneath her breastbone. No matter Arkas's bullheaded biases, the rest of the guild had made attempts to accept her as guildmistress, queen of the Red Knights and lady of the Red Den—frivolous terms Gabriel had laughingly coined but earnestly, seriously imposed.

Gabriel had brought her back to the Den, begged her to stay, and when she'd agreed, he had declared it her home. *"Treat Shyaree as anything less and you will have me to answer to,"* he had announced to all and sundry.

Which was just as well because soon after, she had returned to her clan to discover that her curse-breaking elixir had indeed worked. Her twin had recovered.

And the first thing Reiken did?

Cast her out.

Not for the murder of Hesok and his cronies—their bodies had never been found—but for stealing his dagger and her ill-advised *mating* with an Unseelie. It didn't matter that she could have died in the process of trying to save him. Her brother had discarded her like a worm-infested apple.

She was so hurt that she grew numb from it.

It was ironic how both her and Gabriel's misguided decisions—made for the benefit of their siblings—had led to this. They'd both started in disillusionment, seeking to salvage what was better left to rot.

Then again, had they acted differently, they would never have found each other. Two broken hearts with jagged edges that somehow fit together to create something whole.

Chains jiggled. Back against the stone wall, Arkas managed to shove the platter with a bad-tempered nudge of his foot, splashing the steaming stew close to her own feet.

Caspian hissed. "What in Ozenn's blood . . . I'm going to shorten your chains for that."

Shyaree, having jumped back before the stew could scald her, shifted without hesitation.

She wanted to show the blackguard that she now had control of her inner form—of her venom . . . and, if she was honest, she also wanted to intimidate. She prowled up to Arkas with a snarl that displayed her sharpened teeth. To his credit, he did not so much as flinch, but the slight bobbing of his throat did not escape her.

Satisfied, she snapped her teeth with a low growl.

The former second-in-command only tightened his lips.

Sniffing with disdain, Shyaree turned to the stairs. Caspian could deal with the mess. Before she made it past the first step, Arkas's voice stalled her. "Even as a boy, Gabe had a fascination for all things sharp and dangerous."

Shyaree paused, ears twitching.

"His games terrified me, but I always played along. Always ready to rein him in if he got too reckless." A mirthless chuckle. "I never wanted to admit it, but sometimes, just sometimes . . . I liked them."

It was no apology, but it was the closest Arkas had ever come to speaking words of acceptance. Shyaree met his gaze. She wasn't sure if they could ever be friends. She could find forgiveness in her heart—she could relate to misguided intentions—but she would never forget.

Shyaree issued a noncommittal nod before padding up the steps. She passed through the heart of the Den, where the patrons stared at her openly. Once, she would have found their stares off-putting. But now she cast them a cursory glance before climbing up the next flight of stairs to her chambers.

Gabriel had taken to tying black sashes over doorknobs so she could easily tug and open doors in her pantherai form. He was exceedingly thoughtful, and somehow, still exceedingly exasperating in certain circumstances.

Since moving her into the Den, Gabriel had given her one rule: *"I do not like sharing, wildcat. Not even a peek. If you change into your human form before another man, I will gouge out his eyes."*

She hadn't really believed him . . . until one day she had opted to shift in an empty parlor. She had been seized by a sudden *notion*. She had been so eager to test it, and the privacy of their bedchamber was four flights of stairs away. In her haste, she had not realized a drunkard lay sleeping beside a couch.

The unfortunate male woke just in time to cop an eyeful.

When Gabriel realized what had happened, he had tossed the drunkard from the Den with a warning—and without his eyes.

The fae would regrow his eyeballs . . . eventually. But the poor man would wander sightless for at least a sun cycle first. Since then, Shyaree had been mindful to shift only within the confines of their chambers.

But her *notion* had been right, and tonight she would share it with Gabriel as a surprise.

She was nude and digging through the drawers for undergarments when her guildmaster stalked in. His lips parted in surprise, but he quickly closed the door behind him. His gaze roamed over her, and his lips curved with toe-curling intent.

Shyaree met his lascivious smirk with one of her own.

Purple stained his cheek in an adorable smudge, and the tangy-sweet scent of her favorite fruit clung to him. She didn't need to ask to know where he'd gone or what he'd been up to. If she wandered down to the kitchen, she would doubtless find the pantry stocked with fresh kovi.

She tossed the undergarment back into the dresser and shimmied onto the bed with a coy smile. *"Hello, guildmaster."*

"Hello, darling." He didn't join her on the bed. Instead, he marched around the mattress and picked up the broad silk sash draped inconspicuously on the wooden headboard. "How was your day, hmm?"

Heat pinched her cheeks as she remembered how he'd used the ribbon on her the night before. The beast knew exactly what ran through her mind, because he toyed with the sash and his voice lowered to a sexy rasp.

"Come here, wildcat."

A bald command, but she obeyed. She crawled over on the bed, slowly and languorously, until his eyes darkened to amethyst fire and the strong column of his throat worked.

She'd play his little game the way she liked it.

"Turn around." His voice had thickened.

Smirking, she obeyed again. Instead of binding her arms as he'd done last night, he slid it across her eyes. Blindfolded her.

A thrill snaked down her spine. This was new.

His lips skimmed her shoulders in a soft kiss, his breath tickling her skin, stoking her blood to a sensual simmer. Shyaree sighed and stirred, wanting his hands on her body. He gave her bottom a firm pat. "Patience, darling."

She sniffed.

The wardrobe creaked open, and Gabriel rummaged through its contents. Shyaree's skin tingled. Was he introducing a new toy for their bed play?

He approached her and . . . bundled her up in a cloak.

She yanked off her blindfold, lips pursed. *"What are you doing?"*

He pointed mournfully to the bulge in his pants. "I'm chafing at the sight of you, wildcat."

She stared incredulously. *"I'm right here!"*

He chuckled, pressed a pacifying kiss to her lips, then slid her blindfold back in place. "Later. I have . . . something to show you." His voice wavered. "A surprise. And I want you to see it while the sun is up."

Curiosity sufficiently piqued, she allowed him to lead her off the bed without protest. His shadows wrapped around her like a cool, silken embrace and she knew exactly when they portaled into a new chamber.

Hints of linseed and safflower oil, charcoal and dried vervain—familiar scents that added to Gabriel's innate musk. He led her two steps forward. The wood creaked beneath her soles, warm and inviting.

"Are you ready, darling?" The tinge of nervousness in his tone made her smile. She nodded, prepared to love whatever it was he was about to reveal.

She could hear his breath hold as he slowly, cautiously, undid her blindfold.

Shyaree blinked, and when her sight focused, her smile faded. The attic. The one place he had never invited her into, yet disappeared to with enough regularity to make her wonder. Sunlight cascaded from a vaulted ceiling where wooden beams met in a series of arches to form a circular skylight. Two long rectangular tables dominated the space, occupied by all manner of brushes and miniature tins. A charming space, a little chaotic perhaps, but filled with warmth and light and canvases. So many canvases. Propped against each other, slanted across the walls, but all covered by a white sheet.

Except for one.

The painting was propped on an easel, and it was a full-body painting of Shyaree. Not as she was right now, but with the hodgepodge of pantherai traits and serpenti scales on her skin.

Tears pricked her eyes.

Gabriel paled. "You hate it." Without another word, he plucked a white sheet from the ground and shook it out, ready to shroud the painting from her sight.

She slowed his hand with a sharp shake of her head. She didn't hate it. *"Was this how you saw me?"*

"I know it was a painful state for you, Shyaree . . . but it was beautiful to me. Every form you take is beautiful. I just . . . I painted it because I never want to forget."

Since Duskhall, Shyaree had shifted consistently into a fully formed pantherai. She couldn't shift into her half state now even if she tried.

"It's beautiful." Somehow, the artist had managed to make her appear like some otherworldly creature in spite of the fur, claws, and scales. A goddess. Sensual. Alluring. Mesmerizing.

"*You* are beautiful," he corrected roughly. "You just need to look in the mirror."

Hilarity racked her shoulders as she swiped at her eyes. She looked at her reflection every day, but she had never seen herself this way. Not in this light. But Gabriel's painting . . . made it hard *not* to see what he saw.

"I love it. I love you."

His eyes lit like amethysts under the full glare of the sun. "Do you?"

She nodded earnestly. It seemed to excite him, because he towed her by the forearm like a child ready to show off a collection of toys. "There's more . . . "

That was when her jaw hung.

Gods above, he had done more than one canvas of her. Many more.

She was immortalized in paint in all angles and forms. Moments in time. Captured from his point of view.

There she was, crouched atop a fallen tree, staring into the distance.

Lying on his bed with a white sheet wrapped beneath her arms, glaring from the canvas . . .

"So every time you came up here, it was to paint?"

He smiled wryly. "Believe it or not, guildmaster of the Red Knights was not always my profession of choice. When I was younger, I wanted to be an artist. And being the son of a wealthy duke, I had the privilege of apprenticing with some of the best painters in the realm. But after what happened at the

Winter Palace . . . " A small shake of his head. "I stopped painting for a long, long time after that. Whenever I felt the urge to create, I would turn to charcoal instead. Black felt safer somehow. Like a part of my shadows."

He peeled back another sheet to a smaller canvas. This one of Shyaree seated in a garden laden with yellow and white lilies. Her eyes widened. It was one of the gardens at Amereen Castle. One of Evie's gardens.

Shyaree blinked. *"You painted me even back then?"*

The curve on his lips took a sheepish bend, and the tips of his ears pinkened. He led her to three canvases on the far side of the wall and uncovered them. "I hadn't felt the urge to pick up the paintbrush. Until you."

These were painted from a top-down angle. As though Gabriel observed the scenes from a bird's eye. Shyaree kneeling by the river, drinking from cupped hands. Shyaree with a basket, returning from harvesting wild herbs. And the third one of Shyaree running fingers through her hair, seated on a flat rock in a setting that could have been plucked right from her mind.

"After Arkas sent you home from the mage realm, I uh . . . sometimes checked on you."

"Checked on me?"

"Sometimes I would fly around your clan in bird form, waiting for you to leave your shieldmakers' walls, and . . . " His voice lowered to a mumble. "Follow you around."

Shyaree stared. *"Why? Because you knew I was the blood sacrifice?"*

He shook his head. "I only found out about that when Zion chose to share the prophecy. No, I did that because . . . I missed you."

Shyaree sucked in an incredulous breath. *"You surprise me, Gabriel Blacksage."*

He brushed her hair, watching her intently. "A good surprise? Or a bad one?"

"A wonderful one." She pulled him down for a kiss. They were both panting when she pulled away so she could handspeak. *"But you're not the only one with a surprise."*

He cocked his head.

She grinned and stepped further back. Nervousness filled her gut. What if he recoiled in revulsion? She wet her lip. Why would he? He had already seen her at her ugliest, and he still thought her beautiful. Loved her.

Drawing in a deep breath, she shrugged the cloak from her shoulders. His gaze darkened, and a small, wicked grin crested upon his lips . . .

She changed.

Not into a pantherai.

His mouth parted in shock, but thankfully, not with the shade of disgust. Instead, reverence widened his eyes. "How? When? How . . . how can you . . . ?"

She laughed at his awestruck stuttering, but in her current form it came out as a hiss. She slithered over slowly, not wanting to alarm him, but she needn't have worried. He was already on his knees, reaching for her.

"Oh, Shyaree. Darling. You are . . . so beautiful."

She preened, coiling up his arm and twining near his shoulders so he could better admire her scales. He stroked the length of her, murmuring praises that made her heart swell.

She was not just pantherai but serpenti as well. Perhaps her polymorphic state had always been a result of these two conflicting forms warring within her. Perhaps if she had been allowed to follow her urges as a child and change whenever she wanted . . . if Dapa hadn't tried to beat it out of her . . . perhaps she would have learned to control her change, and to control her inner beasts, sooner.

She slithered away from him and changed back to her two-legged form, breathless and exhilarated. He caught her in his arms and spun her in a small circle before whispering the words that usually flowed from his mouth while they made love.

She had started learning Faerian since, and the syllables were beginning to sound a lot more like words and less like a foreign melody.

"What are you saying? Will you say it in Animatish for me?"

He licked his lips with a small, nervous laugh, but he nodded. "I love you. I will love you until Ozenn draws me back into the sand. I will love you into the next life . . . and the one after that. I will love you even when the five realms crumble to dust and we are no more than an echo in time."

Her heart swelled again, so much that it felt too big for her chest. *"I have never met anyone more . . . "*

He bumped her nose playfully with the tip of his. "Romantic?"

"I was going to say dramatic."

His lips flattened.

She smirked. *"And arrogant . . . exasperating."* She glanced around the attic. *"Hopelessly messy . . . "*

His eyes gleamed with amusement, but he dragged her close and growled a mock warning. The husky sound rumbled over her, raising all the hairs on her skin in the most tantalizing way.

She conceded with a chuckle. *"But yes. Romantic. Insufferably so."*

She wrapped her arms around his shoulders and rewarded him with a kiss that spoke more from her heart than she could ever convey with her hands.

"I love you."

The crooked grin made its way back to his face, smug and satisfied—she had signed those words often.

"I'm not fae, but if I were, I would have chosen you."

That knocked the grin off his face. His lips parted, and his throat bobbed—those words, she had never signed before.

"Now and forever, I will always choose you, Gabriel Blacksage."

Epilogue

Clink.

Consciousness bloomed like bloodstains across his mind's eye. A malodorous scent cloyed the air with nauseating hints of decay and putrefying flesh. He blinked, trying to make sense of the streaks of red amid the blur of shadows and light in his vision. His head throbbed.

Clink. Clink.

A shudder rattled his bones, a chill coursing through his flesh that did not come from the cold but an unshakeable fear. Groaning, he rubbed a hand over his face and winced, but the motion only caused another wave of pain. Every twitch hurt like a laceration in the skin stretched too taut and thin across his skull. His hair was shorn so close to his scalp he was almost bald.

Another soft clink. What was that sound?

He blinked again, and his vision slowly cleared, the blur of shadows solidifying into silhouettes, but the streaks of red did not leave his sight.

Where was he?

Who was he?

He shook his head, trying to recall his name. It danced at the edges of his mind, a whisper just out of reach. He tried to pull himself to an upright position but couldn't manage to lift his head.

"Oh, you're awake," said a female voice. "Finally."

He opened his mouth to speak, but the words that came out were no more than a hoarse murmur. The silhouette drew closer until he made out a face. Through the red striations, he made out the fine-boned features of a woman with moonshine hair and lilac eyes. He shuddered anew as fear scratched down his spine like a skeletal finger. An involuntary, inarticulate sound slipped from his throat.

She chuckled and leaned over him, feminine, floral, and utterly petrifying. "You've kept me waiting long enough. Are you finally ready to tell me where you've hidden it?"

He blinked. A spark of awareness darted into his consciousness like silverfish darting across tattered parchment. A name . . . Iolanthe.

Her name.

Iolanthe lifted a small hand to his cheek, her touch a thousand pricking pins. A moan leaked from him.

"Where have you hidden it, hmm?"

He blinked wildly. Hidden what? He couldn't think. He couldn't remember. He could only shake his head, desperate to shrink from her hand. He shouldn't have, because her delicate features hardened into a mask of cold rage.

Slap!

Agony spread across his face in fiery waves until his vision blackened.

It wasn't until he blinked again that he realized he must have fallen unconscious, because the light slanting into the chamber had faded to a muted glow. His vision seemed better, too. The red streaks no longer obscured his sight. Another blink showed the details of a slate wall stained in darker blotches of gray and black. A small recessed window was the only source of light.

Clink.

The hairs on his skin stood on end.

He shifted ever so slowly toward the sound. His breathing sped, trepidation spiking in his chest.

She was still here. Perched on the edge of a heavy wooden table, polishing a collection of slim silver knives.

"Where is it?" she asked without looking over. The hardness in her tone set his pulse to a fevered pitch.

He opened his mouth, and this time he managed a raspy word, barely a whisper. "What?"

She glanced up, lilac eyes narrowed. "Do not play games with me, my prince. Tell me where the last of the seer's blood is, or I will have no choice but to do it *again*. Do not test me."

Only then did he notice an odd cluster at the far side of the wall. A wall speckled with dark splotches. Another slow blink before he understood what he was seeing.

A cluster of heads. Some more rotted than others . . . but all bearing the same face.

His face.

THE END

Thank you for reading Gabriel and Shyaree's story!
I'd be so grateful if you could leave me a review on Goodreads!
Every review counts, and it really does make a difference :)

Want more?
Sign up for my newsletter at www.holleemands.com for a free copy of Lullaby Scars (a free full-length fantasy romance) and news of the next book!

Reader Bonus

Have you wondered about the letter Gabriel fished out of Zion's pocket?

Last correspondence between the prophet and the Seelie queen

To my beloved Katerina,

Forgive me, my love, for when you read this the Winter Court army will have breached the Marshwood Fort. I will already be gone. I would tell you not to mourn for me and not to shed a single tear, but I have already seen your grief. So I will urge you instead to mourn me the way you have loved me: In your heart.

We will find each other again in the next life. I promise you, Kati. But for now, you must stand strong, if not for yourself, then for your people. This terror does not end with the heinous attack of Jilintree Castle. Your sister's death was only the beginning.

There is so much I cannot reveal, for it is the nature of

sentient minds to try their hands at changing destiny. It would be folly, my love, to pit your intelligence against the threads of fate. My foresight is etched in the sands of time. Irreversible. Unchangeable.

Please know that if I had the power to change it and spare you and our people this anguish, I would. If I could stop it all from unfolding the way the gods have designed, I would give anything, Kati. I would do anything . . . but I am merely a vessel for the gods, a mouthpiece for fate. I will leave you instead with a gift that will aid our people's return: my final prophecy.

The gods are often capricious and sometimes cruel, but they are always discerning. I truly believe everything happens for a reason.

Into the next life, my love. I will find you again.

Forever yours,

Elias

ACKNOWLEDGMENTS

Dear reader,

Thank you for being here. I am so very grateful for you and your ongoing support. When I first started writing, selling a book was one of my wildest fantasies. I've since sold thousands, but whenever I sit down and think about it, it still feels wild. Surreal. So thank you, my dearest reader. Thank you for investing your precious time and energy into reading my words when you could have spent it reading any one of the bajillion other books out there.

I am and will forever be grateful that you gave me and my books a chance.

Gabriel and Shyaree's story hasn't been an easy one to write. I struggled with characterisation, scene setting, and plot. I struggled with the magic system and the world I've established. I spent months writing ninety thousand draft words only to realize I hated the story. Gabriel didn't feel like Gabriel, while Shyaree did not grow into the vision of who I wanted her to be. The characters failed to speak to me the way Declan and Evie/Killian and Mailin ever did . . . so I scrapped everything.

Yep. Ouch.

Starting from scratch was painful, but at the very least, I can put my hand over my heart and say I've given it my best shot. If *Little Fire* was a story from my heart, then *Blood Song* is a story bled from my veins. I've truly poured myself and squeezed every emotion I had to give into these pages.

I hope they resonated with you as much as they finally did with me.

And as with every book, I could never have pulled it off alone.

Kelley Luna

This book is for you, and I so desperately wanted it to be perfect. Ironically, this turned out to be the least perfect book I've produced to date, circumstances being what they are. I am so glad that you love it anyway. I hope you'll forgive me for that mad, mad final rush (I know you do) and I solemnly promise to never put us in that position again (I mean, I'll tryyy), but I really mean it when I say this book would never have been written without you. Thank you, Kels, for everything that you've done for this manuscript—and out of it.

Denali Day

Thank you for that epic eight-hour-long video call where you listened, laughed, and brainstormed with me on *Blood Song*. It has to be the longest video call of my life and one I'll never forget. I appreciate everything you've brought into my life and all the lessons you've taught me. Here is wishing you the very best in all your future endeavors. Blessings to you, dearest Denali.

Tina Emmerich

I am so grateful for everything you've done in this manuscript, I have no words. But since I'm supposed to be a wordsmith, I'll try anyway. This story has been a hard one to write for many, many reasons . . . but your steady presence, analytical mind, and willingness to work through plot inconsistencies with me has saved it from the ditch. Your enthusiasm for the story gave me hope, and your wit kept me laughing when all I wanted was to mope. Thank you for all those hours you've spent stewing over this manuscript that you could—and should!—have been sleeping. Thank you for being the developmental editor I so desperately needed—you made this story shine brighter.

Courtney Kelly

I will never forget the time I was about to hit publish on *Little Fire* and pretty much freaked out about everything indie publishing, and you told me "You're not alone." Those words gave me so much comfort back then, and still do today. Having you and your insights on this manuscript helped strengthen the story and gave me the confidence, once again, to hit that publish button. Thank you for being there for me from the very beginning . . . and thank you for still being here for me now.

Liv Zander

I suspect you are one of those flashy stars I've earned for writing and self-publishing a book because I know I would never have met you otherwise. I expected to make friends along the way, but I never expected to make friends like you. Thank you for stepping in and helping me whenever I need it the most . . . it means more than you know. The snails and their little silver tails exist because of you. *winks*

GiannaMarie Dobson

Thank you for being the most amazing sensitivity reader! Writing a nonspeaking character was not as straightforward as I'd initially, *naively*, assumed it would be. Your insights and your willingness to educate me on nonspeaking culture and hand signing has gone a long way to shaping Shyaree into the character she is.

And to my real-life heroes . . .

Zoe, Su Ee, and Geri . . . I don't think I could have survived those last two months without you. You held me together when I would have broken. I love you all to the moon and back.

Also by Hollee Mands

Warriors of the Five Realms Prequel

Lullaby Scars

Lullaby Scars is a full-length fantasy romance that is free for my newsletter subscribers. Sign up at www.holleemands.com and read for free!

He's the only man she's ever wanted. She's everything he can never have.

Killian's scars are all people see, but with his wretched past, he doesn't want them to look closer. He resigned himself long ago to living as an indentured slave to a powerful and capricious high mage—until a chance meeting with a temptress outside a brothel teaches him to *want*...

If only he hadn't asked her price for the night.

Lady Mailin's escape from her tyrannical father is so close she can taste it. All she has to do is to fake her magical prowess long enough for the high mage to sign a marriage contract and whisk her away. Then she'll lose him and start a new life. The last thing she needs is a tortured bondsman mistaking her for a woman who works on her back...

If only she could forget his gentle, callused touch.

When a stormy sea strands them together on Prison Island, Mailin and Killian's illicit desires may prove deadlier than the convicts out for blood, or worse...

Warriors of the Five Realms Book One

Little Fire

She's broken from a past she can't remember. He's scarred from a past he can't forget.

Declan can kill with a blink of his eye. Jaded and cold, he rules his kingdom the same way he does his heart—with ruthless pragmatism. So why does he risk all to protect a little mortal during a slave-trade uprising? Now stranded in the demon realm, the loss of his powers is the least of his troubles. The woman may have a frustratingly tender heart, but she has enough fire in her soul to thaw the ice in his veins.

He could take her by right, but he wants more than acceptance. He wants her willing surrender...

Evangeline is chained by a past she can't remember. Her fractured memories keep her shy and single. When she is thrust into a savage world in the arms of a deadly archmage, he becomes her only chance of survival. But soon she realizes her unnerving protector may not be as callous as he appears, and her heart may be as much at risk as her life.

His desire for her is no secret, but she wants more than scalding lust. She wants his icy heart...

Can they survive the nightmarish realm long enough to break down each other's walls?

Warriors of the Five Realms Book Two

Winter Sun

He'd do anything to keep her safe...except give her up.

Declan lost her once. Never again. He is an archmage. Fearsome. Terrible. Divine. Yet deadly whispers dare echo in his ear. None more threatening than those of his still-incomplete mate bond and his love's failing health. In a twist of irony, he must now protect his mate from the greatest danger she's ever faced...himself.

Evangeline was raised to be an apothecarist, not an archmage's queen. She knows nothing of the subtle maneuverings of court life, and despite her awakened memories, she remains painfully human. Too human to claim an archmage for a mate. But Declan's contentious council and her questionable mortality aren't the only things she has to worry about. The secrets of her past are catching up, and even her all-powerful lover may not be able to keep her safe...

Winter Sun is the seductive sequel in the Warriors of the Five Realms adult fantasy romance series that will submerge you in a dazzling court of deadly secrets and deception lurking in every shadow...

About the Author

Hollee Mands used to be that kid who sat at the back of the class, scribbling stories and doodling in dreary math workbooks. Much older and still unrepentant, she's now determined to bring her imaginations to life through the keyboard. When she isn't squirrelling away time to write, read, or sketch, she is a communications consultant and proud mom to a tiny dictator who has the speech patterns (and physical energy) to rival a steam train. She currently resides in fickle-weathered Melbourne and is a proud member of Romance Writers Australia.

Connect with Hollee
www.holleemands.com
@Holleemands

Made in United States
North Haven, CT
11 November 2023